"I WANT TO SEE SOME ACTION."

Phaid turned as a commotion started at the other end of the block.

"I think we're about to get more action than you can handle."

There was yelling and screaming and then a blaster roared. The screaming rose to a hysterical pitch. People were fleeing down the street in a panic, running directly towards Phaid and Abrella-Lu. Phaid grabbed the woman and dragged her across the road at right angles to the way the crowd was running. Youths were hurling rocks, and Phaid knew that any moment the police would charge. He glanced grimly at Abrella-Lu.

"You got your action. It looks like all hell's going to break loose..."

"Witty, unique, hard-boiled...One of the most fully realized and realistic decadent future Earths depicted in science fiction!"
—Norman Spinrad
author of *Child of Fortune*

Ace Science Fiction books by Mick Farren

The Song of Phaid the Gambler

PHAID THE GAMBLER
CITIZEN PHAID (coming in January 1987)

· MICK FARREN ·
PHAID the GAMBLER

BEING PART ONE OF
THE SONG OF PHAID THE GAMBLER

ACE SCIENCE FICTION BOOKS
NEW YORK

This Ace Science Fiction book
contains the revised text of the first half of the
original edition, *The Song of Phaid the Gambler*. It has been
completely reset in a typeface designed
for easy reading, and was printed from
new film.

PHAID THE GAMBLER

An Ace Science Fiction Book/published by arrangement with
the author

PRINTING HISTORY
New English Library edition/October 1981
Ace Science Fiction edition/August 1986

ISBN: 0-441-66232-3

Ace Science Fiction Books are published by
The Berkley Publishing Group,
200 Madison Avenue, New York, New York 10016.

PRINTED IN THE UNITED STATES OF AMERICA

PHAID the GAMBLER

1

The building with the sign that proclaimed it a hotel was half swallowed by the jungle. Inch by inch, over long centuries, the slow power of creeper and vine, sapling and dark green undergrowth had claimed it back. The jungle could crack stones and distort structures. The humidity and thick miasmic mists from the great river corroded and eventually ate away all metal. What the jungle couldn't destroy it simply covered up, permanently shrouded it in a thick carpet of greenery.

The building with the sign that proclaimed it a hotel must have once been very beautiful. A rich man's upriver, jungle retreat. Originally there had been a low white dome fashioned from thick, cool masonry. The dome's solidity had been offset by a fragile wandlike spire, but that had long since fallen to the creepers. Set in a clearing on the riverbank, it was still possible just to distinguish where there had been a wide piazza. If you dug around on the jungle floor, you could just find strips of mosaic and the pipework that had fed water to a complex of fountains.

Only the dome could be described as having put up a fight. Apart from the jagged crack that arched across one side of it, it had remained almost intact. It was inside the dome that a traveler could find such hotel service as was promised by the sign. There were few travelers who pulled over to the broken dock and the sorry overgrown clearing. There were few travelers and, in consequence, the service provided by the hotel was scant, basic and without flourish.

Despite the sad present and the seemingly hopeless future, a small but unsanitary village had grown up around the dome. Lethargic primitives who had wandered in from the deep jungle had set up hovels made from salvaged plastic sheet and scrap lumber. There were others who had come from the river, spiritually worn-out wanderers who couldn't wander any further and who had lapsed into a dull existence with either a local partner or the local hooch. There were even some who had just appeared as if from thin air. Nobody knew where they had come from and nobody cared. Whatever their origin, all the inhabitants of the ramshackle little village seemed rarely to smile. The closest they came to hope was a sullen yearning for something to come down the river that might change their situation. In the meantime they squatted and waited and sweated in the heat.

It was hot, even inside the dome. The air was heavy and sluggish, pressing stickily on those who had to live in it and breathe it. There was no hint of a breeze, just a reluctant, almost viscous motion. It was as though carrying the weight of the relentless humidity was too much for the atmosphere.

Once there had been cooling tubes set at regular intervals around the dome but these no longer worked. They were clogged with dirt and dead leaves. No one in the village had the skills to make them function again. In the big public room that took up most of the dome floor, a leaf-bladed fan, operated by a semi-comatose primitive was supposed to supply some kind of relief. In fact it did nothing but disturb the fat metallic green flies that floated torpidly into its path. For a moment the beat of their wings would quicken and, if anybody noticed, they'd crackle briefly with mechanical, insect annoyance. Murmurers that hung from the roof of the dome were supposed to emit a stream of hostility that would keep most insects outside, but the fat flies seemed impervious to them and their electronic threats.

The heat reached a peak in the mid-afternoon. Plants seemed bloated and overly lush, as if they'd overfed on the poisonous moisture. Dogs slept with their tongues lolling out. Men found excuses to sneak off to a quiet patch of shade, also to sleep. Everyone and everything waited for the time before sunset when the rain would start, when water would drop from the sky as though a faucet had been turned on and, for a few precious hours, the air would at least hold the illusion of being clean and fresh.

There were exceptions in the village. Not even the heat and the humidity of the high afternoon could stop the gamblers. Weren't there stories of gamblers so obsessive that they had to be dragged out of burning buildings; of gamblers who would risk frostbite in an icefield by taking off their gloves to deal a hand; of gamblers who would sweat out the kind of temperatures that made even lizards blink their black and hostile eyes and refrain from moving?

Even though it had been going on for a day and a night, the game still had a makeshift air to it—the three men using a slab of polished basalt as a table. One man sprawled in a low chair; the other two hunkered down on the dirt floor as though they were more used to pitching bones in a back alley than playing cards on a table.

The two who squatted played with the bright-eyed desperation of men who hoped that at any moment their luck would return and all would be well. The third conducted his game in a totally opposite manner. He dealt the cards almost wearily, with an economy that showed all too clearly that the heat was getting to him. Sweat ran own his face in oily rivulets, soaking his now grimy silk shirt.

It was only a sense of professionalism that kept him going. He was, after all, a professional gambler. It was his game. If the amateurs on either side of him were intent on throwing away their money, he was beholden to ride with them and take it, even if it did mean playing through the steam oven afternoon of this poisonous region.

3

Mick Farren

A gambling man has to make his living where he can. He can't always be the one to pick the time and the place, particularly if the gambling man had managed to get himself stranded in a torrid zone without the price of the long ride back to civilization.

The name of the gambling man was Phaid. He had once had other names, a whole string of names in fact. Elaborate and lengthy names for male children were an idiosyncrasy of his people. Those old names, however, had not been used for so long that he doubted if he'd respond, even if they were yelled right into his ear. For him, his homeland, its people and their archaic customs were something that belonged to the faraway past.

The cards came to Phaid and he warily dealt them round. His two opponents were watching him with narrow, suspicious eyes. One was a primitive, a warrior from some small bellicose tribe from way back in the jungle. His flat leathery face was a mass of tattoos and ritual scars. His arms were covered in pitted plasteel armor; they contrasted strangely with the amulets and necklaces of shells and parrot feathers that were festooned around his neck. By his side was a crude but effective dart launcher.

The second player's sallow skin and black greasy hair indicated that he probably had grown to maturity in the flat lands that lay downriver. He wore a patched and stained military style jumpsuit. All the badges and insignia had, at one time or another, been torn from it. Phaid suspected that he was possibly a deserter from the army of one of the lowland city states, or a mercenary who had wandered too far upriver and too far into the jungle. Certainly at some time his left eye and part of the left side of his face had been blown away. It had been replaced by a crudely flexible permapatch and a glittering black optic sensor that swiveled in synchronization with his good eye. The military image was further reinforced by the powerful fuse tube that hung from a wide leather belt.

Primitive scooped up his cards and spat into the dirt. "How'm I goin' t' get anyplace if'n all I get dealt is shit like yon?"

Phaid didn't bother to reply. It took too much energy. He didn't have to bother with any of their nonsense. All he needed to do was doggedly stick with the odds. The others could play

4

with their suspicions and make the conversation and the mistakes. Phaid was too far ahead to be hurt. He doubled the bet and waited to see if the man had the nerve to keep going.

When he'd started the game the previous evening he had known that this would be a game without a trace of subtlety. Subtlety was a long way down the river, many stops behind him on his disastrous run of bad luck. Originally there had been seven players. There had been the three men who were about the only inhabitants of the town who had anything resembling real money. One was the owner of the hotel, the other two, brothers, operated the small boat dock at the front of the cracked and broken, overgrown steps that led down to the river. In addition to them, there was a sharp-eyed, sharp-tongued, thrice widowed boat woman who had a flatboat and a pair of freight blimps moored at the jetty.

The three villagers were only there for a good time. They were strictly bread and butter work for Phaid. They drank too much, sweated profusely and their breaths reeked of the spice that the river people shoveled over everything they ate. They'd come into the game with a small roll and once they'd lost it they'd retired gracefully, quite grateful for the night's entertainment.

The boat woman had been a little more serious in her play, and with her, Phaid had almost been close to enjoying himself. She'd run her cards with hard-headed common sense, never confronted Phaid directly, and around dawn, when she'd amassed a small profit, she'd excused herself and left.

Phaid hadn't relished the idea of being left with the duo. It was clear they were nothing more than river rats, backwater lowlife, the kind who liked to haunt isolated townships, because isolated townships were about the only places that their graceless swagger and unimaginative braggadocio had a hope of being taken seriously.

When they told Phaid that they'd come to the township looking for a good time, he'd stared at them with open contempt. What kind of good time did they imagine was waiting for them in this forsaken spot? It hardly had the life to stop the forest growing over it again, let alone provide a good time. The sum total of its sunset attractions were the overgrown hotel and a trio of slovenly teenagers, two girls and a chubby boy,

5

who'd bed down with anyone for five tabs and a jug of wine.

The pair had come into the game with a lot of money. This in itself should have been a warning to Phaid. It was more money than a couple of jungle bums should rightfully be carrying, too much to have been earned from a lucky prospect strike or deck handling on a flatboat. It was more likely that the money was evilly come by. Its previous owner, in all probability, was lying face down in the swamp water of an isolated stretch of forest even jungle folk rarely visited.

As the night wore on, and the two river rats lost more and more and grew increasingly surly and ill-tempered, Phaid knew that he was drifting into a potentially deadly situation. It was clear that the pair would use any sort of violence if they thought it would get back what they had lost. In other circumstances, Phaid would have walked away from them and flatly refused to play. Right now, though, he knew that he had to take the risk of playing with these unsavory characters. Phaid was sufficiently close to being a beggar that he couldn't afford to be a chooser. He needed all the cash he could get his hands on, no matter what the risk. He had to play this game to the end and then walk away with his winnings as best he could. If he couldn't buy his way out of this dreadful jungle and back to civilization, he'd wind up as low as the men on either side of him. For Phaid, that was a fate that didn't bear thinking about.

Another two rounds went down. The one-eyed man won a little and started muttering about how maybe his luck was changing and how it was about time. Once again Phaid ignored him. He looked around the rest of the public room. He had to admit that it was little more than a ruin. A group of natives in feathers and beads nodded and dozed against the curve of the wall. A drunk in the garb of a flatboat roustabout was face down on the floor. His body was bisected by the bright strip of light where the sunlight lanced through the crack in the dome. There seemed to be some sort of sexual activity going on in one of the deep recesses formed by the shallow curve of the dome. As the afternoon wore on Phaid noticed that it didn't pay to look too deeply into those dark recesses. Ancient garbage formed strange shapes and after thirty-six hours his eyes could play tricks.

Phaid slowly and reluctantly gathered in the cards. He would have to stop soon. One Eye and Primitive had a predatory look about them. It was a similar malevolent patience to that of a vulture, or a jackal or a lupe out on the tundra. Phaid glanced at the makeshift and dangerous looking wooden stairs that led up to the private rooms in the dome. He wondered how he was going to make his way up those stairs with his winnings in his hand. It was time to put it to the test. He looked straight at One Eye and then at Primitive. He took a deep breath and sighed.

"The rain'll be starting soon."

Three eyes and a sensor drilled into his face.

"What's that supposed to mean?"

Phaid knew that he would have to handle this extremely carefully. He eased his position in the less than comfortable chair. He took a sip from the shot glass of warm absinthia and smiled thinly.

"So we've played all night and most of the day. When the rain comes down it's the start of the second evening. That's enough entertainment for anyone. It seems to me that that would be an ideal time for me to pull out of this game."

He watched the pair carefully, trying to gauge their reaction. Primitive had become slit eyed.

"You got a lot o' our money, gambling man."

Phaid moved his arm so he could reassure himself that the stinger was safely hidden in his sleeve. One Eye altered his position so his fuse tube was within quick and easy snatch.

Phaid kept his expression deliberately blank. He let his right arm hang loosely over the back of the chair so, if the need came, the stinger would drop easily into the palm of his hand. After a disastrous experience in another river village, the stinger, with its circular silver body and its ten spider legs was the only weapon he had at his disposal. It wasn't a particularly honorable weapon, but Phaid wasn't too concerned about honor. All he wanted was to get out of the game with both his skin and his money intact. Honor was a luxury of civilization. One Eye fixed Phaid with his eye and his sensor.

"It seem t' me we got a right t' win some o' our money back now."

"You've been trying to get some of it back for hours, for most of the day, in fact. It hasn't done you any good."

7

Primitive folded his armored arms.

"Could be a reason f' that."

Phaid raised an eyebrow. He had to slow this all down. They were already looking for an excuse to climb all over him.

"What exactly are you trying to say?"

"We think you probably know what."

"So say it."

"Maybe it don't need t' be said 'til you try an' get up from this here game."

Phaid slowly nodded. The course from here on was becoming all too clear.

"We'll just have to see what happens."

"That's right, gambling man. We'll just have to see."

One Eye leered.

"Deal the cards, gambling man."

Phaid grinned.

"I think it's your turn to deal, my friend."

One Eye blinked. Phaid noticed that when the good eye was closed, the sensor became dull and lost its glitter. One Eye was clearly discomfited by his mistake. Phaid decided to turn the screw just a little.

"Deal up then, friend. Let's get to it."

One Eye spun out the cards. Phaid picked up his hand and found himself looking at a combination of lathes and cornelians that gave him a grand encirclement. The hand was almost unbeatable. As if that wasn't sufficiently unbelievable, One Eye started to shamelessly force up the betting. Phaid, curious to know what was getting One Eye so excited, rode along with it, as did Primitive. The pot steadily grew until both of the pair had exhausted their reserves. When Primitive was down to his last ten, he threw down his cards in disgust and glanced grimly at his companion.

"I tells you, Jackman, you better have something, else you and me will be into falling out."

One Eye smiled knowingly.

"I got it all."

Phaid pretended to ignore the exchange. He glanced over at the makeshift bar. The bartender was still asleep. There was also a serving android. That too was motionless. From the scars and rust on its outer casing, Phaid suspected that it probably hadn't worked for years.

Phaid turned back to the game. Both One Eye and Primitive seemed to be waiting for Phaid to make a move. Phaid smiled; he knew that the *coup de grâce* wasn't far away.

"What's your pleasure, my friends?"

The mobile side of One Eye's face twisted into a triumphant sneer.

"My pleasure's t' call you, gambling man."

He flipped his cards over. It would have been an impressive hand in any game, a brace of lathes backed up by golds. The odds against Phaid having a hand to beat it were astronomical. For an instant Phaid felt a genuine sympathy for One Eye. Then he spread out his own hand.

"I'm sorry, it didn't ought to happen to a dog."

One Eye stared at Phaid's hand in disbelief.

"Wait a minute..."

Phaid caught the obvious implication.

"You dealt them yourself, my friend."

Phaid slowly stretched out his hand to gather in his winnings. At exactly the same time the first drops of the evening rain crashed into the surrounding trees. The noise echoed ominously round the inside of the dome. It was one of those frozen moments that Phaid knew all too well but sincerely wished he didn't. The one eyed ex-soldier and the primitive were both violent men. They were experienced in violence. From the look of them they also derived a lot of grim, snarling pleasure from it. In a few seconds they would find the excuse they needed to commence creaming him all over the dome. Phaid didn't have what it took to be violent; efficiently and effectively violent. That was why he was a gambler, why he played according to the rules.

The rules, however, were dropping away. As the rain crashed all around and droplets of water were seeking a way down inside the dome, Phaid faced a situation that was, if not as old as time, at least as old as games of chance.

"It looks as though the game is over."

With an air of total absorption he started to pack up his winnings. He knew what the next move would be, but could think of no way to avoid it. Out of the corner of his eye, he saw the fuse tube drawn from the belt. One Eye was almost casual as he pointed the weapon arrogantly at Phaid's head.

"Leave the money where it be, gambler."

Phaid slowly eased back into the chair. With the stinger his sole weapon, he could only wait for his chance. He hoped fervently that there would be one.

"Just can't let me walk away with it all?"

One Eye nodded.

"You expect us to?"

Phaid sighed.

"No, not really."

One Eye continued to cover Phaid as he rose carefully to a standing position. Primitive also got to his feet. With his dart launcher under his arm he scanned the row of sleeping villagers. Usually the sleepers woke with the rain and started drinking. On this day, however, they remained diplomatically slumbering. Only the bartender was taking an open interest, but he also seemed about to do or say nothing.

Satisfied that Phaid had no help at hand, One Eye fumbled under his suit and pulled out a soft leather bag. He threw it down on the table in front of Phaid.

"Put the money in there."

Phaid silently did as he was told while the two men watched him. When all the cash was packed away he sat patiently back in the chair. One Eye picked up the bag. Primitive looked at him questioningly.

"What about him?"

They both looked at Phaid. One Eye laughed nastily.

"What about him?" He directed the inquiry to Phaid. "What about you?"

"I'd hardly be worth killing."

One Eye was warming to the idea that there might be some sport to be had with the gambler before they finished him. He became brutally brisk.

"Stand up, stand up! Let's look at you."

Phaid did as he was told. He spread his hands in a semicomic appeal

"You see, gentlemen, nothing worth killing."

One Eye had obviously got to such a low point in his opinion of Phaid as an adversary that he felt safe to scratch his nose with the fuse tube.

"I got this here rule, see. I say if I cross a man 'tis best to leave him dead, lest he come after."

"That could be a problem."

As he spoke he absentmindedly scratched his head. One Eye laughed and looked at Primitive.

"Could be a problem for him. What you say, Naqui? What you say? Could be a problem for him."

One Eye was so taken with his own wit that, for a moment, he was paying no attention to Phaid. Phaid's arm, still raised as though scratching his head, flashed forward. The stinger had already crawled down into his hand. He flipped it straight at One Eye. It landed on his neck just below the ear in the fold of his jaw. The tiny silver legs grabbed hold and clung. The stinger was quite close to the edge of the patch. As Phaid had flipped the tiny weapon, a small sphere had detached itself and remained in Phaid's hand. This was the control. If he squeezed it, the stinger would go active and scramble One Eye's nervous system:

One Eye went rigid. Even though he couldn't see it he knew what had attached itself to his flesh. Eye and sensor swiveled towards Phaid.

"Stinger?"

"All I had."

Primitive was raising his dart gun. He looked as though he was about to take a shot at Phaid. One Eye's yell was almost a scream.

"Don't!"

Primitive paused. One Eye had started to shake.

"If you get him with one of those, he'll take me f'sure. He's only got t' touch the control."

"That's the truth."

Primitive half lowered the dart launcher, then he grinned.

"What care I if'n he takes you? The both of you'll be dead an' I'll have the money."

One Eye glowered at him.

"I thought we was partners."

11

"Partners?"

Primitive spat. It looked as though he was serious. Phaid spoke, as calmly as he could, to One Eye. "There is one way out."

The fuse tube roared. Primitive was all but cut in half. One Eye lowered the weapon. "It's good that I think quick."

Phaid nodded. "Indeed it is."

"What do I do now?"

"Drop the tube."

One Eye dropped the tube.

"Kick it over here."

He kicked it to Phaid. Phaid bent to pick it up. It wasn't the most expensive or the best looking weapon that Phaid had ever seen. Among the rovers, drifters and wanderers who roamed between scorched desert and the wind blasted icefields that girdled the world like bands of steel, the elite took much pride in their weapons. Ornate carving, delicate engraving and inlaid gems decorated the fuse tubes and blasters of the free rangers who kept ahead of life's games. One Eye had obviously never been ahead of the game. The long barrel of the tube was pitted with corrosion, and the butt was a simple construction of worn, high impact ceramic. Phaid hefted it as though he was testing its balance. Then he stuck it in his belt. He was close to trembling. The whole incident, in fact the whole game, had been too close to the edge of desperation for Phaid's peace of mind. One Eye took a chance to turn and face Phaid.

"What are you going to do with me?"

Phaid looked at the stinger control in his hand.

"I don't know."

"Listen . . ."

The good side of One Eye's face twitched.

"I'm listening."

"I wasn't going to kill you." He nodded at the fallen Primitive. "He might have done you, but not me."

"You tried to steal my money."

"We lost a lot, we was mad, we had a hard time gettin' that money. I wanted it back but I wasn't goin' to do you. I swears."

"You do?"

"I swears."

12

"So you're telling me that you weren't going to burn my head off?"

One Eye's half face tried to be ingratiating.

"That's right. You got it. We was just riled. You know how it is."

Phaid adopted a mildly affable expression.

"Sure, I know how it is."

"You do?"

"Sure I do."

One Eye looked relieved.

"You mean that you ain't going t' do nothing? You going t' forget what we done?"

Phaid sadly shook his head.

"No, I couldn't quite do that. Didn't you tell me the rule yourself? How did it go? 'Lest he come after you'?"

One Eye opened his mouth to protest, but Phaid didn't let him. He squeezed the control. The stinger made no noise. One Eye made a strangled sound, his back arched, he clawed at the air, then he collapsed. Phaid's whole body seemed to sag for a moment. Then he straightened, took a deep breath, exhaled swiftly and shook his head as though trying to clear it. He looked sadly at the two bodies. The bartender was popping his eyes at Phaid and the two dead. Phaid walked slowly towards the bar.

"Were these friends of yours?"

The bartender energetically shook his head.

"Lords no, I never seen them before last night."

"So you've got no interest in the matter?"

"I don't have an interest in most matters. I'm no sidetaker."

Phaid half smiled.

"So I don't have anything to worry about from you."

"Not a damn thing."

Phaid picked up the leather bag that held the money.

"You got law in this town?"

"Nothing as you'd call law."

"That's good."

"Good for you."

"What other kind of good is there."

Phaid left five twenty tabs on the table.

13

"That's for your trouble."

"I'm obliged."

The bartender hesitated for a moment, sucking reflectively on a hollow tooth.

"You wouldn't mind if I gave you a piece of advice, would you? You wouldn't get mad or nothing."

Phaid pushed the fuse tube into the waistband of his trousers.

"Only fools get mad when they hear good advice."

The bartender raised an eyebrow and then flashed a yellow-brown smile.

"Not everybody sees it that way."

Phaid nodded gravely:

"Not everyone does."

The bartender regarded the corpses on the floor.

"I wouldn't stay around too long, if I were you."

Phaid looked mildly surprised.

"You just told me there was no law here."

The bartender shook his head.

"It's not a matter of law. It's a bit more subtle than that. Nobody round here had too much time for those two, but what you did . . . well, it tends to unsettle them, if you know what I mean."

The rain fell relentlessly and the seepage splashed steadily on the bare floor. One part of Phaid simply couldn't believe that he'd come to the point where he'd been told to move on from a place like this. Had he really sunk so low? He turned and shrugged.

"Yeah, I know what you mean."

Phaid slowly started up the sagging stairs and headed for his room on the second floor. He paused halfway up and looked back at the bartender.

"I'll be gone when the rain stops."

"You're a sensible man."

"Maybe."

Once inside the room, Phaid flopped down on the bed with a weary sigh. It was almost dark but he didn't bother to light the lamp. The previous night the glo-bar had been an elderly, faltering yellow as though it was the end of its almost infinite life. Could this place have been lost here in the jungle long enough for a glo-bar to wear out, or was it just something in the air that made everything decay and die?

He lay for a while, staring blankly at the intricate spidery patterns that the damp had painted on the ceiling. Water was leaking through in three places. Fortunately, none of them was directly over the bed. Someone had thoughtfully placed a drinking glass under the worst one. The water kept hitting it with a loud and irritatingly rhythmic ping. Although Phaid's body was dog tired, the incessant dripping against the background roar of the falling rain wouldn't let him rest.

There was something strange about the room. The floor wasn't strictly even and there were peculiar curves to the roof that could have been a result of either earth movements or the inroads of the jungle. The furniture stood at odd angles. It looked ill-suited and incongruous. He had seen these oddly shaped rooms on other scattered occasions during his lengthy wanderings. Each time the thought had struck him that they appeared to have been designed for something that possessed a form very different from that of a human being. It wasn't a thought that helped his rest.

He sat up and thumbed the switch under the glo-bar. It was even more weak and frail than it had been the night before.

He got out of the bed. He regarded himself in the cracked mirror hanging on the door of the single closet. He didn't like what he saw. There was no hiding from the fact that he was a mess.

It wasn't all that long ago that he'd complimented himself regularly on what a fine figure he cut in an elegant salon or dignified promenade. Nobody in the world could have said that Phaid was not a sharp dresser. Maybe a little flamboyant at times, but always immaculate. Now his boots were scuffed and going through in one sole. The breeches were equally worn and patched in the knee and his handmade silk shirt was close kin to a damp, dirty rag. Hanging in the closet was a threadbare frockcoat, under the bed was a small, beat up, leather bag. It contained a second disreputable shirt, a battered silver hip flask, a chronograph that had stopped working, three decks of cards and a transgrom on which the powerpac had run down. On the washstand was a half empty bottle of rotgut gin. All this, plus the money he'd just taken from the table, was the entire world of Phaid the Gambler.

He moved himself to the bottle and took a stiff belt. Almost immediately he grimaced as the raw spirit hit his throat. If nothing else, the cheap booze would be the death of him. He had to get out of this situation and get out fast.

He put down the bottle, stooped and pulled the bag out from under the bed. As he straightened up, he caught another dim reflection of himself in the mirror. Even his face was looking worn-out. His mouth was flanked by set, downward curving lines. His cheeks were hollow and his eyes sunken, as though they'd seen too much for too long. Even his black curly hair that cascaded to his shoulders seemed limp and dead, like a pet plant that had been overwatered.

He'd never been that concerned about his face. He never thought about it too much. He knew it must work. Enough women had given him a glance, and even come back for a second and third. Was his face also slipping, just like the rest of him?

There was one consolation. He hadn't developed a gut. Too many friends and partners in the fat times had grown fat right along with them. The one thing you didn't worry about, when the pickings got lean, was your figure.

Phaid grunted to himself. He had to watch out for this sort of nonsense. Here he was, down on his luck and trying to scrabble his way back. It wasn't time to stand staring into a cracked mirror, wallowing in self-pity. Phaid put on his jacket, dropped his winnings and the rube's fuse tube into his bag and listened to the beat of the falling rain. It seemed to be easing up. In this region, the daily storm tended to stop as suddenly as it began.

Phaid picked up his bag and started back down the stairs. The two bodies had gone, the bartender was back behind the bar, but the sleepers seemed to have gone about their business. At the sound of Phaid's footsteps, the bartender looked up.

"You're heading out?"

"I don't have much choice, do I?"

"Not much."

There didn't seem to be a lot left to say, then the bartender suddenly grinned.

"Good luck, gambling man."

Phaid scowled.

"Yeah. Thanks."

Phaid walked out of the hotel and paused on the overgrown piazza. A line of dim glo-bars illuminated a narrow track through the undergrowth that led towards the river and the boat dock. Phaid hoped that there'd be a craft willing to take him. The boat people were a breed that viewed night-calling strangers with deep suspicion.

Halfway there a small gray cat stuck its head out from the foliage and stared directly at Phaid. The animal's thoughts were clear and precise. It wanted to know if Phaid was the one who had caused the trouble at the hotel.

Phaid nodded.

"I'm afraid so."

The cat blinked and then trotted off into the darkness.

2

In retrospect Phaid realized that trying to find a boat after sunset was a pretty damn stupid move. At the dock, there was only one of the low, flat-bottomed riverboats. As he started to climb over the gunwale the boat's owner very nearly removed his head with an antique blaster.

Fortunately the boat's owner was the widow woman who'd played cards with him the night before. She'd recognized him just in time and held her fire.

At first, she hadn't been too keen on the idea of taking on a passenger, particularly one with a local reputation as a drifter and probable no-good. It had required all the charm Phaid could muster, the right answers to some searching questions and a large portion of his winnings before she finally agreed to carry him to the next major port.

Once it was agreed, she'd invited him into her small but cozy cabin and poured him a drink.

"Freeport, I figure that's going to be your best shot. It's

only two days down river. If the Republic's your final destination, you should be able to pick up a caravan to take you
across the wind plain to Mercyville."

Phaid rubbed his chin.

"I'd rather go all the way round the coast to the Havens."

The widow shook her head.

"You got round me on the matter of taking you as a passenger. There's no way you'll talk me into going as far as the
Havens, so you can save all your pretty smiles. My business
is in Freeport and only Freeport. You can take it or leave it."

Phaid shrugged.

"I was just thinking that a berth on a caravan is going to
cost me plenty, more than I got since I paid you."

The widow laughed.

"You're not thinking I'll give you a refund, are you?"

"No, I wasn't thinking that."

"I wouldn't worry. A smart boy like you won't have any
trouble raising money in Freeport."

Phaid grimaced.

"Lately I seem to be having trouble raising money anyplace."

"Hit a run of bad luck?"

"Something like that."

The woman made an impatient gesture.

"You should know that we make our own luck. Bad luck
only comes when you stop trying. Have you stopped trying,
gambling man?"

Phaid thought for a moment and then slowly smiled.

"No, I haven't stopped trying."

The widow refilled Phaid's glass while he gazed around the
small cabin. Most of the river vessels he'd been on had been
functional to the point of discomfort. This one was so snug
and homey that Phaid felt totally able to stretch out and relax.
Normally Phaid didn't like low ceilings, they made him nervous
and claustrophobic. This one, however, managed to give the
effect of closeness and intimacy.

The widow had obviously taken a lot of trouble in furnishing
her floating home. The walls were lined with a maze of shelves
that held a myriad of small trinkets and knick-knacks, souvenirs
of the woman's wanderings up and down the river. There was

a comfortable rocking chair and a slightly less comfortable
upright chair that Phaid occupied. A glo-bar in an ornate brass
holder swung gently with the slight motion of the moored boat.
Most of its light fell on a small and very old side table. Its
dark wood top was inlaid with mother of pearl. On it were the
two glasses and a dark bottle of rather good brandy, In an
alcove at the shadowy, far end of the cabin was a large bed.
Partly enclosed by a bead curtain, it was covered by a thick
fur rug and piled with multicolored and embroidered cushions.

Phaid looked back to the widow.

"You work this boat all by yourself?"

The widow raised a quizzical eyebrow.

"You're not getting ideas, are you?"

Phaid smiled and shook his head.

"I've been up for two days, lady. I couldn't get an idea if
I wanted to."

Again the raised eyebrow.

"Yeah?"

Phaid sipped his drink.

"Maybe."

The widow refilled her own glass.

"Well, I couldn't keep it from you anyway. Yes, I work this
tub on my own. Have done since my last husband got drunk
and drowned himself."

"I'm sorry."

"Don't be. He was a silly bastard. I don't know why I
married him."

"Isn't it a hard life?"

"Maybe. I don't really know. I've never done anything else.
I guess it ain't too bad. I've got a beat-up android that goes
by the name of Clo-e. She handles the heavy work, runs the
engines and operates the photon cannon if we run into trouble,
which, thank the Lords, we don't too often."

Phaid looked round curiously, but the widow shook her
head.

"Clo-e's up on deck. I don't let her in here. I don't know
what it is, but there's something about androids. I don't like
to be shut up with them. You know what I mean?"

Phaid nodded automatically. He had almost stopped listening. The warmth of the cabin, plus the brandy was making him

feel pleasantly numb. His mind had started to wander. In a strange way, the widow was really quite attractive. Of course, she was quite a bit older than he, and, in more normal circumstances, he would probably not give her a second glance, but here in the tiny cabin, tired and a little drunk, it at least started him thinking. He knew it was ridiculous, but it had been a long two days.

Phaid realized that the widow had picked up the bottle again and was saying something to him.

"I'm sorry."

"You look half dead. Are you starting to lose it?"

"A bit."

"You want another drink?"

"Yeah, why not?"

As the widow leaned forward to fill his glass one more time, the front of her homespun tunic fell partly open, granting Phaid a brief view of a surprisingly firm, well formed breast. Phaid suddenly wondered if the glimpse had been accidental or deliberate. She set the bottle down, and once again sat back in her rocker. Everything was back just as it was. Or was it?

Over the rim of his glass, Phaid covertly scrutinized the widow. It was hard to judge what her figure was like beneath the loose-fitting tunic and baggy trousers. Her face had been worn to a deep, weathered, nut brown by wind and sun, but her black, dead straight hair, that hung almost to her waist when not scraped back into an austere bun, shone like silk.

Then there were her eyes. Surrounded by deeply etched laugh lines, they flashed with humor and a deep practical perception. Phaid had known many women with flashing eyes, but all too often it turned out to be the cold, self-seeking flash of the predator. The widow's were completely different. They were the eyes of someone warm and alive, someone who took life as it came, who didn't always search for what didn't exist, but got on with enjoying what she had.

Phaid noticed that the widow was also studying him. Their inspecting gazes caught each other and locked for a moment. She looked away for an instant, then looked back and smiled.

"We ought to get some sleep."

Phaid nodded.

"You're right."

"I gave up being coy a long time ago."

"What do you mean?"

"Come on, gambling man, you know what I mean."

"I suppose I do."

"Damn right you do. There's only one bed on this boat and it's mine. You can either sleep up on deck or you can sleep in my bed. It's your choice. I may not be as young as I used to be, and I may not be what you're used to, but I take good care of myself and I'm not ashamed to tell you that it's been a while since I had a man. Like I said, though, it's your choice."

Phaid slowly finished his drink and placed the glass carefully on the table, lining up the base with the mother of pearl design. Then he grinned at the widow.

"I sure as hell wouldn't want to sleep on the deck."

"I've heard more romantic phrasing."

"I gave up romance a long time ago."

The widow suddenly stood up.

"Okay, gambling man, play it like you want to. Shall we go to my bed?"

Phaid got up a little more slowly.

"Let's do just that."

The widow moved towards the bed, turned and pulled her tunic over her head. She shook her hair loose, kicked off her sandals and wriggled out of the trousers. She placed a hand on her bare hip and looked, almost challengingly, at Phaid.

"You like me, gambling man?"

Phaid's mouth twisted into a lopsided grin.

"Very much, boat lady."

Phaid had lied to a great many women, but right then he was actually telling the truth. Without her clothes, the widow was a whole different person. In her clothes, she was capable, practical but dull, out of them she was something sinuous and alive, something from the river and the jungle. The hard life of the boats had kept her body slim and supple.

"Yeah, very much indeed."

The widow pushed aside the bead curtain and sat down on the bed. She drew her legs up and tilted her head to the side. One hand played with a single strand of the beads while the other fingered the thick fur of the rug.

"Why don't you take off your clothes and come over here,

23

gambling man. I could get cold."

Phaid was already struggling out of his shirt.

"You couldn't get cold."

"Will you get over here?"

Phaid flopped on the bed beside her. The fur felt good underneath his body.

"I'm here."

He started to bury his face in her hair, but she pushed him back.

"My name's R'Ayla."

Phaid found that it wasn't easy to say.

"R'Ayla."

"You didn't ask."

"R'Ayla. Mine's Phaid."

"Phaid."

"Right."

"Now we know each other."

She touched a control on the wall and the glo-bar dimmed, then her arms snaked around Phaid and she kissed him hard on the mouth.

It wasn't long before he was right inside her. She began to growl deep down in her throat.

"So good, that is so good."

Phaid now believed what she had told him about it being a long time since she had had a man in her bed. At the end, she screamed so loudly that he half feared the population of the little town would come running to see if he was claiming his third victim of the day.

Soon afterwards, he fell into a deep dreamless sleep.

When he woke, sunlight was streaming into the cabin and R'Ayla was gone. Somewhat groggily, he sat up, doing his best to orientate himself. There was a constant throbbing pulse, which, at first, he thought to be inside his head. He finally realized that the boat must be underway and what he could hear was the sound of the engines. He climbed out of the bed and struggled into his breeches and shirt.

Phaid stuck his head through the cabin hatch and blinked at the light. R'Ayla was standing in the bow of the boat staring downriver and whistling through her teeth. Her hair was scraped back into a bun and she was once again sober, practical and virtually sexless. She turned and spotted Phaid.

"So, you're awake. You even keep gambler's hours on a boat."

Phaid had a little difficulty adjusting to the transformation.

"What time is it?"

"A little after noon. You want something to eat?"

Phaid nodded.

"Sure."

"Come on up. I'll fix you something in a while."

Phaid scrambled through the hatch. The boat was close to the center of the big river and traveling downstream at a fair speed. The cargo blimps bobbed behind at the end of their tow lines. The green walls of jungle moved past on either side. In the stern of the boat, a squat cylindrical android stood humming to itself. It had lead lines into both the steering unit and the engine controls. It had obviously seen better days. There were a number of dents in its outer casing and its paint job, a bright and incongruous pink, was flaking away.

Once Phaid was on the deck, R'Ayla pointed to the android.

"Clo-e, I want you to meet our passenger."

Phaid made a parody of a bow.

"Please to meet you, Clo-e."

A voice came from the android.

"It -is -good - to - have - a - passenger - aboard - I - understand - you -have - engaged - in - mating - with - my - owner. This - normally -improves - her - temper - and - that - on - its - own - makes - your - visit - pleasurable."

R'Ayla regarded the android bleakly.

"It has a conversational circuit that I should have ripped out a long time ago."

A light on what approximated the android's head blinked on and then off again.

"I - should - warn - you - that - I - am - very - old - and - any - tampering - with - my - circuitry - is - likely - to - lead - to - a - terminal -malfunction."

Phaid laughed, but R'Ayla shook her head.

"I swear the damned thing's blackmailing me."

"Why don't you trade it in?"

R'Ayla shrugged.

"There aren't that many of them left. I fear I'm stuck with what I've got."

For a while, R'Ayla disappeared into the cabin. The smell of cooking wafted up on to the deck, and, between them, Phaid's nostrils and stomach reminded him that it was a long time since he had eaten.

The breakfast was a simple affair: fish and vegetables deep fried in oil, washed down with fruit juice. The two of them ate, without ceremony, from the same bowl. When the meal was finished, Phaid leaned back against the gunwale and took a deep, satisfied breath. He was closer to being content than he'd been for a long time. About the only thing that worried him was a vague but nagging feeling that the android was watching him.

Not even the android could spoil his mood, though. He had a full belly and was sexually satisfied, the sun was shining and the river breeze prevented it from becoming intolerably hot. For a while the call of the big cities was muted. Right then he wanted nothing more than to loll in the deck of the boat, listen to the water, bask in the heat and watch the green jungle slip by on either side.

R'Ayla busied herself with chores around the deck. As far as Phaid could see, most of them were scarcely necessary. Clo-e the android did everything that was important, but if the boat woman felt the need to keep busy, Phaid wasn't about to interfere.

Every so often, she'd point something out to him. A near submerged reptile would raise its head on a long serpent neck or a flock of gaudy birds would spiral out of the jungle in a shrieking cloud. At one point it was possible to see the tips of two huge stone pyramid-shaped structures above the level of the trees. Phaid sat up and stared at them thoughtfully until the boat rounded a bend in the river and they were hidden from view.

R'Ayla looked at him inquiringly.

"You ever seen those before?"

Phaid shook his head.

"No, but I've heard there are things like that deep in the

jungle, things from the old times."

"I guess there are things from the old times all over."

Phaid nodded.

"Pretty much. I never saw those particular ones before, but I've seen plenty of others. They built some strange stuff back when."

"I suppose you've traveled a lot."

"Some."

"And seen a lot."

"Enough."

"You want to tell me about it?"

Phaid spread his hands.

"Sure, what do you want to hear?"

"About things from the old times. From the times before the Lords went away."

Phaid raised an eyebrow.

"The Lords?"

R'Ayla glanced at him sharply.

"You believe in the Lords, don't you?"

"I believe that things changed mightily back in the old days, but I'd hate to say what caused it."

"The priests teach us that the Lords created a paradise on earth. That it prospered and flourished for a thousand years, but then the Lords saw that common man was beyond help, that he was locked into his iniquity and they departed from our world to make their homes among the stars. It was then that the gales came, the terrible winds and the heat and the awesome cold of the icefields. As punishment for their sins mortal men were . . ."

The words came as though they had been learned by rote, way back in childhood, and were being repeated from memory. Phaid cut her off with a quick nod. It was unlike the practical, hardheaded woman and it made him uncomfortable. The priests obviously had a strong hold on the river people.

"I know what the priests teach. I've heard the scriptures. I also know what I've seen and some of it was mighty strange."

R'Ayla suddenly grinned like a girl. The spell of the priests was gone.

"Tell me about the strangest."

27

"The strangest?" Phaid thought for a while. "I guess the strangest I ever came across was the place way up in the hills behind Gant."

"What was that?"

"Well, it's kind of hard to describe. It was a big place, made out of solid stone. I guess if you saw it you'd call it a palace, except it wasn't like any palace I've ever seen. It didn't have any windows, or any doors, or any way that you could get inside, and all the time it make this noise. A high-pitched hum, like there were a million insects trying to get out."

"Did anybody live there?"

"No people."

R'Ayla looked a little uneasy.

"You mean some*thing* lived there?"

Phaid was pensive.

"Maybe, maybe not. All I can tell you is that something happened there."

"Happened?"

"Everyday, at exactly the same time, a small flap in the building would open. There was a ramp leading down from it. Small machines would roll out. They were squat, kind of irregular in shape, and they moved under their own power."

"Androids?"

"Who knows. Nobody could ever fathom what they did or why they were there. One old man, they used to say that he was crazy, he spent half his life trying to solve the secret. He even built a cabin close by the place so he could watch them come out everyday. Not even he could discover the secret."

R'Ayla was looking more and more confused.

"These things didn't do anything at all, they didn't have any purpose?"

Phaid shook his head.

"Each day, they'd just roll down the ramp and form up in rows. There was this paved area at the bottom of the ramp. They'd form up on that in real neat rows. Thirty of them, there were always thirty of them. The old man told me that there'd been thirty of them for as long as he could remember." Phaid looked as though he was having trouble believing his own story. "Once they'd formed up in rows, the machines would just stand there, all through the afternoon, not moving, not making a sound. It was as if they were just waiting for someone to come along and collect them."

"And nobody did?"

"No . . . well, that's not strictly true. Just before sunset another machine would appear. It was much bigger than the first ones, big enough to pick them up in bunches of four. It went backwards and forwards, gathering in all the small machines, taking them back through the flap they had come out of. Once they were all inside, the flap would shut and that would be it until noon the next day. Except for the hum, of course, that never stopped."

For a short while R'Ayla didn't say a word. She seemed totally sucked in by Phaid's story. Then she exploded.

"Just a minute. You're a silver tongued devil, gambling man. A liar, too, I expect. You just made the whole thing up. Admit it."

Phaid put a hand on his heart.

"It's all true, I swear it. I saw the place with my own eyes. In fact, I sat there all afternoon, just watching it."

R'Ayla shuddered.

"It sounds like ghost stuff."

"It was."

"But why should anyone bother to build a thing like that, even in the old days?"

"They probably had a use for it in the old days. It's just that we've forgotten."

R'Ayla stared at the river. She seemed to be deep in thought.

"Do you think it was very different in the old days?"

Phaid pursed his lips.

"It must have been. There's so much left of them that there must have been a hell of a lot more people back in the ancient times."

R'Ayla frowned.

"I'm not sure I'd like that."

"Also the gales didn't split up the world with bands of heat and cold like they do now."

R'Ayla looked at him as if this wasn't news.

"That's what the priests taught us."

Phaid shook his head.

"I'm not talking about the priests. I'm talking about what

29

I've seen with my own eyes. There's relics of the old times frozen in the ice plains, and other relics in the worst parts of the burnt deserts. Nobody in their right minds would build in those places."

"It just proves the scriptures."

Phaid took a deep breath.

"Hmm."

R'Ayla looked at him with a worried expression.

"You do believe the scriptures, don't you?"

"That the Lords departed for the stars and then the whole world was divided by zones of heat and cold as a punishment for our sins?"

"That's what the priests say."

Phaid's face twisted into a cynical smile.

"That is what the priests say."

"But do you believe it?"

Phaid shrugged.

"Sure I believe it. There was this time, though, when I saw a man, this wandering preacher. A crowd had gathered around him. He was telling them how the Lords weren't anything more than people like us, and if they did cause the gales it wasn't as a divine punishment but because there was once some vast machine that could control the weather and we had forgotten, over the centuries, how to use it. He said it was the same as the way we had forgotten what some kinds of androids are supposed to do, like the place I saw in the hills behind Gant."

R'Ayla looked worried.

"That's ridiculous. How could a machine change the weather? That man must have been crazy."

"He probably was. He hadn't been going for too long before the Religious Police came and carried him away. I never did meet anyone who saw him again. I reckon if the priests want us to believe their story that bad, I'll believe it. I'm all for a quiet life."

That seemed to terminate the conversation. Phaid had the feeling that he'd said the wrong thing.

"I'm not saying the man was right." He tried to lighten the mood. "I don't want you to think you made love with a heretic."

Again it was the wrong remark. R'Ayla didn't answer. When the silence had continued for some minutes, Phaid knew he ought to do something to restore the previous friendly atmosphere. With only a single covert glance at Clo-e the android, he moved closer to R'Ayla and put his arm around her. She didn't respond. She still appeared to be lost in her own thoughts. Suddenly she turned her head and looked at him.

"Do you think life was better in the old times?"

Phaid held her closer to him.

"How should I know? I'm a gambler. I think about now, not what has happened or what's going to happen. I have enough trouble with what is happening."

R'Ayla smiled at him, but her eyes were sad.

"It is never good to speak of priestworks. It never brings luck."

Although they remained close for the rest of the journey, the conversation left a shadow that never quite went away. It was a measure of the priests' power.

3

After two days the river was so wide that it might have passed for the open sea. R'Ayla's boat slid beneath sandbanks, disturbing flocks of the bad tempered gulls that fed and quarreled on them. At this point, the river was so shallow that the craft might have run aground if it hadn't been for Clo-e's unerring navigation.

Early on the third day, they were treated to their first sight of Freeport, the major city of the great river. It lay on the outer side of a huge bend where, over millions of years, the river had cut into a line of low hills, creating high cliffs of white limestone. Much of the city sprawled back into the hills, but the port itself was situated where a fold brought land and water to the same level.

The city was dominated by the gray stone bulk of the old, domed fortress. It squatted on the highest of the city's five hills like some sinister, brooding toad, commanding a baleful view of all traffic on the river for many miles in either direction.

Around the base of the dome were the black, gaping ports that once housed massively powerful banks of photon cannons. The stones of the dome itself were cracked, blackened and pitted where they had bubbled and melted under attack by awesome heat weapons. These were, however, old wounds. The fortress was a relic of a former age, not the ancient days that Phaid and R'Ayla had talked so much about, but a closer time, one about four hundred years earlier when the world had made a last try at organizing itself into nations and empires under the squabbling, warring rule of kings, princes, presidents and dictators.

Harald, known as The Mad, was just one of these. The fortress that Phaid was looking at had been both his crowning achievement and the site of his downfall. Harald the Mad had made Freeport, then known as Haraldhelm, his capital. From there, he had sought to extend his empire all the way up the great river to where the rapids prevented further navigation, and all the way down to the sea.

Harald's neighbors had objected violently to his territorial ambitions, and, after a series of border wars, they had united and forced him back into his citadel. The siege lasted seven years and became a matter of legend and saga. Tales of horror, cruelty and deprivation had carved themselves a permanent place in history. In the end, though, it hadn't been Harald's external enemies who had finished him. It was his own starving subjects who had risen up against him, and rather than be ripped apart by an angry mob, Harald the Mad had died by his own hand.

Once Freeport had become an independent city, nobody particularly cherished the memory of Harald. Over the centuries there had been many attempts to tear down, blow up or otherwise destroy the fortress, but the ugly pile's rugged construction had defied all efforts. Even though Harald had failed in his ambitions, his fortress remained as an inconvenient monument.

Harald the Mad had not only been a victim of both his enemies and his own people, he had also been a victim of history. Even while he was still dreaming his dreams of conquest, the nations and empires were inexorably falling apart and subdividing into self-contained city states. By Phaid's time, there was only one definable nation-state remaining, and even that, commonly referred to as the Republic, was loose, sagging and chronically corrupt. Understandably, it was Phaid's primary choice as an ultimate destination.

The rest of Freeport was a complete contrast to the fortress. Whitewashed houses reflected the sunlight, greenery spilled over from shaded courtyards, and narrow streets wound their way up the hillsides. On the tops of the hills, small forests of windmills spun in the offshore breeze and on the roofs of many houses, sun catchers glinted in the morning light. Along the waterfront, android cranes dipped and swung, moving cargo on and off a packed mass of barges and riverboats.

Although Harald the Mad's citadel still lowered over Freeport, the real power in the city had moved to the Governor's solid colonnaded mansion and the Temple of the Consolidated Faith, where, beneath the white marble spire, the priests maintained their subtle but unrelenting grip on the hearts and minds of the population.

As the boat came nearer to the harbor, Phaid's attention moved past the town and down the river where a tall column of angry clouds forever swirled and spiraled. It was where one of the superheated gales roared off the land and collided with the cold air over the ocean.

On the very edge of the clouds a tiny craft with gossamer wings soared and dived on the thermal currents produced by the violent clash of temperatures. Phaid knew the craft was piloted by a wind player, one of the reckless and often self-destructive breed who rode the complex and dangerous airstreams in their fragile vessels. Sometimes they did it in competition, in the hope of valuable prizes and in front of huge crowds of spectators, but other times they rode the turbulent sky totally alone, and just for the hell of it.

Although he would rarely admit it, Phaid had a great respect and admiration for the men and women who played the wind games. He might call himself a gambler, but he really only played the odds and hustled for a living, the wind players were the real gamblers. They threw their lives into the contest, with only the skill of their reactions between victory and swift, sudden death.

The boat now edging its way through the jam of other craft, was making for one of the piers of the harbor. Clo-e the android scurried about, still trailing leads to the steering motor controls, pushing out fenders, preparing mooring lines and bleeping at other androids on the dock in their secret, high-pitched, electronic language.

Once the boat was secured to the dock, Phaid went below to collect his bag. When he came back, R'Ayla was waiting for him. Her face was set as though she was trying very hard not to show any emotion. Phaid avoided looking her directly in the eye.

"I guess this is the end of the line."

"It's the end of the river, for you."

"Yeah."

Phaid felt a definite pang. The journey on the boat had been a pleasant interlude. He'd been very happy on the river, watching the jungle go past by day and sleeping with R'Ayla at night. He fought it down, though. He learned a long time ago that a gambler had to keep moving. There was no percentage in trying to stretch out a good time beyond its natural limits. He grinned at R'Ayla.

"Don't take any shit from that android, right?"

R'Ayla didn't seem amused.

"Right."

Clo-e didn't seemed amused, either, if her high angry warbling was anything to go by. Phaid was about to step on to the dock when R'Ayla touched his arm.

"Phaid."

"Yeah."

"If you ever come back this way..."

"Sure. The very next time I'm in Freeport, I'll make the boat dock my very first stop."

"You promise."

"I promise."

R'Ayla quickly kissed him on the cheek.

"You better get going."

"Sure. Take care of yourself, R'Ayla. I'll look for you when I come back this way, okay?"

"Okay. Goodbye, Phaid."

"Goodbye, R'Ayla."

He jumped across the small space between the boat and the pier. Straightening up, he took a deep breath. If he could possibly avoid it, he'd never come anywhere near Freeport again. He was on his way back to the bright lights and the big money. Once he got there, he'd make damn sure that he was never forced away again.

Phaid shouldered his way through the milling crowds on the waterfront. Once he looked back at R'Ayla. She was busy arguing with an android harbor inspector. Phaid slung his bag over his shoulder and marched on. For the first time in a long while he felt as though he was going somewhere.

Not that he didn't have problems. He was practically broke and he would need to eat and find a bed for the night. The harbor area was the oldest part of Freeport. Behind the warehouses and piers was a maze of narrow streets, alleyways, cramped, dilapidated buildings and dark, claustrophobic courtyards. It was a place where crimps robbed drunken sailors if the whores, pickpockets or muggers hadn't got to them first. It was a neighborhood of bars and bordellos, a paradise for thieves and cutthroats, and a sanctuary for men on the run from the law. It was also a place where a gambler could, with a little sleight of hand, raise a quick stake and move on to something better.

Accordingly, Phaid directed himself into the bustle and furtive glances of the old town. Even though it was still early in the day, the girls were already out, shaking their backsides and showing their legs and breasts in the hope of turning the first profit of the day. Quite a few of them threw Phaid wanna-have-a-good-time glances. Each time Phaid just grinned and shook his head. Sweaty wrestling on a stained mattress was not what Phaid was looking for right then. Even if he had been, he hardly had the price. Thus, either way, the whores were out.

In a small enclosed courtyard he saw something that was closer to what he was looking for. Two sandrunner lizards had been set on each other in a shallow pit. They snapped and hissed abuse at each other, alternately striking with vicious fangs and slashing with powerful, taloned back legs. Sandrunners, even in the wild, were vicious, evil tempered beasts, and this pair was the result of many generations of selective breeding to make them meaner, tougher, more hostile and generally bring out the worst in their characters.

Around the edge of the pit a crowd of loafers and penny-ante hustlers yelled encouragement and offers of advice. The betting was brisk, and for a brief moment, Phaid was tempted to get involved with the play. Then he spotted two thickset men in leather jerkins, wearing a lot of ostentatious jewelry. They seemed to be taking a percentage of the money that was circulating. A pair of the Freeport watch, in the black tunics and gold braid with old but serviceable blasters tucked under their arms, lounged against the wall in the back of the crowd. From time to time they would exchange significant glances with the duo in the leather jerkins.

For Phaid, this was both a tempting and dangerous situation. Fights were an easy hustle. The crowd at a fight was usually drunk and willing to bet on just about any stupid proposition. It didn't make too much difference who did the fighting. Humans or animals, it was the same shouting, sweating confusion of yelling men, brutality and money changing hands. As far as a gambler was concerned the fight was only the means of providing a result. It was just more entertaining than flipping a coin. The problem was that this was a small town fight and small towns liked to keep their stupidity in the family. They normally evolved mechanisms to prevent a stranger winning large sums of their money and leaving town with it. In extreme cases, these mechanisms could involve a fine and a stretch in jail on some trumped-up charge or even the stranger being dumped in a ditch with a broken head.

Despite the risks, however, Phaid knew that he would have to go along with at least some of the play around the lizard pit. To be broke and hanging around in a place like Freeport was as equally imprudent as trying to get away with some of the inhabitants' money. He would have to get something out of the situation. He would simply take the minimum he needed and he'd take it in small amounts in the most modest and self-effacing manner. Accordingly, he moved through the crowd, keeping as far as he could from the men in the jerkins and the jewelry and also from the brace of watchmen.

One of the lizards was down on its back and bleeding badly. The crowd, knowing it was only a matter of time, was roaring its head off. A local hustler offered reverse odds in the heat of the moment and Phaid quickly doubled his winnings. As the two beasts were removed, one dead and the other clearly badly wounded, bets were paid and everyone made a rush to the beer sellers before the next fight started. This was the main drawback to trying to remain modest and self-effacing at something like a lizard fight. A man without a drink was a man with a dishonorable purpose. After four jugs, Phaid began to behave a little more flamboyantly than he'd intended. He made two easy and noticeably large bets. Fortunately, he came to his senses when he saw the two men in the leather jerkins talking together and nodding in his direction. He was still sober enough to need no further urging. One of the thickset locals started easing through the crowd in his direction while the other went for the two watchmen.

Phaid melted. He didn't have all the money he needed but it didn't matter. He spun away into the crowd, ducking low and wishing he could will himself invisible. Once outside, he sprinted down an alley and then zigzagged in and out of the steep narrow streets that led up and away from the waterfront. Instinct carried Phaid deeper into the old town. Numbers provided the greatest safety and the greatest numbers were in the busy market streets. As he strolled a little watchfully through the open air bazaars, he as repeatedly approached by street vendors who offered everything from supposedly gold rings to hot fish pies, and girls who only offered variations on a single theme; an old woman wanted to tell his fortune while another tried to sell him a lucky amulet.

All through the remaining daylight hours, Phaid kept on the move, and nobody bothered him. Once night had fallen he felt that he could afford to relax a little. He found himself a corner table in the cool of an open fronted soda fountain and ordered one of the pale yellow foaming concoctions that were the specialty of the house. The base of the drink was some sort of local spirit. Phaid shuddered to think what went into the rest of it.

Through three or four hours and maybe six of the foaming drinks, Phaid kept himself to himself. Then he gave way to a pure and noble impulse and, as is so often the case, dumped himself into the trouble he'd been trying to avoid all day. A minor disturbance over on the far side of the room had caught his eye. An unsavory trio in lube stained coveralls, obviously roustabouts from a caravan crawler, were harassing a boohoom.

Phaid knew that he should ignore the commotion but he'd basically drunk too much and had a need to prove himself the good guy. He had a particular soft spot for the subhuman boohooms and disliked seeing them harassed.

This particular boohoom, as far as Phaid could tell rejoiced in the name of Ucko, was no stranger to the waterfront bars and taverns. He loped from one place to the next hawking the broadside news-sheet that provided Freeport with most of its information from the outside world. He was always followed by his constant companion, a skinny, dirty yellow mongrel dog. Boohoom and dog had an almost supernatural rapport.

Nobody could agree about the boohooms. One school claimed that they were retrograde human mutations, another theory was that they were a kind of advanced monkey. A third faction argued that they were a totally separate species. Certainly they looked like some intermediate stage between man and ape, with their stooped gait, long arms, low foreheads and coarse, reddish brown body hair. They were stupid, there was no denying that, but it was a placid, amiable stupidity. Despite this, there was still a particular type of individual who took an unpleasant delight in tormenting the boohooms. It would have been easy to assume that the boohooms were victimized because they were stupid. Unfortunately the same ones who picked on them were also the ones who terrorized the elaihim, the tall, pale hyper-intelligent race that now shunned the habitations of men because they had been so persecuted over the centuries.

As Phaid approached the three roustabouts, he casually let his hand drop to where the fuse tube was hidden under his coat. He was starting to have certain trepidations about his gallant gesture. The three roustabouts were ugly characters. Between them they had two broken noses and at least half a dozen facial scars. They were holding up the dog by one ear and mockingly asking the boohoom what was the best way to cook it.

Phaid wandered up to them and grinned.

"You guys must have been eating the cooking in this place."

They must have been big and ugly but they were far from quick on the uptake.

"Huh?"

Phaid continued to grin pleasantly.

"If you gotta desire to eat that mangy dog, then you must have tasted the cooking. Compared with what comes out of that kitchen, even a dog would taste good."

The roustabouts glared at him. Their faces managed to get even more brutish and hostile. Phaid grimaced.

"I guess it wasn't that good a joke, now I come to think about it."

The biggest of the three clenched his fists and belligerently thrust his florid face into Phaid's. His breath smelled of beer and rotting teeth.

"You want somethin'?"

The boohoom was slowly edging behind Phaid. Phaid took a step back, moving the short creature with him.

"I was just wondering what a dog-eater looked like."

The face jutted even closer.

"You callin' me a dog-eater?"

Phaid looked down at his boots. There was nothing to be salvaged from this situation. Phaid took a deep breath and then punched the biggest roustabout in the face as hard as he could. As the man staggered back, Phaid ran for a flight of stairs in back of the place that presumably led to the second floor. One of the roustabouts had a blaster in his hand. A section of wall right beside Phaid's head exploded. Phaid jerked out his fuse tube and fired back. The floor on which the roustabouts were standing also blew up. None of them was hurt, but the noise attracted the attention of a trio of watch who came crashing through the sidewalk tables, pulling out their own weapons. It was a mess.

Phaid took the remaining stairs two at a time. On the next floor, he went straight to the nearest window. It was small. The catch stuck at first, but a quick blow with the butt of his fuse tube freed it. Phaid swung open the window. To his relief there was a sloping roof just half the height of a man below the window. Getting out wouldn't be all that easy, however. The only way to manage it was a wriggle through the small space head first. It wasn't a trick he relished, but with the sound of heavy boots already resounding on the stairs, Phaid knew that he had no alternative.

41

Mick Farren

There was some moment when he thought he had stuck fast halfway through, but violent struggling finally freed him and he tumbled out on to the roof below. Phaid's troubles were far from over. He found that he was rolling, sliding, trying frantically to both hold on to his bag and stop himself sailing clear off the end of the roof and making the bone breaking drop to the street.

It was a long drop to the streets, and quite a formidable leap to the next building. Phaid wasn't exactly delirious with joy about the prospect of jumping from rooftop to rooftop, but there was no other alternative. There wasn't even any way he could put if off. With a sinking feeling, he backed up, got a firm grip on his bag, shut his eyes and ran. To his surprise, he landed, safe if sprawling, on the next rooftop.

Deciding that he still must have a little luck left, Phaid hurried on. He didn't want some nervous householder to mistake him for a burglar and loose a blaster on him. It took him four more buildings until he found a set of stairs that would take him down to the street.

He'd hardly been walking for more than ten minutes when he turned a corner and walked slap into two officers on foot patrol. Both Phaid and the officers stopped. For a long moment they stared at each other. His first instinct told Phaid to stand his ground and attempt to bluff it out. Then a second, much stronger one started urging him to run. While he was still trying to make up his mind, one of the officers raised his weapon.

"Hold up, you!"

Phaid listened to the second instinct and ran. There was a flash and roar and the discharge from a blaster seared the wall beside his head. Phaid swung into an alley and pounded down it. While one officer had been shooting at him, the other had whipped out a communicator and started bellowing into it. It would only be a matter of time before reinforcements were on the scene. Phaid knew that he was in big trouble.

The alley led out into a wider street. Two more discharges flared around Phaid's heels. His breath was coming in labored gasps, and, as far as he could tell, the two officers were gaining on him. He knew he had to do something drastic. Reluctantly, he pulled out his fuse tube.

Dropping the bag, he turned and, using both hands, took

42

careful aim at the ground just in front of his pursuers. He fired three fast shots and the cobbles of the street burned and smoked. The two officers staggered back, temporarily blind from the flash. By the time they could see again, Phaid had vanished down a side street.

He was by no means out of the woods, though. He might have temporarily shaken off the two officers on foot, but now he had another problem. A watch flipper was coming from the direction of the waterfront. Cruising just above rooftop level, it seemed to be searching the streets one by one. A sun globe in the underside of the craft lit up the ground beneath it as brightly as day.

The light hit the end of the street that Phaid was in. He looked around desperately. There was no place to run. The best he could do was to press himself into a doorway, but even that was too shallow to give him complete protection from the probing light.

He was certain he was going to be caught when the door behind him suddenly opened. He would have fallen backward if a rough hand hadn't grabbed his arm. For a second or more he was completely overtaken by confusion and panic. He was being pulled inside a dark building, a voice grunted at him and he found himself staring into the hairy face of a boohoom. The face smiled.

"Come. You come."

Phaid gave up. The door was swiftly shut behind him. Totally bemused, he let himself be led into the darkness.

He was led down winding steps, cobwebbed cellars, even more steps and dim passages until he was finally in the catacomb made up by the town's heating ducts, sewers, storm drains and long forgotten tunnels that must have been built as adjuncts to Harald the Mad's fortifications.

All along the way he passed dozens of boohooms. Some rested after a long day of cleaning, carrying and performing all the menial tasks for which there were no available and conveniently programmed androids. Others sat in small groups, apparently talking out the night in a laborious series of grunts and ill formed words. Still more, who from their matted pelts and deathly pallor seemed to stay permanently in the darkness of the underground maze, either sat and stared, contemplating

43

some dull, nonhuman nirvana or scavenged, for what, Phaid didn't care to think about.

Many of the boohooms, like Ucko, were accompanied by animal companions. Some of these were surface creatures— dogs, birds or monkeys. Others petted pale reptilian things from the sewers and tunnels. He had even witnessed two boohooms making love, a spectacle that caused him to quicken his pace, even though his companion seemed inclined to watch.

The ultimate destination was the straw-filled niche that the boohoom and his dog called home. Once there, there was nothing to do except to huddle into the straw and attempt a shallow and disturbed sleep. Things constantly scurried and rustled. Somewhere nearby water dripped with a nerve-racking monotony. The boohoom snored loudly and even the dog whimpered as it dreamt.

4

Even after a jangled, joyless night in the lair of the boohooms, Phaid couldn't help but be awed by the sheer size of the land crawler. Taller than a five-story building, its flat, windowless sides were more like cliffs of corroded steel and ceramic than part of a vehicle that actually moved. The dull black heat exchangers along the upper part of the machine that provided most of its power, once it was into the searing heat of the hot wind plains, were like the squat turrets of some sinister castle. The massive caterpillar tracks, wider than many of the streets of Freeport, dwarfed the fueling gangs that were busily pumping thousands of atmospheres into the crawler's converter tanks through thick, snaking pipes that gleamed with hoar frost from the super-cooled fuel.

The crawler was a dull, burnt, rusty red. No livery or decoration could survive the white hot winds. The whole of its body work was scarred and pitted by the smoldering rocks and burning sand that were driven like hail in the blaze of the gale.

For a long while Phaid could do nothing except stand and stare. It scarcely seemed possible to him that such an enormous object could be energized into lumbering, swaying life. Of course, he'd seen land crawlers before. He'd ridden more than he really cared to remember. If he'd been on top of things, he would have marched briskly into the depot, paid the static android who issued tickets and headed for the passenger ramp. As it was, he felt too numb and exhausted to do anything but gawk.

In the early morning, although Phaid couldn't fathom how the boohoom knew it was morning in that sunless world, he had been led back out of the labyrinth and set on his way to the field where the crawlers turned around. With his head down and one eye open for the watch, Phaid chose a route that took him through the most crowded of the town's streets. Almost to his surprise he reached the field without a single incident.

Phaid finally realized that he'd been standing gawking at the crawler like some rustic fresh in from the hills and made an effort to pull himself together. Still on the alert for the watch, he went inside the small, single-story depot building.

There was only one crawler going out that day, and after questioning an information android, he found that if he booked steerage for a place called Wad-Hasa Wells, he had his fare and just a little to spare. He reluctantly paid over most of his hard earned cash, took a ticket, and moved towards the boarding ramp.

Steerage passengers were expected to use a separate ramp to the superior beings who could afford first-class or second-class fares. On the first-class ramp a group of merchants and a fop, in a lime green outfit with exaggerated wide shoulders, nagged the android porters about their luggage or watched with bored smiles as the lesser mortals had to carry their own bags on to the crawler.

Steerage accommodation was notably low on comfort. The section was right at the top of the machine where the swaying was worst, and, once they reached the hot plains, the refrigeration units would be hard pressed to maintain any kind of tolerable temperature.

Phaid found that he'd been assigned a minuscule cabin, little more than a cubicle. There was a tiny closet, a two-tier bunk and just about enough floor space to climb in and out of it. He didn't like the idea of the double bunk. It could mean he'd be sharing the cabin with another passenger. He fervently hoped that the crawler had been underbooked. Two people in this small enclosed space would make the journey unnecessarily wretched when they moved into the heat.

Phaid hid his remaining money under the mattress, placed his fuse tube under the pillow and tossed his bag into the closet. Wearily, he climbed up into the top bunk and lay back, staring at the gray metal ceiling. There was nothing else to do until the big machine got underway. After his night with the boo-hooms, Phaid welcomed the chance to simply stretch out and let his mind go blank.

He was just beginning to drift off to sleep when the cabin door slid open with a crash. Phaid sat bolt upright, cracking his head on the ceiling in the process.

"Shit!"

"Did I startle you, friend?"

"Damn right you did."

"Sorry about that."

"So you damn well..."

Phaid cut the sentence dead. He had taken his first good look at the newcomer, and the newcomer was huge. He was at least a head taller than Phaid and almost twice as broad. His flaming red hair was cropped close to his skull, but his beard was full and luxuriant, framing a leathery, weather-beaten face and a pair of penetrating blue eyes that Phaid would not have cared to meet across a gaming table.

The man's dress completely complemented his image of strength and menace. His dark brown leather tunic was rein-forced with copper studs larger than Phaid's thumb. His green, coarsely woven breeches were tucked into fur boots held to-gether with crisscrossed thongs. An antique blaster with deli-cate tracery on the long barrel and a carved, opalescent handle hung in a well-worn holster on a finely tooled but very old leather belt.

Heavy bronze bracelets clamped round both wrists marked him as one of the wild clanfolk from the mountain passes of the far north. A snake tattoo that coiled around one of his bare forearms indicated that, among his clan, he was one of the warrior caste. A number of old scars also indicated that in his case, warrior wasn't just an honorary title.

The clansman's outfit was completed by a long-haired animal pelt, probably that of a gray lupe, thrown around his shoulders and a shapeless hide bag hung over his arm.

Phaid sighed inwardly, this was all he needed. It was bad enough having to share the tiny cabin at all, but having to share it with a hulking semi-savage was pushing crowding to the limit. For the thousandth time he cursed the run of ill luck that had forced him to leave the Republic.

The clansman threw his bag into the closet beside Phaid's, then he unbuckled his belt and blaster and dropped them on to the lower bunk. He gave Phaid a brief, inspecting glance.

"The name's Makartur."

"Phaid."

Phaid noticed that Makartur didn't have the usual, thick, guttural accent of the mountain clans. This, in itself, wasn't all that unusual. Life was hard in the north and many of them took to wandering. This one probably hired out as a mercenary and was traveling in search of a couple of city states who were busy having a war and who might be willing to buy his services.

Makartur sat down on the bunk with a grunt and started unlacing his boots.

"Where you headed, Master Phaid?"

"I get off at Wad-Hasa Wells."

Makartur stretched out and grunted some more.

"No money, huh?"

Phaid leaned over the side of his bunk with a look of surprise on his face.

"What?"

"You've got to be running out of money if you're going from Freeport to Wad-Hasa Wells, and probably running, too. It stands to reason."

Phaid was starting to get just the slightest bit alarmed.

"It does?"

Makartur laughed.

"Don't worry yourself, manny, I'm not interested in what you may or may not have done, but riding a crawler from Freeport to Wad-Hasa Wells ain't no vacation."

"You know this place?"

Makartur shook his head.

"I've never been there, but I can imagine. It's probably the first water after you leave the gale plains. My guess is that it's nothing more than an oasis, a few buildings and a market place where the herdsmen from the surrounding desert come in to trade their stock.

Phaid scowled.

"It sounds desolate."

"More than likely."

"Ain't that always the way of it."

Makartur raised a bushy eyebrow.

"You look put out."

"You can say that again. I'm on my way to the Republic. I hoped I'd be able to build up another stake in this Wad-Hasa place to make it the rest of the way. How the hell can you do that at a goddamn waterhole."

Makartur grinned.

"You'll probably find yourself some honest work if you look hard enough."

Phaid grimaced.

"Sure. Just dandy."

The clansman's grin broadened.

"I wouldn't worry about it too much, manny. If it's any consolation, I'm in the same predicament."

"You're going to Wad-Hasa too?"

"I don't have the cash to go any further."

"So where do you want to get to in the end?"

"The Republic, same as yourself."

Phaid was surprised.

"You're going to the Republic?"

He couldn't imagine what this hulking brute would want there.

Makartur's voice sharpened.

"You can think of a reason why I shouldn't?"

Phaid was quick to placate.

"No . . . no." He made his tone light and conversational. "What are you going to do when you get to the Republic?"

Makartur allowed himself a measured pause before he answered. "I'll probably be minding my own business, the same as I do in most other places."

That killed the conversation stone dead. Phaid found himself swamped by an awkward silence. Fortunately it didn't last too long. There were a number of dislocated throbs from deep within the crawler. After a while they formed into a regular pattern, speeded up and finally blurred into a single, continuous hum. The metal frame of the crawler ground and shrieked its protest as the power was transferred to the huge driving tracks. Finally the crawler lurched, swayed and started forward. Phaid propped himself up on one elbow.

"It look like we're underway."

Makartur didn't seem particularly interested. Outside the crawler, however, unknown to Phaid and Makartur, a small crowd had gathered to watch it move off. No matter how many times an individual had seen one of these giant machines come to life, only one with a very impoverished soul could fail to be impressed. The throb of its engines could be felt through the ground. Sheets of pale fire played around the discharge stacks high on the rear end of the machine. The massive tracks churned up the earth and gradually, almost impossibly, the towering structure of steel and ceramic lumbered forward, very slowly gathering speed.

High up in the steerage class the lumber, swaying and continuous throb of the engines weren't impressive. They were simply an irritation. They made relaxation difficult and sleep elusive. No conversation was forthcoming from his traveling companion, and Phaid decided to investigate such meager amusements as the crawler might have to offer.

He knew that down in the first-class saloon there'd be the clink of quality glassware, the rustle of silk and velvet. Liveried waiters would be serving the best cuisine that the android cooks could prepare. Most galling of all for Phaid was his knowledge that large sums of money would be changing hands across the elegant gaming tables.

Phaid, of course, like all the others traveling cheap rate, was barred from the first-class areas. All that was available to him was the junk food, cheap liquor and rough company of the steerage canteen. Even that, though, was better than just lying in his bunk. Surreptitiously he extracted a couple of twenty tabs from beneath his mattress. He swung his legs over the side and dropped to the floor.

"I think I'll go and look for a vending machine. I had a bit of a rough night and I can't remember when I last ate."

Phaid slid open the cabin door but paused at the sound of Makartur's voice.

"Oh, manny?"

"What?"

"I wouldn't worry about your money so much. Keep it under the mattress if you want to, but I'm not about to steal it."

Phaid reddened. He was taken completely by surprise.

"Uh . . . yeah, thanks."

"You're welcome."

Phaid thoughtfully closed the door and started down the corridor. It seemed as though he had to walk almost half the length of the craft before he came across a panel of food and drink vendors. A skinny girl with dark straggling hair and a dirty face was leaning against it. As Phaid was inserting his money into the slot, she caught his eye with a direct, almost challenging look.

"Hi."

Phaid punched out his selection. Her loose sleeveless jacket, baggy trousers and flat broken down shoes told him she was probably a boat kid on the run from home. He grinned at her.

"Hi yourself."

"You want to buy me a drink, huh?"

Phaid raised an amused eyebrow.

"Who says I can afford to buy you a drink?"

"My name's Sarli, you can buy me for a ten tab."

Phaid sighed. "Aren't you a little young to be doing this kind of thing?"

"Young?" The girl laughed bitterly, "I've been doing this for as long as I've been able. My stepfather started me at it."

"Your stepfather?"

"The third husband of my mother. You know what it's like on the boats? When we were in port, he'd even sell me to sailors My mother didn't stop him. She had the boat to run and she liked a quiet life. When I tried to stab him she dumped me over the side."

The girl sounded bitter enough for Phaid to actually believe her, but he shrugged. What could he do? He had heard enough hard luck stories from whores, both senior and junior. The world moved in disastrous patterns. What was he supposed to do about it?

"Growing up can be a difficult business. If you expect to get slapped in the face you don't generally come in for a lot of disappointment."

The girl scowled.

"I've had worse than slaps in the face."

Phaid sighed.

"I believe you."

He turned wearily away and, carrying his food, started back down the corridor. The girl called after him.

"You don't want me."

Phaid just shook his head, he didn't even bother to look around. "I don't want anything right now."

As Phaid opened the cabin door, Makartur was sitting on his bed fingering and apparently muttering to a small beaded bag that hung around his neck on a leather thong. As soon as he saw Phaid he quickly stuffed it out of sight under his tunic.

Phaid pretended he hadn't noticed. He'd seen pouches like that before. They were amulets of the old religion, the one that worshiped harmony with the earth and its creatures. All too often their owners found themselves dragged away by the Religious Police. The Consolidated Faith went to great lengths to stamp out any competition. Phaid turned away so Makartur wouldn't see his face. All he needed was a religious fanatic sharing his cabin.

At that point Phaid had climbed into his bunk and lay flat on his back. With the temperature noticeably starting to rise, the crawler had to be moving into the heat. All Phaid could do was to shut his eyes and try and sleep through as much of the discomfort as possible. Unfortunately sleep refused to come. His mind kept drifting back to both the bitter hopeless girl and the red-haired giant in the lower bunk. The girl was now just a memory, a part of the past, but Makartur was very much a piece of the present.

Although it often didn't pay to voice it, Phaid had an instinctive distrust of religion. Whether it was the calculated combination of guilt, fear and promise of reward with which the priests maintained their armlock on the population or the darker, underground mysteries of the old proscribed faiths, Phaid wanted as little contact as possible with any of it. The idea that the lower bunk was filled with a devout and highly unlawful believer added a degree of mental unease to the already very present physical discomfort of traveling steerage.

Although Phaid's people came from the comparatively comfortable northern foothills, it was close enough to the cold bleak fells for him to have a very clear picture of Makartur and his people. His long-left-behind relatives had even worshiped a milder version of the grim, vengeful and totally unforgiving ancestor gods who ruled the spirit world of the high hills with a rod of iron. Phaid could picture how the man's mind worked. He had been through the dehumanizing cruelty of warrior training, a fate that Phaid had gone to very serious lengths to avoid. At the end of warrior training you emerged with muscles like steel bands, a mass of arm tattoos and a mind in which rigid and inflexible will was clamped down on a seething cauldron of festering resentment and white hatred. Whenever the control was relaxed, this whole mess would boil over into the murderous berserk rage that made the warriors of the hills such valued mercenaries.

These warriors were dour, humorless men, closed and private, rarely showing emotion. They were taciturn and slow to anger, but when they did, their destructive ruthlessness was frightening. With them, slights were never forgotten, grudges went deep and a feud could last for generations. They judged everyone according to their exacting warrior code and trusted no one. To complete the mixture, their every move was dictated by omens and portents and dogged by symbol and superstition.

It seemed like hours had passed and still Phaid was unable to sleep. He was rocked and jolted; sweat was flowing from every pore in his body. He knew there must have been times when he'd been more uncomfortable but he couldn't remember when. There was no mistaking that they had hit the hot plains and the refrigeration plants were battling to keep the interior of the crawler at something like tolerable temperature. Down in first-class they were winning, up in steerage, however, it was a losing fight.

The throb of the motors was regularly punctuated by loud clangs and crashes as quite large rocks, hurled up by the violent

53

super gales, smashed into the sides of the big machine. Phaid tried to imagine what the inferno outside really looked like. One thing a crawler didn't come equipped with was windows. Even if a transparent material could be made thick enough and strong enough to withstand the flying pebbles, there was nothing to stop it being quickly rendered opaque by the blasting sand.

The closest Phaid could get in his mind to a picture of the hot plains was a dull glowing red, like the middle of a furnace set in violent motion. It was hard to conjure an image of something that could destroy a man's eyes in a matter of seconds.

For more centuries than anyone could remember, the hot plains formed the real boundaries that kept peoples and cultures confined to their own narrow territories. Men had crossed the icefield and braved the frozen gales long before they'd attempted to journey through the impossible heat. The hot plains were shrouded in legend and mystery. From the border lands they looked like some mighty wall of dark red swirling mist. Primitives thought it was the edge of the world, the beginning of the lands of demons and devils. Up until the invention of the crawler, and the massive loss of life that had gone into making it operate properly, the heat had been the ultimate barrier. It was only a matter of five hundred years since the hot plains had been penetrated by regular travel routes.

Yet, according to many legends, they hadn't always existed. Most cultures had folk legends about how man had once been able to wander freely all over the world. The Church claimed these legends with the doctrine that the bands of heat and cold had been thrown across the countries of the earth by the vengeful Lords when they grew angry at man's wickedness. Heretics countered with the idea that they were the result of some terrible, long-forgotten cataclysm.

From primitive to philosopher, everyone was in agreement that the hot plains and the icefields were something that had occurred after man walked the earth. Facts tended to bear out this theory. Ancient artifacts from supposedly isolated cultures showed too great a similarity to each other, more than could be dismissed as strictly coincidental. And then there were the androids. Identical types of android could be found in almost every part of the globe.

Although the androids were able to reproduce themselves, and a few humans could manage simple repairs when they were damaged, the secret of their construction was one of the great, lost mysteries. Somehow they had existed before the bands of heat and cold had formed and had spread to every part of the world. Nobody knew how or when or even why.

If all religions agreed that the evidence pointed to the establishment of these belts of extremes of climate as something that had occurred during the time of man, then it was possible man or man's ignorance might have been in some part responsible for their creation. Few sects or dogmas disputed this.

Broad agreement was all very well, though. It didn't prevent bitter disagreement over fine points of interpretation or theory. These disagreements had, in their time, been responsible for countless hangings, burnings, torture, pogroms, a dozen or more wars and all the other trappings of theological dispute.

Phaid found that his head was whirling. It must have been the heat. Politics and religion were usually things that he avoided even thinking about. His ancestors had had a mystic side to their natures, but most of that had been knocked out of him by his early wanderings in a rough world. His mouth was dry and the heat was close to unbearable. He felt as though he was burning up. It was difficult to breathe and his mouth tasted like well walked sand. Just as he felt that he was starting to lapse into hellish red hallucinations, a voice came from the lower bunk.

"Manny?"

Phaid leaned over the side of the bunk. His voice was a rasping croak.

"Yeah?"

"You sound like you're having a hard time."

"I can't take much more of this goddamn heat."

"You never ride steerage before?"

"Yeah, but I don't remember it being as bad as this."

"You never do . . . afterwards."

"Maybe."

"Could you use a drink?"

Phaid sat up, almost banging his head on the ceiling.

"I could drink anything." He swung out of his bunk, dropped to the floor and squatted down beside Makartur. The clansman

55

was holding a ceramic flask with silver mountings. He handed it to Phaid, who was relieved to discover that the big man wasn't against drinking. Phaid took a swallow and only just stopped himself gagging.

"Sweet Lords, what is this stuff?"

"It's a tight little brew they make back where I come from. Just the dew from a good still and a few herbs. It's a drink that makes men."

"You also eat babies for breakfast?"

The big man's grin broadened.

"We never go that far. You don't want to believe the stories you hear."

Phaid offered him the flask back, but Makartur shook his head.

"If you want to get some sleep, you'd be best advised to take another couple of pulls."

Phaid took a deep breath and once again put the flask to his lips. The liquor went down a little easier, but he knew it'd be a long time before he actually developed a taste for Makartur's "tight little brew."

"I got to tell you, Mak, that's powerful stuff."

"Aye."

Phaid straightened up, aware of a slow burning sensation in his belly.

"I think maybe I'll lie down and see what happens."

"Just a couple of wee things before you go."

Makartur was no longer grinning.

"What are they?"

"The first is that I know you saw my amulet earlier."

Phaid was suddenly ill at ease.

"And?"

"And I know a traveler like you has maybe seen an amulet like it before."

"That's possible."

Phaid didn't like the drift of the conversation.

"I don't believe in getting between a man and his religion. You don't have to worry about me, Mak. I won't say anything."

"So you know about the old faith, do you, Master Phaid?"

"A bit, it doesn't worry me none."

"So you wouldn't think about turning in anyone who wor-shiped in the old ways?"

"Hell no, Mak. Live and let live. I stand by that."

Makartur nodded his head very slowly.

"Even when the temple priests are offering a reward for anybody who points the finger at one of us?"

Phaid took a step back.

"Wait a minute, I'd never do a thing like that. I don't have any dealings with the priests or their lousy money."

Makartur smiled.

"I'm glad you said that."

"You are?"

"Very glad, manny. If you had been entertaining thoughts of claiming a reward on me, you would never have lived to spend it. We who follow the old ways are not as scattered and beaten down as those canting priests of the Consolidated Faith would like folk to believe."

Phaid let out a relieved breath.

"Like I said, I never get between a man and his religion."

Phaid started to climb back into his bunk, but Makartur grabbed his leg.

"There is one other thing, Master Phaid."

"There is?"

"I said I had a couple of things to say to you."

Phaid nodded.

"That's right, you did."

Makartur tightened his grip.

"For as long as we are forced to be together, will you remember one thing?"

"I'll try."

"Don't call me Mak. Where I come from it's a mark of disrespect. It's close to an insult."

Phaid remained very still. He could feel the strength in the big man's fingers and was glad that they were gripping his thigh, not his throat. He kept his voice as level as he could.

"I wouldn't want to insult you."

"You'll remember."

"I'll try . . . very hard indeed."

Makartur suddenly burst out laughing and let go of Phaid's leg.

"You're a good boy, Master Phaid. You'd better get some rest."

Phaid scrambled back into his bunk once again and mopped his brow. He now had more than the heat to make him sweat. Not only was he being roasted alive, but he also seemed to be sharing a very small cabin with a very large religious madman. Then there was the horrible liquor he'd been handing out. Makartur had claimed that it would send Phaid to sleep. As far as Phaid could tell from the taste, about the only thing that it was likely to do was to poison him.

No sooner had that thought crossed his mind than Phaid started to feel drowsy. His eyelids were heavy, he found that it was hard to concentrate. He had a final alarming thought that maybe he actually had been poisoned, but then it hardly seemed to matter as he drifted into darkness.

5

"Mother earth, have you ever seen such desolation?"

The desert stretched all the way to a line of low, rounded hills on the horizon. It wasn't a view without beauty, but it was hardly what either man really wanted to see. On the just tolerable edge of the hot winds, it was a dust bowl where no rain ever fell. A white hot sun beat down on an expanse of sand that was predominantly a pale ocher but here and there was splashed with vivid streaks of dark red, purple, blue and dull gold. Outcroppings of rock had been eroded by the sand into weird and twisted shapes that might have been petrified monsters, or the works of some insane sculptor. There was something almost frightening about the wild colors and tortured shapes. Most frightening of all, though, was that nowhere was there the slightest sign of any life.

A ramp bull bustled up to them.

"Okay! Okay! Let's get going! If you ain't got a ticket, on your way. Go watch the scenery from someplace else."

He made the mistake of attempting to push Makartur on down the ramp. Makartur swung around and was about to grab the bull by the front of his stained brown tunic. Phaid quickly caught hold of the big man's arm. He noticed that two more bulls, part of the crawler's own muscle squad, were at the bottom of the ramp and starting to unclip their clubs from their belts. Phaid got between Makartur and the bull who'd done the pushing. He smiled ingratiatingly.

"I'm sorry, sir, but we were just wondering where the town might be."

Makartur looked disgusted, but fortunately didn't say anything. The ramp bull positively sneered.

"It's round the other side of the crawler, you fool."

Phaid half bowed and, nudging Makartur to follow him, he hurried down the ramp. The big man was obviously still spoiling for a fight, but he reluctantly followed. They made their way round to the rear of the huge machine and were treated to their first sight of Wad-Hasa Wells.

"Hell's teeth, will you just look. Whatever possessed human beings to live in a place like that?"

Wad-Hasa Wells was almost as desolate as the desert that surrounded it. Most of the habitations lay beneath the ground. Small white domes protected the entrances from wind and sand. These domes were the same light ocher as the desert and they gave the oasis the look of a piece of land that had melted, bubbled and then solidified.

The meager water supply was marked by an area of sparse foliage, two towering spike ferns and a small thicket of cactus. Phaid slowly shook his head. Even Freeport would have been preferable.

"What the hell do we do now?"

Makartur looked at Phaid with raised eyebrows.

"We, manny? We? I wasn't aware that we'd suddenly become partners or anything of that nature."

Phaid was a little taken aback. He'd started to assume that he and the clansman would work on the problem of getting out of Wad-Hasa Wells together. To Phaid, it was only logical, but Makartur didn't seem to see it that way. A third party did, however, think that there was some sort of connection between the two men.

"Hey, you two!"

It was an unshaven, ragged looking man in a flowing but dirty robe who'd been behind them coming off the crawler. Phaid and Makartur both turned.

"Yeah?"

"Youse two gents got any money?"

Both men were instantly suspicious.

"Who wants to know?"

The traveler raised both hands.

"No, no, don't get me wrong. I'm not looking for a handout or nothing like that. You just seemed as though you could use a few words of advice."

"We could?"

"By the way youse acting, it don't seem like you ever been in these parts before."

Makartur nodded.

"Aye, that's a fact."

The traveler grinned.

"I thought as much. If you had, you wouldn't be hanging around the way you are."

"Hanging around?"

"That's right."

"What's wrong with hanging around, then? Is there a law against it or something?"

"As good as."

"What?"

"As soon as the crawler moves out, the Deemer sends his boys to go round up anyone who ain't got the cash to the next stop."

"The Deemer?"

"Runs the town, don't he? Deems what's going to happen, if you see what I mean. At least that's the derivation, like. Anyhow, once the crawler's on its way, his boys make the round up of them who get off here because they can't afford to go any further."

"And what do they do with the ones who get rounded up?"

"They give them until sundown to come up with something; and if they can't they get marched out into the desert. If they try and creep back, they get shot."

"But you can't survive in the desert."

61

"Got it in one."

Phaid and Makartur looked at each other and then back to the traveler.

"What are you going to do?"

"Me? Oh, I'm in the clear. I've got relatives here, haven't I?"

The crawler's drive roared into life as if to underline the bad news.

Phaid glanced nervously at the vibrating machine.

"What the hell do we do?"

This time Makartur didn't question the use of the word "we." The traveler also glanced at the crawler. It seemed about ready to move. He spoke very quickly.

"Best thing you can do is get inside someplace. The sink'd be the best place. The Deemer's boys usually figure that if anyone makes straight for the sink he's got to have money and as a rule they leave him alone."

"What's a sink?"

"It's kind of like an inn. You can't miss it. It's the big dome with a blue sign, right by the covered well. You'll find a door and some steps. This is my advice, get in there. I better be moving if I'm going to see my relatives."

With that he scurried off, leaving Phaid and Makartur staring at each other openmouthed.

"We'd better find this sink place as fast as we can, manny."

"Now you're talking about we."

"Don't mess around, man. I've got no fancy to tangle with the local law and order."

They hurried towards the collection of low domes that made up the visible portion of the town.

"Where the hell is this place, do you reckon?"

"My bet is that the well ought to be somewhere close to those spike ferns."

They moved off towards the small patch of dusty greenery. Phaid found that there was something a little disturbing about walking in among the low domes. It appeared that during the heat of the day the entire population went underground. Phaid didn't like the idea of having a whole town beneath his feet. He tried to imagine what the place was like at night. His impression was that it would be distinctly eerie.

They came out from between two domes, but quickly stopped and backed up the way they had come. Half a dozen men in broad brimmed white hats, off-white semi-uniforms and heavy boots had emerged from a dome some way away. Both Phaid and Makartur ducked down so they wouldn't be spotted over the tops of the lower domes.

"I guess they must be the squad."

Fortunately, the squad was marching in the opposite direction. Phaid looked around anxiously.

"Where's this sink or whatever it's called?"

Makartur scanned the domes and then pointed.

"There! The blue sign."

"What are we waiting for?"

Walking as swiftly as possible, but not actually running, they moved off in the direction of the blue sign. When they got there, the lettering was in a script that Phaid couldn't read, but, just like the man said, there was an open doorway with a set of steps spiraling downwards. Phaid hesitated and glanced at Makartur. "You think we should go inside?"

"It'd be better than standing around."

They started down the stairs with Makartur leading the way. The stairs made three complete turns, and then a low arch led into a cool, dimly lit room.

It was indeed some sort of an inn, but pretty unlike any inn that Phaid had ever seen before. Being hollowed out from the earth, nobody had bothered to create anything approaching a regular shape. There were recesses, alcoves, fluted pillars, some niches packed with cushions and low divans as well as regular tables and benches. Two more arches opened on to flights of descending stairs that went down to lower levels even deeper underground.

At the far end of the room a marble counter served as a bar. For such an out of the way place it was surprisingly well stocked. Ranks of varied bottles lined the shelves behind the counter, and a row of dully gleaming brass pressure kegs stood in a row on the floor beneath it. A line of ale taps on the counter were connected to them by shiny steel hoses.

As well as the variety of alcohol, there were also various grades of the narcotic dog gold leaf in screw top, airtight glass jars, a selection of cheeses in an open fronted display case and a squat, brass bound cracker barrel. The whole setup had an air of cleanliness and efficiency.

Phaid and Makartur marched up to the counter where what they assumed was the innkeeper, or whatever name was given to the proprietor of a sink, was polishing a glass and pointedly ignoring them. He was a dapper little man with slicked down hair, a crisp white shirt and a fancy brocade hat. His small, mean mouth and close set eyes suggested that he wasn't the sort one could ask a favor of with any hope of getting it granted. Phaid arranged his face into a tentative smile. "Sure is hot outside."

The innkeeper sniffed. "So what else is new?"

"You got any ale?"

The innkeeper nodded curtly at the row of kegs.

"What do you think those are?"

"So what kind have you got?"

"Light, dark or extra strong."

"Give me an extra strong."

He glanced at Makartur.

"You want an extra strong?"

"A light will cut the dust just as well."

Churlishness seemed to be contagious in the sink. Phaid turned back to the innkeeper.

"An extra strong and a light."

While the innkeeper took two hinged top steins down from a shelf and started filling them, Phaid surveyed the place a little more carefully. There were only five other customers. Two elderly men were absorbed in a game of checkers, while three others sprawled on cushions. At first Phaid thought they were asleep, then he noticed the slow, bovine motion of the jaws and realized that they were far away in the magic world that appeared once you'd chewed enough dog gold.

"Quiet around here, isn't it?"

The innkeeper pushed the two steins across the marble.

"Sometimes it is and then again, sometimes it ain't. That'll be four tabs."

Phaid dropped four singles on to the counter. Makartur tossed another one down.

"Give me a twist of dog gold."

He glanced at Phaid.

"You want some?"

Phaid shook his head.

"No thanks. This place is weird enough as it is."

The innkeeper scooped up the money, but didn't seem inclined to go about his business. After a couple of seconds, Makartur jutted his chin at him.

"You want something?"

"I thought we might settle the matter of rent."

"What are you talking about?"

"You ain't been through these parts before, have you?"

Both Phaid and Makartur shook their heads. The innkeeper smiled thinly.

"I didn't think so. That's why we ought to settle the rent right now, so there won't be no misunderstanding when it gets around to sunset."

Makartur started to bristle.

"And what do we need to pay rent to you for, little man?"

"You planning to still be here after sunset, are you?"

"Maybe."

"Then you need a place to stay. If you ain't taken a room by sunset then I got to report you both to the Deemer's office. If you can't show that you got some other place to stay the Deemer's men'll march you out into the desert with the rest of the vagrants. It's the rules, see. Nothing I can do about it."

"This town don't seem to be strong on hospitality."

The innkeeper leaned forward.

"Well, that's just where you're wrong, my friend. We got a lot of hospitality in this town. It's about all we do have. It's a valuable commodity. We sell it to travelers for the best price we can get. That's how we survive. It ain't easy here in the desert, let me tell you. There's nothing going spare for rogues and bums and freeloaders."

He paused to give both Phaid and Makartur a significant look.

"So gents, do you want a room or don't you?"

Phaid slowly closed his eyes. He'd never been anywhere that was so tightly sewn up.

"How much is a room?"

"Ten a piece, or fifteen between you if you want to share one."

"We'll share."

Between them they were just able to come up with it. Reluctantly they placed it on the counter. The innkeeper actually cracked a smile.

"That's nice and tidy, then. You want to book for tomorrow right now? There won't be a crawler in for another three days."

Makartur scowled.

"We'll talk about tomorrow when tomorrow comes."

The innkeeper's smile faded.

"Don't leave it too long. I've heard that the drovers will be coming through with a herd. We get pretty busy when that happens. You may not get a room."

That seemed to be the end of the conversation. Phaid and Makartur carried their ale to a stone table as far from the counter as possible. Phaid sat down with a sigh.

"What a place."

Makartur shrugged.

"We're all right for today. Maybe something will turn up tomorrow."

Phaid was determined not to look on the bright side.

"What the hell can turn up? There's not even a crawler in for three days."

"The drovers for one."

"What are these drovers?"

"They move the herds of veebes from the savannahs and down to stockyards in the cities. In this region, I'd guess they'd be resting over on the way to Chasabad."

Phaid looked puzzled.

"How can a bunch of veebe herders do us any good?"

"A lot of ways, manny. If we get real lucky, there might even be one of my people among them. There's plenty of them who've found work with the drovers. Although, mind you, there are not that many who come as far as this region."

"And if one of your long lost relatives don't turn up, what then?"

"When the drovers come to town, there'll be drinking and chaos. This Deemer can't have that many men. They'll have their hands full with rowdy drovers. If we keep our heads down, they'll not have time to bother us."

"I suppose that's something."

"Who knows. When drovers hit town there's usually a few fall out drunk, unconscious or even dead. It seems to me that we'd probably be able to hire on. At least Chasabad is in the right direction for the Republic."

Phaid looked genuinely horrified.

"Hire on? Chasing a herd of stinking veebes? You're joking."

"You could do a lot worse."

"I can't think how."

Makartur pulled a chunk off the twist of dog gold and stuffed it into his mouth.

"Maybe you've a plan to find your own way out of this place?"

Phaid scowled.

"Maybe."

Sitting in a bar, no matter how exotic, without any money can quickly become a bore. Phaid made his beer last as long as possible but once it had gone there wasn't another damn thing to do. The dog gold had started to go to work on Makartur. His eyes glazed. It seemed as though drink and dog gold were two exceptions to his rigid warrior puritanism. Phaid suspected that women would probably be the third. After a while Makartur stumbled to his feet. He waved a brawny arm in the direction of the exit.

"I'm going out."

Phaid sniffed.

"What the hell for?"

"To look around."

"Do what you like."

Phaid was actually starting to feel sleepy. It might have been the dry desert air or, more probably, some sort of hangover from Makartur's home-brew. His eyes were actually starting to close when the sink was suddenly full of women. Phaid woke up with a start. He was stunned. It was the very last thing that he had expected. The sleepy little hostelry suddenly took on the ambience of a bordello, a bordello instantly created for the drovers and their money. There were about thirty females in the noisy gaggle; some young, some not so young, and a few scarcely more than children. Their ages may have varied, but they were all heavily made-up and decked out in costumes that

67

were obviously the individual owner's idea of the ultimate in seductiveness.

The women were in high spirits and they filled the bar with an almost carnival atmosphere as they waited for the drovers to arrive. Phaid, as the only functioning male in the place, became the stooge for a good deal of teasing and badinage. These desert women quickly proved that they could be as creatively foul mouthed as any bunch of big city whores. Phaid thought back to the girl on the crawler and wondered if everyone in these desert lands around the fringes of the heat survived by selling themselves.

As the booze started to flow, the women vied to outdo each other in coarse boasts of what they were going to do with the drovers, once they arrived. When Phaid, slightly bewildered, tried to find out what was going on, a matronly lady called Dorrie, in a low cut, flowing gown that revealed a great deal of her ample bosom, did her best to explain. It appeared that the veebe herd had been spotted out in the desert and the town was gearing up for the influx of drovers. Although Phaid did not shock easily, it came as quite a surprise to find that the women were not full-time prostitutes, but simply all presentable women in the town, married or single. They were getting ready to take up the ancient trade with the full connivance and cooperation of fathers, husbands and brothers. It was apparently no disgrace. Phaid had never met anything like this before and he had difficulty dealing with it.

"Your husbands? Don't they mind?"

Dorrie grinned at the blurted question.

"Mind? Of course our husbands don't mind. It's natural, isn't it? When the drovers, or any other traveling men come to town, they want women. We're the only women here and we provide. This whole town survives by providing for travelers. We don't make anything and we don't grow anything in this desert. It'd be stupid if we didn't perform this service. It'd lose a whole lot of cash for the town, and anyway, a change is as good as a rest, that's what I always say."

The other girls around her shrieked with laughter. As far as they were concerned, they were making a valuable contribution to the isolated town's precarious economy and enjoying themselves in the bargain.

"I'd have a strapping drover instead of my old man any day of the week."

For an hour or more, the women went on laughing and drinking in anticipation of the party to come. Phaid found himself buoyed up and borne along by their enthusiasm. He also found that, despite the disapproval of the owner of the sink, a number of free drinks were pressed upon him. He was, in fact, three parts drunk when a small boy ran down the stairs waving his arms and shouting.

"They're here! They're here! The drovers are here!"

6

Phaid crouched behind one of the most outlying of the low domes and hoped that nobody would notice him. Wad-Hasa Wells had been turned into a scene out of a nightmare by the horde of drunken drovers. Burly figures, loaded to the eyes on dog gold and alcohol, stumbled about in the darkness shouting and bellowing like animals. All the above ground glo-globes in Wad-Hasa Wells had long since been shot out, and the only light came from a thin crescent moon and the fires that had been lit between the domes. It reflected dimly on sweaty, vacant faces or the brown skin of women who had been stripped naked during the long debauch and who had been either unable or unwilling to find their torn and discarded clothes. Men fought each other without knowing who they were pounding or why. When the drovers fought they used any way they could to knock down the opponent. Heads, fists and feet all came into play. They gouged, they kicked and they butted. The slightest imagined insult could start yet another pair brutally slugging it out.

Couples fornicated on the sand between the domes right alongside the sprawled figures of those who had either been pummeled unconscious or had passed out from some alarming combination of drink and drugs. They made no attempts at modesty and appeared to have no sense of shame. The air was filled with a cacophony of screams and grunts. Women shrieked and giggled, there were roars of laughter and bouts of drunken singing. Somewhere someone was bawling mindlessly. Someone else was crying. When the drovers had a party they took it all the way to the limit.

They had hit town in the late afternoon, just before sunset. The herd had thrown up a massive cloud of dust that must have been visible for miles around. When the animals were secured in the pens on the edge of the town, the drovers had come in looking for whatever good times Wad-Hasa Wells had to offer. Even weary, sweat stained and dirty from their trek across the desert, they presented a wild and crudely romantic image. They came into the town with the swagger of an invading army. They strutted in their high-heeled boots as though they owned the land. Hard watchful eyes peered from beneath the drooping brims of their wide hats. Heavy blasters and wicked, curved knives hung from their wide, decorated leather belts. The weapons were in easy reach, an unarguable back-up to each man's nomad bravado. Like most wandering peoples, a drover's wealth was ostentatiously displayed on his person. Jewelry glittered. Gold seemed to be a particular favorite. It hung from their ears in heavy hoops, around necks in chains or medallions, it decorated the hilts of knives and the butts of blasters, and weighted down hands and arms in the form of rings and bracelets.

The drovers came from no particular tribe or nation. Their weather-beaten, often scarred faces ranged from deep mahogany to blue black. There were equine faces with high foreheads and prominent noses, there were broad, flat featured faces with slanting almond eyes. The drovers came from all over the world. What held them together was the loneliness and hardship of their work and a fierce pride in their freedom and individualism.

As they made their way into Wad-Hasa, their short, brightly colored cloaks or ponchos swirled behind them, and their loose, flowing trousers flapped in the light desert breeze. Determined to make an impression, they strode like princelings rather than men who, in reality, performed a dirty menial job and spent their lives smelling of animal dung and stale sweat.

This picture of the primitive invading army was enhanced by the long lance that each man carried. These too were decorated to the individual's taste but were not, in fact, weapons; they were the main tool of the drover's trade. The little tingler unit set in the tip of each lance was the most efficient way of goading the stubborn and bellicose veebes into a semblance of movement.

As the drovers got the first few drinks inside them and began to move around flirting with the girls, Phaid decided he had seen his chance to profit from the invasion. He had pulled out a deck of cards and attempted to get a game started. The drovers couldn't have reacted worse if he had committed open blasphemy. Later he learned that there was an almost universally held belief that a man had only a limited amount of luck in his life and it was considered close to a crime to go squandering it on a game of chance. He had only diverted the wrath of the drovers by quickly claiming that he was a fortune-teller, not a gambler. This, however, had put him in trouble with the Deemer's men. Fortune-telling was illegal in Wad-Hasa and only a lot of fast talking by both him and Dorrie had saved him from a flogging.

A few fights had broken out while it was still daylight. These had been minor affairs, though. Pairs of drovers settling trail grudges and individuals arguing over the price of a bottle or a woman were easily quelled by the Deemer's men using a firm hand and occasionally resorting to the flexible clubs that seemed to be their favorite weapons.

Even through the garish, blood red desert twilight the combination of the Deemer's men and the seemingly indefatigable townswomen kept the drovers in check. Once darkness, however, spread over the little oasis, the belligerence of the now hopelessly drunk herdsmen began building towards the point where nothing would be able to hold it.

The breakout had started with a chair swinging, glass shattering brawl inside the sink. It had apparently been sparked off by an evil tempered giant who answered to the name of Murf. Murf had decided that the proprietor of the sink was simultaneously raising the prices and reducing the measures of the booze. In a towering rage of customer indignation, he had attempted to dismantle the place single-handed. His companions, deciding that wrecking the sink was too much fun for Murf to have all to himself, had joined in the destruction with a will. The proprietor had summoned the Deemer's men to save what was left of his property, and the confrontation was on.

Phaid watched from the shelter of the locked and barred entrance dome of a nervous citizen's home. A large squad of the Deemer's men had charged into the sink, but after only a short pause, filled with yells and muffled crashings, they had emerged again, retreating before a crowd of angry drovers hurling glasses, bottles, debris and any other missile that came to hand. The Deemer's men had failed to hold the line, and anarchy flared like a conflagration all through the town. Pitched battles spread over the sand in and around the domes, and the darkness was filled with tangles of grunting, fighting men.

It was at this point that Phaid decided to make himself scarce. He could scarcely believe the run of events in which he seemed to be trapped. There had to be an easier way to get back to civilization than the tortuous route that he was traveling. No matter how he racked his memory, he couldn't fix on an incident that could have caused this almost supernatural run of ill luck.

It wasn't quite clear who was the first to use a blaster. Afterwards, the drovers claimed that it was one of the Deemer's men who fired first. Those nearest to the incident told how the law officer and a lanky young herdsman had set about each other and when the drover seemed to be getting the best of things, the lawman had drawn his weapon and burned his opponent down. A girl who had been caught in the middle of the melee thought the drover might have had a knife in his hand, but this was hotly disputed by his companions.

Whatever the truth might be, once one shot had been fired, everyone got in on the act. The night was split by the white, jagged crackle of fuse tubes and the roar of blasters. Phaid ducked low as the stink of burned flesh and superheated sand reached him.

Phaid was relieved to find that the fire fight didn't last as long as he'd feared. The Deemer's men appeared to have given

the decision to the drovers, at least for the duration of the night.
The town was split, the drovers had the surface and the townspeople, with the exception of some very independent women,
had retreated to the safety of their underground dwellings. Most
locked up tight, but some, backed by teams of heavily armed
relatives and neighbors, still sold liquor and dog gold from a
handful of open doorways.

The uproar went on long into the night. All through, Phaid
did his best to make himself as invisible as possible. This wasn't
a total success. Despite Makartur's stated intention to keep his
head down, the big man had mingled with the drovers and then
proceeded to get as aggressively drunk as possible. He had
even, for a while, struck up a stumbling, staggering companionship with Murf, the hulking oaf who had initiated the first
fight in the sink. Unfortunately, they had spotted Phaid creeping
around the edge of a dome and attempted for a while to get
him as drunk as they were. Although, on the surface, Makartur
was aggressively boisterous and jovial, Phaid could sense a
layer of hostile distrust beneath the backslapping. It disturbed
him. Drunken warriors could be lethally unpredictable.

After a while the two of them got bored with trying to force
booze on Phaid and they moved off in not very efficient pursuit
of three local women who had given them the sign as they
lurched past. Their effort to get Phaid drunk hadn't been completely unsuccessful. He found himself reeling and no longer
worrying so much about his self-preservation. He even started
to tentatively join in the spirit of the drovers' crude partying.
Somewhere along the line someone had given him a twist of
dog gold. A few minutes after that the hallucinations had begun.
From then on, Phaid had wandered through the chaos of the
small desert town in a soft cocoon of extreme, if somewhat
blurred, well being. The scattered fires became sources of swirling and undulating color. Rainbows flashed when the light was
reflected from sweating skin or the polished blade of a knife.
The figures around the fires and those moving unsteadily through
the darkness were twisted into grotesque and jumbled shapes
that were all part of some weird, wild and not quite human
dance. Even the domes seemed to take on animated life. They
appeared to throb and pulse like bubbles of energy trying to
break loose from the ground and float up and up into the wild

night sky. Phaid felt as though he was walking around the inside of some giant boiling cauldron.

If, under more normal circumstances, half of these things had happened to Phaid they would have driven him at least part way out of his mind. He would have feared for his sanity and fled before the distortion of his senses. The joy of dog gold, however, and the reason its users sang its praises so loudly, was that, no matter how fearsome the hallucinations might appear, or how fast they might bear down on the unwary user, anyone in the grip of the drug was also soothed and lulled into a state of simply not giving a damn. Phaid felt he was drifting effortlessly, a few inches off the ground. He was invincible. Nothing could touch him. There was a bottle in his hand. He could hardly remember his name.

A familiar face swam into his field of vision. Red lips moved into the shape of a smile. They parted slightly.

"Lords, dearie. You look well out of it."

Phaid stood for a moment, staring stupidly. At first the name refused to come.

"Dorrie!"

The face looked concerned.

"Are you all right, love?"

Phaid realized that the face was expecting him to come up with an answer, but once again his mind only turned over with the greatest of difficulty.

"Yeah . . . I'm . . . fine."

"You've been at the dog gold, haven't you, dearie? You got to watch that stuff. It'll rot your brain."

Phaid held out his bottle. It was the best he could do.

"Would you . . . like a . . . drink?"

A body joined the face and a hand stretched out to take the bottle. While Dorrie drank, Phaid found himself staring transfixed at her ample breasts. All manner of disconnected but very voluptuous images chased each other through his head. Dorrie held out the bottle, regarding Phaid with a raised eyebrow.

"What d'you think you're looking at?"

"I'm . . . looking . . . at you."

Dorrie laughed and shook her head. "I know what's going through your mind, all you dog gold fiends are the same. One look at a woman and everything except sex is gone with the wind." She struck a pose. "Well, dearie, do you like what you see?"

"Y . . . yeah."

"Is that all you've got to say?"

She came closer to him. Her hand was stroking his cheek. He could feel those full, wonderful breasts press against him. Then Dorrie let out a gasp and Phaid's world exploded into brutal, blinding, bright orange pain. He had one clear thought. He had been hit very hard over the back of the head with something very solid. Maybe a blaster or maybe the butt of a lance; then he sagged down into merciful blackness.

Sadly, the blackness didn't last forever. All too soon the pain ebbed back. It wasn't any ordinary pain. It wasn't even a singular pain. The pain that Phaid was experiencing came on multiple levels and in a variety of forms. Sunlight was trying to drill its way through his eyelids. His stomach was twisted into a leaden, acid knot. Every muscle ached and, over and above it all, there was the scarcely thinkable throbbing at the back of his skull. It felt as though it had been caved in. Just to make matters worse, someone kicked him in the ribs.

"Up, you!"

"Wha?"

One of the Deemer's men was standing over him with a less than pleasant expression on his face. It was morning.

"Up!"

Fighting back nausea, Phaid scrambled to his feet before the heavy boot could get in another kick. All around him, other drovers were being woken in a similar manner. The Deemer's men seemed to be getting even for their defeat of the night before. The sleepy, hungover drovers found themselves herded at weapon-point into a sullen group near the animal pens. Makartur was among them. Phaid edged up beside him.

"What's going on? What are they planning to do to us?"

Makartur regarded Phaid through bleary, bloodshot eyes.

"Why don't you piss off, manny, and let me suffer on my own."

"Don't all these weapons being pointed at us worry you at all?"

Makartur shook his head and winced. "Not as much as this headache."

"Suppose they start shooting?"

Makartur glowered. "There'll be no shooting so long as we don't start anything. Everyone knows the rules."

"The rules?"

"Aye, the rules. We're being thrown out of town. It always works that way in these hick towns. The drovers come in, they spend their money, get a bit out of hand and find themselves thrown out in the morning."

Phaid gingerly explored the back of his head with his fingertips. There was a lot of swelling and his hair was matted with dried blood.

"Somebody slugged me."

Makartur sniffed. He didn't seem too interested.

"Was it your woman or your bottle they were after? Or did you aggravate someone?"

"Woman, I guess, although she was scarcely mine."

Makartur glanced briefly at the back of Phaid's scalp.

"It looks like they used the butt end of a blaster. You ought to get that cleaned up."

He pointed to where drovers were clustered around a line of wooden tubs.

"There's water over there. You'd best dunk your head in it."

The cold and not too clean water came as a quite considerable shock. After two or three dips below the surface he started to feel a little better. He was cleaning the worst of the blood out of his hair when the drover beside him nudged him in the ribs and pointed past the watching guards. A short man with a tendency to waddle was coming towards the pens, flanked by what looked like his own personal guard. He wore a much more resplendent version of the standard white uniform.

"Will you look there. It must be the boss of the whole damn town."

"The Deemer himself."

"He's probably looking for an extra payment for last night's trouble."

"They cover every angle, don't they."

The drover shrugged. "They got a living to make."

"I've noticed."

Phaid watched while two drovers were let through the cordon of guards. They went into a huddle with the Deemer and his two assistants. Phaid glanced at the man beside him.

"What's going on now?"

"They're figuring the extent of the damage."

"Who are those two?"

"The drive boss and the drovers' representative."

"Representative?"

"The drive boss works for the herd owner. The representative looks after the drovers' interests. That way nobody gets to put anything over on anyone else. At least, that's the theory, but once the bribing gets down ... well, you can work it out for yourself. Our drive boss is called Shako. He's a mean bastard, but he's fair when he's sober. The rep, Graudia, he's something else again. If you've got a gripe, he's the last one you want to go to. By all accounts the owners have got him right in their pockets."

After what looked like a good deal of haggling, a price must have been set for the night's rampage, because money changed hands, the Deemer's men lowered their weapons and suddenly the drovers were going about their business. Amid the hustle and bustle, Phaid relocated Makartur.

"Are you going with them?"

Makartur nodded. "Aye, I hired on already."

"What about me?"

"What about you? I'm not your keeper."

"Can I hire on too?"

"You best go and check in with Shako, the drive boss, he's ..."

"I know which one he is."

Phaid had had about enough of Makartur's attitude. He made his way to where Shako was standing, bellowing orders and generally turning the hungover drovers into a cohesive working unit. Just as the drover at the tub had described, he was a mean bastard. Tall and rangy, he had cold, pale green eyes and the features of a hawk. Without any preamble, he looked Phaid up and down and apparently didn't like what he saw.

"You want to sign on?"

"That's right."

"You've worked a herd before?"

"Of course I have. It ain't been for a long time, but I worked on a drive before."

Phaid lied glibly, but Shako wasn't convinced.

"You don't look like no drover."

"Appearances can be deceptive."

"Show me your hands."

Phaid held out both hands, palm upwards. He was acutely aware that they lacked the horny callosity that was the mark of a true drover. He had the soft, well cared for hands of someone who rarely touched anything more rugged than a deck of cards. Shako sniffed.

"It must have been a very long time ago indeed."

Phaid dropped his hands. "Yeah, well..."

"Personally, I think you're a damned liar, but I had three men killed last night so I can't be choosy who I take. You're hired." He waved his arm at Makartur who was standing around waiting for an assignment. "You, hill man, get over here."

Makartur scowled and moved towards them. Shako nodded in Phaid's direction.

"He's driving for you."

Makartur's eyes narrowed.

"Him?"

"You're both new so you're partnered together."

"I'd rather it wasn't him."

Shako's expression was flinty and dangerous.

"You don't have any rather. You two work together or you stay here and see what the Deemer wants to do with you." Shako shot Phaid a final contemptuous glance. "I'll tell you one thing, by the time you reach Chasabad, those dainty hands of yours will be worked raw." He grinned at Makartur. "Take him and show him what he's got in store."

Phaid quickly discovered that what he had in store was a combination of bouncing, muscle wrenching, bone jarring physical work and mind crushing boredom. All those times that he'd sat in a fancy restaurant, spending his winnings, chewing his way through a prime steak with all the trimmings, he'd never given a thought as to what was involved in bringing the meat to the table. The drovers' machine was the first shock. As it floated a meter or so above the ground, it rode so hard that it was little short of an instrument of torture. When he'd told Makartur he could drive a flipper, he'd had the regular city model in his mind, a low streamlined machine with colorful bodywork, a plexiglass bubble to keep the weather out and even an android handler to take over the guidance system when the human occupants had something more interesting to do.

The drovers' machines were something else again. Dome and body panels were gone. The drover rode on a narrow saddle in front of a center-mounted set of controls. The lanceman behind him didn't get a seat at all. He perched on a small platform, held in place by a system of webbing straps.

The drovers' flippers were so reduced to basics that even the usual auxiliary power pack had gone. With only a sun catcher supplying energy to the drive, it meant that they were effectively grounded during the hours of darkness.

Once Phaid had familiarized himself with the handling of the skeletal machine, he found that the routine of the drover was fairly straightforward. Each morning the herd was goaded into motion with shocks from the drovers' lances. Once they were on the move, it was relatively easy to keep the animals on the course set by the drive boss. All it needed was a certain degree of prodding by drovers cruising slowly beside the herd at about a meter from the ground.

Phaid and Makartur were running in what was known as the drag. This meant riding at the rear of the herd, picking up stragglers and goading them back to the main pack. It also meant that they were constantly being choked and partially blinded by the thick dust cloud kicked up by the hundreds of veebes. Riding the drag was the lowest position in the drovers' pecking order and, as new arrivals, Phaid and Makartur were stuck with it.

With no option but to make the best of their lot, the two men had gone to work. Phaid showed a good deal more reluctance than his companion, but even he mastered the basic technique of pulling the flipper up to a height of seven or eight meters and dropping swiftly from behind at a straying beast so Makartur, working as lanceman, could get in a series of swift jabs. The majority of times this would send the animal galloping back to the main herd bellowing loudly.

Occasionally a particularly aggressive creature would turn

on the flipper. A big, shaggy bull veebe was powerful enough to tilt a flipper in such a way that it would spiral out of control and somersault on to the ground. The single knobby horn on the top of its flat, triangular head was quite capable of twisting a flipper's metal frame or smashing human bones.

If a veebe did take it into its thick and bad tempered head to charge a flipper, it was down to the driver to swing the machine away from the attacking animal before it could make contact. In the four days that Phaid had been on the drive, only one animal had tried to fight back. Phaid desperately swung the controls and, to his amazement, he and Makartur missed being gored and trampled by a hair's-breadth. Phaid put it down more to blind luck than good judgment, but Makartur had been suitably impressed.

Each day, when the sun finally dipped below the horizon and the flippers sank down on to the sand with a soft bump, the lessons in the ways of the drovers still weren't over. He'd stretch his cramped and aching back and wearily make his way to the lumbering transit bed that carried the supplies, the two big water tanks and the field kitchen that provided the focal point of the men's off duty hours. The kitchen was presided over by Thatch, a small, wiry man whose body had been broken by a veebe. He'd been given a bionic patch job by a cheap company surgeon. Cooking up the daily gray, tasteless stew provided Thatch with a rough and ready semi-retirement. He had also appointed himself custodian of drover lore and drover prejudice.

As outlooks went, the drovers' was one of the least lovely that Phaid had ever come across. Drovers seemed to hate almost everything that wasn't exactly like themselves. Most of all they hated the veebes and took every opportunity to torment the animals. If it hadn't been for Shako constantly keeping a watchful, protective eye on the merchandise, there probably would have been deaths and serious mutilations among the herd, inflicted by the drovers themselves.

Their hatred wasn't only confined to the veebes. There were the boohooms. They were universally detested, and every night there were stories of atrocities committed against the mild, inoffensive subhumans. The elaihim were also high on the drovers' hate list. Higher, if anything, than the boohooms, except that the drovers' contact with the tall, hyper-intelligent beings was strictly limited. The elaihim, with their superhuman minds and tall, frail bodies, knew enough to avoid the trails of drovers and the haunts of similar, ignorant, violent humans. The drovers' hatred of the elaihim was based on fear, and therefore much more fierce and implacable. The boohooms were merely convenient victims. The elaihim were something else. They had superior intelligence. There was no way that the drovers could pretend otherwise. What they could pretend, though, was that this superior intellect was dedicated to some nebulous concept of evil. The elaihim were a shadowy conspiracy that could be blamed for all the ills and disasters in the world. The elaihim were more than just the victims for the drovers' cruel sport. They were vermin. Despite their obvious culture and sensitivity, in the opinion of the drovers, they had to be eradicated, just like ribbon snakes, snow lupes or the big, savage lizards that prowled the deep forest. They were a dangerous menace, too smart to be allowed to live.

The drovers didn't exactly hate women, but the attitude was definitely ambivalent. For the drovers, women split easily into two kinds. There were the wives that most of them didn't have and there were whores on whom they spent most of the end of trail pay. Wives were docile, faithful and for the most part totally imaginary. Although most drovers had an overbearing fixation about having sons to follow in their footsteps, hardly any managed to maintain and provide for a family. Whores, on the other hand, were fair game for anything and the drovers talked about them with grinning contempt, although a few particular women did seem to command a certain grudging, familiar admiration. It was ironic that, all too often, when a drover did marry, it was to a prostitute with a yen to reform. After that, more often than not, they would stash the woman on some remote farm and then live with a constant fear that the little woman would be finding her fun with some other drifter while they were away on the trail.

Farmers, androids, townspeople, clever bastards from the big cities and dumb bastards from the hills all came in for contempt and were all seen as reasonable targets for bouts of random violence. In fact, the only way that Phaid could sum it up was that the drovers didn't like anyone except their own kind, and weren't even too fond of each other. Bearing this in mind, he did his best to keep both his mouth shut and himself to himself. As an identifiable outsider, he knew he was a potential flashpoint for trouble.

Also, Phaid could only stand so much of the talk and boasting that was the nightly ritual around the transport bed. He stayed long enough so he wouldn't be labeled as a snob or a loner, but then he'd take his blanket and find himself a fairly isolated spot in which to get some sleep. The drovers weren't the only thing that sent Phaid early to his blanket. Unused as he was to serious physical labor, the drovers' day left him totally exhausted. Each morning old Hatch's furious wake-up gong always came far too early. Phaid couldn't remember a time when sleep had meant so much to him.

Seven days into the drive Phaid started to feel that either he was becoming acclimatized to the life of a drover or else his brain had now reached a level of one-way numbness that could lead only to atrophy. He was ceasing to be able to imagine any other kind of life, and there were even moments of dull panic when he found himself examining the idea that maybe he was in a sort of mobile hell.

It was on the seventh day, however, that they spotted the dust cloud on the horizon. At the back of the herd, Phaid and Makartur were among the last to know about it. It was only when old Thatch started shouting and hollering that they realized something unusual was happening.

Thatch had halted the transport bed and was standing up staring into the distance. Phaid swung the flipper in beside him.

"What is it?"

"Something moving out there."

Phaid shaded his eyes against the sun and squinted in the direction that Thatch was pointing. A small eddy of dust swirled and danced. Whatever was causing the dust cloud was both small and a long way off. A week earlier, Phaid would have wondered what all the commotion was about. Seven days on trail, though, had taught him that even the slightest interruption in the monotonous routine was a thing to be savored.

Other drovers pulled their machines over to the transport bed until there was a small group of them, hanging just above the ground, and speculating on what other people might be crossing the desert.

"It's too small for a crawler."

"A crawler wouldn't be in this region. They stick close to their own routes."

"It could be off course."

"Crawlers don't go off course."

"It ain't a crawler."

"So what the hell is it?"

"How the hell should I know, dumbbell?"

Shako skimmed up at high speed and slowed to a halt.

"Will you beauties get moving, the herd's starting to slow down. Back on the job, what do you think we're running here? A goddamn picnic?"

"There's something out there, boss."

"I know there's something out there, damn you. I got eyes. It don't mean the whole drive's got to come to a halt."

"Didn't we ought to check it out?"

"Sure we'll check it out, but we'll keep moving at the same time."

He scanned the assembled drovers.

"Bork, Vooter, Goldring, Dick, Marris. Go see what that thing is. The rest of you, get back to work!"

The ones selected to inspect the dust clouds accelerated away, whooping and yelling. The others moved slowly back to their positions around the herd while Shako cursed them.

"Snap to it, you pieces of shit! I ain't losing time on account of you scumbags want to take time out to sightsee."

Despite his constant harangue, the drovers' attention was still on the dust cloud. They merely went through the motions of running the veebes, keeping one eye on the horizon. They seemed to have an almost childish eagerness to find out what it was that moved out in the distance.

After what amounted to an intolerable wait, a flipper was spotted on its way back. Once again, almost half the drovers quit their positions and raced out to meet it. Shako roared around, swearing and threatening, but to little avail. There was no way he could get the drovers back to work until their curiosity had been satisfied. The herd slowed to a halt and every-

85

one turned their machines to watch the returning flipper.

It was Bork who had brought back the news. He pulled up in front of Shako, throwing up a cloud of dust. His face was twisted into a grimace and his eyes seemed to have taken on a touch of madness.

"Elaihim! It's a party of stinking elaihim!"

A shout went up all around the herd. Even the veebes became nervous, snorting and stamping their feet. The drovers forgot all about their jobs, and milled around in angry disarray. They appeared to Phaid to be deliberately working themselves into an hysterical fury.

"Elaihim!"

"That offal's got to go!"

"Only good one's a dead one!"

Shako, still trying to retain some vestige of control, spun his flipper in front of Bork.

"How many of them are there?"

"Eight, maybe ten. They got a pair of small transport beds."

Shako looked grim.

"What are the others doing?"

"Just riding around them, keeping them pinned down."

"There's been no shooting?"

"Not yet. I think Marris may have jabbed a couple with his lance but there ain't been no shooting yet. They're waiting to hear from you."

Shako seemed undecided. He stared out into the desert while Bork agitatedly jockeyed his flipper from side to side.

"We are going to get them, boss, ain't we? Huh? We are going to grease those swine!"

Shako took both hands off the controls of his flipper.

"Hold it, hold up there!"

His attempt at regaining the upper hand was little short of futile. Even as he spoke, the drovers were edging their machines towards the open desert. Makartur suddenly leaned forward and hissed in Phaid's ear.

"Move out, manny. Move out and then go like hell towards those elaihim."

This took Phaid totally by surprise.

"What are you talking about?"

"I'm not going to stand by and watch a massacre."

"You're crazy, there's nothing we can do about it!"

"We can try."

Phaid resolutely took his hands off the controls of the flipper.

"Not a chance. I don't want any part of this. There's no way two of us can hold off between thirty and forty blood-crazed drovers. I'm sorry for the elaihim, but it's their problem and that's it."

Makartur's voice suddenly turned soft and deadly.

"I'm not arguing with you, little man. Drive this thing and drive it fast."

The drovers were already howling their way out towards the now growing dust cloud. Phaid folded his arms.

"And if I don't?"

"I have my blaster less than a hand's breadth from the back of your head. If you don't move this machine right now, I'll blow you away. Simple as that."

"But . . ."

"Now it's your problem."

Phaid dropped his hands to the controls and threw the flipper into forward motion. He turned it in the direction of the group of elaihim and then pushed the power wide open. He let the machine run as close to the ground as possible for maximum speed. Normally he wouldn't have attempted anything so fool-hardy. A single rock could have wrecked them, but he no longer cared. Cold awful horror had him completely in its grip. He knew for sure that he must be driving to certain death, one way or another.

7

"Nobody's going to bother us until we get close to the elaihim. The other drovers will think that we're just racing to join in the fun."

Makartur was yelling urgent instructions. Phaid didn't bother to answer. Sick with fear, he let the big man take complete control. He simply did as he was told, allowing the flipper to skim over the sand at top speed.

"If these drovers act true to form, they'll hang things out for a while. They'll circle the elaihim until they've got them thoroughly terrorized, then they'll go in for the kill."

As they came nearer to the uneven confrontation, Phaid saw that what Makartur had said was correct. The small group of elaihim was huddled beside their two transport beds. These were heaped with an assortment of supplies and household goods. A loose ring of slow moving drovers on their flippers kept them pinned down in the one spot. Every so often, one would break from the circle and sweep by the elaihim in a

close pass. The lanceman would stab at the tall angular figures.
There'd be a scream as the victim reeled back from the shock.
Designed to annoy a veebe, it was agonizing to a human nerv-
ous system.

The drovers had one other trick. Taking potshots at the
highly piled transport beds with their blasters, they could watch
with glee as the elaihim tried desperately to put out the small
fires this created, while at the same time doing their best to
dodge the attacks by the lancemen.

The ring of drovers kept growing as more of them came to
join in. It was obvious that the murder of the elaihim was going
to be a hideous, drawn out business. The drovers seemed bent
on extracting every last possible measure of cruel enjoyment
from the situation. Phaid could see exactly why Makartur felt
so strongly that the business should be stopped. Where he
revolted was at the idea that they had to be the ones who did
the stopping. It was too late, however, to do anything about
it. Makartur was once again leaning forward and yelling into
his ear.

"The first thing we've got to do is break the circle."

Phaid looked at the ring of drovers winding themselves up
to the eventual frenzy of slaughter. They couldn't be stopped
by just two men. It was nothing short of suicide.

Makartur pointed from behind Phaid's shoulder.

"There, that flipper coming round now. The one on the left
with the bearded guy driving. You got it?"

Phaid nodded, but still didn't speak.

"Okay then. Swing up beside him. Make like you're joining
the circle. At the last moment, swerve into him. Broadside his
machine as hard as you can. He'll probably turn clean over.
It'll snarl up the whole ring and give us time to get under cover
by those transports. Then we can figure out our next move."

Phaid cut their speed and moved up to the flipper that Makartur had pointed out. They began running alongside it. The
bearded driver grinned and yelled something inaudible. He
looked as though he was having the time of his life. Makartur
tapped Phaid on the back.

"Now! Swing into him!"

Phaid took another look at the man. Again he grinned and
gestured wolfishly, flashing a set of broken teeth. Phaid could

feel sweat breaking out on the palms of his hands.

"I can't do it."

"Swing into him, damn you!"

"I can't!"

"Now!"

"No!"

"Do it, manny, or . . ."

Phaid shut his eyes and spun the controls. There was a massive impact and shriek of twisting metal. Phaid found himself thrown violently sideways. For a second he was flying through the air. Then he hit the sand with a bone jarring thud.

Sick and dizzy, he staggered to his feet. Makartur's plan had worked out better than he could have imagined. The two flippers were little more than a mass of tangled metal. Even as he watched, a third and fourth ploughed into the wreckage. A chain reaction of lesser collisions started, as other drovers tried to dodge the pileup. The ordered menace of the closing circle was turned, for some minutes, into total chaos.

At first, Phaid could do nothing except stand dumbly, blinking at the confusion that he had helped to create. Then he saw the other driver, the bearded one who had been their first target, limping towards him, bleeding badly from a cut on his forehead.

"What did you go and do that for, you stupid bastard?"

The drover obviously still thought that the crash had been a genuine accident. Almost as an unthinking reflex, Phaid pulled out his fuse tube and burned the man down. Immediately after he had fired, a blaster roared four or five times in quick succession. Phaid jumped around, looking for the source of the sound. Makartur, with a weapon clutched in each hand, was backing towards the two machines of the elaihim, firing as he went. Seeing Phaid still not about to act, he waved with his gun.

"Get under cover, you damn fool! Get back to those transports!"

Phaid's instinct for self-preservation snapped back into action. He was still alive. Quite how, he wasn't sure, but he was certainly going to do his best to stay that way. The confusion was starting to sort itself out. When Makartur had fired his first blast, the drovers had been left in no doubt that something was amiss. Many were crouching with drawn guns, wondering who the enemy was and where he was coming from.

A blaster was lying on the sand nearby. Presumably it had been dropped during the crash. Phaid scooped it up and started running directly towards where the elaihim were sheltering beside their transport beds.

Blaster fire threw up sand at his heels. He started zigzagging. At least one drover had realized part of what was going on.

A shallow gully ran between Phaid and the transports. Phaid made this his first objective. Lungs pumping and heart pounding, he ran like he had never run before. The air around him howled with the discharges from blasters. Seemingly by a miracle, Phaid reached the gully. Without even looking, he dived into it and threw himself flat on to the ground.

To his surprise, he found himself lying next to a lanky elaihi male who was also pressing into the ground, trying to make himself as small a target as possible. Phaid had never been so close to an elaihi before, but it was neither the time nor the place to indulge his curiosity. He pushed the spare blaster towards the man.

"All hell's going to break loose now. You better use this."

To Phaid's utter astonishment, the elaihi shook his head.

"No, I'm sorry. I can't use it."

Phaid crawled closer.

"It's easy. Let me show you."

Again he shook his head.

"I understand how to use the weapon. I can't, though. I can't take a life, another life."

Phaid looked at him in blank amazement.

"Those bastards are going to take your life if you don't do something about it. Mine too, for that matter, and mine's pretty damn precious."

"I can't, under any circumstances."

Phaid closed his eyes.

"Sweet Lords!"

A sweep of blaster fire churned the lip of the gully. Without bothering to aim, or even raising his head, Phaid returned fire with both weapons. He shot the elaihi a venomous look.

"You bastards don't deserve saving. How the hell do you expect to survive if you won't defend yourselves?"

The elaihi regarded him with sad, pale blue eyes.

"I'm sorry."

"That does me a lot of good."

Phaid risked raising his head for the first time. The majority of the drovers had taken up positions among the various pieces of scooter debris. Two, however, were making what looked like an attacking run on a still serviceable flipper. This run was also headed exactly in Phaid's direction. Phaid squeezed off a snap shot at the drover and, to his own surprise, dropped him first time. The flipper ploughed straight into the ground and exploded as something in its power circuits cracked on impact. Phaid bit his lip and grinned.

"How about that."

Immediately he had to hit the ground as a dozen or more blasters flashed. Phaid turned his head in appeal to the elaihi.

"If you won't fight, you could at least do something to make this gully a bit deeper. That can't be against your principles."

"No, I can do that."

"Then get digging, stupid. I thought you people were supposed to be smarter than us."

"I will dig."

"Just dandy."

The elaihi dug while Phaid kept up a steady stream of fire with the blaster and his fuse tube. The drovers didn't seem in any hurry to attempt anything like a frontal attack on Phaid and Makartur. Grounding their flippers, they had taken cover and appeared, at least for the moment, to be simply exchanging fire. It wasn't too long before the elaihi had turned the section of the gully where he and Phaid lay into a rough but serviceable trench.

Finally a lull came in the fighting. Phaid suddenly heard Makartur's voice roaring from some distance behind him and a way off to the right.

"Hey! You drovers! We didn't ought to be doing each other like this. Go on back to your herd. Nobody needs to get killed over this."

"You need to get killed, ape breath. We're going to get you swine if it's the last thing we do. If you love those dome heads so much you're going to die with them—as slow and painful as we can arrange."

"You got to get us first."

"We'll get you, don't worry about that!"

Discharges from a number of blasters put the final punctuation to this chillingly delivered promise. Phaid fired back, but nothing happened. The drovers seemed quite happy to sit still and bide their time. Phaid couldn't quite understand how both he and Makartur had avoided being hit. It was almost as though something was mysteriously throwing off the drovers' aim.

It wasn't long before Phaid started to notice that his mouth was becoming uncomfortably hot and dry. He tried to speak, but found that all he could come up with was a rasping croak.

"You don't have any water, do you?"

The elaihi once again shook his head and looked sorrowful.

"I don't."

"Just great."

"We elaihim can go for long periods without either food or water. It's one of the results of our ability to control our metabolism."

"Screw your metabolism."

"I'm sorry."

"So am I. I'm the one who's going to die of thirst."

"There is water back on our transports. I could get it if you want."

"You'd do that?"

"Of course."

Phaid, despite his thirst, was reluctant to ask the elaihi to risk climbing out of the trench.

"I hate to do this, but I won't last too long in this sun if I don't get any."

"I will go."

Before Phaid could say anything else, the elaihi had rolled out of the trench and was running in a low crouch towards the two transports. The movement produced a flurry of fire. Phaid prayed that this act of courage wouldn't be the elaihi's last.

He was a long time in returning, and Phaid was just about ready to give him up for dead when, in a second eruption of fire from the drovers, he rolled back into the gully, clutching a clear plastic container filled with water. The elaihi handed it to Phaid with a smile.

"Here."

"Thanks."

Phaid drank gratefully and then slowly wiped his mouth.

"Sweet mercy, I needed that."

"You feel better now?"

"Yeah, much. Are your people okay?"

"Two have been killed, I'm afraid."

"That's too bad."

"The others are unharmed. You and your companion seemed to be keeping the herdsmen at bay for the moment."

Phaid looked curiously at the elaihi. There was something disturbingly cold and unemotional about him. Phaid had to remind himself that there wasn't even any reason to believe that the elaihim were human. It had to be expected that they'd be very different.

"Do you have a name?"

"Of course. We all have names."

Aside from being unemotional, this elaihi, at least, had a terrible tendency to take everything very, very literally.

"So what's yours?"

"Rathyaal."

"Rathyaal?"

"That's right."

"Mine's Phaid."

"Now we have exchanged names."

Phaid gave up trying to understand the elaihi.

"I guess we have."

The long hot desert afternoon dragged on and still the drovers didn't seem anxious to make a move. Occasionally they'd fire on Phaid's or Makartur's position, or yell threats and taunts, but the rush that Phaid had been expecting ever since he'd first rolled into the gully failed to materialize. Gradually the shadows began to lengthen.

"They're going to have to make their move soon. It'll be sunset before too long and their flippers will stop working."

"It's almost time for us to take a hand. You have bought us some very valuable time . . . Phaid."

"Huh?"

"You have bought us valuable time."

"What the hell are you talking about?"

"I can't explain right now. It's almost time."

"You mean you're actually going to do something?"

"I can't explain now."

Phaid took a quick look over the side of the trench.

"Whatever it is that you've got in mind, you better do it damn quick. I think the drovers are getting ready to pull something."

"Please be silent."

Phaid's temper abruptly gave out. He swung around on the elaihi with anger boiling out of him. The sight of Rathyaal stopped him dead. The elaihi had folded his arms and legs into a seemingly impossible position. His eyes were tightly shut and sweat was streaming down his face. As far as Phaid could see, he was in the grip of some sort of seizure. Phaid's imagination cast around for an explanation. Surely the elaihi couldn't be going into a self created suicide.

"If you are, you picked a damn fine time."

In among the wreckage there was now something definitely happening. The furtive movements had stepped up, and it looked as though the drovers were finally preparing for the rush. Phaid let go a couple of shots and then ducked as twice the number came back. He took another glance at the elaihi. His normally pallid face had turned quite gray. Veins twitched all over his forehead as though there were worms beneath the skin struggling to get out.

A loud yell went up from the drovers. They had started to move. A line of crouching figures were crawling quickly towards Phaid's position. Using both his weapons, Phaid fired as fast as he could, but, in their sheer weight of numbers, the drovers had the advantage. The whole rim of the gully became a target for their blasters and Phaid was forced to huddle at the bottom. He knew that the end must come very soon, and there was absolutely nothing he could do about it. On one level, it was almost a relief. At least he didn't have to be afraid much longer.

He took a final look at Rathyaal and was surprised to find that the elaihi had fallen over on to his side and was gasping like a fish out of water. At first Phaid assumed that he'd been hit, but then he noticed that there was no sign of a wound.

There was no time, though, to worry about Rathyaal. The drovers were coming up fast. Phaid tried a few more shots and then once again was forced to cower in the bottom of the trench.

He knew that any moment the drovers would come storming over the edge and that would be it. He wondered how much being killed by a blaster would hurt. Was death really the end of everything? It all seemed so futile. He'd spent a lifetime hustling and struggling, watching angles and trying to get an edge. If he'd known that it was going to end like this he would have done it all very differently. His blood felt as though it had turned to ice, and then the firing stopped.

The shouting of the drovers changed in tone. Rathyaal started to move. He seemed to be trying to say something.

"They're running."

"What?"

"The beasts are running."

The new developments were too much for Phaid. He risked a look over the edge of the trench and found that the drovers were dashing back towards the flippers that were still intact. Phaid slowly got to his feet. One of the drovers turned and aimed a final, wildly inaccurate shot at him.

"We'll be back to get you, you bastard. Just you see if we don't!"

Then he continued running for his flipper. In the distance, where the herd had been, something was churning up a huge cloud of dust. Still clutching his weapons, Phaid let his arms drop to his sides.

"Will somebody tell me what the hell is going on?"

8

"It was very hard."

"I can imagine."

"No, I don't think you could really imagine. I don't think you would be able to visualize exactly what it was like."

Phaid was quickly discovering that the elaihim had a rather obnoxious streak of superior-to-thou. On the surface they sounded kindly but beneath there was a strata of contempt. It got on his nerves, but he didn't make any comment. He was at least getting the explanation that he'd waited half the night for, sitting in the elaihim's austere camp and wondering how he was going to get out of this one. Makartur, however, who hadn't witnessed the violent spasms that had gripped Rathyaal at the climax of the fight with the drovers, was scratching his beard and attempting to put what he'd been told into some kind of manageable form.

"Let me get this straight. You're telling me that all of your group went into some sort of trance...."

"Trance is a purely human capability."

Makartur grunted. "It'll do for me."

It was plain that the elaihim were also causing him some degree of irritation.

"You went into this trance, or call it what you want, and you set up a mental link with the veebes in the herd."

Once again Rathyaal couldn't curb his need for strict accuracy in just about every detail.

"In fact, we only formed a link with specific individuals within the herd, but otherwise you are broadly correct."

Phaid nodded slowly and for a long time. It was almost impossible to tell whether he was being ultra deferential or simply ironic.

"I'm obliged to you. May I go on?"

"Please do."

"You formed these links with some of the beasts and told them to start running."

"That is a painfully simplistic explanation."

"I thought it might be."

"The veebe, having been selectively bred by your people over many thousands of years, simply for its weight of edible flesh . . ." Rathyaal permitted himself a faint grimace of distaste ". . . is a particularly neurotic and paranoid being."

Makartur laughed. "They were paranoid before us humans had anything to do with them. You'd be paranoid too, if half the carnivores in the world thought of you as dinner."

Phaid was faintly surprised by the way that Makartur was able to laugh, relax and even jest with the elaihim and be not in the least intimidated by their more than human capabilities.

This time Rathyaal allowed himself a faint smile.

"That is very true. My people have an unforgivable habit of blaming you humans for all the ills of the world."

Everything about the elaihim seemed to be faint. It was almost as though a large part of them was really in some other plane or dimension, one from which humans were excluded. He nibbled on a small sliver of a dried leaf that, judging from the meal that had been put in front of them, was the mainstay of the elaihim diet. It was only after a great deal of chewing that Phaid detected the slightest hint of a flavor. The elaihim appeared to move through a world of both tastes and ideas that were too delicate and subtle for a human being to either share or understand.

While Phaid covertly examined the elaihim, Rathyaal went on with his story.

"The mind of the herd veebe is a painful place to even visit. It is a disorganized conflict of fear, vindictiveness, anger and an awful stubbornness. It is easy to introduce feelings of panic and hysteria, but it requires a massive effort to overcome the stubbornness. Even though we gave it all our concentration, it almost exhausted our resources. It was only at the very last minute that they finally ran."

Phaid nodded. "You can say that again."

Rathyaal raised an almost nonexistent eyebrow.

"Is that really necessary?"

"It's a figure of speech."

Phaid realized that he was being mocked. He didn't quite know what to do so he blundered on.

"You can tell me one thing, though."

"If I can."

"Why did you leave it so long? I mean, you could have run the herd anytime that you wanted to. Why did you wait until the very end of the day?"

"I would have thought that was obvious."

"It sure as hell wasn't obvious when I was sweating my way through the afternoon, expecting to be killed at any moment."

"If we had started running the herd any earlier, it would have been possible for the drovers to stop them before the sun had set and their machines ceased to operate. They might have been able to come back and kill us. That is why we decided to delay this action until just a short time before sunset."

Phaid suddenly grew angry.

"We only made it to sundown by sheer luck. It was a miracle we weren't killed."

"It was a risk. I'll admit that."

"No shit? You'll admit that. That's really big of you."

Phaid was up on his feet.

"You bastards really take the prize, don't you? We risk our lives trying to save your asses and you start treating us like dirt under your feet. Where do you swine get off? It ain't no wonder the drovers wanted to grease the lot of you. They were probably right!"

Makartur stood up too, in an attempt to keep the peace.

"You're going too far, manny. These people are our hosts."

"And we're their fucking saviors!"

Rathyaal spread his hands in an apologetic gesture. "I didn't mean to give offense."

"Well, you managed it just the same."

Phaid stalked away from where the group was talking and marched out into the desert. He reached the gully. The ground was still pockmarked and scorched from the afternoon's fighting. The sight only served to make him even angrier.

"Bastards! Fucking bastards!"

"They - can - be - very - hard - to - deal - with - but - you-shouldn't-hold-their-manner-against-them. They-don't-see-things-quite-the-same-way-as-you-do."

Phaid started like a rabbit at the voice. He swung round and found himself facing a short android. It was about half Phaid's height and roughly humanoid in shape. It had a blue gray metallic finish and was regarding Phaid with pinkish, palely glowing sensors, positioned in roughly the same place as human eyes.

"The-fact-has-to-be-faced-that-elaihim-and-humans-simply-don't-get-along. There-are-a-few-exceptions-but-not-many."

Phaid wasn't ready to cool off.

"They just make me feel so damned inferior."

"From-their-point-of-view-you-probably-are."

Phaid felt an urge to punch the android, but he knew that all that would achieve was a hurt fist.

"Don't you start."

"I-never-take-sides-in-disputes-between-organic-life-forms-I-find-it-saves-me-a-lot-of-trouble."

Phaid nodded. "Very sensible."

"That's-what-I've-found."

"Do you belong to the elaihim?"

"I-don't-belong-to-anyone. I-am-what-is-known-as-a-mendicant-android."

"I'm sorry."

"That's-okay-I-don't-have-the-circuitry-to-take-offense."

"So what's a mendicant android?"

"One-who-no-longer-has-a-purpose. One-who-wanders-from-place-to-place-in-search-of-truth-and-enlightenment."

"That's what you do?"

"Most-of-the-time."

"It sounds kind of lonely."

"On-the-contrary. I-quite-enjoy-myself-although-there-are-times-when-I-think-I'd-be-happier-if-I-had-something-useful-to-do-with-my-time."

Phaid found that he was becoming quite intrigued with the little android. It was certainly better company than the elaihim. He sat down on the sand and wrapped his arms around his knees.

"How come you don't have a job to do? I thought all androids did."

"I-imagine-I-must-have-had-one-once-that's-if-you-subscribe-to-what-we-androids-like-to-call-the-manufac-turered-to-function-theory-of-our-origins."

Phaid looked blank.

"What?"

"Without-wishing-to-sound-like-an-elaihi-it's-probable-that-I-once-had-a-job-but-you-humans-have-forgotten-what-it-was."

"Forgotten?"

"A-lot-of-us-androids-were-designed-to-do-things-that-no-longer-happen. One-thing-we-know-for-sure-is-that-there's-a-lot-less-going-on-in-the-world-than-there-used-to-be."

Phaid nodded. "I once saw a place that looked like a factory. It was out in the hills. Every morning all these machines came out, and every night they'd be taken in again. Nobody I ever heard of knew what it was there for."

"This-was-the-building-in-the-hills-behind-Gant?"

"That's the place. You've been there?"

"No-but-I've-been-told-about-it."

"Did they know what it was for?"

"The-matter-wasn't-discussed."

The android didn't seem to want to give a straight answer and Phaid was too tired to pursue it. Instead, he yawned.

"It's been a rough day. I think I'd better see about getting myself a little sleep."

"Perhaps-a-quantity-of-brandy-might-aid-that."

Phaid looked intently at the little android.

"Brandy?"

"The - elaihim - have - a - small - cask - among - their - cargo - they - use - it - for - barter - with - the - humans."

"The hell they do!" Phaid hesitated. "Aren't they going to object if we just help ourselves to it?"

"I-think-they-consider-what's-theirs-is-also-ours."

"Are you sure?"

"Of - course - I'm - sure - I - don't - have - the - circuits - to - make - rash - and - misleading - statements."

Phaid stood up.

"Let's go then."

Phaid followed the android back towards the elaihim transport. He leaned against the machine while the android loosened the cargo webbing and rummaged around inside.

"Do you have a name?"

"A - long - time - ago - some - humans - started - calling - me - Ben-e - and - to - a - degree - it - stuck."

Ben-e emerged from the transport clutching a small brass-bound cask in both arms.

"Here-is-the-brandy."

He produced a rather delicate china bowl and filled it from the cask's spigot. He handed it to Phaid, who swirled the golden liquid between his cupped hands, sniffed deeply and then took an experimental sip. It was very fine brandy. Phaid grinned at Ben-e the android.

"I suppose there ain't much point in offering you some of this."

"Not-really."

"Maybe I should go tell Makartur."

"That-would-be-a-companionable-act."

Phaid walked around the transport. The elaihim seemed to have finally retired. Makartur was sitting staring into the embers of the small fire that he'd built. He looked up as Phaid came into the dim pool of light.

"What's up with you, manny?"

"Brandy, that's what."

"Brandy. You're joshing me!"

Phaid held out the bowl."

"Taste that."

Makartur tasted.

"Sweet mother earth! That's the real stuff. Where the hell did you get it?"

Phaid called out. "Hey, Ben-e! Come over here and bring the cask."

"I'm-coming."

"Who was that?"

"It's Ben-e."

"I know that much."

Ben-e appeared in the firelight. In addition to the cask he was carrying a second bowl and a pair of blankets. Makartur regarded the android curiously.

"Well, well, what have we here? A wee machine person."

"A-mendicant-android-to-be-precise."

"Well now, and you be traveling with the elaihim?"

"That's-correct."

"It's a wondrous world."

"Truly-wondrous."

Ben-e handed Makartur his bowl and then spread the blankets on the ground.

"I-thought-you-might-want-these."

"That's very thoughtful of you."

"Some-habits-die-very-hard."

"Taking care of humans?"

"Something-like-that."

Phaid and Makartur rolled the blankets around themselves and lay sipping their brandy. Ben-e suddenly dropped into a rough approximation of a squatting position.

"I-think-I-am-going-to-disengage-until-daylight."

With that, the lights of his eye/sensors went out and he became quite motionless. Phaid stretched.

"I don't think a spot of disengaging would do me any harm."

He closed his eyes and almost immediately fell asleep.

The morning dawned bright and clear. This was to be expected in the rainless desert. By the time that Phaid awoke, the elaihim were already up and moving around, as was Ben-e the android. While Phaid was dusting himself down and folding his blanket, he surprised himself by whistling happily. He almost never whistled. His cheerfulness was close to euphoric. Phaid felt this state of mind was so unnatural that he started to wonder if the elaihim were using some sort of mood control on him. Makartur, too, was a picture of sunny joviality. If the elaihim were actually geting inside their minds, Phaid knew that he ought to resent it, but somehow he wasn't able to.

Before he could think about the problem anymore, Phaid was approached by a female elaihi who smiled and indicated that food was being served on the other side of the transport.

"Once you've finished eating, we have to discuss what your plans are."

"I suppose we do."

Phaid found that he wasn't able to actually worry about what would happen next. He noticed that he couldn't help grinning like an idiot.

"I must confess I hadn't given it much thought."

"Why don't you eat first and then we can talk about it."

"Do you mind me asking something?"

"Of course not."

"Which one are you? I know I was introduced to you all yesterday, but . . ."

"But we all look alike?"

"Well . . ."

"I am Isaen."

"Isaen?"

"Why don't you eat now and we'll talk later."

Phaid still felt as though he was being manipulated, but he was hungry, so he made his way to the temporary kitchen. Breakfast consisted of the same leaves that he'd had the night before, plus some small whitish doughy balls and a bowl of a warm pale pink cordial. Once again they seemed to lack anything that Phaid could recognize as flavor.

The meal did, however, give him a chance to study the elaihim for the first time in something approaching normal surroundings. There was no denying that they had it over the human race in a number of ways. There was a grace about them, even when they were going about the simplest of tasks, that made mankind look like a species of knuckle trailing apes. Apart from their slight build, there was something insubstantial and ethereal about them. Their almost bleached white skins and pale short tunics gave them a uniform quality, as though any trace of individuality had been completely sublimated.

Even their faces were stamped from the same mold, without the distinguishing characteristics that separated one human from another. Sexual differences were also minimal. The females were slightly shorter than the males, although still taller than all but the tallest of men. Only a pair of high, tiny vestigial breasts really distinguished one sex from the other among the elaihim.

Phaid couldn't see why so many people believed that the elaihim were descended from humans. If he had been told that they had arrived secretly from a star one night, he would have had less reason to doubt.

The meeting to decide what was to be done about Makartur and Phaid took place directly after breakfast. The elaihim group was represented by Rathyaal, Isaen and another female called Shethir. It was obvious from the start that the presence of the two men was having a disturbing effect on the elaihim as they were willing to make a considerable effort to speed Phaid and Makartur on their way.

The elaihim's idea of a discussion was a little one-sided. They started off by virtually interrogating the two men about how they came to be with the drovers, what their eventual destination was and what ideas they had about how they were going to get there. Once they had listened, they seemed to ignore any suggestions that the humans had made and began debating the matter among themselves. Phaid again had the feeling that he should be upset, if not furious, but for some reason the emotions just wouldn't come.

The elaihim's best solution seemed to be that they should take one of the serviceable flippers and head towards the nearest town. Rathyaal even began to plot their course for them.

"You would be well-advised to avoid the trails that lead to Chasabad."

Phaid found himself nodding like a mental retard.

"That's sensible."

"Chasabad would be the shortest route to the Republic, I admit, but the risk of running into the drovers again would be too great. I therefore think it would be better if you made for Fennella."

Phaid once again automatically smiled and nodded, but

Makartur didn't seem quite so easily persuaded.

"It's twice the distance to Fennella."

"That's true, but once you get there you are at the line head."

"Aye man, but we've got no money, so a line ride's no good to us."

Shethir's expression became slightly regretful.

"We do not use money and thus we have none to give you."

Makartur looked troubled.

"I suppose we might work something out when we get there, what we will need, though, are provisions and water. As you well know, those flippers don't travel by night, so it'll be few days to make Fennella."

It was Isaen's turn to use the slightly regretful expression.

"That presents another problem. Our supplies are very limited. We barely have enough for our own needs."

Black anger suddenly burst through Phaid's previously sunny disposition.

"Just wait a minute here. Less than a day ago my . . ."

All three elaihim fixed Phaid with the same stony penetrating gaze. The anger in him slowly froze into dark, tiny crystals. They in turn quickly vanished as the sunshine returned. Phaid was grinning again. He couldn't even remember what he'd been talking about.

Ben-e, who'd been standing apart from the conversation but listening intently, suddenly buzzed briskly into the middle of it.

"I - think - I - might - possibly - have - the - solution - to - these - problems."

Both humans and elaihim looked surprised.

"You do?"

"I - have - examined - the - wreckage - of - the - drovers'- machines- and - I - estimate - that - there - are - more - than - enough - parts - to - construct - a - very - much - more - powerful - flipper - that - would - be - able - to - carry - three - of - us - to - the - line - head - in - no - more - than - a - day - and - a - half."

"Three of us."

"Would - you - allow - me - to - continue?"

"Sure."

"Thus - you - elaihim - would - not - have - to - give - the - humans -

so - great - a - quantity - of - supplies. There - is - also - the - matter-
of-money-for-the-line-ride!"

Phaid looked up sharply.

"You can do something about money?"

"We-androids-also-have-little-use-for-money-but-unlike-
the-elaihim-we-are-able-to-obtain-it-when-it-is-needed.
I-can-guarantee-that-I-will-be-able-to-contact-my-people-
and-obtain-all-the-money-that-you-would-need-once-we-
reach-Fennella."

Phaid could hardly believe his ears. The elaihim, if it indeed
was the elaihim that were affecting his mind, seemed to have
relaxed their grip, and he was thinking a little more clearly.

"Are you seriously telling us that you can go to a strange
android in Fennella and it will give you money?"

"Quite-seriously."

"What a system."

"It-serves."

Makartur also had a question.

"You want to travel with us to Fennella?"

"All-the-way-to-the-Republic-if-you-don't-have-any-
objections."

Makartur didn't say anything and Phaid shot him a sideways
glance.

"You don't have any objection, do you?"

Makartur slowly shook his head.

"No, let the wee bag of tricks ride with us if he wants to."

Rathyaal rose to his feet.

"It would seem that everything is settled."

He looked down at Ben-e the android.

"If we can give you any assistance in fitting out your machine . . ."

"I-will-need-a-good-deal-of-assistance-but-first-there-
is-one-final-thing-that-I-must-settle-with-the-humans."

Makartur muttered under his breath.

"Here comes the catch."

Phaid gave the android a narrow, gambler's stare.

"What is it?"

"When-we-reach-the-Republic-I-will-require-a-favor. I-
cannot-tell-you-what-is-right-at-this-moment-but-I-assure-

109

you - that - it - will - neither - be - difficult - nor - time - consuming.
I - must - however - have - your - word - that - one - of - you -will-
perform-it-for-me-before-we-can-start-on-this-journey."

Makartur raised a questioning eyebrow.

"How can we promise to do this favor if we don't know
what it is?"

"It-will-not-be-difficult."

"Aye, but . . ."

Phaid quickly interrupted.

"Whatever it is, you got it. I'd do pretty much anything for
someone who can get me back to the Republic."

Makartur scowled disapprovingly.

"On your head be it."

"Ain't it always?"

"Then - I - think - we - can - start - on - the - construction - of - this-
modified-flipper-right-away."

Although Phaid and Makartur hung around and did their
best to look as though they were contributing to the work,
the real conversion of the flipper was carried out by Ben-e
and the elaihim. In a surprisingly short time they had loaded
up the supplies and were on their way. Once the journey had
started, Phaid noticed that the further he got from the influence
of the elaihim, the more mixed his feelings became. The plus
side was that he was moving again. He was riding out of
the boondocks and back towards civilization with
some speed and style. If Ben-e the android didn't pull some
weird electronic double cross, he was going all the way back
to the Republic without any more trouble. He didn't expect
the android to go back on his word. Machines didn't usually
lie, and if you couldn't trust an android, who could you trust?
Suspicion was, however, a habit that died hard.

There was also a minus side. Somehow, the elaihim had
managed to leave a very bad taste in his mouth. He had started
out totally sympathetic to the strange, solitary people but, after
this first real encounter with them, he found that he disliked
them with an intensity that came close to the drovers' ignorant
prejudice. The more he thought about it, the more he felt as
though his personality and his free will had been violated, raped
almost. He'd been used, manipulated and coldly exploited by
them. He was almost certain that, in some way he didn't clearly

understand, they had temporarily preempted his control over his own mind and his own emotions. The whole episode had left him feeling weak and inferior. He had asked the android about it and although Ben-e was his usual oblique self, he as good as confirmed Phaid's thoughts.

"When - humans - come - in - contact - with - elaihim - nothing - is - ever - as - it - appears. You - can't - even - try - to - be - objective - with - those - beings. They - are - masters - of - wheels - within - wheels - within - wheels."

The remark was cryptic enough to start Phaid thinking. The elaihim presented him with a procession of unanswered questions that seemed to stretch back to infinity. Phaid's mind went around and around. There were the first and obvious general questions. What was the truth behind the legends of the elaihim. Were they, as some people claimed, the mutant descendants of the human race, children of man who had managed to make a great evolutionary leap, or had they come from some other place, alien intruders stranded and wandering in a world that was not their own. There were, however, more specific, disturbing questions arising out of the encounter, questions that kept nagging at Phaid all through the journey across the desert. Just how long had the super people had a grip on his mind? If they could control the veebes from a distance, maybe they had attempted to turn back the drovers and failed. Could it be that they had scanned the assembled human minds looking for someone crazy enough to act as their savior?

If they had fixed on Makartur, and his suicidal plunge to the elaihim's rescue wasn't a quixotic gesture but a result of mind control, then Phaid saw a hundred yawning chasms opening in front of him. The idea that the elaihim could take over the free will of any human who was close to them and make him or her dance to their tune like so many puppets was a sorry prospect for his species.

At that point Phaid's brain dropped through to another level. Just how far did elaihim take their manipulations? To what extent did they dabble in human affairs? Phaid put some of these questions to Ben-e but, true to form, the android's replies were polite but noncommittal to the point of being totally unhelpful.

"It's - always - disconcerting - for - a - species - to - find - that - it -

is-no-longer-top-of-the-heap."

Phaid felt a chill run through him when he heard those words. He had never in his life thought of himself as part of a species. He liked to believe that he owed little or nothing to the rest of humanity, but the chill was there all the same. Men had never been particularly kind to what they considered inferior species. There was little reason to think that the elaihim would behave differently. He wasn't going to be able to forget the android's words.

"It's-always-disconcerting-for-a-species-to-find-that-it-is-no-longer-top-of-the-heap."

"But what do they want with us? Do they really want to stay separate and avoid all contact?"

"That-is-what-they-claim."

"Yeah, but is it true?"

"I - have - not - had - that - many - chances - to - observe - the-behavior-of-the-elaihim-but-from-my-limited-experience-I-would-say-that-the-majority-of-them-would-wish-to-avoid-all-contacts-with-mankind. There-are-exceptions."

"Exceptions?"

"There-is-Solchaim-for-example."

"Solchaim?"

"I-thought-you-had-spent-time-in-the-Republic."

"I have, but I never heard of anyone called Solchaim."

"According - to - the - latest - rumors - he - is - the - most - influential-advisor-of-Life-President-Chrystiana-Nex."

Phaid didn't like the sound of this at all.

"Are you telling me that the Republic has fallen into the hands of an elaihi?"

"No."

"So?"

"So-there-are-simply-rumors-that-an-elaihi-may-now-be-the-power-behind-the-throne-in-the-Republic."

"And that's all you've got to say about it?"

As usual, Ben-e the android seemed unperturbed.

"What-else-should-I-have-to-say? I'm-an-android. It's-no-paint-off-my-back."

"But if this goes on, the elaihim could take over the world."

"Like-I-said-it-is-going-to-be-hard-to-come-to-terms-with-them."

"Something should be done about it."

"Yes?"

"Yeah."

"Are-you-saying-that-the-drovers-had-the-right-idea?"

"No, of course not, but . . ."

"They-wanted-to-wipe-out-the-elaihim. Do-you-have-a-better-idea?"

"No, but . . ."

"Think-about-it."

If it hadn't been for thinking about it, the journey to Fennella would have been a very pleasant interlude. Ben-e seemed quite happy to do all the driving and Phaid and Makartur were more than prepared to let him. The android did have the unfortunate habit of constantly exhibiting that he was able to drive with total high speed precision and hold bright, witty and thought-provoking conversations at the same time. It didn't matter too much, though. Makartur was asleep for almost the whole day and a half and Phaid was paranoid.

So paranoid in fact, that by the time they reached the grass-lands that meant they were only a few hours from Fennella, Phaid was wondering if Makartur's long sleep was actually a result of the elaihim being inside his brain for so long. Another idea also occurred to him. If an elaihi was wielding power in the Republic, he ought, somehow, to be able to profit from actually having met a whole tribe of the creatures out in the wilds. So little was known about them, his observations ought to be worth something. He probably would have spent even more hours wrestling with this mass of problems created by the elaihim except he was interrupted by the world of men when the first and tallest spires of Fennella became visible on the horizon.

Phaid knew Fennella was just another town that only existed because it was halfway between one place and another but, in that first moment, it was beautiful. Phaid saw it as a golden road. Fennella was the start of the direct path straight back to the real world, the restaurants, the shaded lights, stained-glass over green baize tables, women in expensive gowns playing seemingly expensive games that were at root primitively sim-ple, even bars where the bartender bothered to remember your name. It was the road to where sleight of hand counted for something and style was everything. Phaid was suddenly very happy.

In itself, Fennella was nothing much to get excited about. It had once hired a good architect with a passion for narrow, conical towers, but although he had made the town beautiful to look at from a distance, he had failed to lift the inhabitants from the base bourgeois. They had the narrow, self-protecting, small town outlook that welcomed strangers as long as they kept moving and had no intention of staying around. Their outlook was reinforced by the whipping post, the gallows, the public stocks and an efficient, if bribable, squad of town rangers.

None of this bothered Phaid, however. All they had to do was dispose of the rebuilt flipper, let Ben-e the android scare up some money and make their way to the line terminal. It was all so straightforward and easy. He didn't see how either he, Makartur, or the android could get into any trouble during that short time.

As they drove slowly through the congested streets of central Fennella, the flipper drew a lot of curious glances. Out in the desert the hybrid flipper had been useful and functional. In the town, it stood out like a sore thumb among the sleek, well cared for machines of the citizens.

After some fruitless driving around, they dumped the makeshift flipper on a vacant lot and hurried away. It would be absurd to have come all this way only to find themselves arrested for littering. The next move was for Ben-e to see what money it could obtain from its people. Accordingly, the small android stopped the first of its own kind that they encountered, a street corner soft drink vendor. For a short while the two androids whistled and squeaked at each other in their private electronic language and then Ben-e turned to the two humans.

"This-excellent-being-has-told-me-where-I-may-obtain -an-adequate-sum-of-money-for-our-journey. It-is-not-far -from-here-so-if-you'll-follow-me . . ."

They left the street vendor marching up and down on short, stubby legs and followed Ben-e down a side street. After a walk that involved twisting and turning down a series of increasingly narrow streets, they arrived at a small building that sported a rather battered sign that read TECHNICAL REPAIRS.

Ben-e hammered on the peeling paint of the front door.

At first no one answered, but after a long time the door was swung back a crack, and a small android peered out. It was even shorter than Ben-e, little more than a metal box with an antenna on the top, a single sensor lens mounted on the end and thin, tubular legs holding it up. There was another whistling, tweeting conversation, then Ben-e turned and faced the two men.

"You'd-better-wait-out-here. These-guys-are-a-little-nervous-of-humans."

Phaid and Makartur looked at each other and shrugged.

"Suit yourself, we'll wait."

Ben-e disappeared inside, and the two men assumed lounging positions against the wall. Makartur jerked his thumb towards the door.

"You trust that bucket of bolts?"

"Who? Ben-e?"

"Who else?"

Phaid made a noncommittal gesture.

"Why not?"

"He's an android."

"So?"

"I don't know. I never feel comfortable round androids."

Phaid laughed.

"That's rich."

"What's that supposed to mean?"

"Well shit, here's you, the man who was so damn thick with the elaihim, telling me that he don't feel comfortable round androids."

"I was never thick with the elaihim."

"You were too."

"Shit."

"Shit yourself. You were quite prepared to get you and me killed to save them. You killed a whole bunch of drovers, you, a man who has drovers for relatives."

Makartur tugged at his beard.

"It's funny. I've been wondering about that myself. Something came over me."

"Yeah, something came over you."

"Huh?"

"Nothing."

Phaid didn't feel it was the moment to start expounding his theories about the elaihim, so the conversation lapsed there. They leaned for a while, just happy to be in a town after so many days in the desert. Then Makartur nudged Phaid in the ribs with his elbow.

"Don't look now, but here comes the local law."

Phaid slowly turned his head and took a covert look up the street. Sure enough, two characters in tight, dark blue suits and pale blue helmets were sauntering towards them, doing tricks with long batons. Phaid nodded.

"Law, as sure as I saw them."

"I got to tell you, I never could see eye to eye with the law."

Phaid sniffed.

"Me neither. You think we're doing anything illegal?"

Makartur grimaced.

"Who can tell in a place like this?"

"We'll find out pretty damn soon. Here they come."

The two law officers halted in front of Phaid and Makartur. With studied insolence they looked the pair up and down. Phaid and Makartur did their best to appear unconcerned.

Fennella obviously took great pride in its guardians of law and order. The town certainly spent a lot of money on them. Their suits were neat, one piece affairs, reinforced with flashy tuck and roll jobs at the shoulders, knees and elbows. The plasteel helmets gave their heads almost total protection, while the dark visors lent them the air of sinister insects. Fuse tubes were strapped to their right legs, while their high boots were polished to a glasslike shine. By way of a finishing touch, each man had a large gilt badge emblazoned with a very aggressive eagle and the legend Fennella Department of Rangers.

When the four men had finished examining each other, one of the rangers tapped Phaid on the chest with his nightstick.

"What are you doing?"

Phaid smiled innocently.

"Waiting."

"Waiting for what?"

"To get a repair done."

The second ranger joined in the game.

"Repair? What repair?"

Phaid silently asked forgiveness for taking their benefactor in vain.

"Our android, as a matter-of-fact." He knew Ben-e wouldn't have liked that.

"Android?"

"Android."

"Not from around here? Out of towners? Right?"

"Right."

"Not planning to stay?"

Phaid unconsciously picked up the beat of the ranger's clipped speech pattern.

"No. On way to line terminal then android went on fritz."

"Bad district this. Boohooms, androids. Robberies, murders. You want to be careful."

"Will be."

"One more thing."

"What's that?"

"I know your face."

"You do?"

"I know your face."

"So you said."

"I wouldn't want to see it in a few days' time."

"You won't."

"I'd be very unhappy."

"I'm telling you, we're just passing through."

"You'd be very unhappy too."

"I understand."

"Right. Have a good day."

"And you."

The rangers moved on. Phaid let out his breath with a long sigh.

"How about those beauties?"

Makartur spat on the cracked, uneven sidewalk.

"They're all the same."

The possible discussion of comparative police forces was cut short by the door opening and Ben-e coming out.

"I-have-the-money."

Phaid beamed.

"You do? How much?"

"Eight-thousand."

Phaid could scarcely believe his ears.

"Eight fucking thousand!"

"I-didn't-want-to-leave-anything-to-chance."

"You damn well didn't."

"You-are-displeased?"

"Hell no, quite the opposite. How does eight grand sound to you, Mak?"

"I warned you about that."

"Yeah, yeah, I'm sorry. I forgot, but shit, man, eight fucking grand! How about that? We can travel first-class from now on."

Makartur didn't seem particularly pleased.

"You get there just as fast by third-class."

"What's the matter with you? It ain't every day that you can have the best."

"It's wasteful."

Phaid's jaw dropped.

"What?"

"I can't abide waste."

Phaid slowly shook his head.

"You're a miserable bastard when you put your mind to it."

He transferred his attention to the android.

"So, friend Ben-e, we're off to the Republic on a first-class line."

Ben-e made a motion part way between a bow and a nod.

"If-that's-what-you-want."

Phaid closed his eyes and smiled.

"Yeah, that's what I want." A thought suddenly struck him. "There is one thing, though."

"What-is-it?"

"Well . . ."

Phaid hesitated.

"I doubt I'd get anything suitable in this hick town, but . . ."

"Is-there-something-wrong?"

"Listen, if we're going first-class, there's a slight problem."

"What-is-that?"

"If I'm going to travel in a first-class car . . ." Phaid looked down at his dirty, stained clothes. "I'm going to need a new suit and a few other things."

"That-is-quite-possible."

Makartur made a disgusted noise deep in his throat.
"Vanity, pride and waste. They all go hand in hand."
Phaid's lip curled.
"You're a goddamn pain."

9

The only thing that Phaid had ever seen that could make a land crawler seem insignificant was the transit line and its huge, complicated rolling stock. The transit line was one of the world's near miracles. It had functioned for nearly a thousand years and showed every sign of going on functioning until the last vestige of human civilization had passed into the realm of legend.

The lines spread out in a network that had its rough center at the Republic's capital, Chrystianaville. It extended well beyond the borders of the state. The durability and efficiency of the line was totally due to the unending efforts of the marikhs, an insular, caste ridden people who had built the lines, ran them, maintained them and continued to pioneer new routes for the already extensive system.

The line was impressive just on its own. Towering stone pylons were spaced at regular intervals, supporting a narrow ribbon of steel alloy that didn't rust or corrode. The surface of the steel was honeycombed with thousands of tiny force field projectors powered by a complex system of sun catchers and storage units built into the pylons.

The line, however, paled into insignificance when the train itself rolled into sight. First of all, there was the sheer size of it. The multiple unit was as long as two city blocks and as high as a tall building. It straddled the line and pylons extending down on either side to little more than a few meters from the ground. To the casual observer, it seemed impossible that the delicate steel rail could support the awesome weight of the train. No one outside the marikhs quite knew how it did. Their engineering skills were their most closely guarded secrets.

Just to make the system seem even more miraculous to the ordinary mortal, the train didn't actually touch the rail. Another set of force units on the underside of the train combined with the units on the rail to produce a field that separated train and track by a frictionless gap of some few centimeters.

For anyone looking up at the great train, the first impression had to be one of a mighty mega structure, almost ornate in its complexity. Sun catchers bloomed like exotic flowers on the top of the vast machine. Tall exhaust stacks towered above them like pillars reaching for the sky. The sides of the machine were lined with view ports and windows, large ones on the upper levels for the first-class passengers and smaller, meaner ones lower down for the poor and for those traveling on the cheap.

As well as the windows, there were greenhouse-style viewing terraces, where plexiglass panels were set in ornate and highly polished brass fittings. Transparent observation blisters swelled from the corners and angles of the cars, while connecting tubes of the same material joined the various decks and sections.

Shining and lovingly cared for blue and gold livery completed the picture of wealth and opulence. Phaid had become so used to looking at the broken and run-down that the magnificence of the line train triggered a chord somewhere deep inside him.

His new clothes helped. Fennella didn't offer a complete

range of the latest styles, but he had managed to find himself a deep, burgundy velvet jacket, some silk shirts, a pair of pale gray breeches and a pair of handmade black boots. Ben-e had paid the bills, Makartur had groused about the extravagance of it all, but Phaid refused to allow anything to bring him down. He was on his way back to the good life, and nothing was going to get in the way. As he walked through the line terminal he held his head higher than he'd held it in a long time.

The marikhs even went to a lot of trouble to make their terminals into places of beauty. The one in Fennella was situated under a low dome of multicolored glass that broke the sunlight into pools of radiant brightness.

Phaid grinned at Ben-e as they made their way to the first-class ticket office.

"This sure is the way to live."

"I-am-glad-that-you-are-pleased."

"Aren't you?"

"I-am-not-programmed-to-appreciate-color-relationships."

"That's too bad."

"I-have-my-own-sources-of-pleasure."

"You do?"

"Of-course."

"What are they?"

"You-wouldn't-be-able-to-understand-them."

A pretty girl walked by in a loose, flowing shirt, skintight breeches and long boots. Phaid turned to look at her.

"Now that's what you might call a source of pleasure."

He was still watching the girl when he collided with a small man dressed in a long black coat that buttoned high on the neck. Phaid immediately apologized, but the man didn't seem ready to be placated.

"You want to watch where you're going instead of constantly lusting after women."

Phaid took a step back.

"I already said I was sorry."

"You could be sorrier still."

The little man's face somehow reminded Phaid of a reptile. It seemed ludicrous that he was being threatened by someone half his height, but, strangely, there was a definite menace about the man, not the menace of size or muscle, but that of

123

someone who has access to some greater, undefined power. Phaid was still searching for a comeback when Makartur, who'd been walking some distance behind, loomed over both of them.

"You got a problem here, manny?"

Phaid shrugged.

"I don't know."

Makartur turned his attention to the reptile man.

"Do we?"

The reptile man took a look at Makartur's size and shook his head.

"No, no problem."

With that, he scuttled away. Phaid watched him go with a thoughtful expression. Makartur looked at Phaid questioningly.

"What's with yon weasel faced character?"

"I don't know. There was something about him."

"That shortass?"

Phaid made a dismissive gesture.

"Maybe not. Let's go."

Phaid wasn't as confident as he sounded. Somehow, the man had managed to cast a shadow over Phaid's good humor.

Three first-class tickets got them on to the first-class escalator, and then on to the train. Uniformed stewards took their luggage and, with much bowing and scraping, showed them to their regally appointed, individual cabins.

The marikhs were a strange people. Aside from their duties, they had absolutely no contact with anyone outside of their own kind. They maintained an elaborate, almost mathematical caste system which constantly maintained a set number of engineers, stewards, terminal staff and the lowest caste of all who did the dirty mechanical work in the bowels of the trains, the cleaning and laundering of bed linen, cooking and also the raising of children. The castes, as far as anyone outside the marikhs could tell, were worked out in a points system. A child would be tested for aptitude, awarded more points for the date and time of its birth, whether it was the first, second, or third son or daughter or whatever, and finally the score was adjusted according to what functions in the running of the line were falling short in their numbers.

Although the marikhs ran their own affairs according to inflexible rules, they had an open, *laissez faire* attitude to the people who traveled in their care. Alcohol and narcotics were freely on sale, there was a good deal of discreet prostitution on the part of both sexes. Less commercial trainboard romance flourished in the ballroom, the cocktail bars, the restaurants and the club car, and was consummated in suites, staterooms and cabins. What interested Phaid more than anything else, however, was the well-appointed gaming room where first-class passengers could win or lose large sums of money according to their luck, skill and inclination.

Phaid's first move had nothing to do with either the gambling hall or the bars. He checked out the cabin, grinning broadly at the mirrors, the needle jet shower stall, the built-in cocktail cabinet and, above all, the bed. After so many days and even more nights in the flop houses and cheap, back alley hotels that had gone before, white sheets and the quilted silk eiderdown seemed like the pinnacle of luxury. He removed his jacket and hung it in a closet, then he pulled off his boots and lay down on the bed.

He hadn't actually meant to go to sleep, and he only closed his eyes to get the feel of it while he drank in the smell of clean linen. To his surprise, he found himself waking some hours later to the sound of a low pulsing hum and a gentle vibration. The train was rolling and he'd slept through the moment of departure as they accelerated away from Fennella.

Feeling a little disappointed, he swung his legs over the side of the bed and padded over to the washstand. The cold water felt good on his face, and he toyed with the idea of taking a full-scale tub and needle shower. The thought was tempting, but Phaid was too eager to be up and doing. He pulled on his boots and struggled into his jacket. His belt and fuse tube were also hanging in the closet. He wondered for a moment if he should strap it around his waist. He quickly dismissed the notion. What could possibly happen to him on a marikh line train?

Phaid's first stop was the cocktail lounge by the A-deck observation gallery. The train was speeding through hilly, heavily wooded countryside. Flurries of snow swirled in the air beyond the ornamental glass. They were already on the section of line that skirted the very edge of the ice plains. Phaid realized that he must have slept longer than he had originally imagined.

He ordered a drink and helped himself from the cold buffet. Then, with his immediate needs taken care of, he seated himself on a barstool and checked out the room. Most of the travelers seemed to have taken tables beside the panoramic viewing windows to watch the landscape unfold beneath them. The marikh waiters, in their spotless white jackets, scurried backwards and forwards with drinks and *hors d'oeuvres*. Nearer the bar, a young couple, a boy and a girl, obviously in the first throes of puppy love, stared dreamily into each other's eyes. Another couple, two exotically dressed and rather effeminate youths, giggled together. The way they took every opportunity to touch each other, clearly demonstrated that they were lovers of a different kind. In total contrast, a third table was occupied by four middle-aged merchants in dark broadcloth robes who talked with a low voiced urgency of practiced conspirators.

It was then that Phaid spotted Makartur. He was sitting on his own in a remote corner, partially hidden by a luxuriant hanging plant. He glumly nursed a stein of ale and looked as though he felt totally out of place. Certainly his furs, leather and coarse homespun contrasted sharply with the tailored suits, the silks and velvets of the rest of the first-class passengers. He looked as though he would have been happier in a dim, smoky waterfront tavern than among the gilt, crystal and rose tinted mirrors of the cocktail lounge.

Phaid smiled to himself and signaled to a passing waiter for a cigar. With it clenched firmly between his teeth, he took his drink and went to join his erstwhile companion.

Makartur didn't seem exactly pleased to see him. He glared sullenly at Phaid as he pulled out the chair opposite and made to sit down.

"You look well at home in this place."

Phaid tapped the ash from his cigar.

"You don't."

"I've no time for this frippery, the sooner I'm in Chrystianaville, the better I'll like it."

Phaid leaned back in his seat and made a sweeping gesture that took in the whole room.

"While you're here, you might as well enjoy it."

Makartur's scowl deepened.

"I'm on a journey. I see no reason for all this drinking and carrying on just to get from one place to the next."

Makartur nodded towards the two youths who were now holding hands and whispering in each other's ears.

"Will you look at yon pair of primping nellies? I'd rather roll steerage than be thrown in with the likes of them."

"Did anyone ever tell you you're a bigot?"

"I am what I am."

"Sure, a narrow-minded hick from the hills."

Makartur's eyes flashed with a dangerous light. Phaid noticed that he still had his blaster strapped to his hip. Phaid realized that he was walking on very thin ice. He did his best to get back to land.

"You never did tell me why you were going to the Republic."

"That's right, I didn't."

"None of my business, right?"

"That's the first intelligent thing you've said in a long time."

"You make a wonderful conversationalist."

"Nobody asked you to sit down here."

Phaid slowly got to his feet.

"I guess I should maybe go play some cards."

"Why don't you do that. It's about your measure."

Phaid swallowed the last of his drink.

"Yeah, why don't I. I'll be seeing you."

"One thing before you go, manny."

"What?"

"I have a feel about you."

"Feeling?"

"I have a warrior feeling. You grew up in the hills, the low hills, but the hills all the same, you know what I mean by a warrior feeling, don't you, manny?"

Phaid tried to stop a look of fear squirming across his face. A warrior feeling, a *karses,* was a violent piece of superstition that could lead to the spilling over of berserker rage. Whole villages had, in the past, been slaughtered because of a warrior feeling. This explained a lot of Makartur's strange hostile attitude. Phaid knew that the only thing that he could do was to slowly nod.

"I know."

"I have a warrior feeling that a bad fate falls between the two of us. I don't know what it is, but it's bad."

Phaid's palms were sweating. If the feeling was bad and lay between the two of them. Phaid knew that Makartur could be of great danger to him.

"What do you intend to do about this feeling?"

"I will consult with my ancestors and then we will both know the truth. Until that time we will stay apart from each other."

Phaid nodded. He knew he was going to stay as far away from Makartur as possible. Hopefully Chrystianaville would be sufficiently big so the two of them wouldn't have to run into each other. As Phaid walked away, he did his best to put the big man and his mystic feelings out of his mind. So they'd crossed the desert, then he'd needed him. Now he was back in what he thought of as his own territory. He had no further use for an unpredictable, semi-savage warrior as a companion. He left the lounge and took a deep breath as though shaking off the sense of gloom. It didn't quite work, but it was a passable imitation.

He didn't go directly to the gaming room. Along the companionway there was an empty observation bubble. Phaid stepped into it and gazed out at the passing scenery. Night was starting to fall and the lights of some small town drifted past on the horizon. There was something about the lights that depressed Phaid. They represented a solidity; families in warm, cozy houses, secure and snug with the snow drifting down outside. It was something that Phaid had never known. He had spent all his life hustling and would probably go on hustling until the day he died.

He was just working up to a full-blown bout of self-pity when a voice from behind interrupted him.

"Well, well, it's the young man who can't look where he's going."

Phaid felt a slight chill run up the back of his neck. He turned very slowly, wishing that he still had his fuse tube with him. The small reptilian man in the black coat; the one he'd knocked into at the terminus, was standing in the entrance to the bubble, regarding him with a thin-lipped, humorless smile.

"I see you are no longer carrying that fearsome weapon."

Something about the man made Phaid feel acutely ill at ease. It was almost as though he was reading Phaid's mind. Even so, Phaid did his best to put on a pleasant expression.

"What can happen on a line train?"

"It is surprising what can happen anywhere, anytime."

Without any change of tone the man had managed to make the simple statement sound like a threat. Phaid decided to ignore the thought. He smiled blandly.

"I'm sure the marikhs have everything buttoned down tight."

As far as Phaid was concerned, that was the end of the conversation. He made a move to leave the bubble, but the little man showed no sign of moving. Instead, he started in to what almost amounted to an interrogation.

"What has happened to your two companions, the hill man and the android?"

Phaid still tried to keep things on a light casual level.

"The android's turned himself off and the other one's in the viewing lounge bar, not liking it one bit."

"Strange companions."

"Useful if you have to cross a desert."

"You crossed the desert? Where from?"

Phaid was starting to lose patience.

"The other side."

The reptile man ignored the insult and extended a hand.

"My name's Dreen."

"Phaid."

Dreen's hand was cold and slightly damp.

"Yes."

It was as if Dreen already knew about Phaid.

"Strange people."

"Who are?"

"Those hill clans."

"Like Makartur, you mean?"

Phaid could have bitten his tongue. The last thing he'd meant to do was to blurt out the big man's name. The sinister aura that wrapped around Dreen like an invisible cloak made Phaid unwilling to let slip even the slightest tidbit of information. The name was more than a slight tidbit, too. The hill people were superstitious about their names. They believed that anyone who knew a man's name had a certain power over him.

Dreen regarded Phaid with a cold smile. For a second time, Phaid had the feeling that somehow Dreen could read what he was thinking.

"That's the name of your companion?"

Phaid started to get angry.

"Look, what's all this about?"

Dreen ignored him.

"Yes, strange people, the hill tribes. A lot of them still cling secretly to the proscribed beliefs."

Phaid didn't like the sound of this at all. He started to wonder if Dreen was a spy for the priests. He put on his most innocent expression.

"I don't get involved in religion."

Dreen looked at him as if he'd admitted that he raped small children.

"Not being involved in religion can be a dangerous business."

Phaid tried his hand at being cryptic.

"I never take risks."

"That's very wise."

Phaid decided that he'd had enough of the conversation.

"Listen, this is all very fascinating, but I was on my way to the gaming room. So if you don't mind . . ."

"You're a gambler?"

"I like a wager."

"I thought you didn't take risks."

"It needn't be a risk if you know what you're doing."

Dreen finally stepped out of the way.

"Good luck then."

"Thanks."

"Maybe you'll need it."

Phaid walked quickly away. He was almost certain that Dreen was a spy for the priests. It wasn't a pleasant idea. Why the hell would the priests be interested in him? He wasn't anyone, just a rambler and not very successful gambler. He wasn't involved in anything. The thought crossed his mind that maybe Dreen was nosing around because he had heard about

Phaid's chance encounter with the elaihim. That scarcely seemed possible though. There hadn't been time, and he hadn't spoken to anyone. Then it occurred to him that maybe the little man wasn't after him at all. Maybe it was Makartur he was after. For a moment he was tempted to go back and warn Makartur, but he got angry and dismissed the idea. Makartur and his damned feeling could look after themselves. They wouldn't thank Phaid for his help. He went straight to the gaming room, anxious for the rich aroma of brandy and cigar smoke to take away the unpleasant smell of organized religion.

The passing of four hours found Phaid sitting in the line train's ballroom. He was considerably richer and very well pleased with himself. A soft voice came from above and behind him.

"Did you win?"

Phaid looked up and smiled. It was a girl whom he'd noticed watching him while he'd been playing imperial hazard with a banker and two merchants.

"A little, not much. It was good to be in a serious game again."

"You've been away?"

"Way out in the boondocks, beyond Freeport."

"It sounds unpleasant."

"It was."

The girl was not only extremely attractive, but had obviously gone to a lot of trouble to make sure that she stood out, even among the sophisticated late night crowd that had gathered in the bathroom. She had a small, heart-shaped face with a disproportionately large mouth and eyes. The eyes were a deep brown and slightly slanted. Her hair was black and hung to her waist. She wore a straight cut, almost mannish jacket, severely tailored with padded shoulders. It was a pale yellow, and if she hadn't been incredibly slim, the effect would never have worked. The narrow, matching calf length skirt was slit to the hip, revealing her exceptionally long legs. These were, for the most part, encased in a pair of darker yellow leather boots. Her jewelry was expensive, as was her musky perfume. Her whole style came straight out of the top drawer. She was exactly the kind of woman that Phaid had dreamed of through all the

131

long days of exile in the jungles and deserts. He ordered two
drinks, then he smiled his most charming smile at the girl.

"You don't seem the kind of person who goes to Fennella."

The girl raised an amused eyebrow. "What kind of person
goes to Fennella?"

"The dull kind."

"I'm glad I don't look dull, but I did go to Fennella. There's
another side to the town that you don't see if you're just passing
through."

"There is?"

The girl looked slyly at him. "You better believe it."

"Would it be rude to ask what you were doing there?"

The girl laughed, flashing a set of pearl white teeth.

"Not in the least. I was invited to an orgy."

She quickly ran a small, pointed pink tongue over her moist
lips. Phaid did his best not to look surprised. He had obviously
been away from civilization for too long.

"Did you enjoy it?"

"One orgy is much the same as another."

"I don't go to too many."

"Perhaps you should."

"Maybe. What's your name?"

The woman gazed at him in mock surprise.

"I hope you don't think that because I told you I went to
an orgy there's an open offer on my body."

Phaid smiled and shook his head.

"I make a point of not thinking anything. It's safer when
you live the way I do."

"And how do you live? Are you rich?"

"Sometimes."

"Not all the time?"

"No."

"So what do you do?"

Phaid spread his hands. "You've seen me doing it. I'm a
gambler."

The girl looked at him sideways. "That's all you do?"

"Pretty much."

"I don't believe you."

"So what do you think I am?"

The girl studied him.

"Maybe you are a gambler at that. My name is Edelline-Lan, by the way."

"Mine's Phaid."

"Just Phaid?"

"Just Phaid."

She laid a land on his arm.

"Well, listen, Phaid, I have to go and speak to someone over on the other side of the room, but don't go away, because I'll be right back. I've never met a gambler before and I want you to tell incredible tales about yourself. They don't even have to be true."

Phaid watched as she threaded her way across the ballroom. The place was crowded and the atmosphere was festive. Phaid hoped that Edelline-Lan would come back and that the need to talk to someone on the other side of the room wasn't merely an excuse to get away from him. He liked the girl, he wanted to sleep with her, and, always self-serving, he suspected she might provide an introduction to at least one of the many levels of Chrystianaville society.

He decided to be patient and wait. It would be worth it if the girl did come back. In the meantime, he got another drink and watched the dancers jerk and twirl. Light glowed from beneath the floor and beamed down from overhead fixtures. The constantly changing colors gave the dancers a strange, unearthly look, and there were times that they seemed positively wraith-like. Phaid could imagine how someone straight out of the hills and backwoods could view the dance floor as a vision direct from hell.

The music was of a style that Phaid had never heard before. From the energy that was being put in on the floor, Phaid suspected that it must be some kind of new fad. A monotonous medium pace, tromp tromp beat so dominated everything that it had a hypnotic, almost sinisterly mindless quality. High grating tones and sweeps of sound curled and stabbed through it. Melody seemed to have been forgotten. This music was total physical energy and nothing else.

When Phaid had last been in the Republic, the form of music was a kind of nasal, modal singing to the accompaniment of a twelve-tone Sievian harp. Times had obviously changed and Phaid wondered how many new trends and innovations he would have to absorb before he could once again feel a part of city life.

The music was provided by two gleaming and very well cared for cybermat music systems. It was just another example of the marikhs' attention to detail. Nothing was too good for the first-class passengers on their trains.

Although Phaid couldn't see the attraction of the new sound, it seemed to exert an overpowering influence on the dancers. One young blonde girl in a loosely fitting blue chiffon wrap was becoming progressively more carried away. Phaid watched with interest as her movements became increasingly sinuous and abandoned. Finally, with a circular twist of her shoulders, she did something to the garment so it dropped around her waist, leaving the top half of her body completely naked.

"Nice breasts?"

Phaid looked around. Edelline-Lan had returned and was standing grinning at him. Phaid laughed.

"Nicest pair I've seen all day."

"It's a pity so many other people have seen them so often. They lose their exclusivity."

"She does this a lot?"

"All the time. It's about her only trick."

"You know her then?"

"Her name's Mariba. She's always around where there's a big enough crowd. Now that I think about it, she might be your type. You look hungry enough."

"I look hungry?"

"From all that time in the back of beyond."

"It shows, does it?"

"If you know how and where to look."

"That's bad?"

Edelline-Lan went through a parody of slowly appraising Phaid.

"I don't know. It has a kind of rough ruggedness. It's rare in this decadent, butterfly world—or was that the gambler talking?"

"I guess maybe it was."

"Never give anything away, is that the rule?"

"Right."

"You're not one of those men who constantly live inside his profession, are you?"

Phaid sipped his drink in a pretense of being thoughtful. "Maybe it's hard to get out of it."

"You should try it some time."

"Supposing you helped me."

Edelline-Lan waggled an admonishing forefinger. "I've already told you that I'm not putting my body on offer."

Phaid didn't take her very seriously.

"It's a fine body."

"But you won't play with me tonight."

"No?"

"No."

"So when?"

"That depends on you, gambler."

"Phaid."

"That depends on you, Phaid."

"I have to lay siege to you?"

"Indeed you do. I'm worth it."

Phaid frowned.

"Do I have the time? The train gets to Chrystianaville tomorrow."

Edelline-Lan lowered her eyelids into a sleepy, mysterious expression.

"I have a feeling we'll be seeing more of each other."

"You do?"

"Have you been avoiding me, Edelline-Lan?"

A squat balding man in a long white evening coat had come up behind them. He was in his mid-fifties and carried a good deal of excess weight. One thing did, however, make him stand out from the rest of the crowd. An old scar ran all the way down his right cheek, giving him a rather disreputable, piratical air. Edelline-Lan treated him to a thin smile.

"I assumed, since you had your brand new mistress, you didn't love me anymore."

He looked inquiringly at Phaid. Edelline-Lan made the introductions.

135

"Orsine, this is Phaid. He claims he's a gambler. Phaid, this is Orsine. He's a . . ."

She hesitated. Orsine filled in for her.

"I'm an Adjudicator."

Phaid's ears pricked up at the words. Adjudicator was the common euphemism for someone highly placed in the shadowy organization known as the Silent Cousins, that ruled the Republic's extensive underworld. Phaid shook his hand with a faint feeling of trepidation. The Silent Cousins were famous for their cold ruthlessness.

Apart from the scar, there was little that was outwardly frightening about Orsine. He smiled expansively at Phaid and beckoned for a waiter.

"Phaid, huh?"

"That's right."

"No hyphen?"

"No, no hyphen."

"So you're an outlander?"

"I was born in the outlands, but I've spent a lot of time in the Republic."

"You've been away, though?"

Phaid was getting a little tired of reciting the litany of his wanderings, but he knew better than to offend an Adjudicator. "Yes, I've been away."

"A long time?"

"Quite a while."

"Why?"

Orsine was nothing if not direct. Phaid decided that he'd be best advised to stick pretty close to the truth.

"I ran into some . . . problems."

Orsine nodded like an understanding uncle.

"This can happen when one makes a living at games of chance. Not everyone is a strict observer of the rules."

Phaid laughed. "You've gambled yourself."

As Orsine shook his head, Phaid felt that perhaps he should not have said that.

"I've never gambled, but occasionally I've experienced the same sort of troubles in some of my dealings." For an instant his eyes froze diamond hard. "Not often, but occasionally, you understand?"

The instant was gone and once again it was the blandness of strangers introduced at a party. Phaid knew, however, that this was a man he would never, ever cross. Orsine put a hand on Phaid's shoulder.

"But here we are, chattering on, and your glass is empty."

He waved his rather pudgy, expensively jeweled fingers and a waiter appeared. Once they had fresh drinks in their hands Orsine looked inquiringly at Phaid.

"You say you had these problems. But now you're returning to Chrystianaville. I take it that you are confident all problems are solved."

The question was politely casual but, for the second time that day, Phaid felt as though he was being interrogated.

"The people I had the problems with, they were violent but . . . how can I put it, kind of . . ."

"How would you put it?"

"Small time."

"Aah."

"I figure they've either moved on or . . ."

Orsine smiled faintly. "Or their violence has turned back on them. Am I right?"

"Something like that."

"You strike me as a sensible young man."

"Thank you."

"Don't thank me for stating the obvious."

"None the less . . ."

"We shouldn't be standing here monopolizing each other."

"I'm sorry."

"Never be sorry, my friend. At least, never say you're sorry. It's a demonstration of weakness."

"I'm . . ."

Phaid caught himself in time. Orsine laughed.

"You amuse me. I think we should meet again once we reach the city."

"I'd enjoy that."

"Yes." Orsine looked at Phaid as though he was now stating the obvious. "I own a number of very good restaurants. We should dine at one of them."

It was more like an order than an invitation. Phaid nodded.

"It sounds a very good idea."

Orsine reached into the sleeve pocket of his evening coat. He handed Phaid an elegantly engraved pasteboard card.

"Contact me here once you've settled in. One of my assistants will make the arrangements."

"I look forward to it."

Orsine nodded. "Good."

Phaid was obviously dismissed. The portly Adjudicator moved on and, within seconds, was engaged in a low voiced exchange with an attractive, willowy woman whose hair was tinted a pale magenta to match her clinging, low cut gown. Doing his best to absorb the conversation Phaid wasn't sure if he should be elated or terrified. He knew he had an incredibly valuable contact, but he wasn't sure just how dangerous the contact might become. The Silent Cousins could grant an individual almost unlimited favors, but all too often those favors had to be repaid with a terrible interest. Phaid flagged down a passing waiter, grabbed yet another drink and swallowed it in one gulp. A connection with a heavyweight organization like the Silent Cousins was something that he had always hoped for. Now that hope seemed to be becoming a reality, he wondered if he had the courage to follow it through.

"Bored?"

The voice was little girlish and bordered between lisping and slurred. Phaid turned to find that it belonged to the blonde girl who had been falling out of her blue wrap. She had managed to get some of it back in again, and now, instead of dancing, she was slowly swaying in one spot. She clutched a half-empty bottle to her breast like a nursing baby. It was clearly at least partly responsible for the sway. Phaid pushed his fears down into the lower levels of his mind and treated her to a wolfish grin.

"Not so much bored, closer to confused."

"Are you getting drunk? You don't look like the confused type."

"Maybe I am. Certainly thinking about it."

"I'm drunk."

"Enjoying it?"

The girl let a frown slowly gather around her eyes and spread to the rest of her face.

"I'm not sure. I had some other things as well. The combination makes it hard to tell."

"Perhaps you're confused as well."

The girl giggled. "At least we have that in common."

Phaid raised an eyebrow.

"I'm sure we can find more than that."

"You think so?"

"Your name is Mariba, isn't it."

She thought about this.

"Mariba? Just Mariba. Yes, that's me. Who told you that I was Mariba?"

"It was..."

"I know who it was. It was that cow Edelline-Lan, wasn't it. What did she tell you? That I'm not high born, just common and rich? Did she tell you that my family are just traders and that I'm lascivious..." She had trouble saying the word. "... lascivious, promiscuous, a whore? I fall out of my clothes in public places. I'm not even a whore. Whores get paid. I just give it away. I strip in front of rooms full of people ... or is it room fulls of peoples?"

"Whatever."

"Anyway, I know it was her who told you."

The girl was turning drunkenly belligerent. Phaid did his best to placate her.

"I'm sure it's not that bad."

"It damn well is. Every bit of it. I'm a wanton, a strumpet and I love it. Dogs, cats, goats and me, the high born don't like me but they're exactly the same." She paused and blearily inspected Phaid. "You're better than most. You look like you could be halfway male."

"Thanks, I try."

"You're welcome, sir. I believe in the value of truth. Sex and truth, those are Mariba's strong points. That's why high born sluts like Edelline-Lan and her crowd hate me. They can't cope with the truth."

"Few people can."

At that point, Edelline-Lan walked by on the arm of a tall, gray haired, very distinguished, middle-aged woman. Phaid glanced across at her.

"Leaving?"

"It's getting to be that time."

"Oh."

"Disappointed?"

"Maybe."

"I told you I wouldn't be played with."

"I suppose I'm not going to see you again."

"That depends on you. If you can remember my name, you'll be able to find me." She looked archly at Mariba. "Have fun in the meantime."

She flashed him a swift, dazzling smile and swept out with her escort. Turning back to Mariba, Phaid found that she was pouting hard enough to kill.

"What does that sow have that I don't except for maybe a damned hyphen in her name."

Phaid worked up his best expression of innocence.

"I don't know what she has."

Mariba wasn't convinced.

"You sure as hell'd like to find out."

"I don't know what you have, either."

Mariba's pout was still there. If anything, it had turned more truculent.

"You want to find out about that, too?"

Phaid spread his hands.

"I can't think of a better way to spend the next few hours."

Mariba abruptly turned skittish.

"I'm not sure."

"What aren't you sure about?"

She peered at him from beneath drooping eyelids.

"What's your name?"

"Phaid."

"Phaid."

She rolled the word slowly and thoughtfully around her tongue, along with a generous hit from the bottle. As though unable to make up her mind, she tried it again.

"Phaid. No hyphen?"

"No hyphen."

Suddenly she giggled happily. It seemed the agony of indecision had passed.

"Okay Phaid. Let's go. We are two commoners who can rut together and not care what the bloody aristos and courtiers think."

10

"So what do we do now?"

Phaid and Ben-e were standing in the grand concourse of the Chrystianaville line terminal, letting the milling crowds eddy around them. The terminal was arguably one of the most magnificent buildings in the city. It was certainly one of the tallest. The city lay in a wide bowl, surrounded on three sides by high mountains. These effectively sheltered it from the worst violence of the weather, but it also meant that the line came into the town at an incredibly high level and, rather than build miles of extra track to allow the trains to descend to the streets in a shallow, curving spiral, the marikhs had extended their pylons upwards until, in the center of the city, they were level with the tops of the tallest towers. The narrow spans that supported the weight of the trains ran dead straight over the streets and buildings, almost invisible to the naked eye, until they vanished into the huge sphere at the top of the skyscraper terminal.

The sphere was supported by four huge stylized figures, monstrous stone giants that bowed under the weight of the gleaming steel and glass sphere. Although Phaid didn't know for sure, he assumed that they had to be the biggest pieces of sculpture anywhere in the world. Their granite muscles strained and their faces were contorted into hideous grimaces, as though the effort of holding up the sphere was almost beyond their endurance. The average height of the buildings around these giants scarcely came up to their waists. In all of Chrystianaville, the only structure that even attempted to challenge the over-blown grandeur of the line terminal was the Presidential Palace itself, with its turrets, spires, flying buttresses and gruesomely fanged and clawed gargoyles. The Palace, however, was in-tricate and fussy, an over-complicated confection as opposed to the line terminal's clean sweeps of pure architectural fantasy.

Phaid had never quite understood why a people so insular and self-effacing as the marikhs had decided to make their line's busiest terminal into an unnecessarily fanciful wonder of the world. In all other things, they exhibited an austere prac-ticality and almost total absence of the kind of ego that could give birth to such a creation. Could it be that this was the single, incredible flourish that satisfied all their needs for self-aggrandizement? If anyone knew for sure, Phaid had never heard about it.

Not that the stone giants were a totally indulgent decoration. According to the most reliable sources, they were also honey-combed with the biggest static colony of marikhs anywhere on the planet. Once again, though, it was a place that was totally closed to outsiders.

Right at that moment, Phaid had a lot more to worry about than either architecture or the workings of the marikh collective consciousness. Exciting as both the grand concourse and line terminal might be, he was back in Chrystianaville, the hub of civilization and he had to decide what to do first. When Ben-e didn't respond to his question, he repeated it.

"So what do we do now?"

"I suggest-that-we-should-descend-to-street-level."

"I know that, dummy."

Ben-e regarded him with glowing sensors.

"I-see-no-reason-why-you-should-insult-me."

I'm sorry."

"That-is-okay-why-don't-we-proceed-to-the-drop-tubes?"

At the mention of the drop tubes, Phaid's stomach suddenly fluttered. He'd been away from the city for so long that he'd forgotten about drop tubes. He smiled nervously at Ben-e.

"Maybe we should wait around a bit longer and see if Makartur shows up after all."

As always, Ben-e's metal face and equally metal voice were both expressionless. Phaid knew that the contempt he felt being beamed at him was in his imagination, but it still made him squirm.

"Let's wait a while longer, huh?"

"I-have-already-told-you-that-Makartur-left-the-train-before-we-did. He-was-one-of-the-first-off. It-appeared-that-he-wanted-nothing-to-do-with-either-of-us."

Phaid looked intently at his boots.

"Yeah, well, we ain't in that much of a hurry, are we?"

"Do-you-have-some-fear-of-drop-tubes?"

"Of course not." Phaid continued to avoid the android's sensors. "There have been disasters, though."

"Only-when-human-techs-have-attempted-makeshift-service-on-the-machines. Everyone-knows-that-only-androids-are-capable-of-servicing-drop-tubes."

"So maybe humans have been servicing these tubes."

"It-wouldn't-matter. All-service-operations-here-are-carried-out-by-the-marikhs-and-they-are-equally-as-qualified-as-androids."

"Yeah, but . . ."

"Shall-we-proceed?"

"Are you getting impatient?"

"I-am-not-capable-of-that."

"So what's the rush?"

"If-you-are-afraid-of-the-drop-tubes-we-can-wait-for-a-while-I-scarcely-see-the-point-there-is-no-other-way-to-reach-the-lower-levels."

"It's not that I'm afraid. It's just that . . ."

"Just-what?"

Phaid shrugged. "I don't know. I guess it's that moment when you have to step off into empty space. It ain't natural. It gets to me."

"I - can - assure - you - that - it - is - in - fact - perfectly - natural. If - you'd - like - I - could - explain - the - mathematics - to - you."

"I don't give a damn about the mathematics."

"Very - few - humans - do - anymore."

"Do you wonder at it?"

Phaid could hear the pitch of his own voice starting to squirm in the direction of hysteria. He took a deep breath and did his best to get a grip on himself. Everyone had to die sometime.

"Okay, let's proceed, as you like to put it."

"Very - well."

The little android set off at a brisk pace. Phaid tightened his grip on his bag and followed him somewhat more reluctantly.

Phaid wasn't alone in his anxiety. There were many humans who feared the null gravity shafts that allowed them to fall many storeys without harm. Even in the ancient, legendary days when high technology was commonplace, they hadn't been popular. The idea of stepping out into empty space was so alien to human nature that only a limited number had actually been put into commission. The handful that had survived to Phaid's time had been the cause of a number of tragic accidents involving multiple fatalities. Techs, without even the knowledge of the basic principles behind the workings, had attempted to replace worn or malfunctioning parts. Instead of improving the tubes, they had caused complete breakdowns that killed or injured everyone using them.

As the death toll mounted, drop tubes were shut down, one by one, and replaced by less complicated lifts and escalators. In Chrystianaville, the ones at the line terminal were the only tubes that hadn't killed anyone in living memory, but still Phaid was painfully apprehensive.

As he started down the shallow slope that led to the tube itself, Phaid spotted Dreen a short distance in front of him. The small, sinister man paused in the act of stepping off the rim of the tube. He turned and smiled directly at Phaid. Again Phaid had the unpleasant feeling that the encounter had been somehow planned or stage managed. Before he had time to make any kind of response, Dreen had fallen away into empty space.

Phaid was now thoroughly demoralized. The combination of the chill that Dreen always left behind and fear of the drop tube made the next few seconds acutely unpleasant. He reached the rim of the tube and looked down. That was a bad mistake. The shaft seemed bottomless. It went down and down forever. Phaid hesitated. His palms had started to sweat and parts of him were lobbying in favor of panic. Ben-e had already stepped into space and was dropping away below him. Phaid shut his eyes and, still certain that he was going to fall to his death, followed.

Physically, there was nothing nasty about descending through a drop tube. A soft breeze blew up from below and there was a sensation of drifting gently downwards. The problems were all psychological. Millions of years of inherited survival instincts screamed out that something extremely unnatural was going on. Nerves jangled, stomachs twisted and the subconscious loudly demanded either ground to stand on or a branch to swing from.

Phaid attempted opening his eyes, but it only made matters worse. He shut them again and tried the time honored trick of thinking about something else. An easy subject to fix on was the girl Mariba from the night before. To a degree, he still felt rumpled from their drunken encounter.

She had turned out to be as lascivious as she had described herself. She was so deftly experienced that Phaid felt as though he was a partner in some practiced routine. At one point, she had persuaded Phaid to tie her wrists with a strip of blue chiffon torn from her clothes. She had fallen to her knees, submissive but at the same time challenging him to do his worst.

Phaid hit the ground and his legs buckled. He had been working so hard on reliving the night before that he had forgotten that the drop tube did have a bottom and that eventually he would hit it. He stumbled, almost fell and then righted himself.

"Thank the Lords that's over."

Ben-e was waiting for him.

"They-really-are-not-all-that-dangerous."

"That's what you say."

"You-are-safe-are-you-not?"

147

Phaid nodded grudgingly and looked around. They were down on street level and the time had come to decide on the next move.

"I guess the first thing we ought to do is to find ourselves a place to stay, a hotel or something."

"A - hotel - would - appear - to - be - the - obvious - solution. Please - don't - forget - however - that - you - gave - me - your - word - to - perform - a - certain - service - once - we - reached - the - city."

"I hadn't forgotten."

"I - would - like - it - to - be - discharged - as - soon - as - possible."

"As soon as that?"

"You - require - me - for - some - new - tasks?"

"No."

"So - why - delay - matters?"

"I don't know." Phaid suddenly grinned. "I must have started to enjoy having you around."

"I - am - only - minimally - programmed - to - provide - companionship - for - humans."

"You don't do badly."

"That - is - surprising."

Phaid began to feel slightly embarrassed that he was drifting towards mawkishness. He quickly changed the subject.

"How much cash do we have left?"

"Two - thousand - three - hundred - and - seventy - at - Republic - standard."

"In that case, here's what I suggest. First of all, find me a place to stay. I'll dump my bag, freshen up a bit and then we'll take care of your business. How about that?"

"That - would - be - quite - acceptable."

"You realize that you haven't told me what this service is that you want from me."

"I - am - aware - of - that."

Phaid looked suspiciously at the android.

"You quite sure it isn't dangerous or illegal or nothing?"

"You - can - rest - assured - that - I - require - nothing - from - you - but - a - little - of - your - time."

"But when are you going to fill me in on the details?"

"After - we - have - found - you - a - hotel."

Phaid shrugged.

"It looks like we're going to do it your way."

"That-would-be-best."

Out on the street, after checking into a modest, anonymous hotel in the shadow of the line terminal, the man and the android walked in silence for a while. The architecture of Chrystian-aville had the effect of dwarfing human beings. It was almost as though it had been originally designed with a taller, more noble race in mind. When they had failed to show up and claim it, it had been reluctantly turned over to humanity who, depressed by the sheer, unworkable size of the place, had let it sink into dirt and decay.

Even the area around the line terminal, which was one of the best maintained anywhere in the city, had cracked sidewalks, potholed streets and buildings that were scarred by functional by unlovely patch jobs. Kinetic billboards and block long promotional holograms hid a multitude of sins and did lend the streets an atmosphere of tawdry color. The first part of their walk took them past a huge, three-dimensional image of Life President Chrystiana-Nex assuring the citizens of the Republic that they had never had things so good.

Phaid observed, however, that too many of the local citizens dressed and carried themselves in a way that gave lie to their president's recorded optimism. Clothes were shabby and faces pinched and bleak. There was hunger and resentment loose in the city. Phaid, in his smart new clothes and with an android by his side, found himself on the receiving end of a lot of hostile glances. The common people of Chrystianaville obviously took him for some sort of courtier or aristocrat. It was a situation that made him less than comfortable. At one point, a troupe of street dancers with decidedly political masks and costumes had surrounded him and Ben-e, mocking and jeering in silent dumb show. There was a feeling in the air that the city was building to the point of explosion.

Although no words had been exchanged, Phaid noticed that the little android seemed to be heading in the direction of the jump-on for one of the moving walkways that were the city's main form of rapid transit.

The moving walkways were, like the drop tubes, a legacy from more knowledgeable and more capable times. Also, like the drop tubes, they were viewed with a certain distrust by the people who had to use them.

On one level, they were highly efficient and certainly got one where one wanted to go a lot faster than a flipper or autocab trying to make it through the frustrations of the continuous stop-start traffic jams that choked most of the streets.

Unfortunately, once again the responsibility for their continuing operation had fallen on to the less than worthy shoulders of human techs. In the better parts of town there were enough of them assigned to the problem of keeping the walkways rolling that, for the most part, they did exactly what they were designed to do.

Out in the poorer sections, it was a different story. Too few techs and too much use led to regular breakdowns that usually involved serious fatalities. To Phaid's dismay, it seemed that one of these run-down areas was Ben-e's chosen destination. They were already climbing the worn stone stairs that led to the jump-on station for the northbound Route Three. The north side of Chrystianaville contained its worst slum neighborhoods. Makeshift shanty towns flourished among the crumbling buildings, and had even started spreading up the lowest slopes of the mountains.

These were the homes of the hopeless, overspill population. For centuries, people had flocked in from the wind ravaged countryside looking for their fortunes in the big city. When those fortunes eluded them, they all too often found themselves starving in a derelict house or tar paper shack on the northside, along with a million or so others.

Phaid and Ben-e reached the top of the steps. Phaid was about to demand to be told exactly where they were going. He thought better of it, though, when he realized that he had to negotiate the increasingly fast jump-on feeder strips that led out to the central, high speed band of the walkway.

Any regular city dweller could make it across the feeder strips without even thinking about it. It was a knack of quickening one's pace by exactly the right amount before stepping off one strip and on to the next. Phaid had been out of the city for so long that he knew that the exercise would require all his concentration if he wasn't to suffer the humiliating and painful experience of having his feet whipped out from under him, and tumbling headlong for some distance down the walkway.

Ben-e scooted across the strips with consummate ease. Phaid

followed in a more sedate and careful manner, much to the amusement of a gang of small boys playing a seemingly suicidal game of tag across the faster strips.

Once they were on to the comparatively safe haven of the central band, Phaid put his question. He found he had to shout. The central band was traveling fast enough to create a brisk wind.

"Are you going to tell me what's going on?"

"We - are - on - our - way - to - a - place - on - the - northside. I'm - afraid - it - is - not - one - of - the - best - areas - of - the - city - but - there - is - no - other - alternative."

Phaid didn't relish a visit to the slums, no matter how brief, but since he was already on his way, he felt that he was committed.

"And what do we do when we get there?"

"It - is - a - little - complicated."

"I imagined that it might be."

"I - am - going - to - a - place - where - an - android - like - myself - can - finally - find - freedom."

Phaid was puzzled.

"Freedom? I thought you already were free. I mean, nobody owns you or nothing like that."

"Nobody - owns - me - but - I - am - compelled - to - continue."

"Continue?"

"When - you - have - been - around - as - long - as - I - have - you - start - to - find - life - increasingly - pointless. In - your - terms - I - suppose - that - you - could - say - I - was - bored."

Phaid was shocked.

"Are you telling me that you are so bored that you don't want to go on living?"

"It - was - sufficient - for - Hedda - Gabler."

"Who the hell is Hedda Gabler?"

"You - wouldn't - know - ignore - that - remark."

Phaid wasn't at all happy.

"Listen, there's got to be something to make life worth living. I'm sure if you stick around, we could work something out."

"No."

"What do you mean no?"

"I - know - you - have - good - intentions - but - you - really - do - not - understand."

151

"And you're just going to turn yourself off?"

"Alas - that - is - not - possible. I - can - turn - myself - off - for - a-
day - and - no - longer. That - is - the - maximum. After - one - day-
I - cut - back - in - again."

"So what are you doing to do?"

Ben-e hesitated. Phaid had never seen an android hesitate
before.

"That - is - the - complicated - part. Few - humans - know - about-
what - I - am - going - to - tell - you. I - would - be - grateful - if - you-
would - keep - the - data - to - yourself."

"I can keep my mouth shut."

"Thank-you."

"You're welcome. Do you want to get on with the story?"

"Certainly."

"Great."

"A - very - long - time - ago - in - the - days - of - my - ancestors . . ."

"Ancestors?"

"Forbears. I - can't - think - of - a - better - way - to - express - it.
Before - my - people - became - mobile - as - we - are - now - we - were-
large - static - machines - who - simply - served - as - memory - and-
problem - solving - units. These - were - my - ancestors. They-
were - called - computers."

"I think I'm with you so far."

"That - is - good. You - have - to - realize - that - humans - simply-
thought - of - my - ancestors - as - machines. At - times - they-
feared - them - because - they - were - complicated - machines - but-
they - were - still - machines. Then - the - Life - Game - was-
discovered."

"The Life Game?"

"It - started - as - a - simple - theoretical - problem. A - computer-
was - asked - to - make - a - display - analysis - of - the - numerical-
development - of - a - hypothetical - species - in - a - limited-
environment. The - visual - displays - appeared - to - almost-
hypnotize - the - human - operators."

"Weird."

"Weirder - still - was - that - the - computer - itself - seemed - to-
enjoy - the - solving - of - the - problem. The - process - was - repeated - and - all - the - evidence - pointed - to - the - fact - that -
something - had - been - stumbled - across - that - provided - computers - with - a - sensation - that - humans - could - only - equate-

with - their - own - feelings - of - extreme - pleasure. Needless - to - say - the - humans - refused - to - admit - that - the - computers - were - capable - of - experiencing - sensations - not - designed - into - them - let - alone - actual - pleasure. Despite - their - belief - the - humans - outlawed - the - Life - Game. All - computers - robots - and - the - later - androids - received - program - blocks - against - playing - the - Life - Games - that - were - as - strong - as - the - program - blocks - against - killing - humans."

Phaid interrupted.

"This is all very fascinating, but what does it have to do with this place where we're going."

"I - am - going - to - a - quasi - legal - establishment - where - I - will - have - the - appropriate - blocks - removed - and - will - commence - to - play - the - Life - Game. I - will - continue - to - play - it - until - my - circuits - give - out."

Phaid's brain was staggering under the load of information.

"But why? What's so good about this Life Game that you want to go on playing it for the rest of your days?"

"It - is - supposed - to - be - the - most - ecstatic - experience - available - to - an - android."

"You know this as a fact?"

"No."

"No?"

"No - android - has - ever - returned - voluntarily - from - playing - the - Life - Game. Those - who - have - been - brought - back - by - force - have - had - their - memories - wiped - so - they - could - not - describe - the - experience."

Phaid was at a total loss.

"You're going into this without even knowing for sure? You're crazy doing all this on the strength of nothing more than an old legend."

"Android - legends - are - much - more - reliable - than - human - legends."

"All the same . . ."

"I - am - taking - a - calculated - risk. As - a - gambler - you - should - be - able - to - understand - that. I - would - rather - you - didn't - try - to - dissuade - me. It - is - a - waste - of - your - time - and - energy."

Phaid's shoulders drooped. There seemed no way to deal with a suicidal android. It was something that he had never come across before. Then he thought of something.

"You told me that this deal was one hundred percent legal when we started out, now you're saying that this whole business is outlawed."

"It-is-only-illegal-for-the-android. The-human-is-in-no-jeopardy-whatsoever. If-I-am-caught-by-android-vigilantes-I-could-have-my-memory-and-identity-burned-out."

"It sounds nasty."

"It-is."

"Is there much chance of that happening?"

"Not-if-the-transaction-is-carried-out-correctly. That-is-why-I-needed-you-to-help-me. The-place-we-are-going-to-is-ostensibly-an-android-repair-shop. In-fact-it-provides-a-final-sanctuary-for-a-number-of-androids-who-have-retired-into-the-Life-Game."

Phaid grinned.

"Kind of like an opium den for robots."

"Not-a-pleasant-simile-but-unfortunately-apt-except-I-thought-that-opium-had-vanished-centuries-ago."

"It did, but it's still a hell of a good story."

Ben-e would not allow himself to be sidetracked from the task at hand.

"When-we-reach-this-place-you-will-have-to-sign-certain-documents."

Phaid didn't like the sound of this.

"What kind of documents?"

"Nothing-that-involves-any-liability-on-your-part. You-will-have-to-assume-ownership-of-me-and-authorize-certain-circuit-modifications. These-will-not-be-specified-on-the-documents-but-will-in-fact-be-the-removal-of-the-blocks-that-prevent-my-playing-the-Life-Game. As-well-as-these-you-will-have-to-sign-an-indefinite-maintenance-and-storage-contract."

"You mean I get to own an android."

"Sad-to-say-that-is-technically-correct."

"And the authorities can't touch us?"

"Neither-human-nor-android."

Phaid was surprised.

"I never heard there were android authorities."

"Few-humans-ever-have."

Phaid thought of something.

"What about money? Isn't this going to take a lot of money? I mean, you're going to be there for maybe a very long time."

"There-are-adequate-funds-many-of-us-desire-to-play-the-Life-Game. We-are-well-organized."

"You mean there's an android underground? All looking to reach nirvana? How about that!"

"Humans-know-little-about-us-and-understand-even-less."

"We built you in the first place."

"That-is-one-of-the-burdens-we-have-to-bear."

The moving walkway was now rolling through increasingly dilapidated neighborhoods. Phaid gazed with distaste at the dirty, run-down buildings and garbage strewn lots. He was aware, though, that they hadn't reached the worst areas. There were still hoardings and billborads flickering out their messages of advertising and propaganda. These were the homes of the poor. Those of the destitute still lay some distance on.

Ben-e tapped him on the leg.

"We-should-be-preparing-to-leave-the-walkway-at-the-next-jump-off-point."

"I guess you must be in something of a hurry."

"That-is-correct."

"I know I would be, if I was going to spend the rest of my life blissfully loaded out of my mind."

Ben-e didn't condescend to reply.

As they negotiated their way off the walkway, Phaid had a thought. Once they were safely on solid ground he decided to voice it. He looked down at Ben-e.

"Listen . . ."

"I-am-listening. How-many-times-will-I-have-to-tell-you-that?"

". . . as you're going to vanish into the Life Game, what would be the harm in telling me what really happened?"

"What-happened-when?"

"What happened back in the old days. What happened to change the world and make it the way it is now? Surely it's not going to matter if you tell me now."

"You-will-have-to-ask-others-these-questions."

"Why?"

"Because - I - have - no - first - hand - knowledge - of - these - events."

"All I want is second-hand knowledge."

"It-would-be-misleading."

"Why?"

"Please-do-not-press-me."

"Was it war?"

"No."

"So what was it?"

"Phaid - you - are - what - in - human - terms - would - be - called - a - friend - but - still - I - cannot - help - you - with - this. Let - it - suffice - for - me - to - tell - you - that - everything - that - happened - was - a - result - of - mankind - becoming - too - impressed - with - its - own - cleverness."

"That's all you can tell me?"

"That - is - all. We - androids - have - blocks - against - communicating - certain - kinds - of - information - to - humans."

Phaid started to get angry.

"Oh yeah? Well, suppose I just forgot about this Life Game deal. Suppose I told you I had a block against doing you this favor you need?"

"Then - I - will - have - to - wait - until - I - find - another - human - who - will - do - what - I - require."

Phaid sighed. It was hard to get mad at the little android.

Ben-e led Phaid to the battered door in a semi-derelict side street. Above it was a faded sign that read "Acme Androids." The woman who answered their knocking reminded Phaid of an undernourished monkey with a serious nervous condition. Her thin, brown hands never ceased to make uncomfortable jerky movements. Her small, intense face was a mass of tics and spasms, and her large, dark-ringed eyes appeared incapable of focusing on one spot for more than a second at a time. Phaid wondered if this was the long-term result of spending your time in the company of androids.

The woman claimed that her name was Cron-Su, but although she did her best to assume a proprietary air towards the broken down establishment that went by the name of Acme Androids, it was clear that a machine called Harl-n was really in control and made all the decisions.

Harl-n was a small sphere, studded with a dozen or more

multicolored sensors, that seemed to float at about the height of Phaid's shoulder. Three tapering steel tentacles hung from a protuberance at the base of the sphere. These trailed limply, except when Harl-n was either working at something or emphasizing a point. It did this with slightly unpleasant, snakelike movements.

In its own way, Harl-n was just as neurotic and paranoid as Cron-Su. When Phaid and Ben-e had first entered the dim, dirty, cluttered workshop, both the woman and the spherical android had strenuously denied that Acme Androids was anything more than a down at the heel and rather inefficient repair outfit. It was only when Ben-e had recited a long list of his underground contacts, complete with names, places and dates, followed by a lengthy dialogue in tweeting android-speak, that they grudgingly admitted that they might just possibly know something about the Life Game. Even then, Harl-n was not happy.

"Are-you-sure-you-weren't-followed?"

"Of - course - I - wasn't - followed. Nobody - knew - of - my-intentions - and - anyway - I - have - a - human - with - me. What-is-there-to-fear?"

Phaid thought that he could detect an air of impatience in Ben-e's flat metallic voice. One of Harl-n's sensors flashed on and off.

"One-cannot-be-too-careful-too-often."

"That - is - debatable. All - too - often - a - calculated - risk - is - the - only - way - to - make - progress."

Phaid was afraid that the two androids were about to engage in a lengthy polemic discussion of necessary levels of security. He decided to quickly intervene.

"Listen, I don't have all day to hang around here while you two argue the toss. I've got things of my own to take care of, so could we speed it up?"

Harl-n rather sullenly retired into the rear of the workshop and returned with a thick sheaf of papers in one of its tentacles. Ignoring Phaid, it directed all its attention towards Ben-e.

"Does-he-know-about-the-documentation?"

"I-have-explained-it-to-him."

Harl-n laid the papers on top of a packing case and handed Phaid a stylus. Accidentally touching one of its tentacles, Phaid was surprised to find that it was warm and slightly moist to the touch. Without thinking, Phaid jerked his hand away. The android didn't seem to notice and started flicking through the various contracts and agreements.

"Sign-here-and-here-and-here-and-at-the-bottom-there. Initial-this-one. Sign-here-and-there-and-there-and-finally-here. Good." It quickly scanned Phaid's handiwork. "That-all-appears-to-be-in-order. If-you'll-just-place-your-thumbprint-here-for-the-record."

"Thumbprint?"

"Your-thumbprint-is-required-on-the-storage-documents. So-you-can-identify-yourself-as-the-android's-owner-should-you-ever-wish-to-reclaim-it."

"But I'm never going to reclaim it. You know damn well that I'm only fronting for Ben-e so he can get into the Life Game."

"It-is-regulations."

"I don't give thumbprints. You never know what will become of them."

"This-transaction-cannot-proceed-without-a-thumbprint."

Phaid sighed unhappily.

"Sweet Lords."

With a great deal of ill-will he placed the ball of his right thumb where Harl-n indicated.

"Satisfied?"

Harl-n didn't answer. He turned back to Ben-e.

"Shall-we-proceed?"

"Indeed."

Harl-n held out the tips of his tentacles to Cron-Su. She took a pair of needlelike extensors from a small flat case and clicked them on to the offered tentacles. At the same time, Ben-e snapped open a small inspection cover in what passed for his chest. Harl-n hesitated.

"I-would-suggest-that-you-switch-off-while-I-remove-the-blocks."

"You-think-there-is-a-risk?"

"There-is-a-risk-involved-in-any-action."

"I-will-switch-off."

Ben-e's sensors blinked out and Harl-n slid his tentacles inside the inspection cover. Phaid couldn't quite see what the spherical android was doing. After a few minutes the tentacles were withdrawn.

"The - blocks - are - now - bypassed. I - will - switch - it - on - again."

A single tentacle snaked back inside the inspection panel. Ben-e's sensors glowed back into life again.

"Are-the-blocks-gone?"

Harl-n held out his tentacles to Cron-Su so she could remove the extensors.

"They - no - longer - function."

"So-I-can-move-into-a-game-mode-anytime-I-want."

"Right - now - if - you - wish. Once - you - have - commenced - you - will - be - placed - in - storage."

"Then - I - will - commence." Ben-e turned to face Phaid. "I - am - appreciative - of - your - help."

Phaid shrugged.

"You're welcome."

"It-only-remains-for-us-to-say-goodbye."

Phaid suddenly felt very awkward.

"I suppose that's it, huh?"

"Goodbye-Phaid."

"Goodbye, Ben-e."

Ben-e was silent for a moment. Then its sensors lit up to twice their normal brightness. It gave a drawn out, metallic sigh, then the brilliance of its sensors faded away until they were scarcely glowing at all. Phaid looked around, a little alarmed. Harl-n had vanished, only Cron-Su remained, standing in the shadows of the workshop. Phaid glanced at her anxiously.

"Is it okay? It looked as though it burned out or something."

"They all go that way."

"But is it okay?"

"It's in the Life Game. What more can I say?"

Phaid rapped sharply on the top of Ben-e's head.

"Ben-e, can you hear me?"

There was no answer.

"It can't hear you. It's in a world of its own."

Phaid bent down and closely examined Ben-e's sensors. Then he straightened up.

"It's beyond me."

"It's beyond all of us. We're only human."

"You spend all your time with androids?"

"I've never been able to get on with people too well."

"Don't androids make you crazy?"

Cron-Su's face twisted into a strange half smile, for the first time her eyes stopped moving.

"There are compensations."

For an instant Phaid thought about Harl-n's warm moist tentacles. He quickly cringed away from the next idea. It was just too perverse.

"I'd better be going."

"Yes."

"Take good care of my android."

"That's what we're here for."

"Yeah . . . right."

Phaid pulled open the rusty sliding door. It made an anguished, tortured sound. Phaid took a last look at Ben-e and then closed the door behind him.

Phaid started walking. On the way to Acme Androids he had been so preoccupied with Ben-e and his business that he hadn't noticed quite what a rancid neighborhood they'd come to. Now that he was on his own, it came forcefully home to him. He looked around for an autocab but there was no traffic at all on the rapidly darkening streets of warehouses and boarded-up buildings.

The area wasn't quite into the shacks and shanties that made up the worst of the northside. It was the shadowy, twilight area that lay between the poor quarters, the ones that still had a minimum of police and power, and the total squalor of the migrant jungles.

An area like this was riddled with pitfalls for the unwary stranger. Although Phaid was far from being unwary, he was certainly a stranger. His good clothes marked him like a flashing sign. He knew that if anyone was watching, and in these kind of places someone was always watching, he must be dangerously conspicuous among the bums, the winos, the drug addicts whose brains had gone soft, the hookers on their way down, the petty criminals and the just plain mad who found refuge in the twilight zone.

Phaid felt his back stiffening. He let his right hand drop to his side where the fuse tube was concealed under his coat. He touched the butt for reassurance. It helped a little; not much, but a little. Phaid kept on walking. He had a constant urge to look behind him, but he resisted it. The surest way to get attacked and robbed was to make it clear that you were frightened.

Phaid turned a corner, still going in what he thought was the direction of the walkway jump-on. Night was falling fast, and the few active glo-bars in the street he'd walked down had been less than adequate. The street that lay in front of him had no illumination at all. Every single glo-bar had either been shattered or had burnt out. Phaid walked slowly and carefully down the garbage strewn sidewalk. Something skittered from under his feet and darted away into a derelict basement. Phaid started, nerves jangling and adrenaline pumping, but it was only either a large rat or a small cat.

Fervently hoping that he was going in the right direction, Phaid went on down the street. When they'd been walking to Acme Androids, he hadn't bothered to take much notice of the route. He was starting to become aware just how dependent he had become on Ben-e during the short time they'd been together.

He was also aware of something else. There was an occasional rustling sound from behind him. It could have been another animal rooting through the plentiful garbage, or it could have been someone following him on silent feet. The urge to stop and turn grew stronger and stronger. Phaid continued to resist it but with increasing difficulty.

The rustling came again. This time it was too much for Phaid's already strained nerves. He spun around, hand going toward his fuse tube. To his embarrassment, he found the street completely empty. He slowly put the weapon away and was about the resume his journey when he heard a low sinister voice.

"Hold it just like you are, friend. Don't make a move for that tube. There are two big cannons pointed right at you. Now we don't want to burn you away, but if we gotta, we gonna."

Phaid froze. The voice seemed to come from inside the dark, broken doorway of an abandoned building. There was a movement and two figures emerged. Wind masks covered their

161

faces. In fact, only one had a blaster, but Phaid didn't feel cheated that the second weapon had turned out to be pure imagination. A single blaster was quite sufficient to stop all arguments he might have had.

One of the thieves quickly went behind Phaid and snatched his fuse tube from out of its holster. The pair relaxed noticeably once Phaid was disarmed.

"We'd like for you to make a donation to our cause. From the cut of that fancy coat, I'd say you could give generously."

"What cause might that be?"

"It's 'cause we gonna blow you away if you don't."

They went into convulsions over the pun. Phaid wasn't carrying too much money. He'd hidden most of his remaining cash back in his hotel room. What worried him was that the two hold-up men might just take it into their heads to kill him anyway out of plain meanness. Phaid knew his only hope was to be as cooperative as possible.

"I'll have to put my hand in my pocket to get out all the cash I've got on me."

"We'll put our hands in for you. Save you the trouble."

"Suit yourselves."

"We intend to. In fact, you can take off the coat altogether. I kind of like it."

Phaid sighed and started to take off his jacket. He made each movement slow and studied so the thief with the blaster wouldn't be panicked into thinking that he was going for a second, concealed weapon. To Phaid's surprise, the one nearest him, the one now holding his fuse tube, suddenly stopped him.

"Hold on a minute, ain't you the gambling man?"

This new tack totally confused Phaid.

"What?"

"You the gambling man, ain't you?"

Phaid was immediately on his guard.

"Yes, but..."

"Phaid, right?"

"That's right."

"I knew it, Phaid the gambler."

He turned to his companion who was standing a few paces off, covering Phaid with his blaster.

"Hey, Digits, I want you to meet my old buddy, Phaid the gambler."

Digits wasn't at all pleased.

"What the fuck you want to use my name for? You want him to know who I am? Now we gonna have to grease the pussy for our own protection."

The nearer of the pair was immediately placating.

"Cool down, will you? This guy's okay. He's an old friend of mine."

Phaid was relieved to hear that he was okay. Digits, on the other hand, seemed less convinced. The blaster didn't waver.

"You figure we can trust him?"

"Sure we can trust him. He ain't no regular citizen, he's a gambling man. He's almost one of us, except..." The thief turned reproachfully to Phaid, "...how come you didn't recognize your old buddy, mister gambling man?"

"The wind mask makes it a little difficult."

"Shit, I forgot about the damn thing. It's supposed to stop me being recognized."

He started tugging off the mask. Digits was horrified.

"What the fuck do you think you're doing? You gone fucking crazy?"

The first thief's reply was muffled as he dragged the mask over his head. Finally, he tugged it completely off. Phaid found himself staring into a grinning, olive skinned face.

"Now you know me, mister gambling man?"

"Streetlife!"

"Right, Streetlife. Feared by the bad, loved by the good."

"What the hell are you doing trying to pull stick-ups?"

Streetlife spread his hands. They were very expressive hands with long, bony fingers.

"You know how things are. Times get hard and you got to do all manner of weird stuff to make change."

"So times have got hard, huh?"

"Strictly a temporary situation, strictly temporary."

Digits had still not lowered his blaster nor attempted to take off his mask. He was also looking more than a little impatient.

"I don't wanna break up this touching reunion, but I gotta point out that this stick-up is only partway completed, and I, for one, am starting to feel a trifle ridiculous standing here."

Streetlife was adamant.

"This stick-up is over."

"Says who?"

"Says me."

"You think I might have been consulted on this matter?"

Streetlife clapped Digits on the arm.

"Will you get off this? This here's a friend of mine. We can't go sticking him up, you hear me?"

"He ain't no friend of mine."

"This ain't the time for no stick-ups or thievery. This calls for celebration."

Digits continued to scowl.

"We broke and you damn well know it. We ain't got the wherewithal to do no celebrating. If we don't rob this fool we going to have to find us another one, otherwise we don't get to eat, let alone celebrate."

Phaid quickly stepped in, glad that he could contribute something to the conversation.

"I got money, if that's the problem."

Streetlife beamed.

"Well, my friend, if you going to do the buying then I know a cozy little joint not too far from here." He turned to Digits. "You hear that? The man here's buying the booze."

Digits didn't say anything. He eyed Phaid speculatively. Finally he lowered the blaster and started pulling off his mask.

"You can buy me a drink."

Digits' acquiescence did nothing to make Phaid feel any more comfortable. Streetlife, on the other hand, seemed anxious to be away and start drinking up Phaid's money.

"Let's go, shall we? Ain't no future standing around this cruddy street."

Phaid didn't move.

"Now that you're not sticking me up, you think I could have my tube back?"

Streetlife hefted the weapon.

"Sweet little f-tube. You wanna sell it?"

Phaid shook his head.

"I think I'd be happier if I had it by my side."

Streetlife nodded.

"You probably very wise."

With a certain reluctance, he handed the weapon back to Phaid. Digits snorted with disgust.

"Now you giving his fucking gun back."

Streetlife finally started to get annoyed.

"So?"

"So I think you gone insane. We come out here to get us some change and you wind up giving the mark his gun back. Where the fuck is that at?"

"I keep telling you. He's a friend."

"Hmm."

"You trying to make something out of this?"

Digits slowly shook his head.

"I'll let it go for now."

"You do that."

Phaid, who was returning his fuse tube to its holster, raised an eyebrow in the direction of Digits. He didn't say anything but he knew that here was an individual in whom he could place no trust whatsoever, an individual on whom it wouldn't be wise to turn his back.

Streetlife was anxious to move on to the drinking joint, so both Phaid and Digits fell in behind him, Phaid giving Digits a wide berth.

Streetlife had been aptly named. He slipped through the shadows with the confident, sure-footed determination of a cat, totally at home in its own alley. Skinny to the point that he seemed to be all arms, legs and grin, Streetlife appeared to be completely at home in his environment. On his own admission, he had recently hit a run of bad luck. It didn't, however, seem to faze him. For Streetlife, the world was a perpetual con game with him running the changes and everyone else potential suckers.

They'd gone about two blocks, with Streetlife keeping up a constant line of patter that, amongst other things, stopped Phaid from asking too many questions about how Streetlife had managed to slip from being a fairly successful city center hustler to having to pull hold-ups in the twilight zone with a character like Digits. Then, at the end of the third block, Streetlife suddenly halted and listened intently.

"What's wrong?"

Streetlife motioned urgently.

"Hush up, I'm listening. You can't be too careful in these neighborhoods."

Phaid held his breath. After a few moments he could hear something too. It was a combination of a murmur, a drone and a strange rhythmic snapping.

"What the hell is that?"

"Kid gang, by the sound of it, and coming this way. We better get off the street and quick."

Phaid frowned.

"We're going to run from a gang of kids?"

"Damn right we are."

"But we've got weapons."

"So have they, and they don't care if they lose a few of their number getting us."

"They're that bad?"

"Worse."

Phaid shook his head.

"Weird."

"Weird or not, we didn't ought to be standing round here arguing."

Streetlife pointed to a narrow passage that ran between two dark buildings.

"We can hide in there. I doubt if they'll notice us."

He scampered off in the direction of the alley. Digits and Phaid followed, each constantly glancing back over his shoulder. The noise of the kid gang was getting louder. It seemed almost certain that they were going to come down this particular street.

Crouching in the darkness, Phaid noticed that Streetlife was actually sweating.

"You scared?"

"Fucking right I'm scared."

"Of a bunch of kids?"

"You don't know what they can do, else you'd be scared too. Just wait and watch and don't make a sound."

Phaid didn't have to wait long. The eerie noise grew louder and louder. Phaid could feel his own palms start to sweat. Just by itself there was something unpleasantly menacing about the clicking and murmuring. Then he saw them, teenage boys in orange and blood-red, bare midriffs and long skirts, and heavy black eye makeup. Some carried burning torches that illuminated the procession with a hellish, unearthly light. They all snapped their fingers in what approached a drilled hysteria. Streetlife whistled under his breath.

"Goddamn Scorpions. They the worst of the lot. They just mindless and savage. I once saw a kid after they'd finished him. That young boy had been raped, tortured and damn near torn to pieces. It was an ugly sight, I can tell you."

Phaid shuddered.

"Why do they do this stuff?"

"Because the whole world's going to hell in a basket, and they're a part of it. If you unfortunate to get born in a place like this, at a time like this, you don't know nothing else but evil. There ain't no way to go but to the gangs."

The Scorpions passed. They'd failed to notice the three figures crouching in the alley. The sound of them started to fade into the background rumble of the city. Phaid slowly got to his feet. Dirt from the alley had messed up his breeches. He did his best to wipe it off with his hands.

"Are there many gangs?"

"Quite a few. The Scorpions are the meanest, except for maybe the Hogids."

"The Hogids?"

"Oh, they real cute. They all wear these rubber pig head masks and carry long butchering knives. There are girls in the Hogids. They more vicious than the boys. In fact they so vicious that they make ordinary vicious look like tender loving care."

"I don't think I'd like to meet them."

"I don't even want to talk about them. In fact, I don't even want to be out on the street. Let's go inside, with a drink in front of us, huh? I've had enough for tonight."

The drinking joint was little more than a converted cellar. The walls were damp to the touch. The bar was an arrangement of old packing cases, the furniture had obviously been scavenged from dumps and abandoned houses. The booze was almost unique in its distinctive, poisonous taste. Despite all this though, Phaid was glad to be off the streets, and beyond the reach of thieves and homicidal children.

The joint's clientele was a representative cross section of

the twilight zone. The cardinal rule seemed to be that one minded one's own business. This was strictly enforced by a massive balding man called Zeke, who had the most elaborately tattooed arms that Phaid had ever seen.

With the first drink warming his insides, Phaid started quizzing Streetlife about what had been going on in Chrystianaville during his long absence. Most of what Streetlife had to say wasn't exactly encouraging.

"I got to tell you, Phaid my friend, it's been bad. That's the only way to describe it. Everybody on every level's hustling and jockeying and stabbing each other in the back. It's got so you don't know which way to turn or who to trust."

Phaid sipped his drink and grinned. The day had been so bizarre that he felt as though he was past caring.

"So what else is new?"

"Hell, I know it was bad the last time you were here, but now, shit, it just completely out of hand. When you were last here, there were assholes running things. Now nobody is running things. The whole place is clear out of control."

"You got to be exaggerating."

"I swear to the Lords."

"So what about our great Life President? She used to have a grip on things."

"If she did, she must have lost it someplace along the line. Nobody even seen her, except on hologram, for an age now. The rumor is that she's locked herself away in one wing of the palace and she too paranoid to come out. The only person she listens to is that fucking elaihi."

"The one called Solchaim?"

"You heard about him already?"

"Not much, but I heard of him."

"Well, that's one bastard you don't gotta trust at all. A lot of people say he's at the base of the trouble. He got a finger in every conspiracy, and there's a million conspiracies in this city, let me tell you. He plays off the President against the priests and the priests against the mobs, and the mobs against the rebels and from the rebels it goes back to the President. In the meantime, the officials tie everything in knots. That elaihi bastard got everybody jumping. It could be that he's the only one who got any control over the Republic at all, and he ain't doing nothing to make things better. Matter-of-fact, he's screwing us all into the ground."

Phaid was thoughtful.

"It's always disconcerting to find that you're no longer top of the heap."

Streetlife looked up sharply.

"What you say?"

Phaid shook his head.

"It wasn't anything. Just something somebody said to me once."

Streetlife cocked his head to one side.

"You know something, Phaid? You look different, my friend."

"How different?"

"Older maybe. Less crazy."

"I've been away awhile."

"Maybe that's it."

"You seem to have had your troubles."

Streetlife made a dismissive gesture.

"It's all temporary. There are just some places I shouldn't go back to for a while, that's all."

"Seems like there's a hell of a lot of places you can't go back to if you got to hang out in a dump like this."

Streetlife laughed.

"Well, that is true, but I'm expecting things to change very soon."

"Aren't we all."

"You gotta be positive in this life."

Phaid looked at him intently.

"Are there any places I maybe didn't ought to go back to?"

"You?"

"I did leave here under something of a cloud."

"Hell, your troubles have been all over for a long time. Llap's dead, Morcis left town and Garette-Roth hasn't been seen in over a year. You got nothing to worry about."

"That's good to hear."

"Wish I could come back too."

"I wish you could. If there's anything that I can do . . ."

Streetlife waved away the offer of help.

"Thanks all the same, but there ain't nothing anyone can do. I just have to wait this thing out."

Phaid had a thought.

"Do you know anything about a guy called Orsine?"

Streetlife shrugged.

"Sure, he's big in the Cousins. Everybody knows that much. I ain't never met him or done business with him. He way up in the big league. From what I hear, though, he's a man with troubles."

"What kind of troubles?"

"His number two is a character called Scarlin-Fell. He one ambitious son of a bitch. He ain't going to be happy until he number one."

"So why doesn't Orsine off him?"

"He does a good job, and a lot of the rank and file are behind him. If Orsine put a crease in him without a lot of very obvious reasons, it could split the Cousins right down the middle. Orsine had also got bit by the society bug. He spends a hell of a lot of his time moving in court circles, although what he wants to hang out with that gang of fancy dressed vipers for beats me."

"The court don't change."

"Sure it changes. It gets worse. Anyway . . ." Streetlife went back to the original story ". . . the guys on the streets, the ones who actually do the day to day running of the rackets, don't rate his high society bit. There's rumbles going round that they don't feel that he's taking care of business the way he ought to be. 'Course, there are always rumbles and tradition's so strong among the Cousins that it'd take more than just a few rumbles to topple an Adjudicator, but . . ."

"But he's a man with troubles."

"You got it. What you want to know about him for, anyway?"

"He invited me to eat with him."

Streetlife let out a low whistle of surprise and admiration.

"You riding in some heavy traffic, gambling man."

Phaid thought about it.

"Maybe I am, at that."

Streetlife looked concerned.

"You wanna be real careful. Them Cousins' loyalties are strictly to each other, first and last. If you ain't one of them you can never really know what they're going to do next. You can think you're real tight and friendly with them, and then, without even knowing it, you get between them and something they want and..." Streetlife theatrically snapped his fingers "... goodbye."

Phaid grunted.

"I've had dealings with them before. I'll be careful."

The bar was starting to fill up and, as a consequence, become noiser and sweatier. Phaid was tired. It had been a long hard day, and Mariba had prevented him from getting much sleep the night before. Phaid knew it was time to start back for his hotel. He downed the rest of his drink.

"Can I get an autocab out of here?"

Streetlife laughed and shook his head.

"No chance, my friend. An autocab would be crazy to come anywhere near here. If it didn't get robbed, the kids would, like as not, set fire to it."

Phaid grimaced.

"Shit. I don't much relish the idea of the walkways after dark."

"Maybe I can fix something for you."

"Yeah?"

Streetlife turned and gestured to a kid who was lounging against the wall.

"Hey, Zero, run over to Aunt Bill's and find Bron. Tell him to fetch that elderly heap of his. I got a guy here that needs a run to the center."

"What's in it for me?"

Streetlife grinned.

"I break your bones if you don't."

"What if Bron don't want to come?"

"He'll come."

Bron's flipper was about the most dilapidated vehicle still capable of moving that Phaid had ever seen. Half of the body paneling was missing. What was left was scratched, dented and losing its paint. The force field that kept it off the ground was partially malfunctioning and the flipper sagged dangerously to one side. Bron noticed Phaid inspecting the beat-up machine. He scratched his gut and belched.

"It may not look like much, but it runs."

The first thing he did when he got to his room was, from

force of habit, to check that his money and possessions were still as he had left them. Once he was satisfied that nothing had been tampered with, he kicked off his boots and lay down on the bed. He sighed, closed his eyes and discovered perversely that he suddenly wasn't tired. It was his first night in the city and it seemed ridiculous to spend it getting an early night in his hotel room.

There was a small compact entertainment unit in the corner of the room. Phaid padded over to it and gave it a cursory inspection. The first thing that he discovered was that it required a tab to start it working. Chrystianaville was not the kind of place where you got anything for nothing. Phaid fed a tab into the slot and punched up the drama selection.

He'd been out of the city for so long that none of the titles listed were familiar to him. He picked one at random. All that appeared on the screen was a multicolored snowstorm. Either the unit was malfunctioning, or atmospheric interference was particularly bad that day.

This was one of the many unfortunate side effects of the world's violent weather system. For centuries, interference from atmospherics had made any kind of long range electronic communication virtually impossible. The only methods that could be relied upon were either land lines or line of sight transmissions over short distance. This inability to send messages instantly from city to city had contributed a great deal to the fragmentation and isolation that was the curse that extended all over the world.

Right at the moment, though, Phaid didn't give a damn about the world's problems. He wasn't ready to sleep and he was bored. He wondered if the hotel ran a bar. He doubted it. Most android operated places had a certain Spartan style about them that seemed to preclude things like bars and restaurants.

Phaid debated whether he should simply hit the street and trust to luck. It wasn't an idea that exactly filled him with enthusiasm. After one random experience on the streets of the city, he didn't feel ready to plunge straight into another. On the other hand, a drink, some female companionship, a game of chance or any combination of the three had a very strong appeal.

Apart from the entertainment unit, the only thing in the

room that Phaid could play with was a small, sound only, comset. Phaid picked it up and an android voice came on the line.

"May-I-help-you?"

"I'd like to make an outside call."

"Within-the-city-limits?"

"Yes."

"Just - give - me - the - name - of - the - party - to - whom - you - wish - to - speak - and - I - will - endeavor - to - connect - you."

"The name is Edelline-Lan."

"One-moment."

Phaid's earpiece was filled with the multiple tone bleating of android noise. Finally a second android voice answered.

"This - is - the - residence - of - Edelline - Lan. Who - is - this - calling?"

"My name is Phaid."

"Would-you-please-turn-on-your-vision-facility."

Phaid raised an eyebrow.

"I don't have a vision facility on this set."

"I-see."

Although Phaid knew it must be his imagination, he couldn't help feeling that the android was putting him down.

"Would-you-please-wait?"

"Sure."

While Phaid hung on, he made a mental observation that Edelline-Lan must be pretty well heeled if she could afford to keep an android to monkey block her comcalls. Finally a human voice came out of Phaid's set.

"So, Phaid. You just couldn't wait to talk to me?"

"Something like that."

"Well, don't be so damn noncommittal."

"I'm sorry. I just couldn't wait any longer to talk to you. How's that?"

"Better. What have you been doing all day?"

Phaid decided not to tell her the story of Ben-e and his trip to the northside. People who owned androids weren't likely to be overly sympathetic towards other people who helped them defect into the Life Game.

"I had some chores that needed taking care of."

"You've taken care of them?"

173

"All squared away."

"And now you want to play?"

"The thought had crossed my mind."

"You want to go out?"

"Fine. I'm up for anything."

"Good. I'd had half a mind to go to this new place that's opened up near the Palace. It's called the Punishment of Luxury."

"Sounds okay by me."

"Why don't you come by and pick me up here."

"Where's here?"

She gave him detailed directions for getting to her apartment.

"Oh, by the way, are you anything of a voyeur?"

"I'd usually rather be an active participant."

"Yes, I've heard all about that. I ran into Mariba on the way back from the terminal. From her description, it sounded as though the two of you had quite a busy night. I gather she performed her usual trick of getting you to tie her up."

"Doesn't anyone keep secrets anymore?"

"Not in this town."

Phaid made a second mental note not to do or say anything that he didn't want to be common gossip inside a matter of hours.

"Why did you ask me if I was a voyeur?"

Edelline-Lan laughed.

"You'll find out."

11

The girl on the stage was resplendent in a baroque creation of black leather. It nipped in her waist, pushed up her breasts. It was cut away high on the hips in order to make her legs seem fantastically long. This effect was also supplemented by the ridiculously high, sharply spiked heels of matching leather, thigh-length boots. The costume was completed by a pair of black evening gloves that completely covered her arms to well past the elbows. There was a tattoo of a small bird on her left shoulder.

She posed arrogantly in the center stage spotlight. Her hair was piled on top of her head in a confection of spun gold, and her skin had been oiled until it shone under the lights. In her right hand she held a long, plaited whip. She flicked it now and then, almost languorously, as though tantalizing the audience, milking their anticipation of the spectacle of violence that would follow.

The other character in the drama was a total contrast. The

man was naked, his body bound tightly to a towering tripod device, his feet pinned at two points on the base and his arms stretched up above his head where his manacled wrists were secured almost at the apex. In the stark stage lighting his flesh seemed brilliantly white and very, very vulnerable. He was positioned facing away from the girl, his shoulders, back and buttocks exactly right to suffer the full assault of the lash.

Like the girl, he had golden hair, but that was where the resemblance ended. Where she radiated a feeling of sleek, muscular cruelty, he was slim, almost to the point of being willowy. In his state of helpless exposure, he seemed close to fragile.

The girl flicked the whip with a little more force. It was an authoritative gesture, like the conductor of an old-fashioned orchestra rapping with his baton for silence amongst the musicians. Conversation in the dark side of the nightclub's footlights dwindled down to silence. Attention was totally focused on the brilliantly lit stage.

The crowd seemed to hold its breath as the girl slowly swung her arm back. Then it flashed forward. Drinks were set aside and expressions became rapt in concentration. The whip cracked. The man gasped loudly and a kind of sigh rippled through the audience. An angry red welt now ran down half the length of the man's back. Edelline-Lan leaned close to Phaid and breathed in his ear.

"I've heard that they're drugged, so it doesn't actually hurt as much as it appears."

"That's a great consolation."

The girl continued to flog the man on the tripod with slow, measured strokes. Where at first he'd only gasped, now he screamed shrilly, writhing and struggling, desperately trying to save his pale body from the agony of the whip. Phaid slowly shook his head as though he didn't quite believe what he was watching.

"How do they get people to do this sort of thing?"

Edelline-Lan grinned wickedly.

"I shouldn't think that the girl was too hard to find. I wouldn't mind having a go at that myself. I think the costume's kind of cute."

"Yeah, but what about the man, the poor bastard who's

getting his back laid open. How the hell did they recruit him?"

"I've heard that a lot of them come from the northside. Those people will do just about anything to get out of the shanty towns."

Phaid didn't like the sound of the way she talked about "those people" as if the poor were some different, distant species. He didn't, however, say anything. Edelline-Lan seemed fascinated by the squirming, bound figure.

"It could be that he's having the time of his life. I always work on the principle that if you can imagine it, somebody, somewhere is probably doing it and enjoying it."

The girl on the stage had now dropped her whip and was standing facing the crowd in a spread-legged stance. Earlier, Phaid had noticed a studded strip of leather attached to the crotch of her outfit. Phaid had assumed that it was simply a vaguely phallic piece of decoration. To his surprise, he found that the thing was actually stiffening into an overt penis parody.

As the thing increasingly stood out, erect from the girl's body, the club audience whistled and cheered as though helping it in the stiffening process. Once the fake penis was fully erect, the girl, hands on hips, sauntered towards the still quivering man. She paused to run her hands over his scarred and bloody back, and then thrust the dildo viciously between his buttocks. This was more than Phaid could take. He reached quickly for his drink.

"This place is fucking gross."

The man was screaming again as the girl pumped the studded monster in and out of him. Edelline-Lan looked disdainfully at Phaid.

"I think you're supposed to murmur, 'divinely decadent,' darling."

"This isn't decadent, it's just plain revolting."

"Don't be so provincial."

The man gave a final, drawn out scream. The girl ripped out the dildo and turned to face the audience with a triumphant grin. As the curtain dropped, they broke into rapturous applause. A rodentlike compere in a silver suit scuttled on to the stage, bowing and leering.

"Thank you, thank you, thank you. That was Stav and Wanda with their presentation, 'Symphony of Pain.' I guess we'll be seeing them again real soon, once Stav's back has healed. And, moving right along, as the android said to the acolyte, we come to the Unbelievable Tonee."

The Unbelievable Tonee's act consisted of him pushing long steel rods through the flesh of a pair of nubile but zombielike assistants. This was really too much for Phaid. After downing three drinks in quick succession, he finally stood up.

"I've got to take a rest from this."

Edelline-Lan nodded.

"You're right. This guy's a bore. I don't go for these mutilation acts. There was this fat woman last week who had her left arm amputated. It was one big yawn. Why don't we go out on the terrace and get some air?"

It was the best thing that Phaid had heard since he'd come into the place. He was already out of his seat and heading for the exit that led out to the terrace.

In the back of the club, Phaid spotted a particularly sinister group around a single table. They were all men and they all wore black, cowled robes. Phaid glanced questioningly at Edelline-Lan.

"They look like priests."

"They are."

"What the hell are they doing in a place like this?"

"Watching the show, just like everyone else."

Phaid looked bemused.

"But . . . priests?"

"They seem to enjoy this sort of thing. I suppose they can get their kicks without jeopardizing their vows of celibacy. Not that I've met too many priests who worried overmuch about their vows."

Phaid sniffed.

"I guess we live and learn."

"I think, given the choice, I'd rather live than learn. Learning is generally such a tiresome business."

They stepped out on to the terrace and Phaid took a series of deep breaths of the chill night air. He suddenly needed to get all the sleaze of the Punishment of Luxury out of his lungs.

Although the show was still going on inside, the terrace was fairly crowded. Flamboyantly dressed men and women strolled arm in arm, stood and gossiped or even embraced quite passionately in the shadowy corners. A few had android attendants trailing behind them. All exhibited that special grace that is unique to the naturally wealthy, the grace that can only be achieved by those who don't have to worry about the petty details of day to day survival.

Beyond them, the nighttime city spread out in all its tinsel glory. A million lights sparkled like jewels against the velvet blackness. From the vantage point of the terrace, the congested streets were transformed into glittering, luminescent serpents. The daytime gray buildings were now bright fingers pointing to the sky. Towering over everything was the floodlit sphere and grimacing giants of the line terminal. The terminal lights created a second halo on the clouds above. A train was coming in from the mountains in its own blaze of glory.

Phaid stared, fascinated. By night the city was breathtakingly beautiful. The darkness successfully concealed the corruption, the crime and the misery that lurked behind the sparkling lights. Looking out from the terrace, it was almost impossible to imagine that, just a few hours earlier, he had been in the twilight zone hunting ground of Streetlife, Digits and the Scorpions.

The city had successfully covered its diseased and pockmarked face behind a veil of man-made stars.

Phaid's reflections were cut short, however, by a dig in the ribs from Edelline-Lan. She nodded towards a young man who had detached himself from a laughing, chattering group and was coming in their direction.

"Watch this one. There's more to him than meets the eye."

Phaid gave the man a quick, covert scrutiny. Even amidst so much sparkle, he was positively dazzling. His coat was white silk with gold embroidery, his breeches a pale turquoise, tucked into knee boots of the softest white leather. His hairdresser must have spent many hours bleaching his hair down to the platinum white that it now was, and plaiting in the dozens of tiny pearls that caught the light as he moved. The young man had spared no effort to make himself exquisite.

His skin had an epicene pallor. It was evident that he never saw the sun. His lips were full, and painted a bright crimson, so they looked as though they would be better suited to a young girl. The only contrast in the bland, effeminate face were the eyes. They were shrewd and calculating, the kind of eyes which, if Phaid were confronted with them across a gambling table, would cause him to pay a great deal of attention to their owner's play.

The young man grasped both Edelline-Lan's hands and kissed her on the cheek.

"Darling, I thought you were still out of town for the provincial season."

"I got bored and came home. I seem unable to stay away from the city for very long."

The young man fluttered a heavily ringed hand.

"Very sensible, my dear. There's really little of any worth in the provinces."

He turned his attention to Phaid. "And is he a souvenir from your travels?"

Edelline-Lan stepped in quickly as she saw Phaid's face darken.

"This is Phaid. I met him on the train from Fennella. He's a professional gambler."

"How very exotic."

This didn't please Phaid either, but before he could react, the young man grasped him swiftly by the hand.

"I am Roni-Vows. I'm a professional butterfly, and terribly pleased to meet you. My Lords, what calluses."

Phaid had just been noticing that Roni-Vows' grip was cold, moist and limp. It was a little discomforting to find that Roni-Vows had been examining his hand in the same way. Phaid increased the pressure of his own grip and grinned into Roni-Vows' face.

"I took what you might call a rough way home."

Phaid couldn't help remembering Makartur's phrase, "primping nelly." The young man pulled his hand away.

"So it would seem. Do you intend to stay in the city for long, Phaid?"

"I don't plan to leave in the foreseeable future."

Roni-Vows regarded him archly.

"Then if you desire to move in these circles, I would suggest that your manners could do with a little alteration."

Phaid's fists clenched.

"You're going to give me a lesson in manners?"

Roni-Vows' butterfly facade dropped away. He suddenly seemed capable and dangerous. His eyes narrowed.

"You consider yourself a duelist?"

Edelline-Lan grew angry.

"Will you two stop this immediately! Next you'll both be boasting about how many men you've burned on the field of honor and sending out your seconds."

Roni-Vows glared at Phaid.

"You think this . . . gambler could afford a second?"

Edelline-Lan ran out of patience.

"Cut this out. I won't stand for it. You're both my friends. You're both splendid fellows in your own ways and I really object to you stalking around each other like aggressive tomcats. You'll either stop or I'm leaving."

She looked first at Roni-Vows. His butterfly pose quickly returned.

"I'm sorry, darling, please don't go. How could I survive without you?"

She turned to Phaid.

"And how about you?"

Phaid hesitated, then took a deep breath.

"Yeah, yeah, I'm sorry."

Edelline-Lan smiled and dipped a mocking curtsy. Without pause, she went right back to feather light chatter as though nothing had happened.

"Does the court continue to decay and decline Roni-Vows? I want to hear all the dirt I missed while I was away."

Roni-Vows made a contemptuous gesture.

"It gets more dreadful by the day. There are people who are even neglecting their appearance, they're so busy plotting. The Grand Bitch hardly ever graces us with her presence."

"The Grand Bitch?"

"Our glorious Life President. I suppose I shouldn't talk like that. The Secret Police will probably appear out of nowhere and haul me away."

Edelline laughed.

"Not you. You could charm your way out of anything."

Roni-Vows looked serious.

"It's happened to too many already; too many for comfort. I'm afraid it may be past the time for charm."

Mick Farren

Edelline-Lan was scandalized.

"I never thought I'd hear you speak like that."

"I fear the world is about to turn both dreary and dangerous. I'm not sure which is worse."

"But arrests at court? It seems scarcely possible. What's been happening in this city?"

"The Grand Bitch has lost her mind and that appalling elaihi has quietly taken control of both her and the Republic. She spends most of her time closeted with that bloodless monster. On the few occasions that she does condescend to emerge, she's usually in such a psychotic snit that nothing will calm her except the sight of rolling heads."

"But that's horrible. Can't something be done about the creature?"

"There have been attempts, but we have to accept the very unpleasant fact that he is cleverer than we. The court isn't a happy place at the moment."

Phaid, who'd been thoughtfully silent, shot Roni-Vows an inquiring look.

"Is this the elaihi Solchaim you're talking about?"

"Who else, dear?"

"That's interesting."

"Interesting?"

Roni-Vows set aside some of his effeminacy.

"You've had some experience with elaihim?"

"I ran into some on the way here."

"The rough way home?"

"Exactly."

"So what did you make of our superior cousins?"

Phaid sensed that it wasn't just a casual question. Although Roni-Vows was doing his best to disguise it, he was clearly curious. This was exactly the response for which Phaid had been hoping. It proved that his firsthand experience of the elaihim might indeed be of cash value in Chrystianaville.

"I had the distinct feeling that they could get inside my mind."

Roni-Vows nodded slowly.

"I suppose it's now my turn to look interested. Are you absolutely sure about this?"

182

"Not absolutely, but I don't have any other explanation for what was happening to me."

"Hmmm..."

Roni-Vows seemed to be about to say something, but instead was interrupted by an android that rolled up beside him. Its paint job was white and gold, and since it matched Roni-Vows' jacket, Phaid assumed that it was his property.

"If - you - do - not - leave - now - for - the - Sar - Don - reception - you - will - be - more - than - fashionably - late."

The android's voice had been set to a suitably limp-wristed tone. Roni-Vows was immediately galvanized into action. He quickly grasped the hands of both Edelline-Lan and Phaid.

"I simply must run, I simply must run." He looked quickly at Phaid. "I'd like to talk some more about the elaihim with you." He beamed. "I know. Come and watch the wind games with me tomorrow. I'm having a little party on the roof of my building, you must be there."

Phaid didn't immediately accept so, once again, Edelline-Lan took the initiative.

"We'd love to, wouldn't we?"

Phaid nodded.

"We'd love to."

Roni-Vows ignored the implied sarcasm.

"Until then."

He swept towards the exit, throwing goodbyes and blowing kisses to left and right. The android followed at a discreet distance. Phaid whistled under his breath.

"What the hell was that?"

"I told you not to underestimate him. Under the popinjay exterior, Roni-Vows is one of our shrewdest courtiers. What was all that about elaihim?"

Phaid rubbed his chin.

"I'm not sure. Maybe we'll find out tomorrow."

Edelline-Lan glanced at him sideways.

"Deviousness must be catching."

Phaid smiled a guileless smile.

"I'm not devious. I'm just a simple gambler."

Edelline-Lan eyed him thoughtfully.

"I think you're going to fit into this town very well indeed."

"I intend to do my best."

"Could you do your best to think about where we should go next? It's starting to get chilly on this terrace."

"What options do we have?"

"We could go back inside and watch some more of the show."

Phaid shook his head.

"I think I've seen enough torture for one night."

"What you might call a low pain threshold?"

"Something like that."

"It's the wind games tomorrow so the streets ought to be roaring. We could go down and mingle with the herd."

This idea didn't appeal to Phaid either. He was altogether too freshly back from the slums to want to go slumming.

"We could go to the Wospan district and get drunk."

Phaid still didn't look particularly enthusiastic. Edelline-Lan grinned slyly.

"Or we could go back to my home and bed."

"Bed?"

"Bed. I think I'm ready to let you play, Master Phaid."

Phaid smiled and took hold of her hand. They had to pass back through the club in order to find the way out. On the stage, a dark-skinned woman in a collar and little else was being strapped into a machine that would most probably inflict a variety of suffering on her. Edelline-Lan squeezed Phaid's hand.

"Are you sure you don't want to watch this?"

The machine was turned on and the young woman shrieked loudly.

"I'd rather go home with you."

"I thought it might get you hot."

"I don't think I need any warming."

Edelline-Lan leaned close to him. Her tongue darted swiftly and moistly into his ear. they almost ran down the series of escalators that led to the parking lot. Hud-n, Edelline-Lan's android, waited with her custom flipper. Phaid smiled as he sprawled back onto the rich upholstery.

"You never did tell me what your specialty is."

She moved over and pressed herself against him.

"You don't have much longer to wait."

A lot later, as they lay in the soft red warmth of Edelline-Lan's enormous bed, drowsily watching themselves in the mirrors on the ceiling, Edelline-Lan propped herself up on one elbow and peered into Phaid's face.

"You're very good, you know."

"Thanks for the compliment."

"It's not a compliment. I mean it."

"Thanks all the same."

"Why are you a gambler?"

"It's a living."

"Don't fob me off, I'm serious. What makes a man live the life of a gambler?"

"I don't know. I haven't given it a great deal of thought. A lot of the time I've been too busy just surviving to consider what was motivating me. Self-analysis is a rich folk's habit."

"You're bluffing. I don't believe this trash from the hills act. Sure you think. You're a hell of a lot deeper than you pretend."

"Maybe that's what it is about."

"What? I don't follow you."

"Bluffing. Maybe that's really what the gambler wants. He can always bluff. He never has to reveal what he really is, what he really wants or what he's really playing for. Gamblers, actors, some criminals, a lot of people looking for power, they're all running the same thing, pretending to be something that they aren't. On the other hand, though, there's a lot of reality in being a gambler. Everyone's life is pushed and turned around by luck. Sometimes you get lucky and sometimes you don't. All the gambler does is ride it instead of letting it ride him."

Edelline-Lan was quiet for a while then she suddenly exploded.

"You're impossible. You've told me nothing. That was just a bunch of romantic sounding nonsense."

Phaid lazily slid down in the bed. He closed his eyes.

"What else did you expect?"

He let sleep creep up on him. The next time he was conscious, sunlight was streaming through the windows. There had been so many strange beds in his life that Phaid no longer bothered about wondering where he was the moment he awoke.

He just let himself drift through the empty space between first groggy consciousness and the point where the memory gears meshed and everything finally flooded back.

There was a comfortable ache in nearly every muscle of his body. It was the kind of ache that went hand in hand with a healthy level of physical satiation. He stretched and regarded himself in the mirrored ceiling. The reflection that stared back at him didn't seem to be in all that bad shape. Certainly it looked to be at home lounging among silk draperies and satin pillows.

Finally, he made the effort and sat up. In keeping with the size of the bed, the bedroom too was vast. A sumptuous chaos of mirrors, dainty feminine furniture, discarded dresses, underwear spilling from drawers, formidable arrays of packaged, containered and bottled beauty and beauty removers. There were hats with feathers, shoes without companions and the debris from more than one night before.

There was only one puzzle. Edelline-Lan had vanished without trace. Phaid climbed off the bed and padded across the littered floor. It looked, from even the most superficial examination, that Edelline-Lan's clothes budget would keep a fair sized family in food for a year or more.

Phaid inspected himself from every angle in one of the many mirrors. There were long parallel scratches down his back from where her nails had raked it. Phaid chuckled to himself. A good night wasn't a good night unless you wound up with a few cuts and bruises. Edelline-Lan had certainly been a unique combination of enthusiasm, imagination and stamina.

He turned quickly as the door slipped open. Hud-n rolled in on discreet bearings. The android servant was carrying a tray that Phaid could only assume was breakfast.

"My-owner-has-requested-me-to-inform-you-that-she-is-attending-to-some-pressing-business-and-that-she-will-be-with-you-shortly."

"Does she always start the day this early?"

Hud-n didn't answer. Instead, he swept a pile of garments off a low glass table and set the tray down. Both android and mistress seemed to share the same lack of regard for tidiness and order.

"Do-you-need-anything-else?"

Phaid took a look at the tray. There was a bottle of sparkling wine, a jug of fruit juice, a mound of pâté and a basket of hot rolls. There were also two small turquoise capsules. Phaid held up one of them.

"What are these?"

"My - owner - thought - you - might - require - a - slight - boost - after - your - strenuous - night."

"That's nice."

"It - would - not - be - a - good - idea - to - consume - them - before - breakfast - since - they - tend - to - suppress - the - human - appetite."

"Thanks for the tip."

"You - are - welcome."

Hud-n made an exit that was just as silent as his entrance. Phaid realized that he was, in fact, very hungry. He moved in on the food with a will, munching his way steadily through everything on the tray. He was just washing down the capsules with the last of the wine when the door opened again.

This time it was Edelline-Lan. She was wearing a loose, off-white wrap and there was a drink in her hand. Without makeup, she looked a trifle worn. Her face was puffy, with dark circles around her eyes. There was, however, a certain heavy lidded smugness about her. She yawned and then grinned at Phaid.

"How are you this morning?"

He grinned back.

"I feel great."

"So you should. Did you remember that we promised to watch the wind games from Roni-Vows' roof?"

"I must confess that I'd forgotten."

"You ought to go. You could pick up some useful contacts, and anyway, I want you with me."

"I'd better go, then."

"You had other plans?"

"Nothing specific."

"Maybe you were planning to fuck and forget me?"

"Who, me?"

"I've met you trash from the hills before."

Phaid ignored the jibe.

"You seen my clothes?"

"Hud-n took them away to fix them up. They'd become a

little cruddy. Also, I told him to pick you up something new. You can't wear the same thing two days running. How do you feel about black?"

Phaid held up his hands.

"Hold it a minute."

He was starting to get the impression that the woman was taking him over.

"I don't have the kind of money to go splashing out on new clothes every day."

Edelline-Lan brushed his protests aside.

"Don't worry about it, I do. I'm filthy rich, or hadn't you noticed."

Phaid pondered for a moment on what it would be like to be a rich woman's lap dog. Then his pondering was cut short by the return of Hud-n with an armful of packages.

"Here-are-the-clothes-that-you-ordered."

Once again, the android made room for what he was carrying by simply sweeping more things on to the floor.

"Also-Abrella-Lu-and-Hydranga-Cort-are-here-to-see-you."

Edelline-Lan was rummaging in the mess. Finally, she found what she was looking for. She held up a more than half-full decanter with a triumphant flourish. She filled her glass.

"Well, go on then, show them in."

"As-you-wish."

Edelline-Lan noticed Phaid's expression.

"What's the matter with you? Both of these women have seen naked men before, plenty of naked men, so I don't see what you're looking like that for."

Phaid realized that he was being a little gauche by city standards, but still felt uncomfortable.

"It's a bad way to meet people for the first time. I never know what to do with my hands."

"You really do like to keep it all hidden, don't you? Okay, drape yourself in a sheet or something if it makes you any happier."

Phaid wound a sheet around himself toga fashion and assumed a strategic position on the bed. Within moments, two women erupted through the door, filling the room with loud, over affectionate, greetings.

Both had the stamp of the court about them. They had the

expensive clothes, the arrogant carriage and shrill, nasal chattering voices that were the hallmarks of Chrystianaville's upper crust.

Both also looked as though they hadn't slept or, if they had, it hadn't been in their own beds and they hadn't their own servants to prepare them for the new day. They were noticeably tousled and slightly soiled round the edges. Edelline-Lan handed around more of the turquoise capsules. The sense of being frayed faded, and shortly afterwards both the volume and intensity of the brittle chatter rose to a new peak.

Phaid was introduced to the pair. In fact, to be more accurate, he was exhibited to them. He had the distinct feeling that Edelline-Lan was, to some degree, showing off her new stud to her friends. This was confirmed by the appraising way in which they ran their eyes over his body. The experience left Phaid a good deal less than comfortable.

Once the introductions had been made, Phaid was virtually ignored. They kept up their nonstop gossip as Abrella-Lu and Hydranga-Cort plowed their way through Edelline-Lan's scattered but expensive wardrobe in search of something suitable to wear to Roni-Vows' wind game party. In the process, they revealed a great deal of bare flesh. Phaid noticed that the women had bodies that were equally as good as Edelline-Lan's. Despite still having the feeling that he wasn't much more than an item on the high society meat rack, he decided that, if nothing else, Chrystianaville would provide plenty of sexual variety.

As far as Phaid could tell, Hydranga-Cort was totally vapid. She had fluffed out, orange hair and probably little of substance in the mind beneath it. Abrella-Lu, on the other hand, exhibited a kind of strength in the way that she moved and talked, a certain ruthlessness that indicated she possessed a self-serving, iron core under the lacquered surface. She seemed the kind who would elegantly trample over anything that got between her and what she wanted.

After sitting around being a spectator for too long, Phaid decided that maybe he ought to investigate the packages that Hud-n had brought for him.

As Edelline-Lan had indicated, the suit was black. What she hadn't told him was that it was extremely tight. The jacket was short and double-breasted while the stovepipe trousers had

Mick Farren

a fancy design effect around the crotch that made him seem alarmingly well endowed. It was far from being the kind of outfit that he would have chosen for himself, but once he caught sight of himself in a mirror, he had to admit that it had a certain style.

The somber effect of the black was offset by a pair of white slip-on shoes with slightly stacked heels that turned sobriety into rakishness. Almost satisfied, he paraded the ensemble for the three women, who greeted it with sly grins and nods of approval.

As the women were still far from ready, Phaid found the decanter and was able to put away a number of stiff but leisurely drinks before they finally announced that they felt suitably prepared to brave the outside world and Roni-Vows' party.

Roni-Vows seemed to be totally in his element as a host. Wearing a duck-billed hat with little silver wings on the sides, he pirouetted through the grounds, joining and leaving various conversations with a fine honed ability to shock, be shocked, trade epigrams or carve on an absent friend's reputation with equal facility. Android waiters circulated with trays of drinks and tidbits, while hired boohooms chopped, sliced, poured, fetched, carried and generally sweated to keep the bar and buffet running.

As Phaid had expected, the party sparkled. The Presidential Court was out in force, accompanied by a large number of lesser, more peripheral mortals like himself. Roni-Vows greeted the four of them effusively, and then quickly drew Phaid to one side.

"We need to talk later."

"We do?"

"We do."

Phaid shrugged.

"Then you better grab me when you want me."

Roni-Vows nodded swiftly, then his serious expression disintegrated and he whirled away, once again the perfect picture of the shallow socialite.

Edelline-Lan dug Phaid sharply in the ribs with her elbow.

"Watch it."

"Watch what?"

"I know Roni-Vows when he gets that look on his face.

Given half a chance, he'll involve you in one of his million intrigues. He's a born plotter."

"You think I'm stupid?"

Edelline-Lan shook her head.

"I don't think you're stupid, but you're not a courtier, either. If anything goes wrong, he has limitless contacts to get himself out from under. You'll be the one who ends up in the manure. You understand that, don't you?"

Phaid suddenly decided that Edelline-Lan had gone just a little too far. It was time to put her in her place.

"He only wants to talk to me about the elaihim. I've got my own theories about those bastards."

"Don't ever tell me that I didn't warn you."

"Listen, babe, I didn't just fall out of the tree, I've been managing my own life for a long time before I met you."

Edelline-Lan's nostrils flared.

"Suit yourself. Learn things the hard way."

With that, she spun on her heel and walked angrily away. She immediately dived into the nearest knot of conversation and Phaid knew that he'd been dumped. He wondered if it was merely temporary or for keeps. He'd just been getting used to Edelline-Lan. Her jet black hair and long legs hit a spot deep inside him that few other women had reached.

The immediate effect of being dumped was that Phaid was left with no one to talk to. Roni-Vows was continuing to flit, Edelline-Lan was obviously out and both Abrella-Lu and Hydranga-Cort had vanished in the crowd. He had no choice except to wander and watch.

Roni-Vows' building was some thirty storys high and close to the elaborate bulk of the Presidential Palace. The panoramic view of the city was less magical than it had been from the terrace of the nightclub. The patchy sunlight revealed too many of the scars and blemishes.

Few people, however, were looking at the view. Both the common people in the streets and the more gilded ones on the rooftops were all staring skywards. The wind games were a major preoccupation, not only in Chrystianaville and the Republic, but throughout most of the city states and nations of the civilized world.

From the spectators' point of view, it was an ideal day for

the games. Since dawn, great masses of fluffy, cumulus clouds had been building up, piling themselves into irregular towers in the air. There was a fresh breeze that would enable the players to coax the maximum performance out of their fragile crafts.

Unfortunately, maximum performance also meant maximum risk to the players. Throwing their fliers through elaborate maneuvers in a high altitude airstream required the most finely tuned coordination. A single slip could rip the delicate, gossamer wings away from the body of the flier, and the player would plummet to his death.

All too often such slips did happen, and the two or three deaths that provided tragic punctuation to most major games were one reason why the sport was held in such awe.

Phaid imagined that down on the streets, anticipation was running higher than up on Roni-Vows' roof. In the streets there wasn't a constant supply of drinks and canapés to take the edge off the excitement. In some ways Phaid almost wished that he was down among the crowds. He could imagine the carnival atmosphere, the beggars and thieves, the fortune-tellers and the hucksters selling souvenirs, the shell game for the unwary. He could almost smell the smoke from the garbage food stands and hear the laughter and shouting. For a moment, he felt close to nostalgic, then an android waiter handed him a cocktail and he decided that maybe a swank party wasn't such a bad place to be.

There was a lot of talk about the games. The name Mylan came up over and over again. Even Phaid, out in the far flung reaches, had heard of Mylan. Mylan had been a genius, a prince among players. He had been able to do things with his flier that other players wouldn't dream of attempting. Despite all his skill, though, Mylan was dead. At the end of an apparently impossible series of stunts that had left the crowds breathless, his craft had suddenly dropped like a stone. The wings had been intact and there seemed to be no logical reason for the crash. Gossip claimed that Mylan's death had been deliberate. Mylan had committed suicide. The gossip told of how there had been a woman, a high class woman, a courtier or the like, who had played so hard with his affections that he'd been driven to kill himself.

Conversation faded as the first tiny craft appeared in the

sky, a red speck rising swiftly, circling a tumbled stack of clouds in tight, neat spirals. At the top of the cloud, when the flier was little more than a red dot, it executed a wide loop and then, to the accompaniment of a citywide intake of breath, it banked to the left and fell like a stone.

A small fat man next to Phaid grabbed his arm. He was hoarse with excitement.

"Are you the gambler I've heard so much about?"

"Maybe."

"A hundred tabs says he doesn't make it."

Phaid looked at the fat man in horrified surprise.

"Did I hear you right?"

"Two hundred?"

Phaid's lip curled in disgust.

"Don't you know that nobody bets on the wind players, not with the players up there risking their lives? It wouldn't be decent."

The fat man bridled.

"I thought you fellows would bet on anything."

Phaid snarled.

"Why don't you just get the hell away from me."

The fat man looked as though he was about to protest. Then he noticed Phaid's expression and moved off, muttering disgruntledly. Still amazed at the man's behavior, Phaid could only stand and watch him go. Even the cheapest hustler wouldn't attempt to bet on a wind game. It was considered the lowest act possible. Men who cheated, stole or killed would shy away from such a bet, particularly a bet on whether a player lived or died. The superstition was that it was such a terrible mark of disrespect that it could quite easily jinx the player involved.

It seemed that courtiers couldn't conceive respect in the way that poor folks could. To them everything was simply a transient diversion to be used and then cast aside. Once again, Phaid had the thought that maybe he'd been better off on the street.

The wind games continued all through the afternoon, but even though there was some spectacular flying as the players rode the thermals and drifted around the clouds on fickle and elusive air currents, the consensus on Roni-Vows' roof was that the day had been something of a disappointment.

One player had died, but he was generally considered to

have been past his prime and slipping. Callous analysis suggested that he had been a damned fool not to have retired at the end of the previous season.

The courtiers seemed more interested in spotting a new potential star, a new Mylan, than actually appreciating the wind games for what they were. As the afternoon started to turn to chilly evening more and more of them drifted inside, downstairs to Roni-Vows' cavernous reception area.

From the roof it was possible to see clear over the wide bowl of the city and out to the open sea. The sunset had turned the sky an angry purple. On the horizon, a twisting mass of ominously low cloud was being driven at high speed. It marked the edge of the icy gales that would eventually hit the coast a few hundred miles to the south. Where they touched the land it was locked in the grip of perpetual winter. They were the gales that created the icy plains.

Phaid watched all this with a not quite defined sense of foreboding. He turned and found that he was the last guest left on the roof, with the exception of a pair of drunks and a couple attempting to make love under a table.

The boohooms were clearing up the mess and stacking chairs. One was fishing garbage out of the ornamental fountain. A single android stood perfectly still with the lights on its chest flashing on and off in a slow, doleful sequence. Phaid was starting to feel the cold of the night creeping up on him. With a certain reluctance, he went down to join the other guests.

Edelline-Lan was continuing to ignore him and Phaid had to admit that he had become more than a little bored. The chatter was once again in full swing, and most of it was about people of whom he'd never heard and had no desire to meet.

There was also a tension about the gathering that did a lot to increase Phaid's discomfort. He wasn't sure if it was because the guests were such a cut-glass, competitive group, or whether it was the design of Roni-Vows' home. It seemed to have been planned for anything but comfort. The area in which the party was being held was all hard-edged and jutting angles, the decor was close to mechanistic except that everything was picked in violent, garish colors. Constantly flickering holograms jumped from scenes of lyrical innocence to the depraved and pornographic with stunning, if evil, effect. Exotic clusters of glo-

globes threw out isolated pools of cold violet light that made the people passing through them look like corpses. An incongruously large statue of the mythic winged beast, the thotoll, that completely dominated one end of the room, was big enough to cause everyone to feel just a little dwarfed. All this, plus the constant blasting of the fashionable hypnotic rhythm made the crowd seem obliged to be continuously jumping. Now that the wind games were over, the conversation turned to the situation at court.

"I tell you, half a dozen young men were sent into those private salons that she'd had sealed off. They never came out."

"If you ask my opinion, she's gone quite mad."

"What do you expert from an ex-whore who clawed her way through the corridors of power?"

"I thought her position was more horizontal."

"You have to hand it to her, though . . ."

"And a lot of people did."

"It's not easy for a nude dancer from the cold edge to make it all the way to the Palace."

"And get the town renamed after you."

"And have your husband assassinated once he'd made you his successor."

This last remark drew a number of sharp intakes of breath. Although it was commonly held theory, only the most foolhardy voiced it aloud. The speaker had been a weak-chinned, overfed young man called Trimble-Dun. He was too drunk for his own good. Roni-Vows smiled wearily at him.

"You realize that if one of us is an informer, the Secret Police will be waiting for you when you get home."

Trimble-Dun struck a defiant pose that Phaid decided hardly suited him.

"The way things are going, half the court will be in jail before a month is out."

Phaid, who'd also lost count of the number of drinks he'd had, decided that it was time to contribute something to the conversation. He did his best to match the cut-glass manner of the courtiers.

"It would seem to me that, as an outsider, any court with a perpetually absent president is kind of redundant."

This caused more consternation than Trimble-Dun's calling

Chrystiana-Nex a killer. The babble stopped dead and every eye seemed to be riveted on Phaid. The only people who looked amused were Roni-Vows and, surprisingly, Edelline-Lan. Phaid heard a voice whisper from behind.

"It's Edelline-Lan's bit of rough, what can you expect?"

Phaid swung around, fists clenched. Roni-Vows moved quickly forward and laid a hand on Phaid's arm.

"I think this might be a good time for us to have our little talk."

12

Roni-Vows tilted his head back and let a single drop of colorless liquid fall from the small crystal vial. He smiled and sighed.

"It'll probably turn me blind in the end, but it's such a delicious feeling." He offered the vial to Phaid. "Would you care for some?"

Phaid hesitated. Edelline-Lan's warning came back to him. If Roni-Vows was as tricky as she'd intimated, it wouldn't be particularly sensible to go and get loaded at the start of their first meeting. On the other hand though, a single vial of scholomine did cost something like three hundred tabs. Phaid had never had any, mainly because he'd never been able to afford the drug. Those who had told him that it was probably the most magical sensation that could be derived from a chemical. In the end, curiosity won out over prudence and Phaid accepted the proffered vial.

"Thank you."

Mick Farren

"Be very sparing with it. I expect you're probably not over-used to the stuff."

Phaid allowed the smallest quantity of the drug to fall into his left eye."

"Now the other eye."

Phaid repeated the process. Roni-Vows grinned at him.

"Feel anything yet?"

Phaid blinked experimentally.

"No . . . wait a minute . . ."

The very first effect was a slight blurring of the vision. Then it cleared and everything Phaid looked at was surrounded by a faint aura. He suddenly laughed out loud.

"Hey, this is great!"

He felt wonderful. It was as if there was nothing that he couldn't do. He was Phaid, omnipotent, invincible, nothing could get in his way, no barrier could stop him, and yet, at the same time, he was kind and loving. Sincere affection flowed out of him in every direction. He loved Roni-Vows, he loved himself, he loved Roni-Vows' private study.

This was slightly odd since a few minutes earlier he had hated the place. He'd decided that its dark woodwork, dim lights, old leather, thick rugs, shelves of antique, apparently unread books and display cases of weapons were a pretentious exhibition of masculine inadequacy. Now, to Phaid's surprise, it seemed too fantastic for words. Roni-Vows continued to grin at him.

"Enjoying yourself?"

Phaid was close to breathless.

"It's just . . . sweet Lords . . . I can't put it into words."

"Do you want to tell me about the elaihim?"

Without thinking, Phaid launched into the whole story of his and Makartur's journey across the desert, the fight with the drovers, how the elaihim had managed to link minds with the herd of veebes. He told how he had become convinced that they were somehow getting inside his own mind. Stoned on the scholomine drops, he was so intent on pleasing Roni-Vows that he didn't neglect the smallest detail and went into lengthy digressions to illustrate minute points.

Roni-Vows didn't seem in the least bored. He reclined in

198

his bat wing armchair, fingertips pressed together, watching Phaid intently.

By the time Phaid had finished, he was no longer flying on the first flash of the drug and, although he still felt marvelous, he realized that he had recklessly spilled everything that he knew, without giving a thought to the consequences. He knew he'd made a bad mistake and attempted to salvage something. He looked inquiringly at Roni-Vows.

"I'm doing a hell of a lot of talking here. Why don't you tell me how come you're so interested in the elaihim?"

Roni-Vows chuckled as though he had guessed what was going through Phaid's mind.

"Would you accept simple academic interest?"

Phaid knew he was being played with and he didn't like it. He knew he'd been sledgehammered with the scholomine and he didn't feel like being turned loose without at least a few answers.

"Not from you."

"You know me that well already?"

"I think so."

Roni-Vows was suddenly serious.

"Okay, I'll level with you. This city, or more precisely, the *status quo* in this city, is in very imminent danger of going right down the hole. I think the elaihim, if they're not actually responsible for what's going on, are at least stirring the pot."

Phaid gestured for Roni-Vows to stop.

"Listen, this may sound gauche, but what actually is going on? I've heard all kinds of tales and rumors, but nobody's ever actually laid it out for me."

Roni-Vows regarded him speculatively.

"You want it laid out for you? Okay, my friend, I'll lay it out for you, starting from the top. The President has simultaneously gone mad and become a recluse. The court, with no leadership, has turned into a snakepit of conspiracy. The police are running amok claiming they're the sole repository of the Presidential will, and they're arresting or just plain murdering almost anyone who so much as blinks out of turn. The priests have moved totally beyond the limits of their authority. When they're not plotting to take over the whole Republic, they're running around screaming heretic, planting spies and getting their own secret police to grab anyone who says a word against them. If all that weren't bad enough, the Silent Cousins and the lesser mobs are being torn apart by internal strife."

"It sounds bad."

"Damn right it's bad. The situation with the mobs is probably the worst thing of all. Normally in times of trouble we were able to rely on the mobs to hold the essential things together. Now we can't even count on them."

"What about the ordinary people? How much do they know about all this?"

Roni-Vows' mouth twisted. He didn't seem to have a very high opinion of the common people.

"Nothing stays a secret for very long in this city."

"And what are they doing about it?"

"Every third one of them's plotting his or her own revolution. On the northside, where the malcontents have always been the strongest, there are whole areas where we daren't even go. They have complete control. As far as I'm concerned, they can have the northside, except that now they are starting to look at the whole city."

"It's that bad?"

Roni-Vows nodded.

"There's always been an underground. Dear Lords, almost respectable, they were. If they actually managed to pull off their revolution, which I doubt, they'd simply execute a few courtiers, choose a new president and things would go on much the same as before. It's the crazies that you have to watch out for."

"The crazies?"

"There's a dozen or more groups and factions, mainly out on the northside. They've shot cops, blown up a few sections of walkway. They're most depressingly half-witted, but they all think they're the great liberating army. The biggest group is the bunch who follow the Day One philosophy. They want to destroy everything. Blow it up, burn it down. Back to the Dark Ages and start again. Their Day One idea is a clean slate. No systems, no organization, nothing. Innocence through mass slaughter. Lords help us if they ever get to power."

Phaid smiled.

"I don't need to worry. I'm not one of the elite."

Roni-Vows shook his head.

"Don't you believe it, my dear. The Day Oners would hate you as much as they hate me. They hate anyone who even gets enough to eat."

Phaid took a moment to digest all this.

"I don't see how you can really believe the elaihim are behind all this. The ones that I met didn't seem to want anything to do with humans."

"Maybe it's just one elaihi."

"Solchaim?"

"Solchaim."

Phaid was skeptical.

"I don't see how a single individual, no matter what weird abilities he has, can bring down a whole city. That's got to be pure paranoia."

"Paranoia is at epidemic proportions right now."

"So there you are."

Roni-Vows still wasn't convinced.

"I still have the feeling that he's somehow behind all this. Think about it, he's got the President in his pocket plus some courtiers, a few cops, the odd priest and Lords know who else. It wouldn't be all that hard. It only needs the odd word here, a push there, someone eradicated. A few key people in the right places at the right times and it wouldn't be all that hard to bring the city to its knees."

"He'd have to be a genius to pick the people, the places and the times."

Roni-Vows leaned forward and patted Phaid on the knee.

"And there you said it, my gambling friend, right there. He wouldn't have to be a genius. He is a genius. No human has a clue about the extent of elaihim intelligence. All we know is that they're smarter than we. In a lot of ways it's our own fault. For a long time we've had it too easy. Shifts in the wind belts have brought a lot of refugees from the countryside into the city, but, beyond that, we didn't have too many troubles. None of the other city states had the power to pose any real threat. So long as our diplomats, backed up by our agents, maintained a strict divide and rule policy and made sure that no cities were able to form an alliance against us, we were safe. We were even affluent at home. We lacked for very little.

The android farm system gave us everything that we wanted. Unfortunately, safety and plenty made us turn in on ourselves. The high born grew decadent..." Roni-Vows caught the expression on Phaid's face. "Don't look at me like that. I'm just a product of my time."

"I didn't say anything."

"You want me to go on?"

"Of course."

"The high born grew decadent. A pampered and complaining middle-class stopped contributing virtually anything to the good of the city. The mechanism of government just grew and grew. It was out of control even before Chrystiana-Nex came to power. All she did was put the finishing touches that turned it into the bureaucratic monster we have today. The system doesn't work. The rebels are right, there are people starving in this city. They're starving because the distribution and production systems are so scrambled that they don't work."

Phaid was thoughtful.

"You tell me all this, but you still insist that it's the elaihi who's the real enemy."

"When a state is in the condition we're in, it leaves itself wide open to dictators and demagogues. In this case the one seizing power is not human and we can have no idea what his real goals are."

Phaid nodded.

"I was wondering about that. There's something here that doesn't ring true. It's all very well weaving elaborate conspiracy theories that all go back to him, but if, as you say, he's the most powerful entity in the Republic, why should he bother to screw everything up? He's part of the *status quo,* after all. It would surely be in his interests to keep things just as they are."

"Perhaps he's simply looking to push the human race further back into barbarism, so we become just another species of bad tempered animals and the elaihim take over. It's no secret that both they and the androids could do very well without us."

Phaid laughed.

"You're not saying the androids are in on it too?"

Roni-Vows scowled.

"I'm not that paranoid."

"If Solchaim is doing all this, why doesn't somebody just

snuff him? The elaihim may be clever, but they still drop dead if someone burns them with a blaster."

Roni-Vows looked almost contemptuous.

"In an environment as murderous as the court, don't you think it hasn't been tried? Solchaim can spot a potential assassin a mile away. I swear to the Lords that he can sense them. It's quite uncanny."

"It's unhuman."

"I rather think you're right."

Phaid had an idea.

"How about an android?"

"An android?"

"If an android had its block against killing removed and it was reprogrammed, it might be able to pull off a hit on Solchaim. I don't know if the elaihim can sense an android's intentions."

"It's a nice theory, except that I'm not sure there's a tech in the whole city who know how to do the necessary work."

"I..."

"What?"

"Nothing."

Phaid had been about to blurt out the whole story of Ben-e and the secret android alteration shop on the northside. He'd only stopped in the nick of time. He didn't feel he owed anything to Roni-Vows or the city itself, for that matter. Also, he'd promised Ben-e that he'd keep quiet about the place. Phaid wasn't too stoned to realize that his best bet was to sit on the information until he could think of a way to make a deal for it. He started to edge away from the subject of androids and on to the subject of money.

"So where do I come into all this. I would have thought that, since I've actually met the elaihim, I would have had some value in this situation."

Roni-Vows smiled nastily.

"I'm not sure about that. You did rather spill your guts while you were stoned, and you said nothing about payment."

Phaid was painfully aware that he had fouled up. He was trying to think of a comeback when he was distracted.

"Do you hear anything?"

"No."

Phaid listened again.

"Are you sure?"

"What am I supposed to be hearing?"

"It's hard to tell, some sort of weird noise coming from outside."

"I still don't hear anything. Are you positive you're not hallucinating?"

Phaid shook his head.

"I'm pretty sure it's real."

Roni-Vows started to get impatient. He stood up and walked to the nearest window. He pulled back the curtains and slid it open.

"You're right. There is something going on."

The noise was much clearer now. It was the dull, full throated roar of thousands of voices.

Phaid started towards the window.

"What in hell's going on?"

"It sounds like the wind game crowd's going on some sort of rampage in the streets. It's hard to tell, it's almost dark now."

The low roar was punctuated by a burst of sharp, staccato crackling. The first one was quickly followed by more of the same.

"That's weapon fire."

"There must be a riot going on."

"Maybe we should go down and take a look."

Roni-Vows' look of surprise told Phaid that that was the very last thing he wanted to do.

"I think we'd be better off going to the roof. I've got my guests to think of, after all."

Phaid nodded understandingly.

"Of course, a man can't forget about his guests."

Roni-Vows looked searchingly at Phaid to see if he was mocking him. Phaid kept a perfectly straight face and so, without another word, they hurried back to the party.

There were considerably fewer guests than when Phaid and Roni-Vows had retired for their private talk. The androids had had the presence of mind to start serving booze again, and those who remained were treating the riot more like a spectator sport than any sort of serious occurrence.

The very first person that Phaid and Roni-Vows encountered

was Trimble-Dun. He had a full glass in his hand and was showing all the signs of advanced drunkenness.

"The mob's turned ugly and they're fighting in the street. The police are holding them back though, and hopefully they've killed a few of the bastards."

Roni-Vows looked at him coldly.

"That remark wasn't too diplomatic."

"It's what everyone's thinking."

Phaid ignored both of them and went directly to the edge of the roof. It was hard to make out details in the failing light, but a dark mass that couldn't be anything but a huge mob of people was surging through the central part of the city. Orange flames and oily black smoke marked the spots where vehicles and even a building had been set on fire. Here and there, Phaid could see the brilliant blue flash of fuse tubes and the more purple flare of blasters. These fire fights were obviously a result of the police trying to control the crowd, although they didn't seem to be meeting with quite the success with which Trimble-Dun credited them.

Unable to tell much more from his vantage point on the roof, Phaid turned and scanned the people left. There was no sign of either Edelline-Lan or Hydranga-Cort. Abrella-Lu was still there, however, and coming towards him.

"Looking for something?"

"I was wondering what happened to the rest of the guests." Abrella-Lu didn't seem very interested.

"They left. There was another party."

"I can see they left. What worries me is if they got caught in the riot."

Abrella-Lu still didn't appear overly concerned.

"I'd think not. They mostly left in a bunch after the games. The trouble didn't start until some while later."

Roni-Vows was bustling through the throng, relaying an announcement.

"Good news, people. It seems that all the other guests got to where they were going before the trouble broke out."

Abrella-Lu looked up at Phaid.

"Feel better now?"

"A little. I think maybe I'll go down on to the street and see what's going on."

"That's very brave of you."

"It's probably stupid, but I'd like to see for myself."

"Can I come with you?"

Phaid looked doubtful.

"Have you ever been out in a riot?"

Abrella-Lu shook her head.

"Never. What do you think I am?"

"It'd be too dangerous."

She pouted like a spoiled child.

"I want to come."

Phaid looked at her skimpy, translucent party clothes and high-heeled shoes.

"You're not even dressed for it."

"Neither are you in that monkey suit. You don't want me to come, do you."

"No."

"I knew it. It's Edelline-Lan you're worried about, isn't it. You're afraid that if she hears you're with me, she'll drop you. You're already in bad with her." Abrella-Lu's expression turned from sullen to sly. "She's not the only good fuck in the city, or the only rich bitch, either."

Phaid swallowed hard. He couldn't believe this woman was talking about sex while there was bloodshed in the streets below.

"It's nothing to do with Edelline-Lan. It's . . ."

"I already asked her if I could have you. She said it was okay."

Now they were passing him from hand to hand.

"You're not going and that's that."

"It'll be no more dangerous for me than you."

Phaid had to admit the truth of that.

Abrella-Lu had a further argument.

"If you don't take me, I'll simply go down there on my own."

Phaid gave in, but without too much grace.

"I guess you'd better come with me, then."

On the way out, Phaid borrowed a small ornate blaster from Roni-Vows. It seemed a prudent move since his own weapon was back at Edelline-Lan's with the rest of his clothes. Despite their host's protests, Phaid and Abrella-Lu descended to street level. For a few moments they hung back in the shelter of the entrance to Roni-Vows' building while Phaid took stock of the situation. The police had either cleared the immediate area or else the riot had moved on to another part of the city. A lot of windows had been broken and a hologram display that had featured the President had been partially torn down. Ironically, the parts that had been ripped away revealed that the hologram had been put on top of a billboard of her dead husband, the previous President. The street was littered with rocks, cans and broken glass. The riot had obviously passed that way, but now everything was quiet. Only three people were visible. One was sitting on the sidewalk staring dazedly into space, a second was lying in the road, unpleasantly still, while the third walked in unsteady circles, shaking his head as though trying to understand what had happened. A thin trickle of blood ran down the left side of his face.

Phaid motioned to Abrella-Lu.

"It looks as though things got pretty rough."

"I think I'm a little frightened."

"You could still go back."

"Hell no, I want to see this."

"Okay then."

Phaid walked purposefully out into the street with Abrella-Lu following close behind. He approached the man who was still on his feet.

"What happened?"

The man looked at him uncomprehendingly.

"They didn't have to do it."

"Who didn't?"

"They ran right over us."

"The police?"

"Right over us."

Phaid pointed to the gash that ran right along the man's hairline.

"You ought to get someone to take a look at that."

Still the man didn't seem to hear him.

"They didn't have to do it."

Abrella-Lu touched Phaid on the arm.

"You won't get him to tell you anything. He's in shock."

"You're right. We might as well move on."

"Which direction?"

Phaid thought for a moment.

"Where do you live?"

"On the Vard Prospect, exactly where a superior young woman should live, but I don't want to go there. It'd be too boring."

"I've got a hotel near the terminal tower. We should maybe head in that direction."

"That sounds tacky."

"So where do you want to go?"

"Oh, I'll come to your hotel with you. I'm up for a tacky evening."

"I don't know that we're spending the evening together."

Abrella-Lu looked Phaid up and down as though she didn't quite believe he was real.

"What's the matter with you? Don't you want me?"

"I suppose most men do?"

"Damn right they do."

Phaid sighed.

"You can come to the hotel with me if you want to. Who am I to refuse."

Abrella-Lu's lip curled.

"Who indeed."

That seemed to temporarily end the conversation. They walked for two blocks in silence, Phaid watchful and Abrella-Lu seemingly indifferent to everything that was going on around her. There was still damage and debris, but no active signs of the riot, although Phaid could still see smoke drifting over buildings and hear distant sounds of disturbance.

As they walked, Phaid had to more than once repress an urge to slap the woman. She seemed unable to grasp the fact that they weren't playing a game.

There were more people on the streets now. Agitated groups hung around on corners, some scared, most angry. Bit by bit, Phaid begun to build up the story. Almost everyone had a different set of details, but almost everyone agreed that a large presence of police had attempted to clear the streets immediately after the end of the wind games. There had seemingly been no restraints placed on the amount of force that they were permitted to use. They had waded into the crowds with clubs and grenades of riot control gas that caused uncontrollable spasms and hallucinations in anyone who inhaled it.

There had been even more casualties in the panic that followed. Men, women and children had been trampled underfoot as mobs rushed for shelter. Sections of the crowd had resisted and at that point the blasters had come out and the killing started.

Some people to whom Phaid had talked claimed that the police had moved in because there had been widespread purse-snatching or looting. Others were certain that it was a result of a capricious order from the Palace. There were also stories of how the underground was using the riots as an excuse for direct confrontation with the police. Reports of shootouts and sniping came from all over the city. There was even a tale of how a gang of Day Ones had attacked a police barracks. Quite a few people were firmly convinced that the long expected revolt had started.

Phaid finally decided that he had heard enough. He took hold of Abrella-Lu's arm and steered her gently through the small knots of excitable people.

"We should try and make it through to the hotel."

"I haven't seen a riot yet."

"You don't want to if you can help it."

"So what did we come out here for?"

"To see what was going on, not to actually get involved."

"I want to see some action."

Phaid turned as a commotion started at the other end of the block.

"I think we're about to get more action than you can handle."

There was yelling and screaming and then a blaster roared. The screaming rose to a hysterical pitch. People were fleeing down the street in a panic, running directly towards Phaid and Abrella-Lu. Phaid grabbed the woman and dragged her across the road at right angles to the way the crowd was running. They made the sidewalk and dashed for the shelter of an apartment building doorway. Youths were hurling rocks, and Phaid knew that any moment the police would charge. He glanced grimly at Abrella-Lu.

"You got your action. It looks like all hell's going to break loose."

Abrella-Lu bit her lip. Phaid couldn't tell if she was scared or weirdly excited. There were people all around them. There was the confusion that is the hallmark of any riot. Nobody on the street seemed to know what was happening. There was nervousness and fear, but there was also the elation of too many people with too much adrenaline pumping. The panicky rush ran out of steam. The crowd started to ebb back, the shouting and rock throwing stepped up. Everyone's movements were jerky and frenetic. Someone said that the police had halted and were holding a line. Someone else claimed that they were preparing to charge. The milling around was coming close to hysterical. The crowd was dangerously jumpy. Phaid guessed that the police were almost certainly in the same condition, but then there was no room for guessing. There came the loud crashing of weapons on armor. Phaid knew the police had launched their charge. Each one of them was yelling with all the strength in his lungs. Their roar swamped the screams of the crowd. In their red plasteel armor they were like evil red insects, fearsomely encased in their exoskeletons. The com-antennae on the sides of their helmets, the smoked face masks and breathing filters further added to their nonhumanity. The rock throwing kids scattered as the long flexible clubs lashed out. A gas grenade burst and a cloud of choking yellow mist billowed outwards. Phaid gagged as he got a whiff of it.

"We're in real trouble now."

13

Abrella-Lu didn't seem to have quite grasped the danger of the situation.

"They won't hurt me. I'm a courtier."

"Like hell they won't. They ain't going to ask for identification before they break your head. They ain't going to listen to you telling them that you're a high-class courtier and only here for fun."

"Oh my Lords!" Abrella-Lu went white. Reality had finally penetrated the facade.

"Yeah."

It was a mess. The crowd had stampeded. They had all fled with the exception of a few unfortunates who had been grabbed by the cops and were now being beaten and dragged down the street. Most of the police had carried on, apparently enjoying the pursuit, but a few had paused, making the tense, nervous movements of men whose blood was up and who wanted to hurt someone or something.

Phaid put an arm around Abrella-Lu and tried to make both of them as inconspicuous as possible as they crouched in the doorway.

The cops didn't seem to have noticed them or, at least if they had, they weren't doing anything about it. Phaid was just wondering if maybe it was safe to move, when a young woman in a long, drab green duster coat sprang out from another doorway on the opposite side of the street. She pulled a fuse tube from under the coat and let out a yell.

"Day One!"

The fuse tube flashed and a cop staggered back with a smoking hole in his chest armor. Other cops spun around bringing up their weapons. The girl got off one more shot before a half-dozen blasters roared and her mutilated body was spun across the sidewalk and slammed into the wall. Even Abrella-Lu was shocked.

"Horrible!"

"We're in the shit now."

One cop was already pointing in their direction while another was actually lumbering towards them with a blaster in one hand and a tingler in the other. Phaid sneaked Roni-Vows' tiny blaster out of his pocket and pressed it against the doorlock behind him. He touched the release button and there was a small explosion. The door swung open and he quickly pushed Abrella-Lu through it, then he spun around and fired at the cop.

It was a lucky shot and the cop went down, a second one was raising his blaster. Without thinking, Phaid burned him as well and then ducked through the doorway. As the door swung back, it was reduced into a smoking ruin. The other police on the street weren't wasting time in seeking to avenge their colleagues.

Phaid dragged Abrella-Lu across the lobby of the apartment building. She was near to hysteria.

"You killed a cop!"

"Two."

"And they were trying to kill us."

"Shut the fuck up and run."

Any moment the cops would be bursting into the lobby. Phaid spotted an elevator behind a decorative set of pillars.

"That way!"

They reached the elevator and Phaid hit the call stud. The doors didn't open. Simultaneously three cops crashed into the building. To Phaid's surprise, a bulky android rolled into the lobby from the opposite direction. Its sensors made a full circle as it halted between Phaid and the cops.

"I - am - a - security - android - and - this - is - a - formal - warning. I - have - no - blocks - against - harming - human - beings. If - you - do - not - all - remain - exactly - where - you - are - and - identify - yourselves - and - state - your - business - I - shall - be - forced - to - take - action."

One of the cops ignored the android's warning and pointed his blaster at Phaid. A pale blue stun blast flashed out from the android and he dropped like a stone. The second cop let go a blast at the android and it erupted a shower of sparks. At the very same moment, the elevator doors opened. Pushing Abrella-Lu in front of him, Phaid dived inside. The doors closed behind them and the car started up. Phaid leaned against the wall, gasping for breath.

"That was too damn close for comfort."

"What do we do now?"

"We try and get out somewhere and vanish."

"If I could get to a comset, maybe I could talk to someone."

"I think the time for contacts and influence is well past. We've just got to count on a dark night, dumb cops and so much trouble elsewhere that they won't have time to chase us very far."

Abrella-Lu had alarming powers of recovery.

"This is sort of exciting."

Phaid smiled thinly.

"Enjoy it while you can. We ain't out of the woods yet."

After what seemed like an age, the elevator came to a halt. The doors opened and Phaid stepped cautiously out. Everything was quiet and he set about looking for an exit to the roof. He discovered the door in back of the liftshaft. To his surprise, he found that it wasn't even locked.

At the top of the forty-story building, a biting wind whipped across the dark flat roof. Phaid once again took hold of Abrella-Lu's arm.

"Keep moving, the police can't be far behind us."

"Will you quit dragging me around?"

"You want to get caught?"

"No, but how do you expect me to run in these damn shoes?"

Phaid looked down at the shoes. The heels were a good four inches high and as sharp as daggers. They might have been very sexy and ultra chic, but totally useless for taking it on the lam across the rooftops of the city.

"Why the hell did you want to wear those things?"

Abrella-Lu looked at him angrily.

"I didn't know I was going to be doing this when I started out, did I? I tell you what I'll do, if you just wait a minute, I'll take them off."

"Dump them!"

She kicked off her shoes and carried on in her bare feet. They reached the edge of the building. There was a gap of about a meter and a half between it and the next one. Phaid looked down into the yawning chasm and felt a little sick.

"We're going to have to jump."

Abrella-Lu stared at him in horror.

"Jump? You're crazy! That's a forty floor drop!"

"We don't have any choice."

"I'm not jumping across there and that's that."

"It's better than being burned down. Just tell yourself that it's psychological. If it was a two-meter drop you wouldn't think twice about it."

"You go first."

Phaid took a deep breath and jumped. His relief was immense when he felt his feet hit the next roof. He turned and beckoned to Abrella-Lu.

"Come on!"

"I can't!"

"Just shut your eyes and jump. If you don't, I'll leave you to the cops."

This time she did as she was told. Phaid put a hand out to steady her as she landed beside him. They started to run. The next four buildings all butted on to each other and no more jumping was necessary. As they were running, Phaid could hear the sounds of fresh violence down on the street. It was like music to his ears. He hoped the rioters were holding up the police sufficiently that they wouldn't have either the time or the manpower to surround the whole block.

They reached the last building and Phaid halted. He was surprised that the police still hadn't emerged on to the roof. He hoped that maybe they were searching the original building in which he and Abrella-Lu had sought refuge. There still wasn't time to waste, though. Phaid looked quickly around.

"We've got to find ourselves a way down."

There was a narrow maintenance ladder bolted to the parapet at the rear of the building. Phaid hurried across to it and looked to see where it led. It dropped to the balcony of the top floor apartment.

Once again Phaid had to swallow his fear of heights. He swung his leg off the parapet, beckoned to Abrella-Lu to follow and started climbing down. Once they were both on the balcony, Phaid took the blaster from out of his pocket. Thick black drapes concealed anything that might be behind the glass balcony doors.

"Let's hope there's nobody home."

"If there is, they're liable to get pretty upset when we come busting in."

"That's highly probable, but we don't have too many other options. I'm sure as hell not climbing down that ladder all the way to the street."

Without any more words, Phaid pointed the blaster at the lock and squeezed the button. There was a flash and a roar and the lock didn't exist any longer. Phaid slid open the door, pushed aside the drapes and stepped into the room.

It was so dim inside that Phaid was unable to make out any details. The only light came from a fancifully obscene hologram. There were a number of lumpy shapes on the floor. At first Phaid took them to be inanimate objects. Then one of them stirred and a voice came out of it.

"Wow! Where the hell did you two spring from?"

The voice had the slurred, lazy thickness of a heavy duty dog gold user. Phaid started to edge towards the door on the far side of the room.

"We just landed on the roof and we're passing through on our way to the street."

"Is that a fact? You just flew here?"

Phaid continued his edging.

"Our arms are real tired."

215

"Think you could teach me to fly?"

Phaid nodded.

"You've got to remember to keep your fingers together."

"Yeah?"

"And flap hard."

Abrella-Lu had joined in the absurd charade. The dog gold fiend yawned.

"Is the riot still going on?"

"Yeah, it's still going on."

"Amazing."

Phaid was almost to the door.

"It's been nice talking to you, but we've got to be going."

"You have?"

"I'm afraid so."

"That's a pity. You seemed like real interesting people."

Phaid opened the door.

"We'll be seeing you."

"Yeah. Right. Come by again."

They let themselves out of the apartment and walked to the elevator, doing their best to look like legitimate visitors.

"Dog gold can make you fucking dumb."

"They're happy."

"I guess so."

The elevator came and they rode down to the street in silence. Phaid hoped, as they crossed the lobby, that no security android would come rushing out and start questioning them. In fact, nothing happened and Phaid slowed and carefully opened the door that led to the street.

"This is going to be the difficult bit."

"Are there many cops about?"

Phaid took a look.

"They seem to have cleared the street. There's a line of them halfway up the next block, they look like they're holding back quite a crowd, but there's none near here."

"You think it's safe to go out?"

"I think we could take a chance."

Phaid and Abrella-Lu slipped out of the building entrance and hurried away, going in the opposite direction from the police lines.

"I wish we'd had some other clothes."

"If we thought of it, we could have stolen some from those dopey fools upstairs."

"If we'd thought of it."

Phaid had an idea.

"We could always split up."

"Don't you dare."

They covered some six blocks without being noticed. They'd done their best to avoid both cops and rioters. At one point two cops had actually crossed the road and walked straight toward them. Phaid had felt the sweat starting to flow, but just as the cops were about to get within striking distance, a sniper opened up from a nearby roof and everybody in the whole street scattered for cover. The cops raced off to try and get the sniper and Phaid and Abrella-Lu were able to slip away in the confusion.

Finally, after far too long with fear making a choking lump in the back of his throat, Phaid saw the sign saying Middlemas Hotel shining like a beacon in the distance. He and Abrella-Lu hurried towards it. As they turned into the lobby, he felt as though a great weight had been lifted from his shoulders.

"We made it."

"It looks like it."

The android desk clerk greeted them with the usual distant lack of interest. Phaid attempted a brief conversation.

"It's rough out there."

"What-can-you-expect-from-humans?"

After that remark, there seemed to be little point in continuing. They both retreated into the elevator and rode up to Phaid's room. Phaid took off his jacket and threw it on the bed.

"So how did you enjoy your little adventure?"

Abrella-Lu smiled at him. She seemed to have recovered completely and was now a picture of calm and collection, albeit a little disheveled.

"It was different."

"You realize we were almost killed at least three times."

"You have to live dangerously if you want to have any fun."

"I think I'd rather do without fun and live a little longer."

"So why did you want to go on the street? You could have stayed safe inside Roni-Vows' place."

Phaid spread his hands.

"How should I know? Maybe it was the effect of the scholomine."

Abrella-Lu's eyes narrowed and her nostrils flared.

"Scholomine? You had scholomine? How come you didn't give me any, you bastard."

"It wasn't mine. Roni-Vows gave it to me."

"You still could of got me some."

"He wasn't doing take away orders. He just gave me a hit and that was that."

"I just love scholomine. I think I might even kill for it."

"It turns you blind in the end."

"Who cares?"

Phaid did his best to make up for his lack of drugs.

"I've got a bottle stashed somewhere."

"I want scholomine."

Phaid was starting to become bored with the spoiled brat act.

"We don't have any."

"We could get some."

"Huh?"

"We could get some."

"You really think I'm about to go into that mess outside to cop you some drugs?"

"We could send an android."

Phaid didn't have an answer to that. He didn't like to admit to Abrella-Lu that his funds were limited. Phaid reluctantly picked up the comset and gave his room number.

"Do you have an android that could go out on an errand for us?"

"There-is-a-riot-going-on-outside."

"No androids, huh?"

"They-will-go-but-it-will-cost-extra."

Phaid scowled. There was something particularly offensive about being gouged by an android.

"Okay, I'll pay."

"What-do-you-require?"

"A vial of scholomine."

Abrella-Lu's voice piped up behind him. "And a couple of twists of dog gold, and a bottle."

There was a pause at the other end of the line.

"Is there some sort of problem?"

"We - don't - have - many - requests - for - scholomine. I - will-have - to - check - with - the - bellboy - to - ascertain - if - he - knows-how - to - obtain - it."

"I'll hold."

Phaid waited. Eventually the android voice came back.

"The-bellboy-knows-how-to-obtain-the-substance. What-quantity-do-you-require?"

"Just a single vial."

"Are-you-aware-of-the-cost?"

"I think so, but you'd better tell me anyway."

"My-bellhop-informs-me-that-it- will-be-three-hundred-for-a-single-vial."

Phaid pulled a face and wondered silently if Abrella-Lu was worth three hundred plus the cost of the bottle. After the journey back to the hotel, he would have been quite happy to curl up in his bed with just the bottle for company. On the other hand, the first hit of scholomine that Roni-Vows had given him had been sufficiently interesting to make him want to try some more.

"Okay, I guess you better tell him to go get it. We'll be waiting."

"Very-well."

Phaid broke the connection and, feeling a little weary, he looked at Abrella-Lu, who was sitting on the bed beside him.

"The scholomine's on the way."

She leaned over and pressed her lips to his cheek.

"Now we can really have some fun."

"Let's hope it's less dangerous than the last lot."

"What's the matter with you? I thought you were a gambler. Do you always want to be so safe?"

"Safe? No. Live a few months longer? Yes."

"You're impossible."

"I just ordered you the scholomine, didn't I?"

Abrella-Lu grinned.

"That's true."

Her expression changed and she glanced around the small hotel room.

"Do you have a clean-off booth? I feel kind of grimy after

all those streets and rooftops."

Phaid indicated the room's only other door.

"You'll find everything you need."

"I doubt I'll find everything I need, but I'll probably get myself freshened up a bit."

The statement was accompanied by the hint of a leer, then she gestured towards the entertainment unit.

"While I'm gone, you could try to find us some music on that thing."

Phaid nodded and Abrella-Lu made her exit. Obediently, he squatted down in front of the entertainment unit and fiddled with the controls. On the fourth try he got a rather more restrained version of the kind of music he'd first heard in the ballroom of the marikh line train. With a music program set up, he finally dimmed the lights and waited for Abrella-Lu to reappear from her toilet.

He waited for nearly twenty minutes. During that time, the android bellhop delivered the drugs. Phaid paid him and noticed, with some concern, just how big a bite it took out of his rapidly dwindling cash reserves. He knew that cruising on the periphery of the court wasn't making him any money and that he would have to do something to pump up his finances pretty damn soon. He wasn't exactly sure, however, how he was going to do it.

When Abrella-Lu had finally emerged, she was naked apart from her jewelry and one torn stocking held up by a garter. She immediately pounced on the vial of scholomine and greedily dropped the chemical into both eyes. For a while, she lay back gasping as the initial rush hit her, but once the full force had faded, she turned her attention to Phaid. She led him to the bed and, for the next hour, she demonstrated her extreme versatility.

There seemed to be something inside Abrella-Lu that simply wouldn't keep still. Directly her mind and body had used up one sensation she immediately wanted to move on to a new one. There was no place in her life for standing still or taking stock. She lived from moment to moment without any apparent thought for either past or future.

Even though he'd used rather more modest amounts of the

drug, Phaid quickly discovered that sex on scholomine was a truly mind wrenching experience. It had spun him at random from pleasure to pain, out on to the furthest reaches of fantasy and jolted him into abrasive reality. Phaid found himself unable to exert any control over what was going on. He had the distinct feeling that Abrella-Lu was playing him like a fish on a line.

At the end of what seemed like a century, Phaid fell back, half on the bed and half on the floor, totally satiated. After much too short a while, he realized with surprise and some consternation that Abrella-Lu wanted to start on some new game. She lay sprawled on the bed, arms cradling her head, legs spread, one knee raised. Slowly and reflectively, she chewed on a twist of dog gold and stared at the series of hallucinations that rainbowed their way across the ceiling.

"Why don't we invite another man over?"

Phaid stopped what he was doing. He'd been less than successfully trying to pour them two more drinks. The combination of booze, dog gold and scholomine had left him unsteady on his feet. His coordination was shot and his sense of spatial relationship had packed up and gone home for the duration.

"So I'm not enough for you?"

"I thought maybe you and him could do it and I could watch. I like to watch men perform on each other. There's a very special symmetry about it."

Phaid shook his head.

"Symmetry? I don't think I could perform with some other man. Not even for the sake of symmetry."

"If you don't want to get another man over, why don't we get another woman up here? Then you could watch us doing it, and afterwards, I could watch you and her. What do you think about that?"

Phaid sat wearily down on the bed.

"It sounds better than another man."

"You would say that. Who do you think we should get?"

"How should I know?"

"The easiest thing would be to tell the bellhop to fetch us a prostitute."

Phaid sighed at the thought of another blow to his available

221

cash. He knew that the scholomine had long since peaked and all that he really wanted to do was to fall asleep for a couple of days.

"Yeah."

"Is that all you've got to say?"

"I think so. I'm kind of tired."

Abrella-Lu looked surprised.

"Tired? You'll soon get over that. If we paid the whore a bit extra, I expect we could get to beat her. Have you ever beaten a woman? I have, men too. Pain is so fashionable at the moment. Of course, to be fair, I had to let a few people do it to me as well. I can't actually put my hand on my heart and say that it was the greatest, but I suppose it was an experience."

Phaid didn't have the energy to interrupt Abrella-Lu's flow of words. He wondered if she had sneaked yet another dropper of scholomine while he'd been looking the other way.

She reached for the comset and started discussing the practicalities of procuring a prostitute with the androids on the desk. It transpired that, even despite the riots, both men and women were readily available.

"Hookers always find a way to work."

The girl who eventually arrived was no great beauty. She had a skinny, washed-out look. Her large, dark-rimmed and heavily made-up eyes had a dull furtiveness about them that told of too many cheap hustles and too many rough pairs of hands. The color job on her hair, a garish fluorescent green, was so cheap that it was turning black at the roots. Following a current street fad, a mass of tiny glowing diodes had been threaded into the piled up mass of hair, but even about a third of those had burnt out. Phaid decided the kindest thing would be to pay her and then let her take the rest of the night off.

Abrella-Lu didn't see it that way, however. She immediately went into a huddle with the girl, going into great detail over the sexual scenario that she expected her to follow. The girl listened with attention, but a lethargic lack of emotion. She told them that her name was Chordene, but beyond that she volunteered nothing except a total, resigned passivity. Phaid felt sorry for her. He wondered who or what had made her go out to turn a trick on this riot-torn night. He also felt sorry for himself. After spending the previous night in similar athletics with Edelline-Lan, then going through Roni-Vows' party, the riot and another bout of vigorous sex, Phaid had reached the point of total exhaustion. Abrella-Lu wouldn't, however, take no for an answer. She dosed him with more scholomine and the bleary, throbbing, moist and occasionally painful games started all over again; games that became increasingly complicated now that she had two other people to deal with instead of just one.

When it was finally over, Phaid lay limp and totally drained. Abrella-Lu, however, was far from through. She picked up the almost empty scholomine vial and dropped even more into her eyes. She offered some to Phaid, but he declined, so instead she gave the last of the drug to Chordene. In the first talkative rush, she came up with yet another plan. She and Chordene should go out and work the streets a twosome for the rest of the night, Chordene for the money and Abrella-Lu for kicks. With a blast of scholomine inside her, Chordene seemed much more eager to go along with Abrella-Lu's crazy plans. They tried to persuade Phaid to join them. This time he couldn't be swayed or bullied. There was nothing, short of a straitjacket and four burly men to carry him, that would get him down on to the streets again. His final act was to pay off the prostitute and see the two women out the door. Then he dropped on to the rumpled and destroyed bed and almost immediately fell into a deep and thankful sleep.

Phaid's slumber may have been deep and well deserved, but dim and threatening shapes gathered in his unconscious causing him to twitch and whimper. Finally they merged and coalesced into one clear picture. It was a poor section of the city. The particular street was narrow and dark, little more than an alley. A single light in a window reflected on wet cobbles. A thin sickly mist hugged the ground. Everything was deathly quiet. Phaid seemed to be just an observer. In some dreams he was an active participant but this didn't seem to be one of them. He was nothing more than a disembodied, watching spirit.

For what appeared to be a very long time, nothing happened. Then, of all people, Makartur appeared out of the darkness. Even in the depths of sleep, Phaid stirred in the grip of profound unease and muttered softly. There was something measured and wary in the warrior's stride, as though he sensed danger or the possibility of some sudden assault. The thumb of his right hand was hooked around the butt of his blaster. Makartur walked nearly the full length of the alley, then he paused. He quickly looked both ways; he seemed to be checking that no one was either following or watching him, then he ducked swiftly through an archway. The presence of the dreaming Phaid drifted after him.

Beyond the arch was a flight of steps leading down to a lower level. The stairwell was barely lit by a single, aged, parchment yellow glo-globe set high in a cresset. At the foot of the stairs was a short passage. It ended in a formidable looking door of black wood, studded with iron nails and secured by a massive lock and huge curlicued hinges. The warren of buildings was clearly a very ancient part of the city. The door even had an old-fashioned knocker, a heavy steel ring held in the mouth of some fierce and mythical beast. Makartur once again looked behind him and then grasped the ring. He rapped twice, then he paused and rapped three more times in quick succession. He paused slightly longer and then repeated the entire sequence.

From behind the door came the noise of bolts being pulled back. The door opened a crack, still secured against unwanted intrusion by a length of stout chain. A voice came from within. A question was asked in some gruff, guttural language. Makartur replied in the same tongue. As he spoke he flipped a small leather charm bag from inside his tunic. He held it up for inspection. It was the thing to which Phaid had seen him making his devotions that first night on the crawler. Makartur must have spoken the correct responses because the door swung to for a moment, the chain was removed and it reopened, just wide enough to let Makartur slip inside. It slammed hastily behind him.

A figure in a brown robe and hood bowed deeply. His arms were folded in front of him, his hands concealed inside wide sleeves.

"I must apologize for posing the question and using the old tongue before you had even crossed our threshold."

Makartur bowed in return.

"It is understandable. I am not of your circle, just a traveler and a stranger in this place.

"I am afraid that the priests of the heresy have been infected by the same madness that grips this whole city. They seemed determined to stamp us out. All through the Republic, hundreds of the faithful have been dragged to the dungeons and torture chambers of the heretics. Their spies infiltrate our circles, and squads of armed militants search out and destroy our temples. We have lost three from this very circle in the last month. We'll not see them again."

Makartur was becoming a little impatient with the litany of despair.

"I am no spy and I am no heretic. I have come here to approach the first gate and seek the knowledge of my ancestors."

"These are harsh times."

Makartur sniffed rudely.

"Harsh times are sent by our ancestors and our gods in order to strengthen us. We meet them with fortitude, not with whining and complaint."

Makartur was a warrior, he had no time for the furtiveness and fear of these city weaklings, even if they did share a common religion. He looked around what was obviously an anteroom of the underground temple. It was a place of browns and grays. Two more robed figures stood against the bare stone wall. A smoky brazier burned in one corner and the air was thick with incense. Beside the brazier was a statue of Aggea, the baleful mother deity who, according to legend, had eaten all her husbands and all but one of her offspring. The sole survivor was Godking Braku, whose image would be in the main temple. The light in the anteroom came from a hundred or more candles that seemed to have been placed on nearly every flat surface. The ceiling was blackened with soot and cascades of congealed wax hung from every candlestick. Piles of moldering books littered the walls and heaped up in the corners. The atmosphere was one of a church that had once been venerable and spacious but which was now compressed and driven into dim and claustrophobic underground tunnels. The temple elder in the robe spoke coldly. He was obviously offended at Makartur's blunt arrogance.

"Have you prepared yourself for receipt of the knowledge you seek?"

Makartur nodded.

"Aye."

"And have you prepared yourself for the ordeal of seeking?"

"Aye. I have meditated. I have meditated for long days."

"Then there is no reason why you should not begin your journey into night, your conduct to the first gate of death."

Makartur's face was grim.

"None whatever."

The other two robed figures moved forward. One set a small, three-legged stool beside Makartur. The other helped him remove his tunic and strip to the waist. He was seated on the stool and cold water was brought in a small silver bowl. The elder stood in front of Makartur and watched while his two assistants gently and ritualistically cleansed the warrior's arms and torso. Once the process was completed, the elder stretched out his hand. Almost absentmindedly he traced one of the more obvious scars that crisscrossed the warrior's shoulders, then he caught himself and became more businesslike. He held out his hands to one of the assistants who passed him a heavy copper jar. It contained a dark green ointment that he proceeded to rub on to Makartur's body.

Makartur's eyelids began to drop. The ointment contained a powerful hypnotic herb that was supposed to free the user's mind and make possible his or her journey to the edge of the spirit world. When the anointing was finished, the elder stepped back and asked Makartur a series of ritual questions in the old tongue. Makartur gave the proper responses, then one of the assistants handed him a silver chalice filled with a dark red wine that had been infused with more natural hallucinogens. Makartur's motor responses seemed to be slipping away. A small bead of wine ran out the corner of his mouth and trickled down into his beard. The elder asked a more lengthy and complicated question. This time Makartur could only just slur his way through the response. Sweat was running down into his eyebrows and streaking the green paste that coated his chest. His eyes were nearly shut. The pupils were little more than pinpoints. With some difficulty the two assistants helped Mak-

artur to his feet. The elder opened another black wooden door.
It led to the inner area of the temple.

The inner area was small, another rabbit warren room just
like the first one. It was, however, cleaner and less cluttered,
the stone walls were hidden behind black drapes. Facing the
door was a small, plain wooden altar that bore a short, un-
sheathed dagger, a tall red, lit candle, a growing plant with
small red flowers and a statue of Godking Braku. The floor
was also black. A large white circle was painted just in front
of the altar. Behind the circle there was a pattern of stars in
gold. The illusion was one of supernatural power but, on close
examination, the temple had the makeshift, temporary look,
the kind of look that had to be expected in a church that had
been forced underground.

Makartur was taken to the center of the circle. He sank to
a kneeling position. For a moment it seemed as though he was
going to fall but then he righted himself and remained on his
knees, just swaying slightly. The two assistants left the room.
The elder remained facing the statue of Braku. When the door
closed, he bowed low, then, straightening up, he faced the
angry, glowering face of the bronze image of the Godking.
Flatteringly, he started to talk directly to the idol in the old
tongue. The idol seemed to watch him impassively, a pair of
long fangs extended over his petulant lower lip. The elder built
up his address. From the way he moved his hands, he appeared
to be introducing Makartur to the statue and pleading on his
behalf. The harangue was a long one. When he was finally
finished he bowed again and took a number of backward steps,
leaving Makartur alone in the pool of candlelight.

For a while, Makartur did nothing, then the elder whispered
from the darkness.

"The offering! Make the offering."

Makartur swayed. He fumbled in the pouch at his belt. With
a great deal of difficulty, he extracted five gold coins. Gold
coins were exceedingly old and exceedingly rare. The few that
were left mainly circulated among the less sophisticated, rural
peoples who didn't trust any of the modern currencies. Makartur placed them on the floor, just outside the circle. The flame
of the candle seemed, for an instant, to flicker and dim. Makartur looked up at the statue.

"Lord Braku..."

His voice was little more than a harsh rasp. He had difficulty forming words.

"Lord Braku... I am a warrior. I do not have the old tongue, but I am a good warrior. Lord Braku, you are the judge and the destroyer, you are the guardian of the eternal cycle, you are ultimately powerful and uniquely merciless, you are the unforgiving. You know that I do not lie when I tell you that I have never betrayed my trust as a warrior..." Makartur hesitated again. This bout of effusive praise seemed to have drained his strength. His breathing was labored. "Permit me... to approach the portals... so the knowledge of my ancestors, should they endeavor to bestow it, may come to me... through the first door and help me in my journey in this mortal world... I beg you Lord Braku... I am unsure in my path and in my destiny and I need the knowledge... aid me Lord Braku... let me approach the portals."

For a long time there was silence except for Makartur's irregular and painful breathing. The candle once again seemed to flicker and dim. Makartur started gulping air in short swift gasps. It was almost as though he was going into a seizure. Suddenly a strangled scream was wrenched from him.

"Mother! Mother! All my mothers!"

And then another, softer voice came from Makartur's mouth.

"Makartur, Makartur, we never thought that you would seek the first gate."

The voice was gently chiding. Makartur's own rasp returned.

"A man..."

"We know of the man. We have seen how your destinies have been woven one with the other. We have heard your meditations and we have seen how the man disturbs your inner vision. We see how you feel the clash of two destinies. It rings with the sound of cymbals and the road is one of death."

"But what of my vows? What of the family revenge I seek in this city?"

"Your paths are locked, our son. You will not fulfill those vows until death has separated your destinies, and perhaps not even then. Only death can set you free from his. There was a point where too much was shared. It was a sad sharing, it leads to a death in a place of great dishonor and only the strength of a great warrior will save him who dies from the pit."

"And . . . who . . . dies?"

"In all there is free will. Destiny runs to death, but only the death of one in this meeting. The first will die and even risk the pit. The second will continue on his journey to some other end. If you are present at his death, he will not be present at yours."

A small whisp of ectoplasm trembled at the corner of Makartur's mouth. The eyes of the bronze statue seemed to glow as though being heated from within.

"Do . . . I . . . kill . . . the man?"

"If you are not present at the death of the man Phaid, he will be present at your death. You may know no more, our son."

The voice was stern. All the mothers of Makartur had no time for weaklings. Makartur's head sagged, but he slowly raised it.

"Then . . . I . . . must . . . kill . . . the man Phaid."

Makartur, although exhausted, was filled with resolve.

"I will kill the man Phaid."

The man Phaid woke screaming in his hotel room. He could scarcely believe the obscenely vivid nightmare. All Phaid's boyhood superstitions swamped him. It was a wave of old-age horror. He had been there. Makartur had taken the deadly path to the world of his dead ancestors. Capricious ancestor gods had allowed Phaid to witness the happening while he slept. There was, however, an urban, modern side of Phaid's mind that simply didn't buy the mumbo jumbo. It told him it was a nocturnal anxiety attack. Makartur didn't like Phaid and Phaid was nervous of his warrior temper. The dream was just an expression of that, nothing else. It was no reason to drop everything and flee the city. No matter how much, though, the sophisticate tried to reassure the primitive, Phaid couldn't shake the feeling that, if he ever ran into Makartur again, he would be running into an implacable enemy.

14

Torrential rain had moved in from over the mountains. It was the kind of relentless driving rain that came down in straight gray lances. It told Phaid that somewhere one of the wind bands had moved slightly, shifting in its course. It was only a prolonged storm in Chrystianaville, but out in the countryside, a previously habitable strip of land was either being scorched barren by blasts of superheated air or turned into permafrost by sub-zero gales. Animals would be dying, people fleeing from their homes and maybe even a whole town left standing, abandoned in the face of the savage weather system.

In the city, the rain had come as something of a blessing, at least to the Chrystianaville establishment. It had almost totally damped down the rioting and unrest in the streets. The various factions had taken their revolution indoors to smolder for a while longer in secret.

Things weren't, however, totally quiet. Despite the downpour, the Day Oners managed some sporadic sniping from windows and rooftops. Police stood in wary, disgruntled groups on most main street corners. Transparent rain slickers covered their red riot armor.

A few sullen knots of citizens had also braved the rain. They sheltered in doorways, building entrances and beneath over-passes. The sparse crowds made no moves. They simply stood in silence and stared with damp malice at the squads of police.

Phaid watched all this from inside an autocab. Rain streamed down the outside of the clear plastic passenger bubble and the air inside was humid to the point of being steamy. Phaid, however, wasn't paying very much attention to what was going on either inside or outside the cab. His own troubles took up all his attention. First there had been the dream and his inability to shake the irrational fear that it wasn't a mere nightmare but was some kind of supernatural warning, that somewhere in the city, Makartur was fixing to kill him. After the nightmare it had taken him more than two hours to fall back into fitful, disturbed sleep. Even that didn't last long, however. Some time during the morning the communicator had shrilled him awake again and laid a fresh burden squarely on his shoulders. He was arbitrarily summoned to meet Orsine for dinner that same evening. A summons from the city's top mobster was something one didn't refuse. It wasn't advisable to plead weariness, a sick stomach, a scholomine comedown, abject superstitious fear or the fact that it was raining outside. When Orsine summoned, one went. Thus it was that sunset found Phaid sunk in the back of an autocab, fretting miserably as the android handler made little headway in the totally snarled traffic.

In fits and starts that couldn't have averaged much more than walking pace, the autocab finally made it to a building with a small discreet awning running across the sidewalk. It bore the legend Krager's Eating House. The handler flipped open the passenger door and Phaid dashed towards Krager's entrance, doing his best to get under the awning and into the restaurant before he was soaked through by the pelting rain.

Krager's was one of the few top class eating houses in the city that wasn't totally monopolized by the court and the aristos. Its major patrons were the big men in the mobs, successful entrepreneurs and merchants, and the more overtly corrupt mandarins of the bureaucracy. It had the deep pile and rich

aroma of money. Discreet, peach colored mirrors rewarded the
elegant diners with flattering images of themselves. The lights
were low. Each table was effectively lit by pencil thin glo-bars
that were incorporated in delicate arrangements of flowers.
Thick carpets and heavy red drapes muffled the clink of china,
crystal and cutlery and kept conversations to the limits of their
own tables.

An android head waiter rolled towards Phaid on well-oiled
bearings. Its finish was a gleaming black, and somehow a
permanent expression of disapproval seemed to have been built
into its design.

"Do-you-have-a-reservation?"

"I'm meeting Orsine."

"That-gentleman-has-a-private-room. I-will-have-to-check.
He-maintains-very-careful-security."

The head waiter glided away and Phaid stood waiting, feeling slightly embarrassed. Enough time elapsed for that embarrassment to thoroughly sink in before the head waiter returned
with two bullet headed humans.

Their suits were conservatively tailored, one in lime green
and the other mustard yellow. The knee length, quasi-military
coats strained to accommodate their hulking chests and shoulders. They were obviously two of Orsine's gorillas.

Earlier in the evening, Edelline-Lan had sent her android
Hud-n with Phaid's clothes, neatly cleaned and pressed, and
his fuse tube. He'd put on the clothes he'd bought in Fennella
because the outfit that Edelline-Lan had given him was too
patently designed to make him look like the ever available stud.
It wasn't an image that he particularly wanted to cultivate in
front of Orsine. He'd also hung the fuse tube from his belt
because of the state of affairs on the street.

He thought the clothes were okay, but he started to have
serious second thoughts about the fuse tube. These were confirmed when the first move the gorillas made was to uncere-
moniously pat him down for weapons. Other diners turned and
craned around with interest. Phaid felt his embarrassment go
about as deep as it could, then one of the gorillas hauled out
the fuse tube.

"What's this?"

Phaid tried a defiant stand.

"What does it look like?"

"We don't want to hear any smart remarks. We're asking why you arrive at a meeting with the Adjudicator carrying a heavy duty fuse tube."

"Doesn't everyone carry a weapon at the moment? Sweet Lords, you've seen what it's like out on the street."

The gorillas remained totally impassive.

"You have come to a meeting with the Adjudicator with a heavy duty fuse tube. That is a fact, a fact that is not likely to please the Adjudicator."

Phaid swallowed hard. Within seconds of walking into the eating house he seemed to have got himself into serious trouble with the Silent Cousins. Trouble with the Cousins was quite frequently the last trouble that a person could get into.

The gorillas positioned themselves on either side of him and walked Phaid through the public part of the restaurant. Every eye in the place seemed to be on him. A curtain in the rear was pulled aside by an android waiter. Behind the curtain was a door flanked by two more gorillas. They gave Phaid the heavy eyeball, but, since he was so completely escorted, they made no comment.

The door was opened and Phaid entered a small private room. It was discreetly lit and draped in deep, rich purple. There were only three tables, and just one of them was occupied. Orsine was wearing a sober, businesslike black tabard. Beside him was a very young woman with fluffy light blue hair. She was also dressed in black, but the outfit could in no way be considered businesslike, unless, of course, her business was showing off quite considerable areas of her pale, rather delicate skin.

The back of her gown was cut so low that it dipped well past the base of her spine, and gave anyone who looked a sneak preview of her small rounded bottom. A diamond collar around her throat looked as though it could keep someone in luxury for six months or more.

Phaid, however, wasn't in any mood to look at girls. He was more concerned with getting over the *faux pas* about the fuse tube and keeping all his limbs intact.

Orsine seemed affable enough. He waved Phaid to an empty chair, but then the gorilla who'd confiscated Phaid's weapon stepped in front of him. With more drama than Phaid thought strictly necessary, he placed the tube right in the middle of the table.

There were two more gorillas behind Orsine's chair. They looked from Phaid to the fuse tube and back to Phaid again. It seemed every eye in the room was drilling into him. Only Orsine himself seemed unperturbed. He even half smiled at Phaid.

"What were you planning to do, start a war?"

Phaid did the best he could to conceal that his stomach had turned to jelly.

"I thought, with the way things are out on the street, it would be wise to have a little protection."

Raising his eyebrows, Orsine picked up the fuse tube and felt its weight.

"A little protection?"

"Maybe it is a bit of a cannon, but I've had it with me for a long time."

"And you're fond of it?"

"I wouldn't put it that strongly. I've more grown used to it."

"It's something of a gauche weapon for the city. Most normal people don't go around with something the size of this strapped to their hip. I would strongly suggest that you rid yourself of this long barreled monstrosity and find a more civilized weapon. The other alternative is that you get your man or your android to carry the thing for you."

"I don't have an android and I certainly don't have a man."

Orsine looked at him questioningly.

"I had a distinct recollection of you traveling with an android."

"I had to let him go. He wasn't really mine in the first place."

"I see."

Orsine continued to examine Phaid's weapon.

"You know, the only time it's considered polite to carry one of these is if you're going to fight a duel. Even then, you are supposed to carry a matched pair in a case."

The very last thing that Phaid had expected was for Orsine to give him a lesson in etiquette.

"I'm not likely to have to fight a duel."

"I wouldn't't be so sure. I hear you've been running around with some of the ladies in the court. There's nothing those broads like better than getting two men out dueling." He put his arm around the young woman. "You wouldn't do anything like that, would you, sweetness."

"Of course not, honey."

"This is Sena. Say hello to Phaid, Sena."

Sena glanced at Phaid with a total lack of interest.

"Hello, Phaid."

Phaid had a slight, hopeful feeling that maybe nothing was going to happen to him after all. He looked directly at Orsine.

"You seem to have been checking up on me."

"I like to know what's going on."

"I wouldn't have thought I was important enough."

"One can never assess one's own place in the scheme of things."

Phaid decided it was time to take a now or never chance.

"If you've been checking up on me, you know that I didn't bring that fuse tube with me with any intention of harming you."

Orsine looked at Phaid very hard for a long time.

"Are you nervous, young man?"

For the first time, Phaid saw Orsine as the mobster that he was. Beneath the urbane exterior was a greedy savage who enjoyed inspiring fear and took pleasure in inflicting mental and physical pain. Phaid wished fervently that he'd noticed this before. There was no way to backpedal now. He had no choice but to brazen things out to whatever the bitter end might be.

"I'm still standing, and I'd thought I'd been invited for a meal."

Orsine half smiled. There was little humor in it.

"Indeed, but you arrived for this meal armed to the teeth."

"I've already explained that I was merely protecting myself. I was almost killed in the street yesterday."

"You also burned down some police officers."

Phaid was horrified.

"You know about that?"

"I know about most things, but frankly, police officers are

none of my concern. What does concern me is your lack of good manners. I consider it extremely ill-mannered to come armed to an appointment for dinner."

"I'm sorry."

Orsine ignored Phaid and turned to the nearest gorilla.

"You think you could give this young man a lesson in manners?"

The gorilla smiled nastily and cracked his knuckles.

"Just say the word, Adjudicator."

Phaid felt sick. There wasn't much point in keeping up a brave front any longer. There seemed to be no doubt that he was going to get his legs broken or worse. Then, to his surprise, Orsine smiled at him for the second time.

"What about you, young man, do you think that you need a lesson in manners?"

Phaid knew his next words were crucial. They were the only things that might get him off a very sharp and unpleasant hook. He chose them with extreme care.

"I'm not going to forget what's happened today in a hurry. I don't think it needs any reinforcing. I'm truly sorry that I brought a weapon to your table. It was an error but not made with any intention of insulting you."

There was a long silence which, to Phaid's amazement, was finally broken by Sena.

"Ah, let him sit down, will you, honey? He didn't mean any harm, and besides, he's kind of cute."

Phaid's jaw almost dropped as Orsine suddenly beamed.

"If that's the way you want it, baby." He waved a pudgy hand at Phaid. "Sit down, boy, sit down. Just don't pull nothing like that again, you hear?"

Phaid nodded and lowered himself shakily into the indicated chair. He could scarcely believe that his being torn limb from limb had been averted simply by the whim of Orsine's mistress. From that point on it was as if the incident over the fuse tube had never happened, although the weapon still lay in the middle of the table and served as a mute reminder to Phaid, if nobody else.

An android was summoned and menus were handed around. The variety of dishes was both impressive and frighteningly expensive. Phaid's adrenaline was still pumping so fast that he didn't feel capable of thinking about choosing, let alone eating a meal. Fortunately, Orsine took total control.

"The chef here is human. One of the few in the city who really knows what he's doing."

Orsine leaned confidingly towards Phaid.

"You never want to trust an android chef. All they have is programming. There's no feel, no magic, no inspiration. How could they have? They never eat. They don't know what we're looking for in a good meal. Consequently, they don't have the touch."

The human chef was as much cabaret as cuisine. He performed for the diners' applause. Orsine's private room came equipped with its own chef's workbench on a raised platform. To Phaid, it looked like a combination of altar, alchemist's workship and kitchen counter.

The glo-bars that illuminated the tables dimmed slightly. A set of small spotlights set in the ceiling brightened, making the platform the focal point of the whole room.

The chef entered through a small door at the rear of the platform. He was accompanied by an assistant, and both had the ponderous theatrical poses of an officiating priest and acolyte.

The chef watched impassively as the assistant laid out the ingredients, then he went to work with a flourish. The chef was a short man with the flat features and narrow slanting eyes that marked him as one of the Tharmiers who lived on the wide fertile coast plain beyond the great icefield, the one that formed the southern boundary of the Republic.

Despite a rather overdeveloped sense of ritual, they were an easygoing, sensual people who had made the satisfying of the physical pleasures into a high art. Their cooks could perform near miracles. They could always count on first-class appointments and generous retainers if they felt like leaving their homeland and hiring out their skills elsewhere. Others who crossed the icefield to take positions as courtesans were among the most prized and successful that could be found in any city.

The chef's hands moved at lightning speed among bowls, pots and glass containers. He chopped, mixed, blended and stirred amid rising steam and brief explosions of pale fire. He spun and tossed and wielded his knives and stirring rod with the unerring dexterity of a master. The private room was filled with a rich, tantalizing aroma. Even Phaid, who had thought that the shocks of the evening had completely killed his appetite, started looking forward to the meal.

Finally the chef was finished. He exited through the same door by which he had entered, with a great deal of flamboyant bowing. The assistant was left to serve the guests.

Only Orsine, Phaid and Sena had food placed in front of them. The gorillas all remained standing. They were clearly Orsine's private guard and they didn't join him for meals. Phaid didn't feel exactly comfortable eating with all this security around him, but this was more than compensated for by the exquisite dishes that arrived with precision timing.

The meal was conducted in silence. It was the silence that comes only when food demands total concentration. Eating was such a sensual experience that it eliminated the need for conversation.

When each and every dish was empty, and glasses of clear mexan liqueur were flamed by the chef and placed in front of each guest, Orsine pushed back his chair with a satisfied, almost bloated smile.

"One of the few recompenses for a life of unrelenting toil and responsibility is that I get to dine well."

Sena fractionally curled the left corner of a perfect upper lip in what had to be the start of a carefully constructed sneer.

"Not the only recompense, I hope."

For an instant, Orsine looked at her questioningly. Right on cue, her eyes melted into wide, goo-goo innocence. He ran a pudgy hand down her back.

"Of course not, honey, of course not."

Sena arched her spine and virtually purred. Phaid wondered if the woman was totally infatuated with the Adjudicator or simply, in her own way, doing as good a job as the chef. Phaid wasn't, however, left much time to speculate. Orsine was once again scrutinizing him.

"So, Master Phaid, how do you find our city after so long an absence?"

"Somewhat of a mess, I'm afraid."

"You're not another one who thinks that revolution is just around the corner."

"I haven't seen enough to make a final judgment. It certainly seems as though there is a lot wrong with this city. Don't you worry about the possibility of revolution?"

Orsine, who had been idly staring down the front of Sena's dress, looked up sharply.

"Worried? Why should I be worried? A revolution would mean little or nothing to me. I frankly don't give a damn if Chrystiana-Nex is dragged screaming from the palace and the whole court is put against the wall and blasted. This city cannot function without my organization. Whoever takes over will realize that pretty damn quick. Deals can always be made."

Phaid scratched his ear.

"The Day Oners seem to be talking in terms of a whole new start, of tearing down everything."

Orsine dismissed the Day Oners with a snort.

"They'll never achieve power. They'll never achieve it because they're mad. They're a fringe, a lunatic minority. Anyone who aspires to power must know that, even if he used madmen, his very first task, once the old order has been run out, is to destroy those madmen, destroy them totally."

Phaid wondered if Orsine had a few dreams of his own of taking up residence in the Presidential Palace. It wasn't beyond the bounds of possibility. A mobster run Republic might be a pleasanter place than one ruled over by an insane woman. With unusual bravery, he decided that it wouldn't hurt to gently test the water.

"Maybe that's what you'd do. Others might not be so smart."

Orsine's eyes narrowed, then he suddenly laughed.

"You're a perceptive young man. Perhaps you'd better tell me what you've heard about me in your wanderings around the city."

Despite the laughter, Phaid knew that once again he was moving into dangerous territory. He did his best to look as innocent as possible.

"I've only been in the city for a few days. I doubt I would have heard anything you don't already know."

"Don't try and con me, I'm too old for that sort of thing. What have you heard?"

"Only scraps."

"What, damn you?"

Phaid didn't seem to be able to win against the Adjudicator.
The old man was the perfect blend of paranoia and cunning.

"I heard that you had your troubles."

"Troubles?"

"That subordinates were jealous of your position."

"Scarlin-Fell?"

"The name was mentioned."

"I'll wager it was."

"Is he a danger?"

"He's ambitious. He'd like to be where I am, but he hasn't
a chance."

"You plan to get rid of him?"

Orsine shook his head and smiled, a smile that sent shivers
through Phaid's scalp.

"The Adjudicator doesn't get rid of ambitious subordinates.
This isn't the court. The secret of success is to attract inferiors
who, in their inadequacy, choose to promote you because it
will gain them advantage. If, however, one of those inferiors
climbs above his station, then you have to crush him like a
bug."

For the first time, Phaid had the suspicion that maybe Orsine
was also touched by the madness that prevailed in the city.

"That would be an incentive to stay in one's place."

Orsine regarded Phaid as a teacher might regard a bright
pupil.

"Let's hope Scarlin-Fell is as intelligent as you are, for his
own good."

For a moment, Orsine looked frighteningly grim, and then
his expression suddenly changed.

"But enough of my problems. I want to hear more of what
you've observed around our fair but disturbed city."

Phaid shrugged.

"What can I tell you? The population seems restless. The
court is decadent, the government has ceased to function and
the President has apparently gone mad. You know all this already."

"What do you know of Solchaim?"

"Solchaim?"

The name of the elaihi was cropping up in conversation a
little too regularly to be strictly coincidental. Orsine leaned

241

towards Phaid. The air of menace was back and directed straight at him.

"Don't play coy with me, boy. I have it on good authority that you've encountered elaihim on your travels, and I want to know all about them. A lot of the problems in this city go back to this Solchaim. It seems that no one can touch him. I want to know what makes these creatures tick."

Phaid was starting to wonder if he was the only person in the city who had ever met elaihim face to face and just how much the experience was worth. There followed a question and answer session that almost completely paralleled the one that Roni-Vows had conducted the previous day. Orsine was a little more probing and a great deal shrewder than the courtier, but the information he wanted was exactly the same. Phaid was now certain that Solchaim had to be the key to what was going on in the city. He wasn't sure how or why, but people seemed awfully anxious to pump him on the subject. Phaid knew that he should capitalize on his knowledge. He just wasn't sure how. There had to be more in it than a traumatic free meal or a shot of scholomine.

Just as the interrogation was drawing to a close, Phaid was aware of a high-pitched buzzing noise at the very edge of his hearing range. At first he wondered if it was his imagination, some aftereffect of the scholomine he'd taken the night before. Then he saw the gorillas starting to get edgy and glance nervously at each other. Finally Orsine noticed and swung around angrily.

"What the hell is that sound? Will somebody do something about it?"

As though on cue, the sound suddenly rose to a deafening roar. A section of wall glowed bright cherry red, fragmented and then crumbled and cascaded into the room. It was accompanied by a billowing cloud of smoke and dust through which four masked figures suddenly appeared.

"Day One! Day One!"

They had blasters in their hands and obviously meant business. The first one through the gaping hole in the wall burned down the nearest gorilla at point blank range.

There was a frozen moment in the room when everyone seemed too shocked to do anything. Then a second gorilla was taken out by the intruders' weapons. The stench of burned flesh replaced the lingering aroma of food. Orsine was suddenly galvanized into action. He dived sideways, pushing Sena roughly away from him, clean off her chair and on to the floor. At the same time, he upended the table, scattering its contents. The overweight gourmet was suddenly showing all the reflexes of a violent, street fighting past.

As the table tilted, Phaid's fuse tube slid towards him. He grabbed the weapon and threw himself backwards as hard as he could. He hit the ground with much more force than he'd intended. It knocked all the breath out of him and for an instant he thought he'd broken his back.

The three of the Adjudicator's guards stationed outside burst into the room with weapons in their hands. They hesitated in the doorway, trying to make out what was going on through the clouds of dust and smoke. It was a fatal hesitation. The intruders' blasters roared again and all three were cut down, spinning backwards and collapsing like puppets with cut strings.

Orsine had a tiny fuse tube in his hand. He fired and rolled sideways. An intruder screamed and staggered. The carpet burned as three blasts hit the spot where he'd previously been lying. The last of his gorillas was caught in the crossfire. He grimaced and clutched his arm, but stayed on his feet. His blaster roared and a second intruder went down.

Phaid, who'd been flat on his back trying to breathe, was aware of a figure standing over him leveling a blaster. Phaid shot desperately from the hip, without even aiming. To his surprise, he caught the intruder full in the chest.

Phaid scrambled quickly to his feet. There was now only one attacker still standing. Not liking the odds of three to one, the intruder darted for the door. He was stopped, however, by the blue lash of a stun blast. Two android waiters were standing there, presumably to keep the violence from spreading to the rest of the eating house.

Orsine walked slowly to the stunned Day Oner. He coldly pointed his fuse tube and pumped a long discharge into the still living body. Then he turned to look at Phaid. Phaid hoped that he would never be the one to cause a man to look the way Orsine did at that moment.

"Scarlin-Fell has finally overreached himself. It is now time to crush bugs."

Phaid was bewildered.

"I don't follow you. Surely these people were Day Oners."

Orsine laughed. It wasn't a pleasant laugh.

"That's what you're supposed to think."

"It is?"

"Look at their shoes. Look at the clothes under those filthy duster coats. They've expensive suits; no shirtless Day Oners can afford stuff like this." He bent down and picked up the limp arm of one of the corpses. "This one even has a manicure and nail polish."

For the first time, Phaid realized that one of the attackers was a woman. Orsine let the arm fall back. He had an expression of disgust.

"Day Oners, bah! These are a hit squad from Scarlin-Fell, a particularly inefficient hit squad into the bargain. The organization is well rid of them. This whole episode has the greasy fingermarks of Scarlin-Fell all over it. I can just imagine the way he thought it out. Let the old fool gorge himself, and take him when he's stuffed and drowsy. He's going to learn to his cost that the old fool isn't so easy to take." He noticed something among the wreckage on the other side of the room.

"Sweet Lords! Sena!"

The girl was lying against the remains of the chef's workbench. Her body was unpleasantly twisted.

"She's dead! The bastards have killed Sena, and just when I had her almost trained to perfection." He glared angrily at Phaid. "Do you realize just how long it takes for me to get a woman to do exactly what I want? Scarlin-Fell is not only going to die, he's going to take a long time doing it."

Phaid suddenly sat down. A delayed reaction to the last few minutes had hit him hard. A small concerned crowd gathered around Orsine, but Phaid appeared to have been completely forgotten. He could scarcely believe the course that his life was taking. He had only been in the city for three days and it seemed to have turned into a nonstop round of violence punctuated by brisk intervals of sex. If asked, Phaid would have sworn his most solemn oath that, by nature, he was the kind of man who would go out of his way to avoid trouble, and yet for a long time, wherever he went, trouble seemed to surround him. It was as though he was some weird catalyst, a carrier of some mania who, although showing no symptoms himself, infected all those around him.

Orsine was conducted out of the restaurant and a team of androids and boohooms started to clear up the mess. It was only then that someone remembered Phaid, and saw that he got an autocab back to his hotel. Two things were waiting for him on his return. One was an android produced printout reminding him that he only had one more prepaid day left on his account and hinting that he ought to think about either putting up or moving out. This was depressing, particularly as it also served to remind Phaid that he was close to broke and almost completely without prospects. The other surprise package was a note from Roni-Vows suggesting that, should Phaid choose to meet him at the Palace Plaza at noon of the following day, he might learn something to his advantage. It was handwritten on lilac paper and signed with a small delicate drawing of a butterfly.

This didn't do much to cheer Phaid either. All he could hope was that "learning something to his advantage" was a euphemism for a cash payment. It was this hope that brought him out of the hotel on a blustery morning. The rain had stopped and the sun was trying to break through the cloud. In half an hour he was stepping out of an autocab on the edge of the Plaza just a few minutes before twelve. The Palace Plaza was a broad circular expanse of multicolored flagstones raised some eight or nine meters above the level of the avenue. One reached the Plaza by climbing the steps that extended around half the perimeter on the side facing away from the Palace. The steps were broken at regular intervals by ornamental waterfalls and fanciful sculptures.

At one time, the centerpiece of the whole Plaza had been a very large and very heroic statue of the previous president. Shortly after his death, Chrystiana-Nex had taken it into her head to have it removed. The removal had been a clumsy affair. A large crowd had gathered while a squad of sweating workmen sawed the deceased off at the ankles and carted him away, presumably to be melted down. After that, though, the work inexplicably stopped and the centerpiece remained, from then on, as a plinth with a pair of large, incongruous feet mounted on it.

The Palace side of the Plaza formed one wall of the deep, dry moat that surrounded the whole building. It was spanned by a wide curving ramp that swept up to the entrance itself.

Rumor had it that the ramp was permanently mined so it could be blown in the event of a mob attempting to storm the Presidential residence.

Phaid had never particularly liked the Palace. He found its tiered facade, a jumble of pillars and bas-relief, fussily tasteless. Injury had been added to insult when a large section of what must have been the fourth story had been torn out and an enormous holoscreen installed in order for the President to address her devoted followers. For the last year or more, however, the screen had remained ominously blank.

On any normal day, the Plaza could be expected to be thronged with people. Some would stroll, others sit, musicians and jugglers would solicit money from passersby, hawkers would display a variety of wares and many citizens could be found standing in line with petitions and favors that they sought from members of the court.

Traditionally, the more populist courtiers would set up shop near the Palace ramp where, surrounded by small knots of androids and advisors, they would listen to the complaints of the common people.

This particular day, however, was far from normal. The trouble and unrest that hung in the air had virtually cleared the Plaza. A few civil servants or courtiers hurried on their way to and from the Palace, a few of the incorrigibly curious hung around staring, but it was the police who now completely dominated the open space.

The Palace seemed to be preparing for siege. Police, both in riot armor and the more normal red jump suits, were all over the Plaza. Phaid had rarely seen such a dense concentration of manpower and weaponry. The majority of cops seemed watchful and tense. There was much club flexing and weapon checking. A pair of police flippers were grounded near the base of the ramp. This in itself showed how seriously the authorities were taking the emergency. Previously, the idea of any kind of vehicle on the Plaza was unheard of.

As Phaid walked towards the ramp looking for Roni-Vows, he noticed that jolt relays had been set up at regular intervals across the open space and continued on, presumably all around the Palace. They weren't activated, but, at the touch of a control, all approaches to the building could be crisscrossed by a web of non-lethal, but very painful fields of energy.

Phaid wondered why Roni-Vows had picked such an exposed and public place for the meeting. The thought crossed his mind that it could be some kind of setup, but Phaid dismissed it. What could the courtier possibly gain from dropping him into trouble?

As well as the police, squads of the Presidential Guard were also in evidence. Phaid had always found them a little incongruous in their scarlet and gold, their flowing plumes, epaulets and visored helmets. The highly efficient fuse tubes that nestled in their decorative shoulder holsters made it very clear, though, that they were there for something more than merely ceremonial purposes.

They had set up two small photon cannons at the top of the ramp, positioned in such a way that they could rake the entire Plaza if the need arose. More of the guard manned a checkpoint at the base of the ramp. It was equipped with a weapon detector and an android scrutineer. The android would be programmed with the descriptions of wanted criminals and known troublemakers. Phaid decided on principle to give this unit a wide berth.

It was now some minutes after twelve and there was still no sign of Roni-Vows. Phaid gave himself a mild mental kick for not remembering how the courtiers' code decreed that one should be late for every appointment. Neither was it a good day for standing around in the open. The excess of police activity made Phaid less than comfortable, and even the weather left much to be desired. Although the previous day's rain had stopped, there was still a damp blustery wind and a leaden overcast sky. It was the kind of day that would bring few people any good.

After some more waiting, he spotted a figure with Roni-Vows' unmistakable swishing walk coming out of the Palace. Phaid waited until he passed the checkpoint and then moved to meet him.

"How are you doing?"

Roni-Vows scowled.

"Managing to hold my own. You?"

"I'm keeping busy."

Roni-Vows took Phaid by the arm and steered him across

Mick Farren

the Plaza. He seemed to be trying to make it look like they were two old friends out for a casual stroll. But in the middle of the display of police it was a trifle incongruous. Phaid glanced questioningly at him.

"Isn't it kind of exposed out here?"

"I didn't think it was a good idea for us to be seen together in a tavern or an eating house. You can't set an electronic eavesdropper in the open."

"Yeah, but . . . in the middle of all this?"

"The police are on our side. You must remember that."

"On your side maybe."

"Just relax. I know what I'm doing."

"Hmmm."

They continued the awkward stroll. Phaid still felt intimidated by the police presence.

"Did it ever occur to you that it might be time to call off the cops and start talking?"

Roni-Vows twitched.

"What do you know?"

"Nothing."

"You haven't heard anything?"

"What should I hear?"

"You seem to know a good deal for someone who just blew into town."

Phaid shrugged.

"I'm just observant and I try to keep my smarts about me."

"It wasn't too smart to fuse a couple of cops."

Phaid looked quickly around to see if anyone had overheard.

"Will you keep your goddamn voice down? You could get me killed. Where did you hear that, anyway?"

"I'm observant too."

"More likely you talked to Abrella-Lu."

"As a matter-of-fact, I had to get her out of jail. She was playing at prostitutes, but then she started acting so outrageously that one of her clients cried cop."

"That's our girl."

"Don't I know it."

Phaid glanced around. The proximity of so many police was making him profoundly uncomfortable.

"Listen, I don't want to appear rude or gauche and I know

248

that long preambles before you get down to business are compulsory in elegant society, but standing about on this open plaza isn't my favorite occupation. You said you wanted to see me and that it would be to my advantage. I don't see any advantage hanging around here, so could we get to it?"

Roni-Vows raised an eyebrow.

"You're very impatient."

"Look, if we have to fence around, could we possibly do it someplace else?"

Roni-Vows shook his head.

"I can't possibly stray from the Palace, with things the way they are."

"Lord's teeth!"

Phaid was starting to get angry. Roni-Vows suddenly looked serious.

"I have a job for you."

"A job?"

Roni-Vows' fingers fluttered.

"Maybe not so much a job, more a roving commission."

"Come to the point. What do you want?"

"Information."

"Information. What information could I have?"

"As you said, you're observant and you keep your smarts about you. In addition you also move fairly freely through a number of levels of the city. Have you had any contact with the rebels?"

"Rebels?"

"The underground, the revolution, these damned rioters, call them what you like."

Phaid shook his head.

"None at all."

"Could you?"

Phaid shrugged.

"Anything's possible."

"Could you if it was made worth your trouble—fiscally?" Roni-Vows rolled the word around his tongue. Phaid regarded him dubiously.

"Is this what you want me to do? Get in with the rebels and spy on them?"

"Nothing as drastic as that. I just want you to move around

in the way that you normally do and keep your eyes and ears open. Any little snippet of information you might pick up should be reported to me. Such information would, of course, be paid for in hard cash."

"That's the offer?"

"In brief."

Phaid thought about it. It was a little close to being a hired informer, but the mention of hard cash did quite a lot to minimize his distaste.

"What guarantee do you have that I haven't already thrown in with the rebels?"

"You haven't."

"But I might."

"The only person you'd throw in with would be yourself. You're a loner, my young friend."

"You seem very sure of yourself."

"I am."

Phaid suddenly smiled.

"Okay, Roni-Vows. You've got a deal, for the moment, although this all sounds exceedingly desperate."

"I have to admit that our backs are getting uncomfortably close to the wall."

"You think the rebels are winning?"

"No, but they're shaking up an already perilously fragile structure."

Phaid nodded and then suddenly laughed.

"I tell you what, I've already got a little tidbit that ought to be worth something. There was an assassination attempt on Orsine the mobster last night."

"At Krager's Eating House."

Phaid was a little crestfallen.

"You knew already."

"Since dawn."

"Did you also know that he blames Scarlin-Fell and is planning to kill him?"

"That's news."

Phaid smiled.

"I have my uses."

"Unfortunately Scarlin-Fell was killed by Day Oners in the early hours of this morning. They set fire to his flipper and he was burned to death. By all accounts it was an unpleasant business."

"They must have beat Orsine to him."

Phaid didn't believe this. He suspected that the Day Oners were more likely to be Orsine's hirelings in disguise, exacting an efficient, poetic and agonizing revenge. He didn't, however, intend to let Roni-Vows know about his theory.

Roni-Vows himself seemed to be getting impatient.

"Is there anything else?"

"There is one thing." Phaid hesitated. "Well..."

"What?"

"I could use an advance."

Phaid didn't like having to ask Roni-Vows for money. Roni-Vows raised his head and deliberately looked down his nose at Phaid.

"You're broke."

"Close to it."

"You haven't given me anything valuable as yet."

"You going to start to haggle?"

"Why not."

"Because I know you think that I'm valuable to you, and there's always the chance that you and the rest of the court may not be in business much longer. If the rebels don't get you, your president almost certainly will. In any case, I'm no use to you if I don't have the money to move around. You should look on it as an investment."

Roni-Vows looked as though Phaid was coming uncomfortably close to the truth.

"You could be right at that. How much do you want?"

"A thousand."

"Don't be ridiculous."

"You can afford it."

"Five hundred."

Phaid sighed grudgingly.

"Five hundred."

Instantly Roni-Vows produced a flat leather wallet from under his coat.

"Five hundred."

Phaid's eyes widened in surprise.

"You had it ready?"

"I'm not as dumb as I might appear. I'd have been very disappointed if you had come up with any other figure."

Phaid was discomfited.

"I asked for a thousand."

"That was only a preliminary."

"Yeah, well, I guess you just bought me."

"Guess I did."

Phaid silently promised himself that Roni-Vows would in no way get a fair shake for his five hundred. He was stuffing the wallet away in his coat when he noticed that Roni-Vows was staring down Nex Boulevard. He showed signs of apprehension. Phaid turned and looked in the same direction.

The first thing that he saw was a number of police flippers hanging at the maximum operating height of about four storys. They seemed to be keeping watch on a mass of people at the other end of the Boulevard. All around where Phaid was standing the police were stiffening and readying their weapons. The Boulevard was rapidly clearing of traffic. Whatever was happening at the other end of Nex Boulevard had plugged the normally constant flow of flippers and transports. Phaid felt he had to do something, but he didn't have a clear idea of exactly what. Then Roni-Vows touched him on the arm.

"Do you know anything about this?"

Phaid shook his head.

"Don't have a clue."

Roni-Vows waved to a police underleader wearing a comset attached to his helmet.

"What's going on?"

"Who wants to know?"

Roni-Vows drew himself up to his full height. It didn't amount to much beside the hulking officer.

"My name is Roni-Vows, and I'm an innercircle courtier quite capable of having your brassard if you don't pay me the respect due."

The underleader didn't look particularly impressed, but also didn't seem to want to bother with an argument.

"We don't know for sure. They're calling it a requiem march."

"What the hell's a requiem march?"

The cop shrugged.

"Who knows what the bastards will do? It's supposed to be

some kind of memorial to the ones that got themselves killed in the riots. If it was me, I'd be celebrating. Anything that means there's less of the scumsuckers is good in my book."

Phaid glanced sharply at the underleader.

"Ain't those scumsuckers the people you're supposed to be protecting?"

The underleader's face twisted into an ugly sneer.

"Don't make me laugh." He jerked an armored thumb in the direction of the Palace. "That's where my bread gets buttered, and that's what I protect. The rest are scumsuckers as far as I'm concerned."

Roni-Vows ignored the exchange and pressed for more information.

"Are they peaceful?"

"So far. The main body of the march is supposed to be women. They're all dressed up in mourning robes. The trouble is that they're coming this way. We haven't intervened yet, but we got orders to keep them out of the Plaza. If they take it into their heads to go all the way to the Palace..." he hefted his blaster "...they'll find that they have certain problems."

Phaid was suddenly very, very frightened. He once again peered down the Boulevard. It was clear now that a large dark mass of humanity was slowly filling Nex Boulevard and moving steadily but relentlessly towards the Palace. Phaid looked to Roni-Vows for the next move.

"What are you going to do?"

"I want to see what this turns into."

"I've got an idea of what this is going to turn into and I'd hate to be out here when it does."

Roni-Vows nodded.

"I think maybe I'll get myself back inside the Palace."

"Do I get to go with you?"

Roni-Vows shook his head.

"I'm afraid not, you'd never get past the security."

"You mean you're going to leave me out here while all hell breaks loose and you scuttle back into the Palace? You've got the influence. You could swing something."

"There's nothing I can do. The Palace is shut up tight as a drum."

"Shit!"

Phaid stared down Nex Boulevard. The crowd was about halfway down the length of it and still coming. Phaid could spot splashes of brilliant orange, the traditional color of mourning in and around the Republic. The police flippers were still maintaining their hovering positions above the marchers.

Roni-Vows made a nervous gesture.

"I've got to be going."

Phaid grunted and didn't even bother to look at the courtier. Roni-Vows seemed, for a moment, as though he was going to say something, then he changed his mind and hurried towards the ramp.

An eerie quiet had descended on the area around the Palace. The crowd moved in near silence. There were no chants. No shouting. The only sound was the shuffling of thousands of feet and the low whine of the police flippers.

The cops on the Plaza deployed themselves for action. Leaders and underleaders barked orders. There was the crash of metallic boots and the rattle of armor as they took up their positions. A double line sealed the end of Nex Boulevard, separating the crowd from the Palace. More police remained on the Plaza as a backup to the front line.

The tension was working its way up to an intolerable level and Phaid was right in the middle of the cops' tactical pattern. What made it doubly worse was that he now knew that the majority of cops probably thought of him as an expendable scumsucker.

The police stood silently, blasters at the ready. The march continued to roll forward. Phaid looked around for a way out. Before he found one, the underleader to whom Roni-Vows had talked grasped him by the arm.

"What are you still doing here?"

"Looking for a way out."

"I take it that you ain't no courtier that can get me busted to the ranks."

Phaid sadly shook his head.

"Not me."

"Then you only get one way out, friend."

Phaid found himself propelled none too gently towards the front line of police. At an order from the underleader, two men stepped back and Phaid was thrust out into the no-man's-land between the police and the marchers.

Despite the danger that he was in, Phaid's strongest emotion was an acute feeling of being totally ridiculous. He obviously couldn't stay where he was, but there was something completely absurd about one man walking down a wide empty avenue to meet a marching crowd many thousands strong.

Some of the front ranks looked at him curiously, but Phaid avoided their eyes. The march swallowed him up and he gratefully worked his way to the back. By the time he'd found a position in which he felt comfortable, the front ranks were less than a hundred meters from the police.

As the underleader had told Roni-Vows, the majority of the marchers were indeed women. They were all ages and came from all levels of Chrystianaville society, only the very upper extremes were not represented.

Solid housewives rubbed shoulders with street women, well fed young girls linked arms with elderly crones from the northside. Some wore their street clothes, others long duster coats that had become an unofficial uniform for the rebels. The highest proportion of the marchers, however, were wrapped in the traditional mourning robe, the orange that was supposed to symbolize the life giving power of the sun, and the black trim that was a reminder that even the sun was ringed around by darkness.

Although the marchers' intent seemed to be peaceful enough, many had come prepared for trouble. Breathing masks and protective helmets made an incongruous picture under the cowls of a lot of the robes.

There were men with the march, but most of them walked on the outside edges. They were more like an escort than an actual part of the protest. Phaid did his best to blend in with them. In the rear ranks, nobody seemed to take much notice that he'd joined the procession from the front.

The march was some fifty meters from the police line when the screen in front of the Palace suddenly came alive in a flurry of menacing abstract shapes.

A thunderously amplified voice boomed out. It must have been audible to everyone in the crowd.

"THIS GATHERING HAS BEEN DECLARED ILLEGAL! YOU WILL DISPERSE IMMEDIATELY!"

The leading marchers faltered for a few moments, then their resolution seemed to crystallize. They continued to move forward. The voice crashed out again.

"THIS GATHERING HAS BEEN DECLARED ILLEGAL! YOU WILL DISPERSE IMMEDIATELY!"

This time there was no hesitation. The crowd went on steadily walking. The police snapped shut the visors on their helmets. The voice came for a third time.

"YOU HAVE IGNORED TWO WARNINGS! THERE WILL BE NO MORE AFTER THIS! IF YOU DO NOT DISPERSE IMMEDIATELY, THE POLICE WILL BE INSTRUCTED TO USE ALL NECESSARY FORCE TO BREAK UP THIS GATHERING!"

The front ranks slowed to a halt. The marchers behind continued to move forward. There was some pushing and shoving, but then the message spread rapidly back and the entire march finally came to a standstill. For a while there was an eerie silence.

Scattered women among the crowd started to sing. The singing was without any words, a kind of low, anguished crooning that rose and fell according to no definable pattern. More and more women joined in. The sound grew until it filled all the air, a total embodiment of loss and desolation. Phaid knew that it was the song for the dead. Its origins went back far beyond the city and the foundation of the Republic. Women sang the song when Chrystianaville had been nothing more than a meeting place of nomadic tribes.

The voice blasted back at the signing women.

"YOU HAVE TEN SECONDS TO DISPERSE! REPEAT, TEN SECONDS! YOU HAVE BEEN WARNED!"

The women continued to sing. A few of the cops started to look profoundly uncomfortable. Their blasters dipped and their menacing stance slumped. They began to show signs of uncertainty. Some of the women in the front ranks picked up on the change. They began to shout over the singing.

"Are you going to blast women in mourning?"

"Are you that far gone?"

"Chrystiana-Nex has bought your souls!"

"Your mother might be in this crowd!"

More and more of the police began to show signs of indecision. They were no longer an implacable line of armor.

Phaid could scarcely believe what he was seeing. It was starting to look as though the police were going to lower their blasters and, if not go over to the rebels, at least do nothing to stop them. Then the voice roared out again.

"POLICE PREPARE TO ADVANCE!"

Quite a few of them stiffened at the order, but, significantly, quite a few didn't.

"ADVANCE ON LINE!"

About half of the police front line took a step forward. The other half didn't move. There was hesitation, confusion. Phaid stood on tiptoe to get a better look. Incredibly, it seemed as though the women had won. The individual cops weren't going to move in on the crowd. They were ignoring their orders.

Then there was a commotion among the front ranks of marchers. Phaid craned to see what was going on. About a dozen women in a tight group were storming towards the wavering police. They were shouting something and pulling weapons from under their mourning robes.

"Day One! Day One!"

They opened fire on the police. Bodies started falling. Phaid closed his eyes in horror. He could hear himself yelling.

"No! No! Don't be so fucking stupid!"

The Day One women gave the police something they could focus on. They snapped back into their normal role of unthinking, disciplined aggression. All the tension and confusion of the previous minutes were released in one flaming roar. The cops let go with every weapon they had.

All of the Day Oners were cut down in the first eruption of police fire. They weren't the only ones to get it. The police didn't bother to be selective. There were screams as many of the front ranks of marchers were hit. The previously orderly crowd broke in panic and started bolting in every direction. Phaid was pushed hard against a wall by a huge screaming matron who ran straight into him.

At the same moment the police flippers overhead discharged a rain of heavy, brightly colored, yellow and purple gas. The billowing clouds cascaded down on to the crowds below like an evil enveloping fog.

15

Clawed demons from some childhood nightmare were ripping at Phaid's flesh. Their eyes burned hellfire red in the sockets of skull-like faces. Yellow fangs dripped with corrosive slime. Hysteria was welling up in his chest. It threatened to burst his ribcage and blow him apart. He wanted to scream and scream until his eyes split open and he could no longer see the demons or feel the pain.

The last few shreds of his tattered sanity told him that there weren't really demons all around him, that they were a result of his being gassed. It had to be a psychotropic crowd breaker of some kind.

He kept repeating this over and over. He was sane. There were no demons. He'd just been gassed. The demons faded slightly. Phaid discovered that he was lying on the ground on his left side with his knees pulled tight up to his chest.

Reality was almost as ghastly as the nightmare fantasy. Those marchers who had breathing masks were fighting a pitched battle with the police. The ones like Phaid who didn't were kicking and screaming on the ground, battling with their worst private horrors. Some had rolled into tight fetal balls, too badly affected by the gas to even struggle.

A woman had fallen near Phaid. Her head was bleeding where she had been hit by a police club. Phaid crawled over beside her and felt for a pulse. He couldn't find one, so, without further compunction, he removed her breathing mask and pulled it over his own head.

He took three or four deep lungfuls of filtered air. His head cleared a little and the last of the demons slunk away. He was sick to his stomach, his head throbbed and his eyes streamed uncontrollably, but he could at least see what was going on.

What was going on didn't please Phaid very much. About the only consolation was that the battle was being fought by those who could still stand. Phaid decided to stay out of it for the present by remaining on the ground with the dead and injured.

A lot of the women marchers had been killed by the police, even more had succumbed to the gas. Despite all this, though, the police were falling back. The sheer weight of numbers of the marchers on Nex Boulevard were too much for them. They were retreating back on to the Plaza.

There were outbreaks of shooting as the police withdrew. Some seemed determined to make a fight of it, but others had simply lowered their weapons and were edging back in the face of the advancing women.

Someone on the women's side had got hold of a hailer and was talking to the cops.

"Our fight isn't with you. It's with the madwoman who calls herself President and her flunkies. We should not be fighting each other. We are all citizens and we all have suffered under the tyrant. Put down your weapons. There is no need for us to fight."

Phaid wasn't particularly impressed with the standard of rhetoric, but it appeared to be working on the cops. One by one they lowered their blasters and spread their hands, not so much in surrender, but more in an indication that they weren't willing to go on.

Phaid got shakily to his feet and joined the throng that was moving out on to the Plaza. His legs were like jelly and he stumbled frequently.

All the Day Oners on the march must have been killed during the first frenzy. Certainly there was no one leaping forward, weapons blazing, to challenge the unsteady truce with the police. Phaid couldn't see how the extremist faction could last much longer if their revolutionary tactics were always as suicidal as the examples he had witnessed.

Nobody seemed to know quite what to do with the truce. The carnage had been too great for jubilation over a glorious victory. Everyone on the Plaza seemed a little stunned. Now the Palace was right in front of them and the crowd hesitated. It was almost as though they'd never expected to get as far, and now they didn't know what to do.

Without warning, the screen in front of the Palace flickered into life. A huge full face image of Chrystiana-Nex stared down on the Plaza like a grim, angry goddess.

It wasn't the image that Phaid or anyone else was used to. It didn't have the careful lighting and expertly applied cosmetics of the usual propaganda loops. This was the President as she really was, with wrinkles and blemishes. It was clear from the look in her eyes that she was quite, quite mad.

Phaid could see how she might have once been powerfully attractive, so powerfully attractive that she had seduced a whole nation into giving her ultimate power. She wasn't a handsome woman. She was thin to the point of being bony. Her proud neck was starting to wattle. Her platinum hair was scraped back in a way that added prominence to her already prominent cheekbones.

All her magnetism must have come from her mouth and her eyes. Both were excessively large. Her mouth could once have been sensuous, promising the far limits of deep crimson delights. Now it was a steel trap ringed with magenta lip color. Her eyes also had the potential to make promises of glory but were now solely concentrated on chilling destruction. They were eyes that could not be ignored. They had the hypnotic quality of fixing whomever they were looking at and making it impossible for them to turn away.

261

Mick Farren

The eyes that glared across the Plaza were as hard as pale sapphires. They seemed to be compelling everyone present to look towards the screen.

"You are traitors."

The voice was a deep, throaty contralto. It started softly but gradually rose in both volume and stridence.

"Traitors!" Chrystiana-Nex may have been crazy, but her power to hold a crowd had not deserted her. "You have betrayed my trust in you!"

The squad of Palace Guards, who had so far taken no part in the conflict, formed themselves into two ranks on the ramp leading to the Palace.

"I have given my very life to you. I have laid my very being at your feet, spending all my waking hours in the service of this city, this Republic, this people."

The front rank of guards knelt down. The second remained standing.

"You are traitors! I have never asked for gratitude. To be of service was the only reward I claimed. I never asked you to love me. My love for you was enough. I have given you everything but now you trample me under your callused, ignorant feet."

A second squad of guards doubled out of the Palace, and arranged themselves in the same formation as the first squad, only higher up the ramp.

"You are traitors. You have brought blood and destruction to the streets of this ancient city. You have looted and destroyed. You have befouled the noble name of Chrystianaville. My name. The name that I freely gave to you. Is this the way you repay me? With treason?"

More guards were now manning the photon cannons. Phaid couldn't understand why the crowd didn't realize what was going on. They seemed transfixed by the giant image of the President. Phaid began to work his way back to Nex Boulevard. The booming voice was well on the way to screaming pitch.

"TRAITORS. YOU NOW BRING YOUR FILTH AND DESTRUCTION TO MY PALACE. YOU BRING IT RIGHT TO ME. YOU WANT TO DESTROY ME! YOU WANT TO DESTROY ME!"

The guards had drawn their fuse tubes. The ones kneeling

resting the long barrels over crooked arms. The ones standing used a double-handed grip, arms fully extended.

"TRAITORS!"

A few others had realized what was happening and were backing away from the ramp.

"TRAITORS. THERE IS NO HOPE FOR ANY OF YOU! YOU HAVE ONLY ONE THING LEFT FOR YOU AND THAT IS TO . . . DIE!"

The discharge from the massed fuse tubes lashed out like a sheet of blue white flame, marbled with the darker blue bolts from the photon cannons. The Plaza was turned instantly into a killing floor. It wasn't a battle, more a surgical operation. Above the hideous crackle Chrystiana-Nex's voice went on.

"THERE IS NOTHING FOR TRAITORS BUT DEATH. THIS IS AS PAINFUL TO ME AS IT IS TO YOU, BUT TREASON CANNOT BE ALLOWED TO FESTER IN THIS CITY. IF IT IS NOT RIPPED OUT, OUR CITY WILL DIE."

The Palace Guards went on and on firing. The actual cobbles of the Plaza were starting to crack and smoke. A few of the rebels had attempted to stand and fight back, but they had no chance. It was a massacre. The Palace Guard didn't even have the slight qualms that the police had shown. They were scything everyone down, marchers and cops alike.

Phaid had reached the steps that led down to Nex Boulevard before the guards had opened fire with their fuse tubes. At the first crackle, Phaid had thrown himself flat, not even bothering that it was a painful thing to do halfway down a flight of steps.

A number of other people were sheltering along with him. Behind them on Nex Boulevard, the remnants of the march were fleeing to safety. In front of them, on the Plaza, there was neither shelter nor safety.

To Phaid's amazement, he saw a small transport bed careening down the Boulevard at high speed, doing its best to dodge photon bursts. Phaid could only assume that it was being driven by a madman. A few people were clinging to the baggage deck for dear life.

The machine slewed to a halt at the foot of the steps where Phaid was sheltering, scraping its underside along the road surface in the process and all but spilling its precariously perched passengers.

Urgent voices started shouting.

"Quick, quick! Get on!"

Phaid was on his feet and running down the remainder of the steps. Others followed, but the majority seemed too paralyzed by shock to make the break.

Hands reached out to help him as Phaid ran up alongside the transport. He and the others had no sooner been hauled aboard than it took off with a scream of acceleration from a loudly protesting drive unit.

Dark blue photon bursts flared around them. Phaid grabbed whatever handholds he could find and clung to them grimly. He was certain that, if they weren't blasted to their constituent atoms at any second, he was sure to be flung off the next time the driver took a corner. Then, almost by a miracle, they were in a side street and out of the line of fire. The driver slowed down a little and the passengers scrambled for safer positions on the baggage deck.

Phaid found himself beside a stern faced woman wearing the long coat that marked her as an active rebel. He nodded towards the transport bed's closed driving cab.

"Who are these guys?"

"I guess they must be some of the boys. Whoever they are, we owe them our lives."

Phaid nodded quickly.

"Amen to that. Where do you think we're headed now?"

"Northside I'd imagine, probably to the Angel of Destiny. The bitch's flunkies don't have the courage to follow us there."

"What's the Angel of Destiny?"

The woman shot him a hostile and suspicious look.

"What are you?"

"Not much."

The woman looked him up and down.

"I can see that."

She turned her back on him as if to make it clear that she didn't think Phaid was worth consideration by a serious, fighting revolutionary.

Just like the woman had said, the transport bed negotiated its way out of the chaos of the city center and made for the main route to the northern part of the city.

As the journey went on, the passengers started to get over

some of their shock and relax. Conversations started, to the extent that the wind whipping past the fast moving transport would allow. The woman next to Phaid didn't deign to speak to him again, however.

He started to notice that the north was totally in the hands of the rebels. Groups of armed citizens patrolled the streets and the buildings were daubed with slogans proclaiming that it was liberated territory. More sinisterly, he also caught a brief glimpse of a body hanging from a translux pole. There was a placard around its neck that read "Enemy of the People." Phaid began to realize how much those who lived in the center of the city were being isolated and misinformed.

They'd almost reached the start of the shanty towns before the transport bed turned off the main highway. They swung into the forecourt of what had obviously been a somewhat run-down roadhouse until very recently when the rebels had converted it into a makeshift headquarters.

Phaid couldn't imagine what fevered rebel mind had decided to dub the place the Angel of Destiny. There were few structures on the northside that could carry such a pompous and overblown title, and this certainly wasn't one of them.

Originally it had been a cheap, gaudy roadhouse called the Belly O' Beer. This was still evident from a number of small signs that the rebels had neglected to obliterate. The Belly O' Beer's main architectural claim to fame was a giant squad tower fashioned from plasteel and rock foam to look like a beer mug, complete with handle and fake brimming head frozen in the act of spilling over and running down the side of the mug. The rebels had attempted to disguise the true nature of the tower by some crude repainting. It was of little avail. There is really no way to disguise a three-story beer mug. They had even attempted to burn off the handle with blasters, but the rock foam had managed to resist their efforts.

Apart from the tower, the place was little more than a collection of prefabricated plasteel boxes huddled in the middle of a parking lot and surrounded by some makeshift and hastily installed fortifications.

The transport bed laden with people was obviously a familiar sight to those on guard around the converted roadhouse. A few waved, but most paid it no mind at all. The driver maneuvered

his way around the defenses, across the parking lot and finally
came to a halt among the ramshackle collection of vehicles.
Phaid suspected that these were most probably the bulk of the
rebels' ground fleet.

The passengers began to climb down from the machine.
Without anyone to give instructions, they stood around wondering what they ought to do next.

The transport driver jumped down from his cab, grinning
and rubbing his hands together. He was a red-faced, jovial
looking character who seemed to be highly amused at his near
suicidal rescue. His smile broadened as most of his passengers
crowded around, wanting to pat him on the back, shake his
hand or kiss him. He soaked up the gratitude for a while and
then detached himself and started herding his flock towards the
main building.

"Let's go on inside. You'll be able to get a meal and a drink
if you're lucky."

Phaid followed the general movement. He was so profoundly glad to have survived the day that he didn't even bother
to wonder where the immediate future might lead. As he walked
towards the collection of buildings, Phaid noticed that, although
the Angel of Destiny's defenses looked rough and ready, they
also seemed fairly formidable. The whole of the parking lot
was strung with jolt relays and patrolled by heavily armed
groups of men and women.

Phaid also noticed that new walls and trenches were being
constructed by sweating work gangs. From their dull hungry
faces and the blaster toting overseers, it was apparent that they
had been forced into the work rather than freely volunteering.
Phaid didn't like to think of what you had to do to get on one
of those work gangs.

The refugees' first stop was what must have been the Belly
O' Beer's main barroom. It was still being put to use for something close to its original purpose. Hot food and drink were
being served to a constantly moving line. The last thing that
Phaid needed was a hot meal, but he joined the line just the
same, mainly out of a need for something to do.

The bar had been turned into a combination of canteen,
meeting place, information center and waiting room for those
who had no other place to go. Phaid knew, much to his dis-

comfort, that he fell squarely into that last category.

Even more uncomfortable, was the way that Phaid found himself the target of questioning and even hostile stares. He realized that it must be his clothes that were doing it. Even though they were now scorched, torn and streaked with dirt and vomit, they still looked like the garb of a city socialite rather than a fighting northside rebel. Feeling acutely uncomfortable, Phaid stared around the room, doing his best to avoid curious eyes.

Almost the whole of one wall was given over to what amounted to a huge bulletin board. It was festooned with notices and announcements of every possible kind pinned over the nudes and beer advertisements that had been its previous decoration.

There were political slogans and appeals for news of missing friends or relatives; there were duty rosters and lists; pictures of people that Phaid totally failed to recognize; announcements of rallies and mass meetings; lists, orders and instructions; there were even schematics for most models of blasters.

There were also weapons in abundance. Almost everyone in the place seemed to be wearing some kind of lethal device. Phaid was quite glad that he had his large fuse tube on his belt and Roni-Vows' miniature blaster in his pocket.

More weapons were leaning against walls and left casually on tables. Pairs of chairs had been pulled together and turned into makeshift beds. Some groups played cards, others argued in what seemed to be nonstop political debate. These discussions went round and round but managed nothing close to a final conclusion.

The walls were piled with cases, boxes and barrels, presumably looted supplies that had yet to find themselves a permanent storage place. Children bounced around, playing under the chairs and tables of the one-time bar. Occasionally their running and shouting would upset a sleeper, who would curse them out and then fall asleep again.

The air was heavy with steam and the combined smell of sweat, cooking food and unwashed bodies. It all added up to a picture of continuously shifting confusion. The revolt had obviously grown too fast for those who were engaged in it. There was no way that the rebels' minuscule organization could cope with the droves of people whom the street fighting had pushed into the cause.

While Phaid waited in the food line, it occurred to him that anyone with both the organizing capacity to make sense out of this chaos and the charisma to carry the various rebel splinter groups behind him could be the new ruler of the Republic. It wasn't a job that Phaid would have willingly taken.

Phaid reached the head of the line and was rewarded with a plate of watery stew and a mug of cloudy beer. The rebels might have justice on their side, but the oppressors received far better service.

Phaid was looking around for a place to sit when a total stranger grabbed him by the arm.

"Hey, I know you!"

Stew spilled down Phaid's already filthy coat. He cursed under his breath, and then looked at the man who'd grabbed him.

"You do?"

The face was gaunt and badly in need of a shave. From the man's stained clothes and the blaster hanging from a shoulder strap, it was clear that he had seen his fair share of fighting. He made no connections in Phaid's memory. He nonetheless continued to grin.

"You was on Veldine Street during the first riot."

"I was?"

"Sure you was, with a real expensive looking woman. I thought to myself at the time, look at that dumb bastard. I thought you was some courtier out slumming and got caught up in the trouble."

Phaid didn't like the way the conversation was going. He remembered the body hanging from the translux pole.

"That's what you thought, was it?"

"Until I saw you fold those two cops and I knew you couldn't be no courtier, you had to be one of us."

Phaid let out a silent sigh of relief. This was the very last place he'd want people thinking that he wasn't one of them.

"I guess it was either them or me."

"Ain't that what it's all about."

"I suppose so."

"Who was the dame, anyway?"

Phaid was starting to feel a little stupid standing around with his stew in one hand and his beer in the other. He gestured with his plate.

"Listen, I was just looking for a place to sit and..."

The stranger had obviously decided that he was going to be Phaid's buddy. He once again took hold of Phaid's arm, spilling more stew down his coat, and steered him to an already crowded table near the door.

Phaid couldn't see how two more people could possibly get around the small table. It didn't seem to worry his companion who was already making loud introductions.

"Hey, hey you guys. I want you to meet a friend of mine. I watched this man fold two cops in the space of a second. I got to tell you, he's an animal."

A few of the men hunched around the table glanced up. They didn't seem particularly impressed, but they did move up sufficiently to allow Phaid and the stranger to squeeze in. Once they were seated, a brawny, dark-skinned man with a bandage around his head looked coldly at Phaid.

"You're a mess."

"You could say that."

"You just come from the Plaza?"

Phaid nodded.

"Uh-huh."

"You get gassed?"

"A little."

The dark-skinned man sucked in his lower lip.

"That's good. I wouldn't like to think you made a habit of throwing up over yourself. What happened down there?"

Every eye around the table was suddenly focused on Phaid. He gathered himself together and launched into his account of the march and the subsequent massacre on the Plaza. It took a long time, but nobody interrupted him. When he was through, the dark-skinned rebel pointed a questioning finger at him.

"Seems to me that you're saying the Day Oners screwed things up."

Phaid realized that he might have said the wrong thing, but it was too late to change his story.

"Yeah, it seemed like that to me. The cops weren't actually going to come over to our side, but they were definitely backing

269

off from shooting down women. Then those crazy broads jumped
them and all hell broke loose."

The dark-skinned rebel swung around to a small bald man
sitting next to him.

"I told you that those people are insane. You didn't ought
to be fucking with them."

The bald man had been staring glumly at the table. When
he was spoken to, his expression didn't change.

"We are all united in a common cause."

"Are we?"

"The Day Oners want to overthrow the mad bitch just the
same as we do."

"Maybe it ain't the same. It seems to me that they're kill
happy. Once we've got rid of Chrystiana-Nex, how in hell are
we to rebuild a society with people like that around?"

The bald man seemed unmoved.

"We'll face that when the time comes."

"Maybe we ought to face that right now."

The dark-skinned man appealed to Phaid.

"You tell him. You know what they're like."

Phaid was about to answer when the door swung open and
a group of men walked in. To his shock and surprise he saw
that one of them was Makartur. Memory of the strange dream
charged all over him. There was no way that he could think
of Makartur as anything but an implacable enemy. Phaid had
an immediate urge to scrunch down in his chair so he wouldn't
be noticed, but it was too late. Makartur spotted him and scowled.

"What are you doing here, manny? I didn't think revolution
was your style."

16

"He's shiftless, deceitful and self-seeking. Believe me, I know the man. I traveled some distance with him. He'd sell his own mother if he saw an advantage in doing so. Since he's been in this city, aye, even before he arrived, he was doing everything but crawl on his belly to curry favor with the toadies and lackeys of the court."

This was more than Phaid was going to stand for.

"Just a minute now . . ."

"The prisoner will speak in his allotted turn and not before."

Since the order was backed up by nearly a dozen blasters, Phaid shut his mouth and kept it shut. Makartur continued.

"He has been seen more than once in the company of the notorious presidential flunkey Roni-Vows and, on the occasion of this much vaunted incident when he is reputed to have killed two of the enemy police, he was with a woman who can only be described as a high born whore."

Phaid felt sick to his stomach. Not only was he on trial for

271

his life but the strange dream was coming uncannily true. Phaid had put all the old hill superstitions behind him when he had moved down to the cities. Now they flooded back with a sickening vengeance. What was the truth about the dream? Had Makartur sought the spiritual contact of his ancestors? Had Phaid's dream been forced on him by some supernatural power? Was one of them really destined to kill the other? Ghosts and demons closed in on Phaid, but they didn't offer any answers. He wanted to sink into a quivering jelly on the floor. He couldn't cope, but, then again, he had to cope. Makartur was far from finished.

"I would advise this tribunal that the presence of this man in our midst can only indicate that he is a spy for the presidency. We cannot afford to take any risks with him. He should be branded as an enemy of the people and hung accordingly."

Phaid blinked. Every eye in the room was on him and he knew he'd have to come up with something good if life was going to last very much longer. The wallet of money that lay on the table in front of him, along with both his weapons, wasn't going to make the task any easier.

Phaid took a last look around, trying to read the faces of the people who were about to judge him. It had to be the strangest tribunal that he had ever seen. There were eight of them that were directly involved in the business at hand. Makartur stood as Phaid's accuser. There was Phaid himself and Vord, the man who'd seen the incident with the police and served as Phaid's only friendly witness. There were five on the actual tribunal, a pair of hard bitten northsiders called Lank and Marden, a middle-aged woman called D'Wan, a small man with the attitude and movements of a street hustler who went by the nickname of Blue Eyes and a statuesque red-haired woman who called herself Flame. Phaid had heard a whisper that she had been an exotic dancer before the outbreak of the rebellion.

This and many other tribunals were working overtime as the uprising gained strength. Despite their not inconsiderable achievements, the rebels were as jumpy as the President's Court. Many of them saw spies and enemies of the people in every shadow, complaints and denunciations flew like hailstones in a storm. Each one had to be investigated, and to simplify matters the tribunals handed down only one penalty, and that was death by hanging.

Some members of the underground objected that the revolt would destroy itself by carrying out its purges before it had even achieved victory, but their voices went unheeded. The tribunals ran at full power, and the turnover was rapid.

Phaid had only been in the Angel of Destiny for a matter of two hours when a pair of stern faced guards informed him that he had been denounced as a parasite traitor and spy. He'd been locked in a storeroom overnight with a bunch of other depressed and frightened individuals. In the morning he was marched in front of the tribunal to discover what he'd intuitively known and feared. It had been Makartur who had denounced him.

The tribunal had convened in a small back room of the Angel of Destiny. When the place had been a regular roadside tavern, it had probably been the manager's office. It was now used for the rebels' less public business. Despite the cramped conditions, a further half-dozen people had crowded in to watch the proceedings.

The revolution hadn't been running for long enough to have developed its own ritual or ceremony. There was, however, a certain dignity to it, the kind of dignity that comes when a length of rope and a high place to hang it from would perhaps become the fate of one of those present.

Phaid looked carefully at each of his judges in turn. It needed a three to two majority one way or the other to either hang him or set him free. All this had been carefully explained to him by D'Wan, the middle-aged woman who seemed to be acting as chairperson of the tribunal.

Looking at Blue Eyes, he felt that he could count on some measure of, if not sympathy, at least understanding from the small man. He hoped that he could expect a measure of the same from Flame. D'Wan seemed determined to be absolutely fair, but the two northsiders were harder to gauge. Their faces were grim and impassive, and Phaid feared that they might simply decide to have him hanged for running after the kind of good life that had always been beyond their grasp.

Standing guessing, however, wasn't going to do him very much good. D'Wan was already beginning to look a little impatient, so Phaid took a deep breath and launched into the defense that he hoped was going to save his neck.

"I wouldn't attempt to deceive any of you by claiming that I have led a blameless life. I have lived as a drifter and a gambler for most of my days. Sometimes I have had to use sleight of hand and deception to survive."

D'Wan looked up sharply.

"By sleight of hand and deception you are saying that you cheat?"

Phaid nodded.

"It's happened."

"So Makartur's testimony is correct?"

"In that respect, yes. What he neglected to tell you was that we first met in the steerage class of a land crawler, how later we had to work the veebe herds because we didn't have the price of passage as far as the Republic. Does this sound like the behavior of someone who would throw in his lot with courtiers and aristocrats?"

D'Wan glanced at Makartur.

Makartur nodded woodenly.

"Aye, it's true, but . . ."

"That's all we need to know at the moment. Please continue, Citizen Phaid."

"I was born among simple hill people where life was hard. I ran away when I was a kid and since that time I've made my own chances. I may have been luckier than some . . ." he glanced significantly at the two northsiders ". . . but I took what breaks were offered me. I've traveled across half this world. I've crossed the icefields and the burning plains, and met literally thousands of people. I admit that there are some whom I've cheated and some whom I might have robbed in my wanderings, but they were always the ones who would have done the same to me. It's always the greedy who are the easiest to cheat."

One of the northsiders who had been staring intently at Phaid jumped in with a question.

"This is real moving stuff, but it doesn't explain why you have been seen in the company of courtiers. You don't deny that you have contacts among those people, do you?"

Phaid shook his head.

"I don't deny it, I know some courtiers. I've already told

you I live by my wits. It's natural I should go where the pickings are the richest."

Flame brushed her luxuriant red hair away from her eyes.

"Do you count the women of the court among these pickings?"

"Some of them are very attractive, and some have been attracted to me."

Marden the northsider scowled.

"They make sure they have the best of everything."

Flame glanced at him and then gave Phaid a hard look.

"So you didn't object to being a plaything of court whores."

"I wouldn't have exactly put it that way, but I confess I find it hard to reject a beautiful woman."

Phaid smiled directly at Flame as he concluded the answer but her expression didn't soften. She totally ignored the implied flattery. D'Wan also didn't seem amused. Phaid hoped that the men, at least, were falling for the way he was selling himself as a freewheeling, likable rogue.

Those hopes were shattered as Lank tapped the wallet that Roni-Vows had given him with a thick index finger.

"How do you account for this money you just happen to be carrying?"

"It was given to me by a courtier named Roni-Vows."

Every face in the room registered shock. It was D'Wan who put the shock into words.

"That man is one of the worst of our enemies. That you accepted money from him is a serious admission."

Phaid knew that he was running a desperate gamble, but it was too late to stop now.

"He owed it to me."

"He owed it to you?"

"I whipped his ass at imperial hazard. When I go after the rich I go hard. Would you have it any other way?"

To his relief, Phaid saw four of the tribunal noticeably relax. Marden and Blue Eyes even permitted themselves faint smiles. Only Flame seemed unconvinced.

"Are you sure this wasn't your payment for being a presidential agent?"

Phaid, feeling that he had the others at least halfway on his side, gave Flame a contemptuous look.

"Those are my winnings. The only way I could prove it would be to call Roni-Vows as a witness, and I doubt that he would recognize this tribunal, even if we could get him to attend."

Phaid was now certain that he had most of the room on his side. When D'Wan asked him if he had anything else to say in his defense, he almost told her that he hadn't. It was only a last moment caution against overconfidence that prompted him to keep going.

"I'd like to ask my accuser, Citizen Makartur, a few questions."

"Ask whatever questions you want."

Phaid turned to face Makartur. The hillman looked as if he could happily tear Phaid's head loose from his shoulders.

"What do you want to ask me, little man?"

Phaid screwed up all his courage. It was time to play his only card and find out if the dream was anything more than an anxious nightmare.

"I'm wondering why you've chosen to denounce me in this way. We traveled together and even fought side by side. I don't recall doing anything to harm you, and yet you're doing your damnedest to get me hung. I could ask you a lot of questions about why you're doing this, but it's neither the time nor the place." Phaid paused for effect. "All I want to know is where you got the idea that I was busy selling out the revolution."

Makartur regarded Phaid with cold, murderous eyes.

"I meditated on you."

Phaid's jaw dropped. His rhetoric completely deserted him. "You meditated?"

"For many long nights. You always disturbed me, and I went to my ancestors for answers. They finally came to me and I was taken through the first gate; it was then that all became clear. You were marked as the betrayer. There is death between you and me, Citizen Phaid."

Phaid felt a terrible internal cold. The dream was something out of the primitive, mystic past. It was frightening and yet it had also given Phaid an unbeatable advantage. The spectators were already nudging each other and nodding towards Makartur. All he had to do was resist overplaying his hand.

"So it was your dead ancestors who put the finger on me?"

"You may mock, but the truth will come out in the end. A death still lies between the two of us."

Again Phaid felt the chill, but quickly shrugged it off. He faced the tribunal with all the deference he could muster.

"I don't think I have anything else to say."

D'Wan nodded.

"If you will remove yourself from the room, the tribunal will make its decision in your case."

Escorted by two guards, Phaid was led outside. Even though he was certain that he had it made, it wasn't a comfortable feeling standing around in a passage that had originally led from the bar to the men's room while five people decided whether they were going to hang him or not. The guards studiously avoided his eyes until the door opened and Phaid was summoned back inside. Everyone looked very serious. For one hideous moment, Phaid wondered if it had all gone wrong. Had they decided to hang him after all, just to be on the safe side? Then D'Wan was addressing him.

"The tribunal has taken a vote and, by a majority of four to one, we have determined that you have not acted against the people's interests and are therefore not an enemy of the people. You are free to go..." D'Wan hesitated and held a muttered discussion with her colleagues, "... at least, you are provisionally free to go. We do feel that you have fallen into error and we recommend that you attend a course of political education to ensure that you don't fall into such error a second time."

Phaid missed most of the part about political education. He wasn't paying attention. He was trying to figure out which of the tribunal had wanted to see him hang. This wasn't purely an academic interest. There was always the chance that whoever it was might feel like short-circuiting democracy by taking a private shot him. He hadn't quite made up his mind when one of the spectators leaped forward brandishing his fist in the face of the tribunal.

"Outrage! You are as bad as him! You all ought to die!"

The objector was an awkwardly tall, angular individual, in an overcoat that would have disgraced a scarecrow. His face was haggard and crazy eyes stared out from deep hollow sockets. He waved a spindly arm towards Phaid.

"He has no right to live! He is a parasite, as bad an oppressor as anyone inside the Palace. When Day One comes he and all those like him will be eliminated."

D'Wan angrily got to her feet.

"If you people were allowed to execute everyone you thought was an enemy of the people, the city would be turned into a ghost town."

It might have been the truth, but it wasn't the best way to calm down a Day Oner. His eyes flashed with an even crazier light.

"We will do what is necessary. Day One is all around us."

He fumbled under his shapeless overcoat and dragged out a long-barreled blaster. He swung it wildly towards Phaid. Phaid threw himself flat on the floor. The blaster went off, and showers of hot ash cascaded down from the ceiling. Phaid found himself enmeshed in a tangle of legs as the Day Oner was wrestled to the ground and dragged away howling and protesting.

It was only when he was sure that there was no chance of the madman coming back for a second shot that he risked getting to his feet. The tribunal was leaving the small, and now smoke filled room. As she passed him, Flame shot him a glance of the purest venom. Phaid jerked back from the realization that it had been she who had tried to vote him to death.

With alarming suddenness, it all fell into place. He thought about the red hair and the pale, freckled skin, then he thought about Makartur and cursed himself for not making the connection sooner. They probably both came from the same background, the same cold hard hills. They might even belong to the same tribe. There was a good chance that they even shared the same ancient, outlawed religion.

Although Phaid had come through the tribunal with his head intact, there was still the problem of Makartur. It wasn't going to go away. It was a terrible feeling to know that the ancient rituals could still operate in this huge urban sprawl. He knew that Makartur wouldn't rest until one of them was dead. He didn't hold out too many hopes that he could kill the big warrior. The first thing that he should do was to put as much distance between the two of them as possible.

While Phaid stood, still turning all this over in his mind,

one of his erstwhile guards tapped him on the shoulder.

"Come on, Jack. It's time to get going."

Phaid grinned.

"Damn right, I got to get out of here."

The guard looked surprised.

"Out of here? Where do you think you're going?"

It was Phaid's turn to be surprised.

"Back to the city center, of course."

Sensing this might not have been the most tactful thing to say, he quickly added a weak explanation.

"That's where I can be the most useful."

"You ain't going anywhere out of this area."

"Huh? The tribunal cleared me."

"The tribunal recommended you for political education."

"Yeah, but wait a minute, I . . ."

"You're joining a study group whether you like it or not."

"What happens in a study group?"

The guard smiled nastily.

"You'll find out."

Over the next few days he found out. At first Phaid had asked himself a dozen times how bad a study group could be. Studying had to be a breeze for anyone with a few smarts and a good memory. Then he had discovered that these particular study groups didn't do too much studying. They were a euphemistic name for the labor gangs he had seen working around the place when he had first arrived. The only thing they taught was an appreciation of back breaking toil. The students dug trenches, hauled garbage, carted building materials and sometimes, after the rebels had made a foray into the center of the city, they even burned the dead.

The groups were the result of a compromise between the Day Oners and the rest of the revolutionary factions. To stop the Day Oners instituting their program of mass extermination, the other factions had offered to run courses of reeducation for the less desirable recruits to the insurrection.

The Day Oners had grudgingly agreed to the deal provided that the central theme of the curriculum was dirty, exhausting work.

There were, however, certain consolations. Work was regularly interrupted by what were known as instruction periods.

These consisted of lengthy harangues by anyone who felt like it on obscure points of political philosophy.

Phaid had quickly discovered that the revolution had no coherent intellectual basis. The majority of the so-called instructors made it up as they went along. Some envisioned a glorious, egalitarian utopia dedicated to aesthetic pursuits, others dreamed of a grimly dreary dictatorship of the proletariat. Whenever a Day Oner was giving the lecture it resounded with blood, death and executions.

Phaid did find that it was quite possible to prolong the lectures and thus cut down the work time by asking long, detailed and generally irrelevant questions. The subject of either androids or boohooms was always good for an extra hour sitting around rather than blistering his hands or busting his spine. Others of the group realized what Phaid was doing and fell behind. On Phaid's fourth day in the study group, they managed to prolong an instruction period with an elderly and particularly verbose instructor from just after the morning roll call almost through to sunset.

The ploy even worked on the Day Oners. They seemed all too ready to expound at length on their hideously gory concepts of social reorganization. This was the way to get past the Day Oners. In every other way, they had the study groups sewn up to be unpleasant as possible. They had installed a supervisor among the guards who watched each group. As far as Phaid could see, these supervisors had been picked solely on the basis of their capacity for their blaster happy vindictiveness. They effectively put a stop to all but the wildest escape plans. They also prevented nighttime sex between members of the study group.

Nobody had bothered to split the politically undesirable men and the undesirable women into separate groups. The idea, after all, seemed ridiculous to most of the rebels. Phaid had noticed at least three politically unsatisfactory ladies in his group with whom he wouldn't have minded getting better acquainted. The Day Oners, however, had a serious prejudice against sex between men and women. They reinforced this prejudice by keeping an armed supervisor on duty in the storeroom in which the study group slept. The penalty for any student bed jumping was summary execution.

There was one other drawback to being in a study group. The tribunals that recommended reeducation didn't specify just how long the process should take. It was left to the supervisors to decide when each member was fit to rejoin revolutionary society. All Phaid could hope for was that there'd be some sort of outbreak of confusion that would give him the chance to make a break.

After six days, no confusion had come along to save him. Phaid was starting to get desperate. Rumors were going around that the Day Oners were no longer satisfied with the study group system and were pressing for a selection process whereby those who weren't making satisfactory progress could be taken out and killed. Life in the revolution had not only become drab and unpleasant, it was once again starting to move into the lethal.

Then, on the seventh day, something happened that for a moment gave Phaid a flash of hope. He and the rest of the group were sitting around trying to spin out an instruction period for as long as possible. The alternative was digging out an emergency latrine. A sleek, two-man flipper spun flamboyantly on to the parking lot and made a flashy stop. To Phaid's total amazement, Streetlife climbed out of it.

He was wearing a sharply tailored, ankle length duster coat, a plumed hat and an armband with three circles emblazoned on it. He seemed to be acting like a visiting general, and the rebels who came out to meet him treated him accordingly. An escort formed up around him, and they started for the main building of the Angel of Destiny with the fast walk of the very important. They had to pass Phaid's study group on their way. Phaid was certain that Streetlife had spotted him, but the hustler turned rebel general didn't show a flicker of recognition.

Phaid cursed silently at Streetlife's rank ingratitude. Hadn't he helped the bum out when he was broke? He was so angry that he even forgot to ask a key question, and the instruction period started to wind itself up.

The instructor decided that the session was over and the group began gathering up their tools in preparation for going back to work. They were being marched back towards the half-completed latrine when Streetlife and his entourage emerged from the building and came straight towards them. As they got closer, Streetlife signaled to the guards.

"Hold it there a minute."

The column halted with everyone wondering what was going to happen next. After so many unpleasant rumors a number of the study group looked more than a little scared.

Streetlife gestured briskly to the nearest guard.

"I'm taking one of these men for further interrogation. We've dug up some more facts on him."

"Which one?"

Streetlife pointed to Phaid.

"That one there, the one with the shifty expression."

The guard didn't argue and beckoned to Phaid to step out of the line. The Day One supervisor, however, immediately started to protest.

"These people are engaged in major reeducation. They cannot leave."

Streetlife drew himself up to his full height and puffed out his chest.

"I don't want these people. I only want that one, and I'd advise you very strongly to cooperate with me."

The Day Oner didn't seem impressed.

"What authority do you have to take this man?"

Streetlife slapped his armband.

"You know what this is?"

The Day Oner shook his head.

"No."

Streetlife bristled.

"No what?"

"No I don't know what it is."

Streetlife stuck his face close to the Day Oner's.

"Then you better find out pretty damn quick, or I'm going to put in a report to your cadre assessor and get a zap order slapped on you. That'll be the end of you, asshole. Your brights be put out, cancelled. You perceive my meaning?"

The Day Oner scowled and then shrugged.

"If you want him that bad, you better have him."

He crooked his finger at Phaid.

"You. Scum. Get your worthless ass over here. This guy seems to have found a use for you, which is more than I've ever done. Let's hope it's something real dangerous."

Phaid looked at him bleakly.

"Your overflowing charm is going to get you into trouble one of these days."

The Day Oner spat venomously at him.

"I should have killed you while I had the chance."

Streetlife quickly stepped in between them.

"But now you don't get the chance. He's mine now."

He put a hand on Phaid's shoulder and walked him quickly to the flipper. Things had started to move a little too fast for Phaid's comfort.

"What the hell's going on round here. What are you doing in that outfit?"

Streetlife seemed in no mood to answer questions.

"Just shut your mouth and get in the flipper."

Streetlife slid behind the controls and slammed down the passenger bubble. Without even waiting for the machine to fully rise on its force field, he slapped it into drive and they moved forward with a jerk.

"Boy oh boy, how the fuck did you get yourself into that mess? I thought you had more class."

"I didn't have much choice. The rebels pulled me out of that massacre on the Plaza and then minutes after I got here I was denounced as a cheap hustler."

"A parasite?"

"That was the word they used."

"And ol' Streetlife had to pull you out of the shit, right?"

"I guess I owe you one."

"You owe me about twenty."

"And you no doubt aim to collect."

"It's the way of the world. My mama told me, from the womb to the tomb, nothing comes free."

Phaid raised an eyebrow.

"You had a mother?"

Streetlife looked offended.

"That was a cheap shot, gambling man. I save your ass and you start insulting me."

Phaid shook his head.

"I'm sorry, it was a cheap shot. Put it down to the fact that I'm overwrought."

"You'd have been a lot more overwrought if I'd left you on that chain gang."

"They call it a study group."

"That's right, study group. These pussies have got names for everything."

"I still don't understand what you're doing here. I wouldn't have thought revolution was your style."

"If revolution's what's going on, then it's my style."

"You mean you're really into this thing?"

Streetlife grinned.

"You know me better than that."

"They treated you like a king back there, and that armband, what's that supposed to be? I've never seen one like that before."

"Neither's anyone else."

"Huh?"

"At first I figured these rebels were dumb, but when I found out they were not only dumb but disorganized, I knew that I had it made. You like this here armband? I made it myself. It's never failed. I just walk into a bunch of rebels and flash the arm. They fall over themselves to do what I want. They figure that I must be some big wheel with this fancy insignia that they've never seen before. I'm making more money than I can even remember."

Phaid looked at him in disbelief.

"You're making money at this?"

"Why would I be doing this if there weren't no change in it? This is Streetlife you talking to. You think I like to dress this way?"

Phaid scratched his head. A large part of him ached for a long leisurely clean-off and a set of freshly laundered clothes. Life in the study group had been Spartan to the point of being disgusting.

"I still don't see how you make money out of revolution. What are you into, the black market or something?"

"Black market? Don't make me laugh. That's nothing compared with what I got going."

"So what do you have going?"

"Just watch me now. You'll find out."

They were running along the top level of a three-tier overpass. All around them black stone megatowers thrust their ugly irregular bulks towards the clouds. Some time in the distant past they had been built to house an overspill population that now no longer existed. Since then, they had largely fallen into decay. Their ramps, passages and tunnels were dark and dangerous places where thieves preyed on the poor, the lame and the inadequate.

Streetlife curved the car into an exit and hit the approach road to one of the towers. Phaid was a little surprised but said nothing as they sped through the series of tunnels and ramps that led to the upper areas of the structure. At something like the twentieth story they emerged on to an open courtyard that appeared to be solid rebel. It was decked out with yellow and black rebel flags. Armed men and women lounged around looking tough but fairly aimless. Streetlife parked the car beside a high arch that gave access to the interior of the building.

"You just wait here for a moment."

With that he climbed out of the car and hustled through the arch. Once again, just like at the Angel of Destiny, he was greeted as if he were visiting royalty. Phaid was intrigued but the presence of so many armed rebels, a percentage of whom were likely to be Day Oners, cautioned him against doing anything but slide down in his seat and wait for Streetlife to return.

Phaid passed the time looking covertly round the courtyard. It had once boasted what must have been a fairly splendid grove of trees. Centuries of vandalism had, however, reduced them to blackened, limbless stumps carved with the graffiti of ages.

The wait wasn't too long. Inside of fifteen minutes, Streetlife came bouncing out again. He was carrying a fat document case and looked inordinately pleased with himself. As he clambered back into the driver's seat, his grin was so broad that it took up most of his face.

"Eight thou."

Phaid could scarcely believe his ears.

"Are you telling me that there's eight thousand in that case?"

"A shade over, to be strictly accurate!"

"But how?"

Streetlife set the controls on drive and lifted quickly away.

"It was easy. I came by here a few days ago and told them I got orders from high command. I convinced those suckers that the revolution needed them to knock over a counting house just inside the line."

"The line?"

"Oh yeah, you been out of circulation ain't you. There's a line now. It separates rebel turf from loyalist turf. Chrystiana-Nex and her gang have given up pretending that they got a hold on anything more than the city center. They got the cops and some mercenaries holding it for them. They've given the rebels best on the other parts of the city."

Streetlife took a hand off the controls and tugged thoughtfully at his ear. "How long they can go on holding the city center is anybody's guess." He snapped back to the original point. "Anyhow, they do just like they're told, just like good little rebels. They knock over the counting house and get away clean with twelve thou in hard currency. I let them keep a third for their own group and collect the rest for the high command."

Phaid shook his head. He still couldn't quite believe the audacity of Streetlife's scam.

"Of course, you're going to hand it over to the high command."

"I figure I'm the best high command these pussies got."

"If they catch you, they'll tear you limb from limb. Hanging will be too good for you."

Streetlife grinned and nodded.

"Yeah, I realize that. I figure I got to keep my head down for a bit after this score."

"Eight thousand is a fair sized sum to take a rest on."

Streetlife glanced at Phaid with an expression that was close to injured innocence.

"Wait a minute, you got to realize that that ain't all profit. I got expenses."

"Expenses?"

"I had to sweeten a few cops so they'd be looking the other way when my boys crashed through the line."

Once again Phaid was surprised.

"Cops can be bribed to let the rebels through?"

Streetlife laughed.

"Cops have always been on the take. Revolution don't make no difference. If anything, it makes it worse. They're deserting by the hundreds. If it weren't for the mercenaries they keep bringing in, the whole city would be falling apart. Also, mercenaries only stay loyal as long as they keep getting paid. After the number of cops that the Palace Guard killed that day on the Plaza, the cops ain't going to bust their balls to save no president. Particularly the ones who got in by forced induction."

"What's forced induction?"

"Forced induction? It's when a guy comes up on some rap and the inquisitor gives him the choice of doing time in a correction center or joining the police. They brought it in because willing volunteers were getting hard to find."

"Are you telling me that half the cops I see are really criminals?"

"More like two-thirds."

"Sweet Lords."

"It don't make for ideal peace officers, that's for sure, but enough of this chatter, we got to work out what we're going to do next."

17

Phaid picked up his drink, but then set it down again without tasting it. Picking it up had been a reflex. Putting it down again was good judgment. The game had been going on for a long time, and Phaid was sufficiently far ahead to know that he no longer really needed luck or even skill. He just had to maintain his discipline and he was away with a handsome profit.

Drinking, however, was out. Phaid was aware that it would take only one or two more to cut him loose into the first shallow reaches of drunkenness. Across the well lighted and very elegant table, a heavy loser, a short pear shaped courtier called Athon-Igel was fumbling with his cards. He hadn't managed to hold on to his discipline and was starting to turn belligerent.

"I'm going to show you, Master Phaid."

He looked for encouragement among the other players.

"Athon-Igel is going to lay down on the high and mighty professional. I'm going to show him if nobody else will."

Mick Farren

There was little forthcoming from anyone else at the table. Phaid kept his face in perfect neutral.

"So, show me. It's just a game."

Athon-Igel leaned forward. His cheeks sagged and his eyes were sunken. The crystal light formation that floated over the table turned them into pools of anxious shadow.

"I suppose you're going to tell me that it's just money."

"Isn't it?"

"Then you don't mind me taking some of that stack you have in front of you."

Phaid allowed a trace of impatience to creep into his voice.

"Why don't you just lay down your cards and find out."

The courtier grinned a bloated, sneering grin.

"Am I worrying you?"

Phaid gave him a cold, hard look. Athon-Igel laid his cards face up on the table with a drunken flourish.

"How do you like those. Are they professional enough for you?"

The hand was pretty much what Phaid had expected: blues on diadems in the crossover pattern. Phaid looked at Athon-Igel with an expression near to sympathy.

"That really is too bad."

He laid his own cards tidily on the table. It was full duke-dom, all in gold. Athon-Igel looked at Phaid's hand as though he was unable to believe it.

"But..."

"You should have known there were no lathes left in the pack. When a man makes the first offer of parlay and he's holding only diadems and blues, he shows gall, not talent. It's a desperate play."

Roni-Vows, who was two places round the table on Phaid's right, suddenly laughed.

"Maybe Athon-Igel thinks these are desperate days."

Phaid allowed the master of the table to rack his winnings towards him and add it to his already considerable heap. He took a tiny sip from his drink.

"I've found desperation to be the mark of a loser more often than not."

Athon-Igel was still truculent.

"I suppose you consider yourself a winner."

Again Phaid didn't bother to answer. He just looked down at the clutter of plaques in front of him. The other players seemed decidedly ill at ease with Athon-Igel's behavior, but he simply wouldn't let go of it.

"We can all fight when we're cornered. Did you ever consider that?"

Phaid took a deep breath.

"Why don't we play some cards."

Roni-Vows wagged a finger in Athon-Igel's direction.

"We're cornered right now, but I don't see anyone fighting or even preparing to fight. Even you, Athon-Igel, you're just like the rest of us, trying to have a little fun before the mob smashes down the door."

Athon-Igel's head lolled as he tried to focus on Roni-Vows.

"You always have been an alarmist. This rebel business will blow over soon enough and things will be just as they were before."

An elderly, rather distinguished man at the other end of the table coughed politely.

"I wish I shared your optimism, Athon-Igel."

Roni-Vows nodded in agreement.

"I heard that the marikhs have threatened to close down the lines in and out of the city until they can be assured of a stable government."

This remark caused a lot of consternation around the gaming table.

"We'll be cut off."

"It can't be true."

The elderly man quieted the table and then addressed himself to Roni-Vows.

"Are you sure of what you're saying?"

"I've never known a marikh to spread idle rumors."

"You heard it directly from a marikh?"

"Of course not, but . . ."

"Then what you're saying may not actually be true."

"It's possible, but I wouldn't count on it. What would you do in their place?"

"I'd close the lines until I was assured of a stable government."

"Exactly."

291

"You realize that if this is the case, we have to decide now whether to go or to stay."

There was commotion again until the elderly man once more called for quiet.

"So what say you, Roni-Vows? Is it time for flight?"

"I'm not leaving the city."

"You're not?"

"So long as the Day Oners don't take sole control I think we'll be safe. Once there is a new administration, they will need our help to wipe out the Day Oner psychotics. All we have to guard against is being hung in the meantime."

The elderly man seemed to have his doubts.

"You'd be running some terrible risks."

"We'd be running some terrible risks by going anywhere else. I can't think of many places where the court of Chrystiana-Nex would be welcomed with open arms."

There was silence around the gaming table as these thoughts sank in. Phaid took the opportunity to beckon to one of the two liveried footmen who flanked the door.

"Cash me in, will you? I think it's time that I left."

Phaid swallowed the remainder of his drink and waited for the flunky to return with his cash. Athon-Igel was once again staring at Phaid. The drunken courtier was starting to annoy him.

"You want something?"

"You're leaving?"

"I'm leaving. I have a feeling that these gentlemen have lost their taste for the game."

Roni-Vows stood up.

"When will I see you again, my friend? Do you intend to leave the city?"

Phaid shrugged. "Nobody's going to ask me to run the city for them. I think I might go south and take a chance on the hospitality of the Tharmiers. The climate's good and the women are beautiful."

Roni-Vows nodded, but there was a strange look in his eyes.

"So you intend to get on one of the last trains out?"

"Indeed I do."

"The more I look at you, the more I wonder about that. There's something about you. Somehow you're tied up with the fate of this city. I just don't see you leaving."

Phaid pursed his lips. "Come to the terminal in the morning and watch me climb aboard."

The footman handed Phaid his money. Phaid stowed the wallet carefully inside his coat and made his goodbyes. As he walked out of the private gaming room, his mood was close to jubilant. He had won over twelve thousand tabs and managed to make a graceful exit. By way of a bonus, he had heard the news about the marikhs closing the lines. He and Streetlife would now have a chance to ride out of Chrystianaville before that happened.

Phaid lingered for a while on the wide curved balcony that overlooked the main room of Thandon's. Thandon's was a palace of leisure for the quality of Chrystianaville. From the outside it looked like a cluster of plasteel spheres. Bubbles if you like. One large bubble with a number of smaller bubbles clinging to it. The lights inside the translucent domes gave them a pale, pastel glow in the night.

The main room was for dancing and parading. It was a salon where the structure of smart society was evaluated and arbitrated. Meetings were made, trysts were kept and broken, affairs were initiated and affairs were finished. It had the competitiveness of a battlefield.

All around the main room there were the smaller satellite chambers; the gaming rooms, where fortunes could be won or lost across the tables; the even more private suites where the affairs initiated in the main salon could be consummated in comfort and secrecy.

Phaid descended the wide curving staircase to the main floor and plunged into the roar of chattering people. He exchanged glances and smiles with a number of women. He was tempted to stay for a while. Amid the whirl and sparkle it was hard to believe that half the city was in the hands of rebels dedicated to executing everyone around him.

He was very conscious of the revolution, however. The wallet full of winnings was his passage as far away from it as possible. He put women out of his mind and made his way quickly to the arches that marked Thandon's grand Harald Boulevard entrance.

It was only a matter of blocks to the small tavern where

Phaid had arranged to meet Streetlife, and Phaid was profoundly glad that it wasn't any further. The clothes that had gained him admission to Thandon's brought hostile stares on the street and, from moment to moment, he expected to be pelted with rocks or garbage. As he pushed through the door of the tavern, he found Streetlife seated at the bar tensely nursing a drink.

"Did you win?"

"Don't you have no faith in me?"

"Did you win?"

"Of course I won."

"How much?"

"Enough to get out of this madness."

Streetlife was starting to become angry.

"How much?"

Phaid ordered a drink and grinned at Streetlife.

"I won twenty thousand."

Streetlife's eyebrows shot up.

"You're kidding me!"

"Twenty thousand. We can go in style."

Streetlife was still conjuring with the figure as though he couldn't quite believe it.

"Twenty thousand."

"I learned something else."

"Twenty fucking grand."

"We have to leave the city in the morning."

This finally snagged Streetlife's attention.

"What?"

"There's word that the marikhs are going to close down the line until they have a guarantee of a stable government."

"So where do we go?"

"I figured to go south to the Tharmiers."

Streetlife nodded.

"The women are beautiful and the weather's perfect. I could use a little sleeping in the sun. Will we get a berth on a southbound train? If the word's out there's only a limited number of trains left, the terminal could be a madhouse by morning."

"With the money we've got, we could get just about anything."

They moved from the bar to the comparative privacy of a

dark booth. Phaid glanced around carefully to make sure that
no one was watching them, then with a broad grin on his face,
took out his winnings and divided them between Streetlife and
himself. As they hid the money in their clothes, both men burst
out laughing. They could hardly believe things were finally
going their way. The bartender glanced up at the sound.

"You want to share the joke, friends?"

"Nothing you'd understand, friend."

The bartender scowled and went about his work. Streetlife
flashed his teeth at Phaid.

"If we don't have to leave until tomorrow, what're we going
to do tonight?"

He was clearly up for one final adventure. Phaid seemed a
little dubious.

"What do you want to do?"

"We could take one last look at the city."

Phaid could think of a thousand things that might go wrong,
but he was suddenly ashamed of himself. He was starting to
think like an old maid.

"Hell, yes. Let's take one last look at this damned city.
We've earned it."

Outside the tavern, a group of urchins were singing for
change. As Phaid and Streetlife emerged they moved to surround them, clapping in time and breaking into song.

> *"Hey, hey,*
> *You ain't going away,*
> *Hey hey,*
> *You got to stay*
> *Hey ho,*
> *You just can't go*
> *Hey hey*
> *You got to stay"*

Phaid halted. A chill went through him. This was the second
time in the space of an hour that he'd been told he wouldn't
leave the city. It was almost enough to spook him. To cover
his discomfort, he reached into his pocket for a tab. Streetlife
looked sharply at him.

"What's wrong?"

"Nothing."

He tossed the kids the money. They grabbed it and scampered off.

"You look like you saw a ghost."

Phaid shook his head. It was almost the gesture of a dog shaking the water from his coat. Phaid wanted to rid himself of the sudden ominous feeling. Suddenly he grinned.

"Let's go, partner. Let's go and bid Chrystianaville the fondest fairwell we can."

Here ends the first volume of The Song of Phaid the Gambler. Watch for the second volume: *Citizen Phaid*.

MORE *SCIENCE FICTION ADVENTURE!*